BLACK HEART

A Black's Bandits Novel

LYNN RAYE HARRIS

Printed in the United States of America

First Printing, 2022

For rights inquires, visit www.LynnRayeHarris.com

Black Heart
Copyright © 2022 by Lynn Raye Harris
Cover Design Copyright © 2021 Croco Designs

ISBN: 978-1-941002-65-0

Chapter One

IAN BLACK STOOD ON THE TERRACE OF HIS VENETIAN palazzo. He was supposed to be inside, mingling with the masked crowd of arms dealers he'd invited for the evening. Instead, he was thinking about a woman.

Not just any woman. Natasha Oliver—aka Natasha Orlova, aka the assassin Calypso.

Which made no sense because she wasn't the woman for him. She was more than ten years younger and she worked for a group of people he despised. They were on opposite sides of *everything*.

He'd tried to recruit her, sworn to protect her if she left her masters in the Gemini Syndicate, but she hadn't taken him up on the offer. He wasn't going to stop trying, though. She knew things about the Syndicate that he wanted to know.

Needed to know if he was going to stop them from hurting people and ruining lives.

The water of the Grand Canal gleamed like diamonds as it lapped the walls below. The city reclined beneath a full moon like a satisfied lover, her languid form soft and beautiful. Behind him, the noise of a party in full swing drifted through the open terrace doors. He took a swallow of Scotch and let it burn its way down his throat.

He didn't care for the people here tonight, but that was the job. Since BDI operative Brett Wheeler had failed at his quest to infiltrate the Syndicate's human trafficking arm last year, they'd gone deeper underground. Tonight wasn't about human trafficking, no matter how much Ian might have wished it.

One day he'd make it so hard for them to trade in human lives that they'd stop doing it, but this wasn't the day. Not yet.

Tonight was about the global demand for illicit weapons. Ian was himself—the wealthy founder and CEO of Black Defense International. On the surface, a legit businessman.

Beneath the surface, he was a known trader in guns and a major backer of causes the real him despised. But it was the job, and Ian believed in getting the job done. Whatever it took, even if he sometimes felt like the job was crushing his very soul.

He adjusted the mask over his eyes. It was the barest of black silk eye-masks, but it did the job. He wasn't precisely anonymous, but he also wasn't as obvious as he would have been without it.

It was nearly Halloween, not Carnival, but the people attending tonight appreciated the opportunity to hide their faces. It made some of them bolder than usual.

Ian's people circulated, working as serving staff or pretending to be guests, watching the crowd and making careful notes of any conversations or interactions that needed to be examined later. Unless something needed his immediate attention, they had it under control.

As if on cue, Tyler Scott strode outside holding a tray.

"May I offer you an appetizer, sir?" he asked, sticking to his waiter persona for the night.

"No, thanks." There was no one on the terrace but the two of them at the moment. "How's it going in there?"

Ty lowered his voice. "You've got scumbags eating your food and drinking your liquor, but other than that, I'd say it's okay."

Ian snorted. "Part of the job, my man."

"I know, but I still don't like it."

Ian swirled the Scotch. "It's not the Marine Corp, is it?"

Ty shook his head. "Not in the least."

"You regret leaving?"

"No. It was time. I'm proud of being a Marine, but this feels bigger. Not more important, but different."

"Understand."

Ty gazed into the distance. "Do you think we ever learn to forgive ourselves for our mistakes? Or are we doomed to keep replaying them over and over?"

Ian considered the question. It was something he grappled with often. "I think it's possible. But not always. Some things stay in the back of your mind forever. You learn to live with it, but you don't get over it. You don't forget."

Ty nodded and hefted his tray again. "Sure you don't want an appetizer? I hear they're fucking delicious. This is Italy, after all."

Ian laughed. "Okay, sure, when you put it that way."

Ty strode inside again and Ian popped the small tart into his mouth before washing it down with Scotch. It was probably time to mingle, but before he turned to go, a gondola caught his attention. It glided across the canal toward his palazzo, cutting through the water with purpose. The gondolier stood on the rear of the craft, dipping and swirling his oar in that magical dance with the water that only seemed to happen in Venice.

A woman sat in the middle of the gondola, back straight. He could tell it was a woman because of the way she held herself. She was covered in a cloak that hid her defining features, but then she lifted her gaze and her hood fell back, revealing an ornate mask that obscured most of her face.

A late comer to his little party, then. Perhaps the wife or mistress of one of the powerful men who'd gathered here tonight.

Or, hell, perhaps she was the wife or mistress of one of the powerful women. There were a few, though they weren't as numerous as the men. Ian watched the craft glide up to the small inlet beside the palazzo, and then he heard the muted sounds of voices as the woman disembarked.

He finished the Scotch and turned to stride inside again. The woman didn't matter. His mission tonight did.

Ian entered the palazzo with its soaring, vaulted ceilings painted with Renaissance frescoes that never ceased to delight him. Sparkling Murano glass chandeliers reflected the light off gilded surfaces, illuminating bodies dressed in silk and fine-spun wool. No one had worn a mummy costume or arrived as a witch, but elaborate masks in the Venetian style decorated many of the faces. Some wore silk masks like he did, but most took their opportunities to sport the custom paper mâché beauties that Venice was known for.

Where else could you do such a thing?

Ian worked his way through the crowd, chatting amiably with people who supplied weapons to terror groups and didn't blink at genocide so long as they weren't included, and felt his insides grinding with anger. The CIA would make sure the weapons didn't fall into the worst hands, and perhaps take down some of the middle men while they were at it, but there would always be guns that slipped through the cracks.

Always guns, always deaths. It couldn't be stopped completely.

The woman he'd seen stepping onto the dock a few minutes ago entered the room. He knew it was her from the mask. She'd shed the cloak, and her body was encased in a form-fitting white sequined dress that covered her from neck to mid-thigh. Her legs were long and lean, and she wore heels that gave her a good three inches of height. Her hair was dark, falling in a sleek waterfall over her shoulders.

A hush descended for a moment as men and women alike sized her up. She surveyed the crowd like a queen, and he felt a flicker of interest stir deep inside. It stunned him, that flicker, because he hadn't felt it in a long time.

Except for the times he'd encountered Natasha.

The woman tossed her hair and lifted her chin as she sauntered into the room. The crowd parted like the Red Sea for Moses. A buzz started in the back of Ian's brain as he watched her progress and the room's reaction. It worked its electric path through him, raising all his senses into high alert.

Would Natasha come here so blatantly, exposing herself to scrutiny? To discovery?

Except it wasn't blatant, was it? She wore a mask and her arms were covered to her wrists, which meant there was no mermaid tattoo to give her away. She could literally be anyone. Or she could be Natasha, here to assassinate someone. Or just to taunt him with her presence.

She took a glass of champagne a waiter handed her and sipped it lightly from beneath the half-mask she wore.

The top of the purple mask was ornate, decorated with white feathers and sparkling jewels. The lower half was gone, revealing a plump set of cotton-candy pink lips.

Her gaze surveyed the crowd, but he couldn't tell what she was thinking. A man approached, putting his hand against her back, and disappointment thrummed in Ian's veins. She was indeed taken. And not Natasha.

He recognized the man, despite the red and white paper maché mask he wore on the top half of his face. Tommaso Leone was the son of Ennio Leone, a Roman who'd built a fortune in plastics and ranked near the top of billionaire lists the world over. Ennio had never been linked to illegal activities, but Tommaso was seen quite frequently in the company of arms dealers and traffickers.

The son might be doing the father's bidding, or the father turned a blind eye to his activities. Ian hadn't figured it out yet, but it was unlikely Ennio had no idea what was going on in any case. It wasn't an important distinction to Ian. The Leones were represented here, and that was enough.

Tommaso bent to whisper something in the woman's ear. He slid a hand down her back and over her ass.

Ian was about to turn away when Tommaso yelped. The woman removed his hand from her body, twisting Tommaso's wrist and shoving it between his shoulder blades. He couldn't do anything but stand on tiptoe as he tried to relieve the pressure. He was clearly in pain, and cussing her loudly. If anything, she jacked his arm higher until his voice became a whine.

Ian started toward them, intending to rescue—who? Her? Him?

But she said something to Tommaso before shoving him away. The crowd swallowed the Italian up and the woman took a delicate sip of her champagne, feathers completely unruffled as people murmured.

She'd managed everything without spilling a drop.

His interest was piqued. She could be anyone.

He plucked a champagne glass from a tray and strode toward her.

Chapter Two

NATASHA HAD TOLD HERSELF MORE THAN ONCE THAT coming to Ian's palazzo was a bad idea, and yet she'd done it anyway. As she sipped her champagne and glared at the retreating form of the man who'd dared to put his hand on her ass—as if she were his for the taking—she felt a disturbance in the air around her.

The hairs on the back of her neck prickled in warning, but it wasn't the warning she got when danger was imminent. More like a warning that a predator was at hand and moving closer. In this crowd, it could be anyone.

And yet she knew who it was before he arrived. She'd been looking for him when she'd entered, certain she'd find him without too much trouble. She'd felt him then, too, but she hadn't seen him.

Ian Black moved toward her with the lethal grace she'd come to expect. He was a tall man, his body beneath his suit lean and taut. Not that she'd ever seen his body, but she knew. She'd felt it when he'd pressed her against him a few months ago and kissed her.

She hadn't expected that kiss, and yet a day hadn't gone by since that she hadn't relived it at least once. Usually more often, though. She sometimes went to sleep with the ghost of that kiss on her lips, and woke with the phantom touch of his body against hers.

It was maddening. And it was the reason she was here. *Part* of the reason.

She had to get him out of her head. He claimed to want to protect her, to save her.

But she didn't need protecting, and no one could save her. Certainly not him.

He was one of the reasons she'd gone to prison in the first place. He'd admitted as much to her the first time they'd met. If not for him, if not for his involvement with her parents and their stupidity in turning against their mother country, they wouldn't have been arrested. And neither would she.

She'd still be in Russia, her parents would be alive, and Nikolai would be there too. Her family would be whole. *And who would protect Daria now if you'd never gone to prison?*

Who indeed?

Natasha sipped her champagne carefully, coolly, as if she were made of ice crystals. Inside, her heart thrummed harder than she liked. He was nearly there, his focus on her alone. She'd expected it, dressed to attract him, and yet she'd worked hard to disguise herself too. She didn't want him to know who she was. She wanted to talk to him, survey him in his habitat. And she wanted to do it anonymously.

She'd covered her arms, put on a dark wig, and inserted contacts that took her eyes from their usual hazel to a piercing blue. She'd plumped her lips with a makeup gloss that contained an irritant to swell them. Not too irritating, of course. Even now she could feel the tingle of the gloss, though she also wondered if part of it was the memory of kissing him.

Her pulse fluttered in her throat, but there was nothing she could do about that. Her heels made her seem taller than her five-feet-four-and-a-half inches did. Her body was unencumbered by padding or inserts, however. Her form tonight was all her. She'd considered wrapping her breasts to seem skinnier, but ultimately had not done so. Everything she had was on display for him, and her ears grew hot at the thought of all that scrutiny.

Scrutiny that even now was happening. His eyes gleamed hot and dark from his mask, and she wondered if they were his real eyes or not. She'd seen him with different colors every time, so she did not know. Like her, he wore disguises. So many disguises.

It was why she did not trust him. Which Ian Black was the real one?

A small puff of air forced out between her lips reminded her that she did not care. She wasn't there to find the real Ian. She was there to kill him.

Eventually, anyway.

Once she'd punished all those responsible for what'd happened to her in prison, she *might* be satisfied. She wouldn't go so far as to say she would be happy, but anything was possible.

The list she'd kept in her head for so long had only one name left. His.

Yet still she hesitated. *Why?*

That was the question she could not answer.

"Signorina," Ian said, his voice like warm honey dripping down her spine. He took her hand and brought it to his lips. She let him.

"Signor," she replied in a breathy voice, pitching it into a lower register than her own.

"Is everything okay?"

"Of course."

He studied her, still holding her hand near his mouth. "It's just that I thought someone was bothering you."

"Not at all, I assure you."

"You seem to be alone. Allow me to be your escort tonight."

"I am not alone," she lied. "I have simply not found my date yet. He told me to be here at this time, but I do not see him."

She could speak English without an accent, but she put on a slight one that could be vaguely Italian or Spanish. She also made sure not to use contractions very often. These were the sort of minor details that could make or break a disguise.

Ian tucked her arm into his and led her into another room, toward the massive buffet that was laid out against one wall. "Until he arrives then."

Natasha told herself to play harder to get, but Ian was already guiding her where he wanted her to go. She didn't feel like resisting anyway. "Very well."

"My name is Ian," he said as he picked up a plate and put a few choice delicacies on it.

She didn't bother telling him how easy it would be to poison the entire spread. He would already know.

"And you are?" he prompted.

"Anna," she said, picking a name that could belong to just about any culture.

"Anna," he repeated, his voice a rough purr that scraped along her nerve endings and made butterflies swirl in her belly.

Why? Why, when she hated him?

She had to remember that he was the reason she'd spent two years in a dank, dark, depressing cell. Until she'd met him, she hadn't known why. But he'd admitted it to her. Told her that he'd gotten her brother out of Russia before he could be arrested—which meant he'd left her and her parents to rot. She'd lost those she loved and she'd changed from a girl whose most pressing problem had been what to wear to the club to a woman who killed people for a living.

Bad people most of the time, though she feared the day she was sent to assassinate an innocent.

She wouldn't do it, of course. No matter what they did to her.

But it would be Daria they'd punish, wouldn't it? Which meant she'd do it in the end. She'd kill whomever they told her to kill, so long as Daria was safe. She'd promised.

"Are you okay, Anna?"

It was Ian's rough purr cutting through her thoughts, reminding her she was currently basking in the lap of luxury and not back in prison with her cellmate. *Poor Lena.*

"Yes," she said evenly. "I'm fine. Just thinking."

He handed her the plate and she took it, surprised that she was actually a little hungry.

"About the date who stood you up?" he asked.

Was that a teasing note in his voice?

"I could not care less about him." She took a delicate bite of a small pastry filled with something savory, the flavors bursting on her tongue and grounding her in the present again. She wasn't really worried about a poison buffet. What would be the point of it? It was like using a sledgehammer to perform brain surgery. If you wanted to

12

take out a target, you focused on the target, not on everyone around the target.

"That's good," Ian said, "because I couldn't either."

Her stomach flipped at the hint of sensuality in his voice. Paradoxically, jealousy flared hot and bright.

Ironic.

Ian Black was flirting with her, but he didn't know who she was. He thought she was this Anna person who'd been stood up by her date and he was moving in on her. Which pissed Natasha off because he clearly hadn't been thinking about *her* the way she had about him.

For him, that kiss beside the Tidal Basin in DC had simply been a kiss. For her, it had been both a revelation and a dagger to her soul. She hated him, and she wanted him too. Wanted more of the way he'd made her feel. She was like a rat in an experiment, hitting the button for more drugs while ignoring the food because the dopamine hit from the high was so good.

"Are you trying to seduce me?" she asked, more ice than she cared for creeping into her voice. She reminded herself to be warm, because he wouldn't expect warmth from Natasha. She didn't want to do anything that made him think of the real her.

It was vital she maintain her anonymity. Vital because she didn't want to answer his questions. He'd been looking for her since their last encounter. Probably because he wanted her to give him information on the Syndicate, nothing more. But it wasn't that easy for her. Nothing was. She had responsibilities he didn't know about.

She'd heard the whisperings across the network these past few months, but she hadn't dared to respond. It was too dangerous.

It was dangerous now, too. Yet here she was.

The heat in his gaze flared at her words, and she found

herself caught. Staring as he bent his head closer to hers. His mouth ghosted along the side of her cheek, and she hardly dared move. And then his voice whispered in her ear, hot and sensual, and shivers rolled down her neck and into her core.

"Is it working?"

Chapter Three

Ian didn't know what she was playing at, but everything inside him told him this woman was Natasha Oliver.

Natasha, dressed to the nines and wearing a mask, crashing his party for reasons of her own. Or maybe she really was expecting a date. One of her Gemini Syndicate bosses who would parade her around like a trophy, all the while laughing inside that he had the deadly Calypso on his arm and no one knew it.

Her hair was long and silky, dark—and real. He'd touched it to be sure. Jace had told him that Natasha was a blonde, so either she'd colored her hair or she was wearing a natural wig. Either scenario was possible.

He itched to pull her sleeve up and see if the mermaid was there, but she wasn't going to let that happen.

While he was about ninety-eight percent certain she was Natasha, based on his reaction to her, there was always the two percent that could be wrong. He wasn't a monk, after all, and he enjoyed women.

He'd enjoyed his share over the years, sometimes more than one at a time. Sometimes more than two.

Lately, he hadn't cared enough to go through the motions. He knew how to take care of business when he needed to, and he knew how to find a willing partner if he needed that too. It wasn't difficult. It never had been.

"Maybe," she said, her voice soft and low, and a thrill of desire tingled in his balls.

He had an urge, such a dark urge, to sweep her into a hidden corner and wrap those legs around his waist while he fucked her hard and deep. Would she welcome it? Or was it his fantasy alone?

"Careful what you say to me, beautiful," he told her seriously. "I'm not a man who enjoys games or half truths."

Not about something as serious as seduction, and not with her.

Her chin lifted. "And what makes you think I'm playing games?"

Everything. But he didn't say that. "It's just a warning, Anna. If you want to take this farther, we can go upstairs and get to know each other without interference. See what happens. Or we can flirt a bit without really meaning it, dance a little, and then you can climb into your gondola at the end of the evening, safe and sound—and unsatisfied."

Her eyes flashed. "Do you usually come on so strong?"

"Only when I want something."

She seemed to consider it. "You said we could go upstairs. Is this your place?"

"It is."

"So you are Ian Black then."

"The one and only."

"I've heard about you."

"Good things, I hope."

"Not all of it," she said with a sniff.

He chuckled. "The important parts are good, I promise you."

She nibbled on a tiny sandwich he'd put on her plate. "Perhaps I will find out. But there are rules, Mr. Black."

"And what are those rules, lovely Anna?"

"The masks stay on. And if I want to leave, you let me leave."

"I wouldn't dream of keeping a woman who wasn't delighted to be in my company."

"And the masks?"

He was convinced she was Natasha. Now more than ever. She was too prickly not to be. Besides, the masks were a critical part of her disguise. That she didn't want to give them up in private spoke volumes.

"A bit uncomfortable, I'd imagine. But whatever revs your engine, baby."

Her eyes flashed again, and he suppressed a chuckle. She picked up her champagne and took the tiniest sip. No doubt to keep her wits about her.

"You get ahead of yourself, Mr. Black."

"Do I? I thought we were discussing the terms of your surrender."

He could see the moment she made the decision. She set the plate down, but held onto her glass. Then she took a step toward him and put one hand on his chest. He could feel the burn of her touch through the layers of his bespoke tuxedo. He hadn't felt a burn like that since Natasha had touched him.

He wanted to rip the mask off her face and ask what game she was playing, but it occurred to him that her plan could be one of two things. Either she'd been as obsessed with him as he had been with her, and was approaching him as safely as she could—or he was a target for assassination.

Hell, maybe it was both.

She tilted her face up to his, her eyes clear and bright blue in the holes of her mask. He thought he detected the edge of a contact, but she blinked before he could be certain.

"Perhaps you should kiss me. Then we'll see if there's anything worth surrendering for."

He dipped his head toward hers, then stopped when he was only inches away. Her eyes had closed, but she opened them again when she realized he wasn't kissing her. There was a question in them. Confusion.

"I want to, lovely Anna. More than you realize. But how do I know you aren't an assassin? I have enemies. Powerful ones. And I didn't get to be this age by pretending they don't exist."

He thought she might react to that, but she only said, "Search me then. Have your people search me. I have no weapons."

"Poison?"

"I don't have that either."

"You expect me to believe that?"

She licked her lips. The sight of her pink tongue startled him. Aroused him.

"There," she said. "If I have poisoned my lipstick, then I'll die first."

He wrapped an arm around her waist and tugged her close, melding her body to his, uncaring of those around them who might be watching. "But what a way to go, sweetheart."

This time he didn't hesitate, and she didn't resist. He took her mouth swiftly, surely, his tongue sweeping against hers. She sagged against him for a moment, and then she met him with as much passion as he gave to her.

It was fucking exhilarating.

And there was no way in hell this woman was anyone other than his Calypso. His body knew, even if his mind had doubted. No more, though.

He didn't know what she was up to but he wanted to find out. She wasn't in disguise without a reason. She never did anything impulsively, least of all enter his domain and give herself up to him.

He broke the kiss first, setting her away from him gently, his fingers tracing the line of her neck before falling away. Her chest rose and fell a little quicker, her pulse fluttering in her throat. His lips tingled ever so slightly, and he knew she'd used something to plump her lips.

"Shall we ditch the party, Anna? Or do you wish to dance and flirt and disappear at midnight like Cinderella?"

"I'm willing to ditch the party. But if I decide I wish to go, you must let me."

"Will you leave a glass slipper to remember you by?"

Her lips curved. "Perhaps I will."

"I'll let you go," he said, though he didn't intend to give her a reason not to stay. "But I don't think you'll want to."

"So arrogant," she replied. "I might leave simply to prove a point."

"You might. I guess we'll find out, won't we?"

"I guess we will."

He put her arm in his again, then escorted her toward the ornate stairs that led up to his private rooms. Tommaso Leone was with another woman, a hot blonde in a red dress and matching red lipstick, but he looked up as they walked by, his eyes blazing with fury as he glared at Natasha.

If she noticed, she didn't dignify his anger with a reaction. Cool as fucking ice, this woman.

Ty caught his gaze and frowned, jerking his chin toward the party. Ian ignored him.

He was done with these people anyway. Ian Black answered to no one, and certainly not to anyone here tonight. His team would learn all they needed from the guests as the hours went by and the alcohol continued to flow.

No one would notice he was gone—and he didn't care if they did. Not with Natasha so close. He didn't know when the next time he'd get her alone would be, and he couldn't lose the chance to press her for information, however subtly.

Besides, Colt Duchaine was currently working the room as the Compte de Duchesne, his hereditary French title, and letting it be known he'd gone into business with BDI. Most people had no idea the title had no money attached to it. Even if they did, they didn't know he hadn't made a fortune elsewhere. He was as good a representative of BDI's success and global influence as anyone.

Natasha glided up the stairs beside Ian, never faltering in her heels. He walked slowly for her, but she moved so elegantly that it seemed not to matter. When they reached his private quarters, he led her into the sitting room and closed the door behind them. The lights were on, and the doors were open to the private balcony that looked out onto the Grand Canal.

"Very pretty," she said as she moved around the room, casually caressing the furniture and artwork. "You are a wealthy man, Mr. Black."

He shrugged as he went over to the bar and poured Scotch into two glasses. He didn't have to worry about anyone tampering with his liquor. He had a system and knew if anything had been touched. It had not.

"I do well enough."

"A palazzo on the Grand Canal is more than well enough," she said with a hint of disdain so slight he might not have noticed if he'd been a different man.

He handed her the Scotch and took a sip of his. "There are a lot of bad people in this world, Anna. And there are a lot of people with money who are willing to pay for protection when they need it. I'm good at what I do."

"No doubt. But sometimes the people paying for protection *are* the bad people, don't you think?"

"True enough." He itched to ask her what she wanted from him tonight, but he had enough experience with Natasha to know it wouldn't work. If he wanted to figure it out he had to let her play her game.

And be on his guard. He didn't kid himself that she wasn't lethal, or that she had a special fondness for him that would prevent her from attempting to kill him. Especially if she'd been sent to do so.

"That doesn't bother you?"

"Sometimes it does. But who am I to say who's good and who's bad? It's all a matter of perspective, don't you think?"

She nibbled her pink lower lip and a bolt of desire shot through him, tightening his balls. "I suppose it is."

She turned away and drifted out the open doors and over to the stone balustrade. The moon had moved higher in the sky and the sequins on her dress glittered like fire. He went to join her.

"It's a lovely view. You are very lucky."

"I don't spend much time here, to be honest. But yes, it is."

"Where do you spend your time, Mr. Black?"

He sipped the Scotch. It was a single malt, peated, and expensive. "Here and there. And you, Anna? Are you Venetian?"

"Hardly. I live in Switzerland. When I'm not working."

"Do you? How interesting."

That explained how she'd gotten to Brett and Tallie in the Brenner Pass a few months ago when they'd been trying to avoid detection. Assuming she was telling the truth, of course. He thought she might be since she didn't seem to think he knew who she was. It rankled him on some level that she thought him so gullible. Then again, she'd fooled him once in London when she'd impersonated a flower seller on the Embankment. He wouldn't make that mistake ever again.

She took a sip of Scotch, as if realizing she'd said too much. She didn't cough or make a face, and his admiration for her ticked up. "I like Switzerland," she finally said. "It's peaceful."

"And known for its neutrality in all matters," he added. The perfect place for an assassin to call home, provided she was careful. "What do you do, Anna?"

"International banking," she said without hesitation. "I travel and I meet a lot of people."

"Like your date who stood you up."

She shot him a look. One corner of her mouth tipped up. "That was a lie. I came tonight because my bank is always looking for wealthy clients, and there are many here."

"You crashed my party to make a sales pitch?" He laughed. Natasha was nothing if not inventive.

"Do you intend to throw me out?"

"I should." He let his gaze slide down her body, enjoying the way the fabric and sequins hugged her form. "But I can think of better things to do with you."

Chapter Four

NATASHA'S HEART THRUMMED AT HIS NEARNESS. THE SCENT of his custom soap mingled with his own body chemistry to create something that was uniquely him. If it were pitch black without a single flicker of light anywhere, she would recognize him by smell alone. A moment of panic seized her as she wondered if he might be as attuned to her scent as she was to his, but then she relaxed when she remembered that she'd used a different soap in the shower earlier for precisely that reason.

She could never be too careful. She'd learned that in prison, and then she'd learned it again when she'd trained to be a combatant.

Never let your guard down. Never.

Constant vigilance was the price for staying alive. So was being willing to do whatever it took to survive.

Ian took the glass from her and set it on the wide balustrade. He placed his own there as well. When he reached for her mask, she took a hasty step backward, then cursed herself for showing so much emotion.

"I wasn't going to remove it. But I would like to know

if you have any hidden weapons there, Anna. A syringe in the feathers, perhaps? A small nail with a poison tip secreted somewhere?"

"I'm a banker, not an assassin."

His grin was sardonic. "In my line of work, everyone is potentially an assassin."

"And what if I have a knife between my breasts? Do you intend to look there too?"

"I definitely intend to look at your breasts, Anna. If you'd like to strip for me, I can get busy examining you for weapons before we move on to the main event."

He was infuriatingly arrogant. But that wasn't what was making her angry. No, it was the casual way he intended to fuck a woman he'd just met. He might have kissed her that night in DC, but it hadn't meant a thing to him. He didn't know she stood before him now. He thought Anna the banker was a hot lay just waiting to spread her legs for him like so many others must have done.

He wasn't thinking about her—about Natasha—at all. Perhaps she should pull out one of the hat pins she'd used to secure the ties of her mask to her hair and stab him in the throat with it.

Except, no matter what he thought of her, she didn't kill that way. She preferred shooting to stabbing in all cases. Poison worked too. But stabbing was too personal. Too messy.

"Your foreplay leaves much to be desired," she said acidly.

"Ah, but haven't we been engaging in foreplay from the beginning?"

A wave of heat flared inside. He wasn't talking about every time they'd met as Ian and Natasha, but that's what she was thinking about. And, oh my God, it *had* been foreplay. Every encounter, every look and every word—and that kiss beside the Tidal Basin in DC. All of those things had been foreplay.

She was suddenly, achingly, aware of her own need. Her own desire. For him. For Ian Black, the man she hated. The man who'd ruined her family and left them to rot in the darkest hell of a Russian prison. She needed to kill him, not kiss him.

Natasha closed her eyes and sucked in a breath, willing her chaotic emotions to still. To let her think and act as the stone cold operative she'd been trained to be, not as a weak woman who desperately desired this man's touch.

Not that she'd come here tonight to kill him. There were better places and better ways. Besides, she'd pushed her luck the night she'd killed Dr. Roberto Broussard—the Butcher—on the mountaintop in Spain. If she killed Ian Black without permission from her handler, there would be more than hell to pay.

"Natasha," he said softly.

Her eyes snapped open to find him watching her. Fresh heat flared inside, only this time it was the heat of shock and shame.

She hadn't fooled him at all. She was losing her touch. She started to whirl away, but he grabbed her arm.

"Yes, I know it's you." He turned her and tugged her against him until their bodies were pressed chest to hip, the unmistakable hardness of his arousal thrusting against her.

Dear God…

"How?" she choked out. "How did you know?"

"How?" He kissed her hair at her temple tenderly, and she wanted to weep.

Do not be deceived by him.

"Because I know you. My body knows you. I felt the pull between us almost instantly, but you fooled me at first.

I thought maybe I'd been spending too many nights thinking about you, wanting you, when here was someone else who made me feel that same electric pull of attraction. That I'd only needed to wait for her to walk into my life so I could forget you."

Natasha shook inside. She hadn't expected so many words. Such sweet words. She wasn't accustomed to sweet words like those.

She gripped his biceps and bowed her head, examining every moment since he'd approached her at the party. She'd felt the attraction too, but she'd thought it was only because she knew who he was. She hadn't thought he would know her the same way.

She needed to push away from him, but it felt good to be held. She was never soft, never relaxed. She couldn't be. She had to be strong—but sometimes she wished for someone stronger than she was. Someone to take care of her. Just for a little while.

"When did you know?"

"I suspected it the minute I saw you. I knew when I kissed you."

"Why did you let me keep pretending?"

"Would you have stayed if I'd recognized you?"

"No."

He tipped her chin up and made her look at him. "Did you come to kill me?"

"No."

Not this time.

He must have believed her because he asked, "Then why?"

"I was curious."

"About what?"

What could she say to that? She searched her mind,

but embarrassingly enough, it was the truth that popped out. "Why did you kiss me? In DC, I mean."

He studied her for a long moment. "Because I had to."

Her heart hammered and her skin felt as if it'd been electrified. She didn't want to keep thinking. Didn't want to analyze everything to death. She wanted to feel safe and protected. And loved, dammit. Not that Ian Black was capable of that. And not that she wanted him to be.

Not him.

But, holy hell, she *wanted* him. She hadn't wanted anyone in a very long time now, so to feel this way was shocking. The pull of him was magnetic. Like she was the moon and he was her earth, anchoring her to him while they circled each other. She'd felt it from afar, and she'd answered the call by coming here tonight.

"Kiss me again," she said before the feeling went away.

He didn't hesitate. His mouth settled on hers, his tongue thrusting into her mouth to stroke her own. Natasha moaned as she wrapped her arms around his neck and kissed him back with all the passion of so many lonely nights.

He broke the kiss first. She gazed up at him, disoriented. Her head swam. She thought maybe he'd spiked her Scotch. But no, she was simply drunk on him. What a sensation.

"I want you," he said. "I want to strip you out of that dress and explore you for hours. But if that's not what you want, then you need to go. Now."

Natasha sucked in a breath that was heady with the scent of him. She curled her fists into his lapels. "I want you out of my system. I want to go back to my life without you invading my dreams every night."

"You think spending a few hours in bed with me will cure you? Or will it make it worse?"

That's what she didn't know. In truth, when she'd begun this journey tonight, she hadn't known what to expect. But she was here now, he knew who she was, and he wanted her.

"I don't know," she said, her body humming with arousal. That was something she hadn't felt in a long time. And never quite like this. "But I intend to find out."

Ian's sensual mouth curved in a wicked smile as his fingers found her zipper and slowly tugged it down. "From your lips to God's ears, kitten."

Chapter Five

NATASHA GRIPPED THE DRESS BEFORE IT COULD FALL. "NOT here. Anyone could see."

They were still standing on the terrace, and Ian chuckled. "That's part of the fun."

She looked scandalized. "You're a bad man, Ian Black."

He could hardly believe she was here, or that he was touching her. He turned her until she was facing the Grand Canal, then he ran his hands up the sides of her legs, pushing her dress upward as he went, shaping her hips, then caressing the sweet roundness of her ass. She wasn't wearing panties, and he groaned as he dropped his mouth to her neck. She tipped her head to the side, gasping.

"Ian…"

He pushed against her with his hips and she rocked back into him, sending shivers of delight straight into his balls. "No one can see us from mid-torso down. Should we do it here, with the tourists floating along the canal below —or should we retreat to my bed where I can spread you out and devour you slowly?"

He thought she might finally snap to her senses and pull away from him, but she surprised him with her reply.

"Mmm, what if I ask for both."

He ran a hand over her hip again, then dipped down her abdomen to the seam between her legs before she could change her mind.

"God, you're wet."

She gasped as he caressed her clit, her head falling forward as she tilted her hips and moved against his hand, seeking more. He nibbled the skin of her neck, obliging her with extra pressure. She moaned brokenly—and then bit back a cry as her body stiffened in his arms.

"Jesus. Did you come already?" He knew the answer, but he wanted to hear her say it.

"You got lucky," she told him a few seconds later.

Ian laughed. "So lucky." He tugged his zipper down and grasped his cock, sliding it into the wet folds of her pussy. This entire thing was madness, but he was as caught up in the heat of the situation as she was.

And he didn't want to let her go in case the madness evaporated. Still, he hesitated at her slick entrance, his body throbbing as he held his need in check. Below, he could hear the tinkling of laughter from the party. The scent of a cigar wafted by on the breeze and was gone. The moon shone down on them, illuminating everything.

He almost stepped away from her and zipped his pants. He hadn't lied that no one could see what was happening on the balcony. The balustrade was massive and it hid the important parts from view. But this wasn't how he'd envisioned the moment when they finally gave in to the desire between them.

He'd thought there would be more care, less desperation.

"Don't stop," she whispered, and all his good intentions evaporated.

"I don't intend to," he growled as he slid inside her body.

Good heavens, she was wet. Wet and hot and tight. So perfect he could feel his pulse in his cock, feel the pull between them as if it were a physical tie binding them together.

"Oh my God," she said. "I didn't know…"

He nipped her ear and sucked the lobe. "Didn't know what?"

"That it would feel like this."

Ian circled her clit rhythmically as he began to move deep inside her. God help him, he hadn't known it would feel like this either. Some part of his brain told him he was playing with fire, but the other part—hell, most of it— wanted to burn in the flames.

It didn't take long for her to come again, shaking in his arms as she gasped. He pulled her against him, holding her tightly, moving harder, quicker, until his own release built to a crisis. At the last moment, he jerked from her body and spilled his seed onto the stone at her feet.

Then he zipped his trousers and turned her in his arms. "More, angel?"

She still shuddered from her last orgasm. "I'm not an angel."

He chuckled. No, she wasn't. "You didn't answer the question."

Her eyes glittered behind her mask. "Yes, I want more. Take me to your bed, Mr. Black. Make me forget every-thing but you for a few hours."

He swept her into his arms and strode inside with her cradled against him. "I think you'd better start calling me

Ian, don't you?" he asked as he slid her body down the length of his and set her on her feet.

"If you prefer it."

He laughed as he stripped her naked. He untied her mask and pulled it free, catching the pins she'd used to secure the ribbons to her hair. When her face was revealed, he kissed her forehead, her nose, her chin, while she untied his mask and dropped it on the bed.

When they faced each other without masks, they let their eyes roam each other greedily.

Then Ian swept her up and lay her on the bed. He started from the beginning and worshipped her the way he'd dreamed about for so long. He lost track of the hours as they made each other delirious with pleasure.

Later, as they lay entwined on the rumpled mattress, sated and drowsy, he whispered into her ear, "Stay with me."

She turned to face him, tangling her naked limbs with his, and burrowed into his arms. It felt more right than anything he could recall. But she didn't answer.

When he woke sometime later with the first rays of sunlight stealing into the room, painting the covers of the bed golden, he knew instinctively that she was gone.

Cinderella had vanished.

Chapter Six

Natasha wrapped herself in her cloak and leaned against the window of the first class train compartment. She was shaken in a way she hadn't been in years. She hadn't gone to Ian's palazzo with the intention of spending the entire night wrapped in his arms, lying beneath him, on top of him, feeling the powerful thrust of his body inside hers over and over again.

It hadn't been her intention at all. Not like that.

Yes, she'd thought she would go and see him again. See if the magnetic attraction was still there, and then she would kiss him, find out if her memory was all it'd cracked up to be. She'd even envisioned fucking him to get him out of her system. But she'd pictured being in charge, taking what she wanted and then discarding him like a bad memory.

It had not happened that way at all. She'd been in charge of nothing.

Her body still tingled with the memory of his. Her nipples were sensitive, aching where they pressed against her clothing. Her skin was tender where his beard had scraped. Her pussy—well, that particular body part was somewhat sore. She hadn't had sex with a man in a very long time until last night.

But oh, what a way to climb back on the horse. Sex with Ian Black was very satisfying. She could wish it had been any man other than Ian, but too late now.

Natasha yawned as the train slid from the station. The first rays of dawn were painting the sky in ridiculously pink and purple colors, and her heart lifted at the beauty of it.

There was much beauty in the world, and much ugliness. She tried to focus on the beauty as much as possible. It was the only way she kept going from day to day. Until she'd turned nineteen and experienced life in prison, she'd had no idea the depth of ugliness that existed in the world.

She'd survived, but it hadn't been easy. Without Lena, her cellmate, she wouldn't have survived at all. It was Lena who'd protected her, Lena who'd told her what to do when the guards came for her, Lena who'd diverted the attention to herself whenever Natasha had thought she might crack if one more guard touched her.

Rape was a fact of life in prison, but Natasha had Lena to thank for surviving it. She'd managed to go somewhere in her head whenever it happened, but mostly the guards went for Lena instead. It had helped that Lena was older and more knowledgeable. She'd been a sex worker, so she'd used that skill to her advantage. She didn't get paid in money in prison, but she got paid in favors and special treatment.

The guards all knew she'd been there for killing a man who'd beat her, and they'd seemed to pay her more deference because of it. Or maybe it was just that Lena was so good at sex.

Natasha shoved the memories of that time away, unwilling to mingle the ugliness of rape with what had happened between her and Ian last night. She made her own choices these days, and Ian had been a choice. A bad choice, maybe, but still hers. She just hadn't expected to be consumed by it.

She imagined Ian waking alone, his dark hair mussed, a day's growth of stubble on his impossibly handsome face. He would look for her, and a twinge of regret pierced her at the thought of him realizing she wasn't there. He'd asked her to stay.

Or had he told her to?

Nevertheless, it was impossible. Even if she wanted to, she couldn't have done so.

But she did not want to.

The train picked up speed, putting Venice farther behind her with every kilometer. Natasha was determined to put everything about last night behind her too. It was merely sex, and the wanting should stop now that she'd sated it so thoroughly.

Several hours later, when the train pulled into the station in Zurich, Natasha grabbed her small suitcase and exited with the crowd. She was herself again, blonde and hazel-eyed, but she usually kept her tattoo covered. It had been an indulgence, but it also covered scar tissue and she loved it. Still, she was careful. No short sleeves for her.

Her persona in Switzerland was that of Elena Weiss, a single woman who worked as an international banker. Anna the party girl hadn't lied to Ian when she'd told him her profession.

Natasha hailed a cab and sank into the backseat after giving the driver her address. She thought of all that had happened in the past twenty-four hours. It had not turned out how she'd thought it would. Far from being a fading memory, Ian Black was now a constant thought in her head. She could smell him, taste him, and rather than being finished with him, she realized with a shock that she wanted more.

But she was nothing if not strong and determined. She might want him, but she wasn't going to let herself be weak where he was concerned. Not ever again.

The cab came to a stop before a house that overlooked Lake Zurich. Natasha paid and then watched the cab drive away before turning her attention to the beauty of the snow-capped Alps in the distance. This was her happy place. Her sanctuary.

The door opened and a little girl ran outside. "Mommy! Mommy!" she cried. Her nanny, a French woman named Lissette, watched with a smile as the dark-haired girl hurtled herself into Natasha's arms.

Natasha hugged Daria back, laughing. "You almost knocked me over, sweetie. You're getting so big!"

Daria's cheeks were red with exertion. She must have been playing in the yard behind the house when the cab arrived. "I'm only six and a half. I'm not very big."

"Maybe not yet. But you will be."

"I know. My mommy in heaven was taller than you, and I might be tall like her," Daria said matter-of-factly.

"That's right," Natasha said, taking Daria's hand and leading her toward the house. "Your mommy in heaven would be very proud of how you've grown."

Sadness squeezed her at the thought of Lena. She wished her friend would have lived to see Daria growing up, but it did no good to dwell on what could not be changed.

"Did you bring me a present?" Daria asked.

"Of course I did," Natasha said as they walked inside. She unzipped her suitcase and handed the little girl a box. Daria giggled as she tore at the wrapping paper. Inside was an ornate paper maché mask fit for a child and a small velvet cloak. "From Venice," Natasha said as Daria turned the mask over in her hands. "Let me help you put it on."

Daria handed Natasha the mask and turned to face away from her. Natasha tied the mask in place, then fitted the cloak over the child's shoulders. When she turned Daria around again, the little girl was practically bouncing with excitement.

"I want to go see in the mirror. May I?"

"Of course," Natasha said. Daria turned and ran up the stairs, the cloak flowing behind her, and Natasha laughed. "But you look like a princess if you ask me," she called out.

Lissette peeked out of the kitchen. "I have prepared hot tea and some pastries, if you'd like, Miss Weiss."

"Oh yes, thank you so much," Natasha said, going into the warm kitchen where the light streamed in from the huge windows facing the lake. She took a seat and waited for the tea to be poured, then sipped the hot liquid.

Lissette watched her carefully. "Your business in Venice was successful?"

Heat crept into Natasha's cheeks. She hoped it didn't show. Even if it did, she wasn't going to explain. "It was a beginning, shall we say."

Lissette nodded. She was the closest thing Natasha had to a friend, if a meek nanny who wouldn't call her by her first name, no matter how many times Natasha had asked, could be a friend. Of course Lissette had no idea what Natasha really did for a living, just like she had no idea that Natasha's name wasn't Elena Weiss.

She believed that Natasha was an international banker and traveled extensively for work. If Lissette had had the slightest clue Natasha was really a paid assassin on a tight leash, she would have probably run screaming. Not that Natasha would have blamed her.

To keep her lives as separate as possible, Natasha maintained an apartment in Zurich that contained her weapons and disguises. When she needed to work, she went there first. She had weapons in this house, but mostly for protection should the need arise. Thankfully, Lissette didn't question why a banker would have a gun or two lying around.

"Oh," Lissette said as she put a pastry on a plate for Natasha. "I almost forgot. A gentleman stopped by yesterday. He said he was an old friend of your parents'."

The hairs on Natasha's neck prickled. Nothing about that last sentence was any good. Her parents, God rest their souls, didn't have old friends. "What was his name?"

Lissette blinked. "I'm not sure he ever said, come to think of it. He said he'd stop by another time."

Goosebumps chased up her arms. It was a warning from her masters in the Syndicate. There was no other explanation.

They knew where she lived and where Daria went to school. They knew everything, which was why she couldn't do what Ian Black wanted and give him information. If anyone found out she'd told him anything at all, it wasn't only her life on the line.

A knot of apprehension coiled tight inside. If they knew where she'd gone yesterday, she likely wouldn't be sitting here now. It didn't matter that she hadn't told him anything useful, and that she didn't plan to. Only that she'd been with him.

She trembled inside as she picked up the tea and took a sip. She couldn't see him again.

Not ever.

Chapter Seven

"Who was she, boss?" Ty asked at breakfast.

Ian looked at the former Marine. He was casually buttering his toast.

Colt blinked as his gaze bounced between them. "Who was who? What'd I miss?"

"No one," Ian said. "You didn't miss anything. I took a woman to my room. We had sex and she left. End of story."

"Damn," Colt said at the same time Ty said, "Whoa."

"Was she hot?" Colt asked.

Ian didn't have to work to keep his voice even. It was what he did. Turn off the emotions and do the job. He was an expert at it. Had been since he'd been a child. It was his superpower. One of them anyway.

Except he'd said too much this time. Way to overreact to a simple question. He knew better, which made it worse.

"She was hot, and now she's gone. It was sex, not a marriage proposal." Ian sipped his espresso.

"I thought you were going to tell us she was a contact,"

Ty said, still looking a bit surprised. "The way Tommaso Leone was glaring at the two of you, I figured she was someone important."

She was, but Ian wasn't admitting that. "So you missed him hitting on her earlier?"

Ty tilted his head. "I heard that some woman made him scream like a little pussy. Was that the same woman I saw you with?"

"One and the same."

"Jesus, she didn't look capable of getting the jump on a belligerent asshole like Leone."

"It was classic self-defense 101," Ian said, remembering how Natasha had turned the tables on the fucker. Man, it'd been awesome too.

Colt took a bite of his pastry. "Shit, I missed everything. Some woman kicking Tommaso's ass and you leaving with her. I never noticed you were gone. Had my hands full with the Turkish contingent."

"Nice segue. Now why don't we discuss the party? Where's Jace and Dax?"

"Right here," Jace Kaiser said as he strode into the breakfast room. "Dax is coming."

"Ian had a hookup last night," Colt said, grinning. "Took a hot babe to his room while he had a house full of douchebags and spent the night doing more fun things than talking to any of them. God I wish Angie was here. Would have made the whole night better if I could have been with her."

"For real?" Jace asked, blinking at Ian.

"For real," Ian said casually. Jace was Natasha's brother, but Ian didn't care. First, he didn't have weird rules about that kind of thing. Second, Natasha was a grown woman who could make up her own mind. And she had, at least for a night. Third, it was none of Jace's business. Or anyone's. "Now can we please stop speculating about my sex life and get on with business?"

"We could, but where's the fun in that?" Ty asked. "Never seen you leave an active operation with a hookup before."

"First time for everything. Are you telling me you kids didn't have it under control?"

"Nope," Ty said. "We did. Just seemed pretty intense between you two. I thought for sure she was here to give you some top-secret information. Don't know why I didn't think it was more basic than that."

"Because you haven't gotten laid in so long you can't remember what it's like?" Jace said with a grin.

Ty rolled his eyes. "*Har har.* I get laid plenty."

"Sure you do, buddy," Jace replied.

Colt turned his attention to Ian. "Intense, huh? So that means it was good, right?"

"Yes, it was intense," Ian replied in clipped tones. "That's why we had sex. I'm not a hermit. Any of you care to discuss the women in your lives and what you get up to in the dark, or are we done with the subject?"

Colt ran his fingers over his mouth like he was closing an imaginary zipper. "Nope. That's private."

"My point exactly, gentleman. Let's discuss the party and what we know, and leave the sexy bits where they belong."

"I think the Syndicate is about to host a big auction," Colt said, all seriousness now. "I heard two of the Turks hinting about it."

"Jesus," Dax Freed said, entering the room in time to hear that much.

Ian couldn't have expressed it better. The auctions were

a disgusting display of extreme wealth at its worst. Billionaires gathered to bid on human beings, usually women, though sometimes young men too, as their own personal sex slaves.

Sometimes the people being auctioned agreed to it since the money could help families in distress. But other times—many times—they were snatched from their lives the way Tallie Grant had been. Still, it didn't matter whether they agreed or not—the entire thing was exploitative and disgusting.

Ian knew he'd never stop every trafficker out there, but if he could hit the big ones and make it extremely unpleasant to continue, maybe he'd make a difference in vulnerable lives.

"Then we need to find out when and where," he said coolly, though his belly twisted with anger. "I intend to make it impossible for them to hold it."

"I'll get onto the dark web," Dax said. "See what I can find."

"Good. Hey, I've heard that Calypso lives in Switzerland," Ian added. "See what you can find out about that while you're chasing rumors."

Jace was frowning. "Switzerland? Where did you hear that?"

"Can't say, but I think it's credible."

Jace shook his head and leaned back in his seat. "I appreciate what you're trying to do for her, but I don't think it'll work. How long's it been since you offered her your protection in exchange for information? More than a year now. She's not taking the bait. I think she's a lost cause, and it pains me more than anyone to have to say that."

"It's up to her to come to us," Ian said. "But that doesn't mean I don't want to find out if she really does live in Switzerland. It'd be good to know where she is so we can watch her closely. Maybe she'll lead us to someone in the Syndicate hierarchy if we're patient."

"I think that's a good plan," Colt said. He rubbed a spot on his arm absently, and Ian knew it was where Natasha had shot him when she'd kidnapped Maddie Cole from his protection. That she hadn't killed him was a miracle. It also gave Ian hope. Hope that she wasn't as indoctrinated in the ways of the Syndicate as it sometimes seemed.

"Yeah, fine, I get that," Jace said on a sigh. He let his gaze slide over everyone there before resting it on Ian. "She's my sister, and while I can't forget that she nearly killed Maddy and Angie—not to mention me and Colt here—I still care about her. But I don't kid myself that she's redeemable. Too much water under the bridge, and too much programming."

Ian knew what Jace meant, and yet he wasn't as certain. He remembered Natasha last night in his arms, the way she'd sighed and moaned, the way she took her pleasure when she wanted it and the way she gave it back to him when she was ready.

She hadn't been polished at all. She'd been uncertain of herself at times, and she'd tried to cover for it by being overly bold. He hadn't been fooled.

Natasha was twenty-eight and not a virgin. But she wasn't so experienced the sex seemed mechanical. Somehow, everything with her felt fresh and new. As if he weren't forty-one and so jaded by life that he no longer believed in much of anything. That in itself had been a revelation.

He wanted more of that feeling.

"No one's past redemption," Ian replied. "Not even her."

Jace shook his head slowly, considering. "I'm not so

sure. Sometimes, the shit that happens to you is too much. Some people are just broken beyond repair. Sometimes you have to admit that and move on."

Ian nodded. "Might come down to that. But for now we're going to give her a chance."

Chapter Eight

Six weeks later....

The first time Natasha threw up her breakfast, she didn't think anything of it. But when she kept being queasy in the mornings, when her breasts started to ache and she couldn't seem to drag herself out of bed, a dark suspicion began to unfold in her brain.

"You are not feeling well again this morning?" Lissette asked when Natasha came down to breakfast.

Natasha shook her head as she pushed the eggs away and grabbed a slice of plain toast. Lissette put a hot cup of tea in front of her and a hand on her forehead. It brought back a memory of her mother doing the same when she'd been a child. Natasha's first instinct was to lean into that hand and close her eyes, but she pulled away instead.

Lissette frowned. "No fever. Perhaps it's a mild stomach bug that doesn't want to go away."

"Yes, could be," Natasha said.

Daria bounded into the room, dark pigtails bouncing. "Are we getting a Christmas tree after school today?" she asked as she plopped into her chair.

Natasha forced a smile, though she felt green inside. "Of course we are, sweetie. We'll go into the *Altstadt* and browse the markets, and we'll find our tree while we're there."

"You're coming too, Lissette, right?"

"I wouldn't miss it. Now eat your breakfast and let's get you to school so we can have fun this afternoon."

Natasha made it through breakfast, then accepted Lissette's offer to walk Daria to school. Natasha usually did it whenever she was home, but she definitely didn't feel like it today. Once Lissette and Daria were gone, Natasha took a deep breath and opened her laptop. She googled her symptoms, her belly turning over again at what they could mean.

But it wasn't possible. Even if Ian hadn't used a condom, which he had except for that first time when he'd pulled out of her body before he came, she wasn't capable of getting pregnant. She knew it for certain. If she'd been able to get pregnant, then why hadn't it happened *before*, when she'd had no choice about what happened to her body?

She slapped the laptop closed and put on her boots. She had to go to the *Apotheke* and buy a test. It was the only way to remove doubt.

Half an hour later, she sat in the bathroom, her heart throbbing as the impossible was confirmed.

One line that changed everything: *Pregnant.*

Tears blurred her vision as she sat and thought. She could fix it easily enough. Make an appointment, and it would be as if it'd never happened. That was probably the wise thing to do. She couldn't be pregnant, couldn't carry a child to term and still do what she did. She couldn't walk away either.

The Syndicate wouldn't allow it. She was theirs to

command so long as Daria was alive, and they knew it. Even if she managed to take time away to have this baby, that would give them yet another hold over her. Yet another way to keep her in line.

She pressed her hand to her abdomen, her thoughts warring with each other. Perhaps she could have the baby in secret. Pass it off as Lissette's.

But that wouldn't work either, because they would use Lissette against her too. So long as Lissette was Daria's nanny, then she was also a way to keep Natasha in line. And there was no way Natasha could hand over her baby and expect Lissette to take care of it as if it were her own.

Lissette was a fabulous nanny to Daria, but she could always walk away from the job if she wanted to. A baby would change everything, especially if Lissette had to pretend the baby was hers.

Natasha swiped away tears. What the hell? There was truly only one answer, and though it surprisingly wasn't the answer she wanted, she was going to have to make the hard choice.

She sniffled again. Maybe she should tell Ian.

But that was madness. He couldn't change anything. He couldn't make the Syndicate go away, though heaven knew he was trying. She'd been hearing grumblings lately that he was more of a thorn in their side than ever—not that the rank and file knew he was behind it. Someone had been sabotaging computer systems, chasing after leads that would uncover the big players behind the crime ring. It was a serious challenge to the status quo, and there were powerful people who weren't going to take that lying down.

Go to him, her inner voice said. *Let him help you. He promised he would.*

"He promised," she muttered. "But he is not God."

His help had been nothing to her family before, except

for Nikolai—Jace now. Ian Black couldn't be everywhere, and he wouldn't be able to stop the Syndicate from finding her and Daria in the end.

If she could get Daria away without them noticing in the first place.

Which she could not. As good as she was at disguises and disappearing into thin air, she couldn't do the same for Daria and Lissette. She'd thought about it many times, but how could she endanger the child by attempting it? So long as she did what she was told, everything was fine. She had a decent life here, and Daria was well cared for.

She'd been working on a failsafe plan for the past two years, but it wasn't good enough. Not yet. She had a great deal of money in a secret account in the Caymans, fake passports—for her only at the moment—and she'd researched places she could disappear if she had to.

Alaska. British Columbia. South America. Australia.

She could disappear. But taking Daria with her would draw too much attention. Daria spoke German, French, and English, but she was very clearly a European child. She wouldn't fit in, and that would draw attention. Add Lissette into the mix, and it was impossible.

Natasha stood and wrapped the test in a paper bag, then stuffed it into the trash. She washed her face and scrutinized her reflection in the mirror. Hazel eyes peered at her from a face surrounded by a cloud of golden blond hair. Her skin seemed to glow, or perhaps that was her imagination. She frowned at herself, then turned and went downstairs.

Lissette wasn't back yet and Natasha glanced at her phone to check the time. Perhaps Lissette had gone on an errand after dropping Daria at school. Not that Natasha remembered Lissette saying so, but then she hadn't heard a lot of things Lissette had said lately since she'd been caught up in her own thoughts.

She texted Lissette to tell her she had to go downtown. What she really intended was to go to the apartment and have a look at her things. Maybe she'd come up with a new plan, something she hadn't considered before. Maybe she *could* disguise Daria long enough to get her out of the country if only she tried hard enough. If she called Ian, told him to send a plane for them—

But no, she couldn't trust that he would comply. He'd been as obsessed with her as she had with him that night in Venice, but the obsession might be over now. Easy come, easy go.

She'd never been certain she could trust him, and she wouldn't start now. Not with Daria's life at risk. The price for failure was too great.

It wasn't until a couple of hours later, when she was in her apartment in downtown Zurich going through her disguises, that the text from her handler came. And even then, it took a long moment to process what it said. What it meant.

It was precisely what she'd always wanted. But the order didn't make her happy.

Instead, it filled her with dread.

Target is Ian Black. Dossier to follow. Terminate immediately. Proof required.

Chapter Nine

I NEED TO SEE YOU. ASAP

Ian stared at the text message blinking on his private cell phone. He hadn't heard from Natasha in almost two months now. Not since the night he'd taken her to bed and then woke up alone. He'd had his people scouring the Swiss countryside for Cinderella—and the Lichtenstein countryside too since it was close—but they'd turned up nothing.

No Natasha Oliver. No Orlova either. Not that he'd expected to find either one. He'd grilled Jace on possible aliases, but Jace didn't have a clue.

He opened the message window and read it again. Though it was the number she'd contacted him from before, he wouldn't blindly accept that it was her.

How do I know this is you? he typed back.

His phone rang. He swiped to accept the call and leaned back in his chair. It was a little over a week until Christmas, and he was at home for a change. Home today being a sprawling estate with a view of the Chesapeake Bay that never ceased to delight him.

"It's me," she said without preamble. "Who else?"

"Who else indeed?"

She blew out a breath. "I can't talk long. They're watching me. But I need to see you."

Ian's skin prickled. Was it a warning, or excitement? He didn't ask who was watching. He knew what she meant. "Okay. Where are you?"

"I'm in Frankfurt. But I can be in the States in a few hours if you're there. Or anywhere. Tell me where to go."

Ian frowned. "What's wrong?"

He heard her voice hitch in. "Nothing I can explain over the phone."

"I haven't heard anything from you since Venice."

"What more was there to say?"

He didn't like the pinprick of annoyance that question caused. "I stayed, you know. A week longer than necessary. Wondering if you'd return."

There was silence for a long moment. "I couldn't. What happened—it shouldn't have gone that far."

"And here I thought you enjoyed it." He couldn't help the hint of sarcasm.

"I have to go. Please tell me where you are. Please."

"Fly into BWI and call me again. I'll send someone."

"No, it's too risky. I'll text you when I arrive. We can arrange to meet somewhere."

"Don't you get tired of the cloak and dagger routine, kitten? Wouldn't you like to behave like a normal adult for a change?"

"I don't know what that's like. I suspect you don't either, so don't you lecture me like you're anything other than a hypocrite when you say things like that."

"Ouch," he said, laughing. "Fine, have it your way. Text me when you land. We'll figure it out. Any hints for me so I know what to expect?"

"No."

The line went dead and Ian dropped the phone. Not a day had gone by since October that he hadn't thought of Natasha Oliver and her sexy little moans. He remembered what it had felt like to slide into her wet, slick heat, and it made him hard all over again.

It also pissed him off because he remembered what'd happened next.

She'd run away. Ghosted him in the morning like a bad memory she wanted to forget.

Until this moment, he hadn't heard a word from her even though he'd put out feelers on the dark web. Messages she would understand but no one else would. She hadn't replied to a single one.

Not that he was fucking chasing her down. He just wanted to be sure she was okay.

Ian picked up the phone and called Ty. Jace wasn't the man for the job, plus he was too close to Colt and Brett. They would not keep secrets from him.

Or not this kind of secret anyway.

He could have called Jared Fraser, but this was Jared's first Christmas with his fiancée. Libby was a dynamo, and she was planning a big party in a few days. Jared was helping even though parties weren't typically his thing. Though for Libby, he would do anything that made her happy.

That left Ty, Dax, or Rascal—and Ian chose Ty.

"Yo, boss, what's up?" Ty said.

"I need you to help me make some arrangements."

"What'd you have in mind?"

"Meeting with someone tonight."

"Can you tell me who?"

"Natasha Oliver."

Ty whistled. "Calypso. You sure that's a good idea, boss?"

"No, but it's the only one I've got."

"Okie doke. Maybe we should get the team involved, set up a perimeter—"

"Call Dax and Rascal. But I don't want anyone else onboard. Especially not Jace or Colt."

Ty hesitated. "If that's what you want. She's dangerous, though."

Ian thought of Natasha in his arms, her body burning like liquid flame. "Trust me, I know."

"Where are you meeting?"

"Not sure yet. I'll try to get her here. If not, the harbor in Annapolis. It'll be packed tonight. She'd be a fool to try anything."

"Copy. I'll give Dax and Rascal a shout. We'll be standing by."

"I'll be in touch," Ian said, ending the call and dropping his phone on the desk.

After nearly two months of silence, Natasha was flying to DC specifically to see him. He wasn't optimistic enough to think she was ready to flip sides, or that she had a special fondness for him. She wasn't flying all this way for a booty call, though he'd be happy to oblige if she was. No, he'd bet she had an ulterior motive.

And he intended to be prepared for anything.

Chapter Ten

NATASHA WAS TIRED WHEN THE PLANE TOUCHED DOWN AT
BWI, but she wasn't so tired she needed to rest before
getting on with her mission. She'd flown back and forth
across time zones many times. She'd crisscrossed the world
for the Syndicate, and she'd done what they asked as efficiently and quickly as possible. She did the job, got the hell
out, and got paid. And Daria stayed safe and sound in
Switzerland, living the life of a normal little girl. Natasha
feared every day that Daria would be snatched into a
nightmare world, the way she'd been, and she worked to
keep that from happening.

She would do the job, and she would do it well. If she
did it quickly, perhaps Daria and Lissette would be home
for Christmas. Because this time the Syndicate had taken
them. Along with the dossier on Ian, her handler had sent
a photo of them. They were happy and healthy, thank
God. They'd been told that Natasha had an unexpected
assignment, and they'd been taken to a luxury hotel in the
Alps to spend a few days enjoying all the amenities.

Natasha recognized the hotel—the Grand Hotel Schoenburg had once been a palace for a minor royal—and she'd toyed with various scenarios to break them out, but ultimately she'd decided it was too risky. She was one woman, and she didn't know how many guards the Syndicate had watching them. Or what the price would be if she defied orders so blatantly.

She'd tried calling Lissette, but her calls went to voice mail. Texts went unanswered, which made Natasha think that Lissette's phone had been confiscated. Yet another indication the Syndicate meant business.

Killing Ian would only hurt a little bit. She'd always intended to make him pay for abandoning her and her parents to the Russian prison system while saving Nikolai. She'd wanted to do it on her own timetable though, not someone else's.

Now that the hour was nigh, there was a pit in her stomach that kept growing bigger with every kilometer she traveled. Inside her, a tiny life grew. A tiny life that was part Ian Black's as much as it was hers. For that reason alone she would not have killed him just yet if the choice had been hers.

It wasn't.

Natasha surreptitiously adjusted the lanky brown wig she'd donned, and grabbed her bag from the overhead compartment. She didn't carry weapons with her, but she knew where to obtain them. The Syndicate had people everywhere, even in the American halls of government. Which meant they had people in the local area willing to provide her with weapons and shelter.

She didn't need a gun because that wasn't how she intended to kill him. Instead, she had a small vial of poison to inject him with. She didn't know what was in it, but death would be swift. It wouldn't be pleasant, which she imagined was part of the design. Her handler had been very specific about the method.

Yet another aspect of this job that was different than most.

Natasha caught a glimpse of herself as she walked past a large mirror that ran along one wall. She looked like a grungy college kid home for the holidays. She had the lanky wig, a pair of round glasses, and she'd put in a prosthetic to make it look like she had an overbite. She wore a military style green fatigue coat, Chucks, and a pair of ripped jeans with an oversized black T-shirt with long sleeves. Her passport was American, and her name was Kimberly Branson.

Once she was through customs, she headed for the exit. She took her phone out as she walked into the taxi line.

I'm here. Where do you want to meet?

The reply was swift. *Tell me where you are and I'll send a car.*

Natasha nibbled her lip as she stopped to answer. Someone grumbled as they passed her in the taxi line. She paid them no heed. *A car to take me where?*

Ian: *My place. Unless you'd rather meet in public?*

Natasha: *You trust me enough to let me come to your home?*

Ian: *You've seen me naked. Slept beside me. Are we really going back to distrusting each other now?*

She wanted to shout in all caps *YES! DON'T TRUST ME! DON'T LET ME INTO YOUR HOUSE!*

But of course she didn't. She simply stood and considered the implications. Easier to jab him in private, especially if they got naked first. She could inject him once he fell asleep, then make her escape the same as last time.

Or she could meet him in a public place, poison him when the time came, and make her escape when he fell and people rushed to help him. It would be both harder and easier that way. Harder because they'd be in public. Easier because she wouldn't have to spend any time alone with him first. Wouldn't have to kiss him and touch him and let him inside her body first.

But if they met in public, there was always the chance she wouldn't get the opportunity to act. And if she didn't, then Daria would remain in the Syndicate's control. Besides, her handler had been specific about that too.

Proof of death required.

Not possible for a public venue. Any other circumstance, and she might risk anger by not following instructions to the letter.

Give me the address. I'll take a taxi, she replied.

Her phone buzzed in her hand, startling her. It was him. "What?" she growled.

"No taxis, angel face. No Ubers."

Natasha snorted. Her breath frosted in the cold air. "You enjoy ordering people around, don't you? I'm standing outside the airport, near the taxi stand. I can be on the way in five minutes, for fuck's sake."

"Which airport?" He managed to sound bored.

Natasha blinked. "BWI. Does it matter?"

He laughed and she cursed herself belatedly for giving away the information so easily. She hadn't lived as long as she had in this profession by being careless. He'd told her to fly into BWI, and she had, but not because he'd said so. She'd done it because it was the most convenient.

"It might."

A moment later, a sleek limo turned the corner and rolled along the access drive. It stopped near the taxi stand, idling. "Is that yours?" she asked, somewhat stunned and not quite sure she was right anyway.

"It is." He didn't even have to ask her what she meant.

"How did you know I'd be here?"

"I didn't. I know I told you to use BWI, but believe me I don't make the mistake of thinking you'll do as I say."

"Wise man."

"I guessed based on your location when you called earlier. You could have gone to Dulles, or Reagan, but BWI isn't as busy as Dulles, and Reagan isn't an international arrivals point."

"I might have flown to JFK or Philly. Or even Atlanta, and backtracked."

"You might have, but you didn't. Now are you getting in or would you prefer the taxi?"

"I'm thinking."

The back window rolled down. Ian's handsome face was suddenly visible across the distance, and her heart tapped the inside of her chest with a hard thump. "Think fast, angel. No one will know it's you. Not looking like that."

Natasha's stomach rolled. Not entirely from his words, she imagined. "Looking like what?"

Because it could be a game. He would be waiting for her to betray herself when he really had no idea what she looked like or which of the thirty or so people milling about was her.

"Like a college kid who hasn't had a shower in a week, and who buys her wardrobe at the army surplus store."

Natasha lowered the phone from her ear and made eye contact with him. He shot her that cocky grin of his that made her insides melt. She sighed and tapped the screen to end the call, then looked both directions before sauntering over to the limo. Ian didn't get out, but he did open the door and slide across the seat. Natasha tossed her bag inside and climbed in.

"How did you know?" she asked, ignoring the crazy beating of her heart at his proximity.

The limo pulled away from the curb as he handed her a drink. "Here, have a shot to loosen some of the tension of that long trip."

She took the glass, contemplating the liquid. If she was ending this pregnancy anyway, did it matter? She handed it back to him, shaking her head. "I can't. My stomach is queasy from something I ate on the plane. I feel like that would send it over the edge."

"Bubbly water?"

"That would be wonderful."

He gave her a bottle of Perrier and she opened it, savoring the cool lemony flavor as it went down. "You didn't answer me," she finally said. "How did you know it was me?"

His eyes—blue this time—gleamed hot. "Because I can sense you, Natasha. It's an itch beneath my skin, a tingle of attraction that doesn't abate. I know you when I see you now. And you know me."

She was very afraid she did. She closed her eyes and took another sip. This wasn't helping.

Not the water, but him. Seeing him like this. How the hell was she supposed to kill him?

Because you have to. Because it's what you do. Because Daria's life depends on it.

"I don't know what you mean," she lied.

"What was so urgent you needed to see me?" he asked, ignoring her answer. Knowing she lied, probably.

She glanced at the barrier that had been raised between them and the driver. She couldn't see the driver, but it didn't matter. "You're pissing off people in the Syndicate. You need to be careful."

He laughed. "You came all this way for that? I already

know it, angel. I've put a stop to at least three human auctions in the last two months, and someone isn't happy. Where else will obscenely wealthy men get their premium sex slaves?"

Natasha shivered at the leashed violence in his tone. It wasn't obvious, but it was there. She suspected there weren't many who could hear it, but she did. It made her wonder why it was so personal for him.

"There are always places for such things. You aren't stopping it, merely making it more difficult. And costing some people a great deal of money."

"So you've come to plead the poor innocent trafficker's case? Seems like an odd choice of ambassador to me. Surely you don't approve of what they're doing. Then again, you do their bidding elsewhere, so why not?"

His tone was angry and bitter, and she pulled in a breath. Then she reached up and tugged off the wig, tired of the way it itched her scalp. She removed the overbite from her mouth and tucked it into a pocket.

"What happened to being anonymous?" she demanded. "To being just another lowlife like they are?"

She'd been stunned at how much information the Syndicate had collected on him. Someone knew at the highest levels that he wasn't what he pretended to be. She didn't know how widely that information was known, but how could he be so foolish as to let his disguise slip even a moment?

Ian's gaze seared into her, scanning her from tip to toe. "Anonymity only goes so far," he told her. "Besides, they aren't entirely certain I'm not a lowlife. Just this morning I got a query about sending guns and fighters to yet another skirmish between warlords in yet another hotspot."

"Maybe not, but someone knows you have a hot button. Trafficking is something the mighty Ian Black doesn't engage in, no matter how many other immoral things he does. Or maybe he's biding his time until he can start his own operation. That's another possibility that will have occurred to someone."

"They think I'm competition, huh? Good."

"How is that good?"

He didn't reply. Instead he reached over and slipped a finger beneath the net cap she wore, pulling it off her head before he started work on the pins holding her hair in place. She didn't stop him, and soon her hair spilled free, the golden blond length of it reaching to just beneath her shoulders.

"Feel better?" he asked.

"Yes. The wig was hot and itchy."

"Stinks too," he said, eyeing it on the seat between them.

"Sorry, but if I want it to look greasy and unkempt, I have to make it so." She sighed. "Yes, I do their bidding. I've told you before that I do what I have to. It's about survival. I think you know what I mean."

"I do. And I've offered you something different, but you won't take it. Yet you won't tell me why."

Natasha fixed her gaze on the window that obscured the driver. So many things she wanted to say. And none that she could. "We all have our secrets, Mr. Black."

Too many secrets these days. Like the fact she was pregnant, and the baby was his. Like the fact she was here to assassinate him, and that this baby would not survive either. A wave of despair dragged her beneath the surface and choked the breath from her lungs.

She was a killer, nothing more. She didn't deserve a chance at happiness, no matter how fleeting.

A sob welled in her chest. She turned her head and clenched her fists tight, digging her nails into her palms to stop it from escaping. It was stupid to cry. Stupid to wallow in self-pity. But the pain of her fingernails wasn't enough, and soon her shoulders shook with silent tears.

Ian didn't say anything. He simply pulled her into his arms and let her cry.

Chapter Eleven

Ian held her as she cried. It wasn't like her to crumble, not in his limited experience, yet here she was sobbing like her heart was broken. It was possible she was playing him for some reason, softening him up, but he'd never gotten the impression that Natasha cried easily. If anything, he'd have said she worked hard to repress her emotions. So what was this about? The only way to find out was to let it happen.

He rubbed a hand up and down her arm, soothing her. He said nothing as she curled her fists into his shirt and shook in his arms. If she was acting, it was a damned good performance. He didn't think it was, though. There was real emotion behind the breakdown, which meant someone was leaning hard on the lever that controlled her.

He could tell when she began to get control of her emotions. The shaking subsided and her breathing grew more even as she pulled herself together. Eventually, she slipped from beneath his arm and sat up straighter. The only concession to her chaotic emotional state was that she shredded a tissue in her hand, possibly to keep herself from letting more tears fall.

He didn't press her to speak. He sensed that doing so would tip the balance again, and she'd be crying once more. He wanted to know why, and he wanted to fix it if he could, but pushing her wasn't how he was going to make that happen. He sat silently instead, waiting.

"I'm sorry about that," she finally said. "I'm tired. It was a long journey and I didn't get much sleep on the plane."

"I understand."

She shook her head. "I shouldn't be here with you. If they knew—" She gulped the words back, dropping her gaze to her lap.

"They'd hurt someone you care about, wouldn't they?"

He could see her go still, see how every line of her body suddenly subsided from nervous energy to calm control. "What makes you say that? I don't care about anyone but myself."

"You told me once that they had something of yours. About the only thing I can imagine you'd care about more than your own freedom would be a person. Specifically, a child."

Her entire body was stiff now. She'd stopped shredding the tissue. She merely sat, breathing slowly. He recognized it for a calming technique. He wanted to grab her and shake her, disrupt that calm utterly, but she was perilously close to the edge and he wouldn't push her over it.

Yet.

"How imaginative of you. Perhaps it's money. Did you ever think of that?"

"I did, in fact. But money wouldn't make you cry."

"It would if it were a great deal of money."

He scoffed. "If money's all it is, then come work for

me. I'll give you the money you're so upset about, and you can start over."

She didn't say anything. She also didn't look at him. "How generous of you, Mr. Black."

He was getting closer to shaking her, his temper simmering just beneath the surface. She got under his skin like nobody else had in a long time. Maybe ever.

"I think you should call me Ian, don't you? We spent an entire night fucking each other senseless—even if you did disappear the next morning."

Her gaze whipped to his. There was color in her cheeks. Her eyes flashed. Brown eyes. He wondered if that was really her color or if she'd donned contacts as part of her disguise.

"I had to go. It's not a matter of choosing to stay. *Ian*," she added, exaggerating his name. "The Syndicate has spies everywhere. For all you know, your driver is one. They could already know I'm here."

He tilted his head. "He's not, I promise you. But why *are* you here? Just to warn me? You could have done that in a text or sent a coded message."

She turned away again, her chin dropping so that she studied her lap. The tissue was turning to confetti again. "I wasn't sure you'd get a message. Or take it seriously enough."

He shrugged. "So what happens now? I pinky promise to stop bothering the bad guys and you go tell them you got me to swear to it, then everything's cool and we go back to pretending we don't know each other?"

She swore under her breath. He recognized the words as Russian.

"You wish to anger me, don't you? I came to warn you, and all you do is talk in circles. It's no wonder people don't like you," she finished with a sniff.

He wanted to laugh suddenly. "Fine, you've warned me. Now what? Do I take you back to the airport, or would you like to stay at my place for a couple of days before heading home again?"

"I'm tired. And hungry. Maybe one night will do."

He studied her. "Color me surprised. I thought you'd want to go and stay in a flea-hole to maintain your cover. Especially if you're worried the Syndicate's watching."

She made a dismissive noise. "You assured me your man is not a spy, so that's good enough. I want a bath and some dinner, and then I want a few hours sleep. I'll trust you enough for that."

"And will you trust me enough to tell me what hold they have over you? If I know, maybe I can help."

"No one can help—and I will never be free."

"You keep saying that, but you have choices, Natasha. Choose to accept my help, and I'll move mountains for you."

"Like you helped my parents?" she flung at him, her cheeks suddenly flushed with color.

He felt the blow like she'd hit him with her fists. Like she'd sucker punched him in the gut. He deserved it. "Not a day goes by I don't regret what happened to them. And to you."

She hugged herself. "But you saved Nikolai. How did you save him and not us? I was nineteen," she finished on a cracked whisper.

"I know. It's complicated."

"Then make me understand."

He sighed. Raked a hand over his head. He wondered how much to tell her. Then he decided, fuck it, she deserved to know all of it.

"Your parents became disillusioned over time. They felt like everything they'd done, everything they'd fought for

66

and sacrificed as double agents for Russia—including your life and your brother's as you knew them in America—was no longer important to those in power. Yes, they were ripe for the picking, and I was part of the team who picked them. I was younger then, more idealistic, and I believed in right and wrong. I also believed I knew which side the good guys were on. I thought it was us, and I didn't see the danger until too late. There were more people than you and your parents swept up in the purge, and I will carry the guilt of that to my grave."

He dragged in a breath, surprised he'd said so much. But he'd been carrying the burden for a long time now, and he'd never spoken of it to a soul outside of the CIA team he'd been a part of back then. They'd made mistakes, been too arrogant, and people had suffered. He'd learned a lot in the years since, and he'd spent the time working hard to make the world a better place.

Natasha stared at him now, her eyes big and liquid, her lip trembling. She'd been one of those who'd suffered. He didn't realize he'd made his speech in Russian until she answered him the same way.

"So you admit you caused it?"

She sounded small and wounded. He would do anything to change what'd happened, but he couldn't. He could change her future, though. If she'd let him.

Chapter Twelve

"I was a part of it," he said. "We didn't protect their identities well enough, and we didn't learn about the arrests until too late. I did what I could for your brother, but we were told that the three of you had been executed. I didn't know you were alive until we captured you the night you kidnapped Maddy Cole and her friend."

Natasha's stomach twisted. Did she dare to believe him, or was he lying about not knowing she'd still been alive?

He'd do it if he thought it would help persuade her to leave the Syndicate and join him. He'd say anything to make that happen.

"They were executed. I was not."

She gritted her teeth and refused to break down again. She'd been taken to the firing squad with her parents and several others, but she'd been pulled from the lineup at the last minute. She'd heard the shots as she'd been led away. It was something she would never forget for as long as she lived.

When she trusted herself to speak once more, she went

on. "I didn't know who you were until that night when your people rescued Maddy. I didn't even know you were involved until then. And I've hated you since."

Her heart throbbed and her eyes stung with fresh tears. She was overtired thanks to these stupid pregnancy hormones, and she'd said too much by admitting she hated him.

What next? Would she tell him she had a vial of poison and she was supposed to assassinate him with it? That she damned well *intended* to do it because, if she didn't, then she was dead and so was her innocent daughter? The Syndicate had no mercy when betrayed. She knew it well.

"You needed someone to hate, and better me than your brother. It wasn't his fault."

She clenched her fists in her lap. "No, I know that. But I was angry for the life he got to have while I endured a prison sentence for things I did not do. But I shot him and threatened to hurt the woman he loves, so there will be no forgiveness. I don't expect it."

"Maybe you should try. Tell him you're sorry."

She shook her head. "It's better this way."

He sighed. "Your call."

The limo slowed, then turned into a drive with big iron gates. They were motionless a moment as the driver spoke to someone in the guard shack. The gates swung open and the car began to move down the drive. Natasha turned to look behind her at the gates swinging closed. Ahead, a big house sat on a hill, light blazing from its windows. It was an imposing house, made of stone and brick, sprawling across the hill it perched upon like a dragon sitting on its hoard.

"Are we at Wayne Manor?" she asked, thinking of the rich billionaire who transformed into a caped crusader whenever anyone turned on the Bat Signal.

Ian snorted. "Cute. It's not that big."

She began to wonder if she'd made a mistake agreeing to go to his place. She'd expected a house on a street somewhere, even a big house, but a mansion on a hill, surrounded by iron fencing and guarded by security, had not crossed her mind. The dossier hadn't gone into detail about his house, though the address had been there. Her fault for not doing more research. It was going to be a lot harder to sneak out of a place like this than it had been his Venetian palazzo.

They reached the house and the driver stopped. Natasha was out of the car before anyone could open her door. The driver rounded the front of the car, throwing a hard look at her as if he intended to stop her from doing anything.

She recognized him. He was one of Ian's commandos. He'd been at the palazzo in October, and he'd been on the mountain in Spain when she'd handed Tallie Grant over.

Ian joined her on the pavement, shouldering the backpack she'd forgotten in her haste to get out of the car.

"I can take it," she said, reaching for the bag.

"It's no trouble, kitten."

"You're going to search it, aren't you?"

He handed the bag to the driver. "Standard procedure."

She wasn't worried. The moisturizer bottle was very real, and the vial didn't rattle inside. Unless he knew how to take that apart, she would still have the poison. And the syringe since it was concealed in the handle of her hairbrush.

She shrugged as if it was no big deal. "Whatever."

Ian put his hand against her back and her skin tingled beneath his fingers. She ignored the sensation as much as possible and walked up the stairs toward the front door. It swung open and another man stood there. She recognized this one from the mountaintop as well.

She gave Ian a sideways glance. "You don't trust me, do you?"

"I don't trust anyone," he said, not pretending he didn't know what she was talking about. She liked that he didn't make excuses. "It's part of the business."

"And I have just said that I hate you."

"So you did."

He ushered her inside the house, stopping to speak to the man who'd opened the door. Natasha took it all in. The house was decorated in sleek modern lines, with glass and pale woods such as maple and oak. The accents were steel. It wasn't as sprawling as it appeared on the outside, but it was still impressive. A rich man's abode. Not unlike some of the dwellings she'd been forced to visit on Syndicate business.

She didn't know who pulled the strings inside the Syndicate, but she knew there were powerful men involved. Many of them were involved for reasons of self-interest. Promises of business opportunities and ways to cover certain criminal activities and perversions. They financed some of the Syndicate's interests, but weren't part of the decision-making process.

Being here made her insides tighten. Was it the thought of the Syndicate and the fact they held Daria's life in their hands? Or were the lines blurring, making one rich man seem very much like another in her eyes?

What lengths would Ian Black go to in order to achieve his aims? Was he as ruthless as the Gemini Syndicate?

"You wanted a bath and food," Ian said, leading her down a hallway. "Let me show you to a room. Come out when you're ready."

They stopped in front of a maplewood door. She tilted

her head back because he was too tall to look in the eye. "I don't have any clothing. You took my bag."

"You'll have it in time to dress. I'll put it inside the door."

"Will you be watching me?"

"Cameras? No. I don't have them in the bedrooms. Other areas of the house, but not the private spaces. I also wouldn't make any phone calls if I were you. Those we intercept."

"Then I should text my evil overlords for instruction instead of calling them?"

Ian grinned. She liked that grin. Far more than she should.

"That'll work just fine. But no promises that we won't see those too."

She felt as if a noose were tightening around her throat. "Okay, so no communications in or out that you don't see. Am I a prisoner?"

He didn't move an inch, but she felt his presence against her body as if he'd backed her into the door. It was somewhat intimidating. And strangely exciting.

"Only if you want to be."

Her stomach chose that moment to get queasy. She felt herself turning green.

Ian's eyebrows narrowed. "I was kidding, Natasha. You aren't a prisoner. You can leave whenever you like."

She pressed her hand to her stomach. "I'm sorry, it's not you. I just, uh, my stomach has been upset. I might have eaten something a bit off, you know?"

He looked concerned. "Do you want some antacids? Something to stop the nausea?"

She almost said yes, but she didn't know if his something to stop the nausea would be bad for the baby. Was he talking about a drug?

"Maybe an antacid."

"What can you eat?"

"I don't know… Soup, maybe. Crackers. Nothing spicy or acidic."

"Okay, I'll see what I can find. Take that bath. Text me if you need anything."

"Thanks."

"I'll bring a tray to your room. Don't worry about coming to the kitchen."

"I want to see your house." Needed to see it so she'd know how to escape. "I'll come out unless I really can't. I'll let you know."

He frowned down at her. "All right, if that's what you want." He ran a finger down her cheek, and her skin tingled at his touch. "It's good to see you again."

"Yes, it is."

She almost said she'd missed him, but what the heck would that have been about? She hadn't missed him. She'd missed the way he'd made her feel for a night, but not him. She could get that feeling somewhere else. Just because she hadn't yet didn't mean it wasn't possible.

"Thanks for coming to warn me about the Syndicate. Means a lot, even if it was unnecessary."

Guilt pricked her. "I had to do it."

Silence fell between them. She stared at him, unwilling to look away. Or unable.

"I want to fix things for you, Natasha," he said softly. "But you have to let me in. You have to trust me."

Hope flared, but she squashed it. He couldn't fix it. No one could.

"Says the man searching my bag."

He laughed. "True. But we'll get there. We just have to try."

Chapter Thirteen

IAN WENT TO THE KITCHEN TO SCROUNGE FOR SOUP AND crackers. Not the kind of thing he usually did, but Natasha wasn't his usual guest. He had a very efficient housekeeper who stocked the pantry, and he was certain he'd seen soup at some point. He looked up as Ty walked in holding Natasha's bag.

"No weapons. I can't help thinking there's something I'm not finding, but damned if I can figure it out."

"Let me see," Ian said.

Ty emptied the bag onto the island. There were her travel documents, three shirts rolled into tubes, a sweatshirt, a pair of jeans, socks, and underwear. Six pairs of panties and two bras. Ian didn't remark on them and neither did Ty. The only toiletries were a toothbrush and toothpaste, a shampoo/conditioner combo, and a bottle of moisturizer. There were hairpins and another lace cap to cover her hair, as well as a short black wig, and a hair brush. She was traveling light for a master of disguise, which meant she didn't intend to be gone long.

Ian turned the brush over and tapped the handle. He

examined the toothpaste and brush, the shampoo, and the moisturizer. He considered keeping the toiletries since the guest bath was stocked, but it wouldn't build trust if he did that.

"If she has something, it's in here," he said, pointing to the bottles and tube.

"Poison," Ty said.

"Calypso has been known to use it before."

"We should analyze the contents."

"No time."

Ty frowned. "You're just going to give everything back to her and let her roam freely around your house? What if you're the target?"

He'd considered it. "I'll watch her closely."

"Boss," Ty said, shaking his head. "I don't know about this. Why not just take her to BDI and shake her down? We can find out why she's really here, who she works for —everything."

He could do that. Probably should do that. But he wasn't ready for it. Not yet. There was something about those eyes and the pain in them that got to him.

"Put everything back and I'll take the bag to her room. I'll need you to stay, though. If you're here, she likely won't try anything since it'd make escape harder."

"She could kill us both if that's the case."

Ian shook his head. "No, her style would be middle of the night. Kill and disappear before the household wakes up."

Ty didn't look convinced. "I don't like it. What if you're wrong and she comes out here gunning for you?"

They both knew he meant figuratively since Natasha hadn't carried a weapon on a commercial airliner. But that didn't mean she wasn't deadly anyway. The woman had skills.

"I'm not wrong," Ian said with the kind of certainty that came from years of experience. "Pack the bag. I'll take it to her, then fix the food. She's planning to come to the kitchen so she'll see you. Two of us will make her hesitate."

"Unless she poisons me too," Ty grumbled.

Ian resisted rolling his eyes, but barely. "You were Force Recon, and you're worried about a tiny woman who's tired and maybe a little sick? She's not getting the jump on us. Avoid getting close to her. Treat her like she's got Ebola or something. I'll do the serving and you stand in the corner with your sidearm, looking fierce."

"I could wish you hadn't sent Dax home just now," Ty said, still grumbling.

"We don't need him. Besides, he'll be monitoring the dark web for any hints about the Syndicate's plans or her real purpose. If he finds something, he'll call."

"Still don't like it, but you're the boss."

Ty finished packing the bag while Ian found the soup and crackers. He handed Ty a can opener. "Start that for me, would you?" he asked as he shouldered the bag.

"You forgot to give me the sedative to dump in here," Ty called out as Ian walked away.

Ian laughed. "Stop being a pussy, man."

"It's called being smart. That woman is trouble, mark my words."

Yeah, she was. And Ian wasn't forgetting it for a minute.

He took the bag to the guest room and knocked.

"I'm in the tub," she yelled. "Be out in a bit."

Ian opened the door. "It's me. Brought your clothes."

"Okay. Leave them on the bed, would you?"

He dropped the bag on the end of the bed and strolled into the bathroom. Steam curled up from the tub. Natasha leaned back against the rim, eyes closed. She'd found bubble bath—probably the housekeeper's doing—and her body was hidden from view. All he could see were her collarbones above the bubbles. Her eyes opened slowly, languidly. Ian perched on the edge of the tub. She arched an eyebrow.

"You think because we slept together once there are no boundaries?" she asked him coolly.

Her tone pleased him, mostly because it meant she was feeling normal again. He'd wondered about her when she'd turned green a few minutes ago. He'd thought she might puke on his shoes for a second, but now she looked perfectly healthy. Perfectly, sarcastically, Natasha.

He put a finger in the water and trailed it through the bubbles before blowing them off his hand. "I've seen the goods, angel. You ever hear that saying about toothpaste?"

She blinked. "What saying?"

"You can't put it back in the tube."

She snorted and closed her eyes again, clearly not bothered by his presence. "Which means now you get to walk in on me naked whenever you please?"

"So long as you're in my house, sure."

"You're a bad man, Ian Black."

"So they tell me. But don't worry, I understand how consent works. Seeing you naked is different from having sex—and I don't expect it, though I wouldn't turn it down if you wanted me to scratch your itch."

Her eyes snapped open again. They were… hazel. Green eyes with brown flecks around the iris. Could be her real color, or she could have changed contacts again. There hadn't been any in the bag, but that didn't mean she wasn't carrying a small kit in her jacket.

"What?" she asked as he studied her.

"Your eyes."

She dropped her lashes, covering them. "What about them?"

"Is that your real color?"

"I don't know. Is blue yours?"

"I don't know."

She rolled those pretty hazel eyes and frowned at him. "Whatever. And no, I have no itches that need scratching. You may go now. I'll be out soon."

He chuckled as he got to his feet. "I'll be in the kitchen. If you change your mind about that itch, text me."

Chapter Fourteen

THE BATH FELT GOOD. SHE'D PLANNED TO SHOWER, BUT when she'd seen the huge tub sitting empty, she'd thought that sinking into a hot bath would feel even better. She'd been right.

Natasha unplugged the drain with her foot, then stood and grabbed the fluffy white towel she'd gotten from the linen closet. She glanced at the bathroom door, but Ian wasn't lurking there. She'd heard him shut the bedroom door behind him as he'd left, but still.

He was trained in subterfuge. He could have faked the whole leaving thing.

"For what? To see you naked?" she muttered. Since he'd already done that, it defied logic.

He'd told her he had no cameras in the bedrooms. She'd checked to be sure. Not that he couldn't have something cleverly hidden, but there'd been nothing she could find. The mirror wasn't two-way, and there were no red dots anywhere.

Ian wasn't a perv recording her drying off, and he wasn't lurking outside the door. He was the sort of man who'd saunter in, lean on the doorframe and cross his ankles, whistling softly while letting his eyes slow walk down her body and back up again.

Natasha wrapped the towel around herself and went into the bedroom to retrieve her bag. It'd been gone through, but everything was there. She didn't find any listening devices or trackers. The moisturizer bottle still had the same weight as before. She pressed the hidden seam and the top popped off. The vial was still nestled in its hollow tube inside the creamy liquid. A quick check of the hairbrush revealed her syringe and needles.

She let out a breath and put everything back again. She still had the poison, and she could complete her mission and go home. Daria would be safe. It was all she wanted.

Nausea threatened for a moment before subsiding when she pressed her hand to her belly. She needed to try and eat. Perhaps that would help.

She dressed quickly in jeans and a long-sleeved tee to cover her tattoo, put on her Chucks, and tucked her hair behind her ears. Then she went in search of the kitchen.

Ian looked up when she walked in. She stopped in her tracks when she spotted the other guy leaning against the counter beside the refrigerator. He'd been the driver tonight.

"Natasha," Ian said. "Meet Tyler Scott."

"Ty," the man said. He was tall like Ian, with dark curly hair and green eyes that studied her with barely disguised dislike. He didn't hold out his hand for her to shake, and she didn't offer her own.

"You were on the mountain in Spain," she said.

His eyes widened a fraction. "Are you guessing or do you know?"

They'd been wearing greasepaint and dark clothes, so

he was thinking she shouldn't know. But he had a scar that curved from his left nostril down and around his mouth, stopping just beneath the corner of his lip. It wasn't a new scar. It looked quite old, really. The kind of thing you wouldn't pay much attention to under ordinary circumstances. But she noticed scars.

"I know it, though you may deny it if you wish. It doesn't matter to me."

Ian dragged a chair back from the island. "Here, come try the soup. It's from a can, but that's the best I can do."

Natasha went over and took a seat. There was a placemat with a bowl of hot soup—looked like chicken noodle—a sleeve of crackers, and a spoon. Ian had given her another bubbly water, this one plain instead of flavored.

"Thank you," she said politely as she picked up the spoon.

"You aren't worried we've poisoned it?" Ty asked when she had the spoon halfway to her lips.

She shot him a grin and put the spoon in her mouth. She understood his kind. He was a warrior, the kind of man for whom black and white was a given. There were no shades of gray with him, and he didn't like her.

She knew why. And she didn't care. Being liked was for high school. Being feared was far preferable. Kept people away.

"No, I'm not worried," she said once she'd taken the bite. "Poisoning me will not get you any of the answers you seek."

"Who said I'm seeking answers?" he snapped out.

Ian sighed. "Children, please. No fighting at the table."

Natasha rolled her eyes. "All I'm trying to do is eat this soup and not puke it back up. Your Neanderthal friend over there is the one with the problem."

Ian dragged out a chair for himself and sat. He filched one of her crackers and popped it in his mouth. Ty watched them, looking all flinty-eyed and cold.

"My friend is convinced you've come to kill me. He's a bit protective at the moment."

The cracker Natasha had just bit into seemed to swell until it threatened to choke her. She swallowed hard. "Why would I come to your house to kill you? Far safer to arrange one of our secret meetings and take you out there, don't you think?"

Ty's gaze narrowed. "Secret meetings, boss?"

Ian waved a hand. "We've run into each other in different locations. I'd hardly call them secret meetings."

"If I wanted you dead, I could have killed you in London," Natasha said, her cheeks feeling hot suddenly. "Remember that?"

"Not likely to forget it. That disguise was very good, by the way."

"Thank you. I rather thought so."

Ian folded his arms on the counter and leaned on them, looking up at her from beneath long dark lashes. Too attractive, that man. Her heart flipped as if to say *"Yep."*

"Thing is, though," he said, oh so casually. "It's not if *you* want me dead that I have to think about. It's if your bosses do."

Color flooded her cheeks. She cursed herself for the too obvious response, but it couldn't be helped.

"And why would I come here to warn you about crossing them if that was the case?"

"Don't know, kitten. Is it hot in here?"

"A little," she said. "Or I might be feverish. Honestly, I'm not sure I'm not coming down with something."

"Then eat as much as you can and go to bed. You're

safe here." His phone rang and he picked it up. "Gotta take this. You two behave."

He walked out of the room, talking to someone in… was that French? She strained to hear the words. Yes, definitely French.

"But are we safe with you?" Ty asked once Ian was gone.

Natasha kept eating her soup and shot him a glare. If he was scared of her, good. But really, she suspected he wasn't scared at all. He was just trying to get a rise out of her. Which she wouldn't give him. She'd encountered her share of posturing men over her career. Men who hated that she was good at what she did, and who took every opportunity to undermine her.

Not that this one was doing that, but she could tell when someone didn't like her or when they thought she wasn't worth the time it took to speak to her.

"Are you friends with my brother?" she asked.

He blinked, and she wondered if it was possible he didn't know. But, no, she imagined everyone in Ian's inner circle knew the truth. If he'd been around the night she'd shot Nikolai and his teammate, then he'd know.

"We're friends."

Natasha finished the soup—or as much as she could stomach—and pushed the bowl away. "I don't really care if you don't like me, you know. It's unimportant."

He put his hand on his side and she knew he was touching a concealed weapon.

"I don't like you. And just so we're clear, I'll have no problem putting a bullet in you if you give me a reason."

She forced ice into her veins, forced herself to rely on her training.

Be cool. Be aloof. Don't let them see your fear.

"Then I guess I better not give you a reason. But just

remember it goes both ways, *Ty*. You give me a reason, and I'll come for *you*. You don't want that to happen, believe me."

His eyes flashed, but he didn't answer.

Natasha pushed her chair back and stood. "Tell Ian I went to bed, would you?"

It wasn't until she was in her room with the door shut that she lifted a hand to push her hair from her forehead—and found it shaking.

A moment later she was in the bathroom, losing everything she'd just eaten.

Chapter Fifteen

IAN ONLY HALF PAID ATTENTION TO THE FRENCH billionaire who was about to fork over a ridiculous amount of money for protection from an obsessed former lover.

Instead, he thought about Natasha. He wasn't an idiot, no matter what Ty might think at that precise moment. He knew she was dangerous, and he knew he had to watch his back. Until he knew precisely what hold the Syndicate had over her—and how to end it—she could be used against him.

Against anyone.

Presidents, generals, religious leaders. He didn't like to think about it, but it was possible. She was a living weapon, and she was deadly. When Ian had soothed the Frenchman's fears, he ended the call and returned to the kitchen.

"She went to bed," Ty said.

"Did she eat everything?"

Ty shook his head. "About half the soup."

Ian frowned. "I'm going to my office then. You can go home if you want."

Ty looked at him disbelievingly. "Right. No way. I'm staying."

"Suit yourself. Pick a guest room. I'm not sure how long I'll be."

"I'll guard the door," Ty said.

"You don't need to guard the door. I'll know if she leaves her room. Once I put the cameras on night mode, I'll get an alert if she crosses the threshold into the hallway."

Ty huffed a breath. "Okay. But I'm still staying."

"I expected as much."

Ian went to his home office with the great view of the Chesapeake, not that he could see it tonight but he could see the lights of boat traffic, and made some phone calls. He didn't need more than four or five hours of sleep, so he typically spent some of his evening talking to his teams and clients in other parts of the world.

He sometimes missed being out there as much as he used to be, but the bigger his business grew, the more he had to be home to handle it. He had a trusted team, and they could run things for him here when needed—and often did since he had skills that came in handy in danger zones—but he still found himself in the DC metro area more frequently than he used to.

It was why he'd bought this house six months ago. Plus he'd taken one look at the view and thought it was a place he'd love to show a special woman some day.

He leaned back in his chair and stared at the lights illuminating the lawn as it gently sloped toward the water. A woman? Or Natasha in particular?

He wasn't surprised at the thought, even if it disconcerted him. He'd recognized something in her soul the instant they'd met. Something that also resided inside him.

That didn't make her his fated soulmate or anything, but it did make the whole thing damned interesting.

And more than a bit complicated.

He glanced at the computer monitor with the camera feeds from the rooms of his house. No bedrooms, as he'd told her. That was crossing a line into creepy. But he was the kind of man who couldn't be too careful, so he had cameras that recorded the activity in his house. Just in case.

There was nothing to see. No lights warning that someone was in the zone. Natasha's door was closed, and there was no light coming from beneath it. She hadn't breached the exterior because he would have definitely known that. The alarm would have triggered if she'd opened a window. Or broken it.

He thought of her pale face earlier. The way she delicately ate, as if she didn't trust her stomach not to bring the food back up again. The way she'd grown hot when he'd mentioned the Syndicate sending her to kill him. She could simply be sick, or it could have been a reaction to what he'd said.

Especially with the way he'd been shitting all over their plans lately. If they were ever going to make a move, the time would be now. And who better to send than the legendary Calypso?

Part of him wanted to know if she would really try and kill him. He wanted to know if the woman who'd lain beneath him, who'd moaned so sweetly in his arms, was still capable of killing him after the night they'd shared.

Logic told him she was. Hope wanted to believe otherwise.

But experience, that bitch, told him that hope was a futile thing in this world.

He knew it better than most.

Chapter Sixteen

SHE SLEPT THE SLEEP OF THE DEAD, AND THEN BOLTED upright when her old friend nausea came calling.

Natasha shot from the bed—not an easy task when you were still groggy—and barely reached the toilet before losing the absolute nothing she had in her stomach. When she was done, she sank onto the cool floor and leaned against the tub, focusing on breathing deeply and regularly.

This being pregnant shit was for the birds. How the hell did women put up with this crap? It was a wonder anyone ever wanted to get pregnant. Or, if they didn't know how it was going to be, it's a wonder they did it more than once.

When she felt like she wasn't going to puke again, she stood on shaky legs and turned on the shower. After standing beneath the cool spray for a while, she dried off and dressed again. She put on what she'd worn to the kitchen last night. Since she hadn't worn it long, she figured it was fine.

Besides, she was supposed to be a college student who

shopped army surplus, not a fashionista. Well, mostly a college student since she hadn't donned a wig or the over-bite. She also didn't put the contacts in. Ian had seen her eyes, so what was the point? Besides, he still didn't know if it was her real color or not.

What was his real color? She really wanted to know.

Natasha moved carefully, until she was sure she wasn't going to lose it again. She eyed the moisturizer bottle on the counter and considered retrieving the vial, loading a dose, and secreting it on her body. If the chance arose, she could inject him and be on her way.

Assuming Ty with the terrible scowl wasn't lurking behind the furniture, waiting for her to strike.

But no, she couldn't count on being ready if the opportunity presented itself. She also couldn't be sure she'd get away feeling like this.

If this pregnancy experience went the way it had been going for the past few days, she'd feel normal again for a few hours late this afternoon. That might be the time.

She didn't dare turn on her phone in case she had an incoming message from her handler. Ian had said they could intercept cell phone messages. She didn't know if it was true or not, but she wasn't testing his technology when she was an easy target in his lair.

She had to be patient and wait. Daria and Lissette were in the Alps, being treated like queens at a gorgeous hotel. They weren't in a prison cell. They were having afternoon tea, skiing, and shopping. Daria would have missed getting a tree for all of an hour, until she'd walked into that hotel and been greeted by the massive tree in their lobby. The hotel very likely had trees in every suite as well.

The only nagging worry was why the Syndicate had

taken Daria in the first place. It wasn't like they'd never been able to count on Natasha doing the job.

Maybe it was a response to the fact she'd been chafing at her restraints lately. She'd declined jobs, suggested they use someone else. And they had since she wasn't the only hired assassin in the business. There were plenty of others who could do the work.

And did. So why not send one of them? Why send her, and why use her child as a lever?

Natasha pulled in a slow breath and made herself calm down. She was reading far more into this situation than she needed to. This was definitely about control, but it was probably about her killing of the Butcher in Spain. She'd gone rogue on that one, and they knew it. This was a show of force to reel her back in and remind her who had the power.

Ultimately, they were giving her permission to do what she'd wanted for the past year. The opportunity to kill yet another person who'd contributed to the peeling away of her innocence. Hunting down all those who'd hurt her—who'd hurt Lena—had been her secret mission for years now.

It's what had kept her going during the darkest times.

Natasha gritted her teeth as she looked at her face in the mirror. She had to stop thinking about her demons and start thinking about how she was getting out of here alive. Killing Ian wouldn't do her any good if she couldn't escape.

Her eyes were bright, and her cheeks were pale. The bags under her eyes made her look exhausted.

Hell, she was exhausted. She'd never been so damned tired in all her life.

She pulled in a deep breath for support and marched over to the bedroom door. There was no one in the hall, but the smell of coffee tugged her toward the kitchen. She put her hands in her jeans pockets and then took them out again. Made her look like she had something in there, right?

Ian was at the island, a paper spread out on the white marble countertop. His dark hair shone in the light coming in from the window. She watched him, wondering at the feelings spiraling through her.

There was dislike, of course. But there was also admiration, and attraction, and even a feeling that hinted at contentment. Weird.

Ty was nowhere to be seen, but she knew he must be close by. Maybe watching her on Ian's cameras.

"You haven't heard of the internet?" she asked, moving fully into view.

Ian looked up. He wasn't startled, or fearful, or wary. He simply looked up and shot her that gorgeous grin of his. She almost thought she wouldn't mind seeing his smile in the morning more often.

Almost.

"Morning, kitten. How's the stomach today?"

"Okay. For now." He'd called her kitten and angel, and though she thought she should tell him to stop, she couldn't make herself say the words.

Because you like it when he says those things.

He folded the paper over and stood. He was tall, handsome, imposing. She had a sudden memory of him in a tuxedo, a black silk mask over his eyes, and her heart thumped like a moth beating its life away around a street light.

"I like reading an actual paper," he said, shoving his hands into his faded jeans as he answered her earlier question. They hugged his hips like a lover, and she found herself having to drag her gaze upward to his face. He wore a black button-down shirt with sleeves rolled up so that his forearms were visible. What was it about a man in rolled sleeves that made her feel all gooey inside?

Except it wasn't *a* man in rolled sleeves. It was *this* man in rolled sleeves.

She had to work to drag her attention back to the topic. A paper? What?

Oh yeah, she'd asked him about the internet.

"Whatever, grandpa. The kids are reading their papers online these days, or hadn't you heard that?"

He snorted. "I'm aware. I also read them online—but I still like to spread a paper over the island and really explore it, you know?"

Uhhhh…

"Whatever works for you."

"It definitely works for me. I like spreading things out, really touching every single part. It's so satisfying."

Oh my God.

Was she blushing? She felt like she was.

"Is there coffee?" she blurted.

"There is. Do you feel like you can drink it, or would you prefer something milder? Tea maybe."

"Oh, tea would be better. Just tell me where to find it and I can fix it myself."

"You're my guest, Natasha. Sit down. I'll fix it."

She took a seat at the island, torn between watching the muscles rippling beneath his shirt as he moved, and looking at the gorgeous view of water beyond the picture frame windows. The grass was green, but the trees had lost their leaves. A flock of Canada geese flew low over the water, then lifted and wheeled south.

It was almost Christmas, but it didn't seem like it. Ian didn't have a tree or decorations of any kind. Then again, why would he? If not for Daria, she wouldn't either. It made her too sad when she remembered her childhood Christmases and how happy she'd been back then.

"I've got English Breakfast or Earl Gray. Which one do you want?"

She chewed the inside of her lip. Surely a little caffeine wouldn't hurt. It wasn't as bad as coffee. Plus, she remembered Lena telling her once that a small amount while you were pregnant was fine. It was drinking too much that was the problem.

"English Breakfast," she said, baffled as to why she was even worrying about this. She could *not* keep this child. But a part of her sat in a corner inside and cried—because, strangely enough, she wanted to.

My child. Mine.

She looked at Ian as he filled the kettle and plugged it in. Tears stung her eyes.

Our child.

He set a sugar bowl in front of her, then pulled a carton of milk out of the refrigerator and held it up in question.

"Is there any other way to drink tea?" she asked.

He came over and set it down in front of her. "Nope, not in my book." He frowned as he looked at her. "What's going on, Natasha?"

She sniffed and turned her head away, wiping her eyes on her sleeve. *Dammit.*

She had to stop this. Now.

"Hormonal shit," she told him boldly. "Haven't you heard those are a bitch?"

"I've heard. There's probably some, uh, products in the guest room. Margo keeps things stocked around here."

A little flare of jealousy reared its head. She'd thought he lived alone. Maybe she was wrong. "Margo?"

"She's my housekeeper."

"Oh. Okay. Um, I think it's fine. But thank you."

The kettle chimed and he poured boiling water over a tea bag, then slid the cup toward her. She occupied herself swirling the bag around. "Where's your grumpy friend?" she asked after a few silent moments.

"He's around. I expect he'll walk in any minute."

"He doesn't like me."

"He doesn't trust you."

"Do you?"

"Should I?"

She dropped her gaze. "Probably not."

"That's honest. Hey, you hungry?"

Her stomach growled. It was also about one wrong smell away from heaving again. And by wrong smell, it could be absolutely anything. "I am. But I think I should take it easy. Toast, maybe?"

He walked into the pantry and came out with a loaf of bread. Then he set about making toast.

"What about you?" she asked when he buttered the toast and set it in front of her.

"I ate a couple of hours ago. With Ty."

Natasha blinked. "What time is it?"

She couldn't turn her cell phone on so she didn't know. If Ian had a microwave with a clock in his kitchen, it wasn't visible to her.

"It's eleven-thirty, angel. Almost lunch time."

"Are you kidding?"

He shook his head. "No. You slept about twelve hours."

She took a bite of the toast and gagged. "Oh God. I think I'm going to be sick again."

Ian wrapped a strong arm around her and took her the few steps to the island sink. She gripped the edge of the

countertop and stared at the bottom of the sink. Nothing
was coming up and the nausea slowly subsided.

"What's wrong with you, Natasha?" Ian's voice was
soothing, like a cool hand on her brow.

"It's nothing. A twenty-four hour bug."

She heard footsteps and knew that Ty the Terrible had
returned. His words confirmed it.

"Jesus, boss, what the hell are you doing?"

"She's sick. Call Knight and let's get this figured out."

"No," Natasha said. Or moaned, maybe. "Really, it'll
be fine. I just need to lie down."

"Shit, someone could have infected her with a
bioweapon," Ty said. "She could be contaminating us right
now."

"It's not a bioweapon," Ian said coolly. "Call Knight.
Tell him to bring his medical kit."

Natasha straightened, determined. "No, you don't have
to do that. I just need to rest. Maybe I can try the toast
again. Or the tea. I should drink more tea. I'll be fine."

She pushed away from Ian—weakly, of course—and
went back to her seat. Her stomach roiled, but she didn't
let it get to her this time. She sipped the tea, reluctant to
try the toast for fear it would overwhelm her again.

"See, already better," she said, forcing a smile. Natasha
closed her eyes and willed the room to stop spinning. If she
failed at this mission, she was as good as dead. Which
mean that Daria was dead too. And Lissette, who didn't
deserve it any more than Daria did.

"Knight," Ian said. "Now. Tell him to get here ASAP."

Ty took out his phone. "I'm on it, boss."

Natasha opened her eyes and glared. Ian shrugged.

"Sorry, angel, but I take care of those who need it.
Whether they like it or not."

Chapter Seventeen

Jared Fraser, otherwise known as Knight, arrived within the hour. He'd brought his fiancée, Libby. Ian hadn't said not to, but maybe he should have considering the patient was a notorious assassin. Not that Libby knew that. Besides, she was bright and bubbly, not the kind of person to make anyone feel bad. Maybe she'd be good for Natasha. They were close in age and completely opposite.

After the small talk, Jared slanted his gaze from Ty to Ian and back. "Okay, so what's the problem?"

"I have a guest who's a little sick," Ian said. "Can't seem to hold down any food, even something as mild as toast. She's tired, maybe a little more emotional than she typically is. She flew in from Europe last night, but this seems a little more intense than jet lag."

Jared's eyebrows climbed a little higher. "Uh, okay. Could be a few things, but the first thing I'd like to eliminate is a simple one. Is she pregnant?"

And just like that, Ian felt as if someone had taken a big fat club and swept his legs out from under him.

Fucking hell. Why hadn't he thought of that possibility?

Two months since they'd slept together. He'd used a condom—except for the first time. It was possible, even if highly improbable, that he'd gotten her pregnant.

It was also possible she'd been fucking someone else. Probably the case, actually. It wasn't like they were a couple, or exclusive. They had a connection that was physical, and they'd acted on it. Didn't mean anything.

Still.

Jesus.

"Actually, I haven't the faintest clue," he said, his voice as cool as he could make it under the circumstances. He hadn't been with anyone since that night, but she could have been. "She didn't mention it."

Jared set the medical kit down on the coffee table and rummaged through it. "Okay, well, I have a test here if she wants to pee on it. Or we can draw blood and I'll take it to the lab. That's the more certain way."

"How about the blood then?"

Jared's brows drew down. "That's fine, but don't you think we should ask her what she prefers?"

In any other circumstances, yes. But Ian was undergoing a shift inside. A shift that those around him often called beast mode. He was about to enter the *fuck the consequences and take no prisoners* phase. He wanted answers, and he wanted them now.

"We can ask. But you're drawing blood even if we have to hold her down."

Jared looked like he was about to say something.

"It's Calypso," Ty said.

Jared shot a look at Libby, then back to Ian. "You could have fucking told me that. I wouldn't have brought Libby."

It was Libby's turn to frown. "Why not? Is she an old girlfriend of yours or something? Because you know I don't care about that."

Jared put an arm around her and pulled her against his side. "No, she's not an old girlfriend. She's just someone we don't like much."

"Okay then," Libby said brightly. "You may not like her, but she's sick. And you're here to help. Where is she?"

"I'm right here," Natasha said.

Ian turned. They all did. She was standing in the entry to the living room. She'd gone to her room earlier, saying she needed to be still and quiet. Ian had let her go, watching as she walked away on unsteady feet.

Pregnant? Jesus.

"Hi," Libby said. "I'm sorry for anything you over-heard. Really."

She started toward Natasha, hand held out, when Jared grabbed her by the arm and tugged her back again. "No, baby. Best not to get too close."

Libby crossed her arms and gave Jared a look. "You're being kind of dickish, which isn't like you. Why?"

Jared looked uncomfortable. "She might be contagious. That's all."

Libby tapped a foot. "Pregnancy is contagious? Who knew?"

"Who said I'm pregnant?" Natasha snapped. But her face had paled again.

Ian was barely holding in his anger. His hurt. That was an emotion he hadn't felt in so long now that it took him a moment to identify it. Not much had the power to hurt him, but this was, shockingly, one of those things.

"Jared's a medic, Natasha. Your symptoms sound like pregnancy to him."

She snorted. "Oh, so now you can diagnose pregnancy just by hearing symptoms? There aren't sixty other possibilities? Some medic."

"He's going to take your blood," Ian told her. "We'll know soon enough."

Her eyes widened. "No, I don't think so. I told you it's a stomach bug. I'll be fine when it runs its course."

Ian stalked toward her. Her nostrils flared but she didn't move. She folded her arms and watched him coming. He stopped when he loomed over her. Maybe it was a cheap move to use his size against her, but he was holding onto the shreds of his temper by the barest of threads.

"Roll up your goddamn sleeve, Calypso," he growled. "Or I'll hold you down and do it myself."

Her face turned red and then white. Her lips tightened until they were white too. "You wouldn't."

"Test me. I'll fucking do it."

She searched his gaze while he glared at her. The air between them was thick. Hot.

He wanted to kiss her. And he wanted to lock her in a room and not look at her until he calmed the fuck down. He didn't often lose his shit, but he was on the verge of it now. And it wouldn't be pretty if he did.

"Are you pregnant?" he asked, switching to Russian because he didn't want the others to understand the conversation. "Tell me the truth."

She didn't say anything for a long moment. And then she did, one word that burst from her in a puff of air. *"Da."*

"Is it mine? Or someone else's?"

He wasn't prepared for the slap. Maybe he should have been, but he wasn't. His head rocked to the side and his cheek stung. He held out a hand behind him to stop Jared and Ty from rushing over and taking Natasha down.

"Who else's would it be?" she hissed. "You think I crash parties and fuck random men as a pastime? Or do you think perhaps you got careless when you didn't use a condom the first time and here we fucking are?"

He couldn't argue with her. He had been careless. And yet the hurt throbbed hard in his soul.

"I don't know what you do when you're off wherever it is you go, Natasha. I don't even know you. You won't tell me a fucking thing, and you won't tell me what they have that keeps you dancing to their tune."

Her eyes looked sad. So sad and helpless. In that moment, he wanted to do anything to fix it for her. But she wouldn't let him in.

Except she had no choice now. She was pregnant, and it could be his. If so, he wasn't letting her go. He wouldn't abandon his child, and he wouldn't abandon her. They'd figure out the details later, but for now she wasn't going anywhere.

"You can't fix it, Ian. If I left, they would come for me and they wouldn't ever stop." Her eyes shone with tears. "I'm sorry. So sorry. I have to protect her. There's no other way."

He didn't know what she was talking about. And he didn't get the chance to ask before she whipped her hand up with lightning speed, the light flashing on something metallic as she aimed it at his body.

All he could do was react.

She was fast. He had to hope he was faster.

Chapter Eighteen

SHE DIDN'T WANT TO KILL HIM, AND YET SHE HAD NO choice. For Daria.

Once Ian had sent for his medical person, she'd gone back to her room and taken the vial from the bottle, filling it with a lethal dose. She hadn't planned to do it now. She'd just wanted it on her so she could be prepared. If she had an opportunity, she had to take it.

But acting out of emotion was the surest way to fail, and this time was no different. Even as she thrust the syringe at his jugular, she knew the attempt was doomed.

Maybe that was why she'd done it. Or maybe she was just foolish and stupid.

Ian stepped back and to the side, letting her momentum carry her forward. He didn't trip her, though. He grabbed her wrist and twisted, dragging her backward against his body and forcing her to drop the syringe.

It was over in seconds.

Natasha struggled against Ian's hold, but it wasn't enough. His arms were steel bands around her, and yet somehow he held her gently. As if she were fragile.

"I knew you were here for a reason. And it wasn't to tell me I was going to be a father." He still spoke in Russian. He sounded detached, clinical.

Dread pooled in her stomach. Whatever softness he'd had for her was gone. She shouldn't care, and yet it hurt to think she'd ruined everything between them. No more kitten or angel. No more mischievous grins. No more sexual innuendo that made her melty inside.

She'd tried to kill him, and she was worried that he wouldn't call her kitten anymore? Ridiculous.

Ian's men had started toward them, but they took a step backward as Ian subdued her. They were prepared for violence, though. If Ian told them to take her outside and tear her into pieces, they would do it. Happily.

She glared to let them know she wasn't afraid, even if she was.

Never show your fear. It makes you weak.

Her fear wasn't because of them, though. It was Ian. She'd never pushed him this far, and she didn't know what he would do. He had a reputation in the dark underworld she inhabited of being ruthless and black-hearted. She'd thought it was exaggerated since she'd only ever dealt with the man who wanted to save her from the Syndicate.

Now she feared she was about to encounter the other Ian. The one who made others fear to cross him.

The woman—Libby—darted her gaze between them all, looking a little bit wild and a lot confused. "What the hell just happened? What is that thing?"

"A syringe. I believe she tried to kill him," Ty said casually. "Pretty sure she wasn't administering a flu shot."

Libby turned big eyes on her. "Why? Why would you do that? What's wrong with you?"

Natasha shuddered but didn't answer. Libby had been her ally briefly, but no longer. Not that Natasha needed an ally. She did what she had to do, and she didn't care what anyone thought of her.

Anyone but Daria.

She repeated it to herself over and over, but it didn't help her feel any better about what she'd done.

Behind her, Ian's body was rock solid. She could feel the anger rolling from him in seismic waves. That didn't help either.

"Someone is holding a person Natasha loves hostage. They're threatening to kill this person if Natasha doesn't do their bidding." His voice was very cool. "Killing me is their price."

Libby hugged herself, frowning. "I don't know what it's like to be forced to do something terrible to save someone, but I do know what it's like to be taken against your will and threatened. I'm sorry for your pain, Natasha."

Natasha's throat knotted. She didn't dare try to speak. There was nothing she could say anyway. She'd failed, and Daria was still in danger. The Syndicate would retaliate when they found out.

She should have taken more care. She'd planned to, and then he'd asked if the baby was his.

It had been more than she could take and she'd lashed out. Stupid to be so prideful. She'd doomed herself, and she'd doomed the one person she loved. The tears she'd been holding back spilled down her cheeks.

Ty came over to pick up the syringe. He handed it to Jared.

"Do you have more?" Ian asked in that voice of his that wouldn't melt ice cubes.

Yet it still managed to send shivers of anticipation down her spine.

"No comment."

"The toiletries," he said. "Take them to the lab."

Ty nodded. "Sure thing, boss. Want me to call and get a cell prepared for her?"

Natasha didn't like the way he said *her*. With disdain. As if she were a cockroach he intended to smash.

She felt the tension in Ian's body as his voice whipped into the air. "She's fucking pregnant. I'm not putting her in a cell at BDI."

"You can't trust her," Jared said. "And you can't let her go."

Ian bent until his mouth was beside her ear. "I'm not letting her go."

Natasha shuddered again, but not from fear or revulsion. He was ruthless, but he'd also defended her to the others. In a way. Her body hummed from being so close to him. Goosebumps rose on her flesh. The hairs on her arms stood up. It took her a moment to understand what was happening. When she did, shock reverberated into her bones.

How? How could she still want him when his very existence endangered her daughter's life?

"What are you going to do with me?" she asked, the words barely more than a whisper.

"Keep you," he replied, his voice low and deep.

"You can't." There was panic in hers.

"Try and stop me, kitten. Try and fucking stop me."

Chapter Nineteen

IAN WAS IN A RAGE. SHE'D TRIED TO KILL HIM.

Fucking tried to inject him with poison and kill him. In his own damned living room. A week before Christmas, for fuck's sake. In front of his team. How the hell did she think she was going to get away with it?

The truth cracked through his brain. *She didn't.*

It was almost as if she'd wanted him to stop her.

Ian growled as he raked a hand over his scalp. That was fucking wishful thinking. It wasn't that she'd wanted him to stop her. It was that she'd acted out of emotion because he'd pissed her off. Stupid of her, really. But damned good for him.

He didn't like to think what would have happened if she'd been on her game. It wasn't the first time a woman had tried to kill him. Thankfully, that one hadn't succeeded either. It was a memory he'd managed to shove deep, but for some fucking reason it was back.

Probably because he'd trusted Natasha more than he should. Believed in her. Believed in the magnetic pull between them. It was clearly one-sided and he'd been a fool.

He didn't like being a fool. Pissed him off to no end.

He stood in his living room, staring at the water beyond the windows as it sparkled beneath a sunny December sky, and his mind raced. Jared had taken a blood sample and left. Ty was very wisely not saying anything. Dax and Rascal were on the way over.

And since Jared had been a witness, that meant that Jace, Colt, and Brett would be on their way too. Ian hadn't bothered to tell Jared not to say anything to them. It wouldn't have mattered anyway. Jared would have disobeyed that order. He'd have found a way, like a damned atomic particle, to exist in two states of being at the same time. He'd have told them without telling them.

And the shit would have hit the fan anyway.

Natasha was in the guest room. Locked in because he wasn't letting her roam his house when he had knives and forks in the kitchen. He also had guns, but those were in a safe. Well, most of them. He had guns tucked away in different places in the house for quick reach, but they weren't obvious to anyone but him.

She could find them, though. Given enough time.

It wasn't ideal to keep her here. But he wasn't putting her in a cell at BDI either. Better to take her somewhere remote. Somewhere she couldn't escape.

One way or another, he was getting her secrets out of her. The time for gentle persuasion was over.

Ian's phone rang. He answered with a clipped, "Yeah?"

"She's definitely pregnant, boss. Almost nine weeks along."

"Nine weeks," he repeated, not really understanding the words as he said them.

"Pregnancy is estimated from the date of the last

menstrual cycle, so conception would have likely occurred a little less than seven weeks ago. In case you want to know the actual date for any reason."

Ian heard the curiosity in the other man's tone. He wasn't in the mood to confirm or deny anything. "Thanks."

Natasha had said she was pregnant, but after everything she'd done, he wasn't going to believe a word she said unless he got it confirmed. Guess she hadn't lied about that one.

"Be careful. She's still dangerous."

"I know."

He ended the call and stalked toward the guest room where she resided. Ty didn't go along, but then he'd checked every inch of the bedroom, bathroom, and closet to make sure there were no weapons. They both knew she could use a clothes hanger or a lamp cord as a weapon if she so chose, but Ian didn't think she was going to try it yet. She knew she wouldn't get out of here alive if she did.

Staying alive was important to her, even if she'd acted stupidly when she'd tried to kill him. It wasn't a mistake she'd make again.

And yet she was a cornered animal, and cornered animals were unpredictable.

He knocked on the door. She didn't answer, so he unlocked it using the keypad and thrust it open—and found her sitting on the bed, leaning back against the headboard, her eyes closed. She wasn't sleeping, but she wasn't acting like she cared he was there either.

He closed the door behind him and shoved his hands into his pockets. "Almost nine weeks," he said. "That's how pregnant you are."

"I know how pregnant I am, thanks. And I know when it happened. It was *not* nine weeks ago."

"I know. It's the way pregnancy is calculated. It happened in Venice."

The corners of her nostrils flared. Such a tiny gesture. Like she was working on control. "I'm aware of when it happened."

"Who sent you to kill me? Or was that your own idea?"

She didn't flinch. "No. I'm pregnant, not stupid."

"So who then?"

"Who do you think?"

"The Syndicate. But *who*?"

Her eyes snapped open. "I don't know. I don't get told that. I got a text message and a dossier. You were the target."

"And you were going to go through with it."

Her expression tightened. "I had no choice."

There was so much about that statement he wanted to unpack.

"Who are they holding, Natasha? Do you have a child? Is that their hold over you?"

Her lashes dropped, covering her eyes. When she looked at him again, there were tears shining in those eyes. Such pretty hazel eyes. He could drown in them under different circumstances. Except that she clearly didn't feel the same. She'd tried to kill him. Would do it again if she could.

His heart was stone in the face of that. *Impenetrable.*

"My adopted daughter. She's six and she's innocent. She doesn't deserve any of this."

His insides twisted. He didn't want to feel any softness toward this woman, didn't intend to ever again. But he couldn't condemn an innocent child. He knew what it was like to be condemned when you'd done nothing wrong.

"No, she doesn't. And what about the child you're carrying? What was the plan there?"

"I was going to make an appointment at the clinic," she said, sniffling and wiping her eyes on her sleeve. "I couldn't let them have this baby. *Use* this baby."

Rage flared in his soul. He understood what she was saying, and yet… "You would make that decision without telling me?"

"Why would I tell you?" she snapped at him, her face reddening. She smacked her hand to her chest. "*I'm* the one who would be responsible for this baby, the one who would carry it to term and make sacrifices to keep it. *I* would be the one who worried every day that the Syndicate was going to come and take it away from me. What would you do? What *could* you do?" She snorted. "Nothing, Mr. High and Mighty Ian Black. *Nothing.* There are too many of them, and too few of you, and they want you dead."

He took deliberate steps toward her, stopping when he came to the end of the bed. She looked up at him, her face a mess of red cheeks and salty tears, and a chink grew in his armor until he slammed it closed again.

"Do you honestly think this is the first time anyone's ordered my death?"

She stared. He kept talking.

"I've been in darker places than you imagine I have, Calypso. I've seen things, heard things—and done things. And I will never, *ever* give up or let those fuckers get me."

"You can't stop them."

"I can. I will. You're going to help me."

She shook her head. "No. No way. I won't give them any reason to hurt Daria. Kill me if you must. Send my body to them. They won't blame me then. She'll be free."

He shook his head. "If you really believed that, then you wouldn't have hesitated to kill me the first chance you had. Even though Ty would have killed you for it."

She clasped her hands in her lap and dropped her chin. He knew as well as she did that the Syndicate wasn't inclined to be forgiving. If she failed, it wasn't just her who paid the price.

"I hate you right now," she rasped.

Ian snorted. "Just right now?"

"No."

"I didn't think so."

He turned to leave. She called out behind him. "What are you going to do?"

He stopped and faced her again. She had no idea what he was capable of. The lengths he'd go to in order to protect what was his.

No idea.

"Do? I'm going to burn the world to the ground if I have to so I can find the people responsible for hurting you. Then I'm going to make sure they never threaten either one of us again."

Her throat worked. "And what about me? What are you going to do with me?"

He let a slow smile spread over his face. It wasn't meant to be friendly.

"I told you earlier. I'm keeping you, Natasha. You're mine now, like it or not."

"But what does that *mean?*" She sounded fearful.

He didn't care. Let her stew in it for a while.

"I'm not quite sure. But I guess we'll find out, won't we?"

Chapter Twenty

THE LIMO CAME HALF AN HOUR LATER TO TAKE THEM TO the executive airport where one of Ian's jets waited.

Natasha was still wearing her army surplus outfit as she boarded the plane and flopped into a seat beside a window. Ian stood in the front of the cabin, talking to the pilot. A flight attendant asked if she'd like something to drink. Natasha told him no thanks and stared out the window.

The jet engines were warming up and she listened to them drone, thinking how it'd only been a few hours ago that she'd been flying in from Europe. And a few hours before that when she'd last seen Daria and Lissette. She wished she'd been the one to walk Daria to school. Perhaps the Syndicate wouldn't have taken her then.

Except that was nonsense because they would have gotten her anyway. Maybe not then, but the instant Natasha's back was turned. After she'd left the school and walked home again, someone would have waited until they found an opportunity.

Ian entered the main cabin and took a seat across from her. He accepted a drink. He really was gorgeous, damn him, with his dark hair silvered at the temples. It wasn't much, but it was enough to indicate he wasn't as young as she was. Not that it mattered. He was still the most attractive and interesting man she'd ever met. She'd give anything if that weren't the case, but it was.

It just was.

"Where are we going?" she asked when he didn't say anything for five minutes. Low level anxiety bubbled beneath the surface as she thought of Daria and how the clock was tick, tick, ticking.

Ian looked up, his brown eyes—brown this time!—giving her a bored once over. "To a safe location."

"The moon? I believe the Syndicate can't quite reach us there."

"Not the moon."

There was a commotion at the front of the cabin and a man stalked toward them. Two more followed him. Natasha's heart flipped as she recognized her brother.

"What the fuck, Ian?" Nikolai demanded.

She gave her head a tiny shake. She had to think of him as Jace. That was his name now.

Ian's expression was cold. "I assume you have a real question in there."

Jace scrubbed his hands over his face. Colt—she'd shot him once—looked equally angry. Not that she blamed him. Getting shot would do that to a person.

Jared was behind them, a small plastic bag in his hands. He looked fairly calm to her, but then he'd been angry earlier. Murderously so, she imagined. Unlike these two, he'd had time to come to grips with it.

Jace flung his arm out, pointing at her. "She tried to kill you. And you're taking her to Colorado. Alone?"

Colorado.

Her heart fell. She'd hoped they were going to Europe.

That he was somehow magically going to get Daria back for her even though she didn't really think he could.

"I need you here."

"She wants you dead, Ian. She won't stop trying."

Emotion boiled inside her at the way her brother talked like she wasn't even there. Ian had told her not to hate Jace. Right now she despised him more than she did Ian.

"It must be so nice to be able to read minds," she snapped. "Did the *Spetsnaz* teach you that? Or does Ian have a secret program he's failed to tell me about?"

Jace glared at her. "Deny it then."

"I am denying it."

"Liar."

Natasha folded her arms and rolled her eyes. She didn't feel as brave as she pretended, but she wasn't accustomed to backing down from a fight. "Deserter."

Jace's expression tightened. Was it her imagination, or did he look wounded for the barest of seconds?

"I didn't desert you, Tasha. I thought you were dead, and I wanted to live."

"And you did. Yay, you."

"These are for you," Jared said, elbowing his way past her irate brother and handing her the plastic bag with two bottles in it. "For nausea. It'll help. Also, a prenatal vitamin. You need to take them for good fetal development, and for your own health."

"And now you're pregnant too," Jace threw at her with utter disdain. "Unbelievable."

She took the bag, ignoring him. "How do I know these aren't poison capsules?"

She was only half joking.

Jared gave her a severe look. "I'm a medic, and I take my oath seriously. If Ian wants you dead, he knows how to do it. He doesn't need me to give you poison pills."

She believed him. Besides, if there was a pill that could cure this nausea, she wanted it. Maybe she could think if she got that under control. It'd be nice to feel normal.

"Thank you."

"You're welcome."

"Anything else you kids need?" Ian asked mildly. She wasn't fooled by his tone. He was in control of his temper, but he was very angry. It was a wonder the others didn't cringe in response. Though maybe they didn't feel the spark in the air the way she did.

"We've got a departure time fast approaching," he continued in that same tone. "And the flight attendant needs to close the door."

"Don't go dark, Ian," Jace said. "Stay in touch with us. And you," he barked at her. "I'll hunt you down myself if you do anything to warrant it. Pregnant or not, I won't be merciful."

Heat flashed through her. "I expect nothing less from you, Nikolai Alexandrovich."

He stiffened. "That's not who I am. I never was that person. You think about that, Tasha. You don't have to be what they made you into either."

"So easy for you to say. You know nothing."

He turned and stalked away. Colt and Ian spoke for a moment, then he and Jared were gone too. The cabin door closed, the engines fired higher, and the plane started to move. Natasha waited for Ian to say something—anything —to soothe her jangled emotions.

But he didn't speak at all. Somehow, that made everything worse.

Chapter Twenty-One

IAN DIDN'T SAY MUCH ON THE FLIGHT TO COLORADO. HE spent his time online, looking at a computer screen and making phone calls. If he got up and walked away, then she knew it was something he didn't want her hearing. Strain though she might, Natasha couldn't hear a word.

If he sat in front of her and conversed with someone, it wasn't about anything interesting. She thought about asking him questions, but he ignored her so thoroughly that she decided to ignore him as well.

She was worried about Daria and Lissette, but there was still time to make a plan. Her handler—code name Pluto—never expected her to complete a mission within hours. He knew it could take time. Especially a mission that involved someone like Ian Black who was constantly surrounded by security.

Once she took the nausea pill Jared had given her, she fell asleep. But when she woke, she felt much better. Not precisely energetic, but not like she was going to lose the non-existent contents of her stomach. Which meant she could think now. Plan.

Maybe she could escape. She would have to watch for the right moment, but it was never hopeless if you were determined.

An hour later, the plane started to descend. When they were on the ground and the jet door opened, a rush of cold air swirled into the cabin and made her shiver.

She wrapped her arms tighter around herself as Ian fixed his gaze on her for the first time in hours. He'd gotten up and gone to the front of the cabin, but now he was looking directly at her. She couldn't read his expression. Was he angry? Tired? Suspicious?

She had no idea.

"The car's waiting."

Natasha shoved herself to her feet, happily surprised when her stomach didn't lurch. She went to join him. He took her hand, and an electrical current zapped through her. If he felt anything, he didn't show it. He simply led her out the door and down the stairs. She held the rail and his hand on the way down, but once they set foot on the pavement, he let her go. He strode to the waiting SUV that idled nearby.

She looked for a possible escape route, but nothing revealed itself. If she tried to run, they'd catch her laughably quick. She followed Ian instead, trying to take in her surroundings. It was dark and she couldn't see beyond the lights of their immediate vicinity, though she could tell that everything beyond was covered in snow.

Not a good place to try and hide, especially dressed as she was in clothing that wasn't meant for this climate. Out of habit, she studied the things she could see. The flight line workers, the buildings, the planes nearby. In her profession, you always looked for trouble.

For the high ground where a sniper could be waiting for the kill shot.

Nothing happened, but that didn't mean she could relax. She stayed on her guard as Ian opened the passenger door. He turned and motioned to her, indicating she should get inside. There was no chauffeur and no armed bodyguard in the interior as she climbed in. He shut the door with a soft thud and walked around the front of the Mercedes. Natasha clipped her seatbelt as he got into the driver's seat.

"Wow, no chauffeur? I'm shocked, Mr. Black."

He shot her one of those inscrutable looks of his. "Not this time. It's just you and me today."

Somehow that made her more nervous than when he had people around him. She didn't like Ty, but having him around had meant Ian would act a certain way.

Now? She had no idea what this man was capable of. He'd said he would burn the world to the ground, and she believed him. But would she turn to ash in the blaze?

"You aren't afraid I'll wait for an opportunity to knock you over the head and steal your car? What if I leave you on the side of the road somewhere? You could freeze to death."

He put the vehicle in gear. "Not afraid, Natasha. First, you aren't getting the jump on me. Second, you have no idea where you are and no money. You don't even have a cell phone."

They'd taken that from her when she'd tried to kill him. She didn't like to think about it too much. She'd been out of contact with Pluto for over twenty-four hours now. That wasn't unusual, but she didn't like being without a way to communicate. Lissette never called her when she was 'traveling' for work. The nanny knew if there was an emergency to do everything she could and damn the expense. Natasha had made that clear from the beginning.

"But you do," she said, thinking of the phone in his pocket. "And you have money."

"You can't use my phone. You don't have the code to unlock it. And money? I'm not carrying cash. Where we're going, I'm your only chance for survival. Kill me, and you'll die trying to escape."

She shivered at the truth in those words. He'd thought of everything. And it frightened her more than it should have. "You sound like one of *them* now."

He didn't look at her. "You mean I sound like a billion-aire who doesn't give a shit about anything but my money and my personal agenda?"

"Exactly."

"For all you know, I *am* one of them. What if this entire assignment was a test—and you failed it?"

Ice crusted in her veins. Her heart throbbed. She blinked, turning to look straight ahead. Studying the snow and the headlights coming at them while she processed what he'd said. Was it possible? Was Ian Black really a member of the Syndicate? It didn't seem likely, and yet...

Anything was possible. She'd learned that when she'd been nineteen and her entire world came crashing down on her head.

She concentrated on breathing, on slowing her heart rate to something reasonable. "Then I suppose I'm doomed."

There was silence for several moments. "I'm not a member of the Gemini Syndicate."

His voice was soft and hard at the same time. And sexy. How the hell did he manage that?

"But that doesn't mean I'm any less formidable. It's time you start trusting that I'm the only man who can protect you, Natasha. It's time to believe I'm your best choice for survival, and that I can get your daughter back."

Her heart pinched. She wanted to believe him. So badly. But she'd lost her ability to believe in miracles a long time ago. It was less painful that way.

"I'll believe it when I have her in my arms again."

"The only way that's going to happen is if you tell me what you know about the Syndicate. I can't make a plan without information."

Panic threatened to close her throat. Long years of training were ingrained in her very bones.

Turn on them and you die.

"I don't know anything. I don't get involved. I do the job, I collect my money, and I stay alive."

"You know more than you think. I want to know everything you know. It's the only way to win."

She sucked a breath into lungs that wouldn't inflate. Dammit, the nausea might be under control, but her hormones were still for shit. She wasn't going to let fear make her cry. She'd choke before she cried in front of him again.

"I'll th-think about it."

They reached the highway and the Mercedes leapt forward like a race horse bursting from the gate. "You've got until we arrive at our destination."

Alarm twisted her stomach. It was a different feeling than nausea, but just as unpleasant. "What if I don't know anything that's helpful? You'll have wasted precious time when you could have been figuring out how to rescue my daughter."

The look he shot her was utterly without sympathy. "Then I guess you're going to have to dig deep and give me something to work with, aren't you?"

Chapter Twenty-Two

THEY DROVE FOR OVER TWO HOURS THROUGH A SNOWY landscape until they came to a mountain road that took them upward. Natasha never saw a house before they were sitting inside a vast garage, the door rolling down behind them and sealing them in.

"Where are we?"

"My house. It's a secure location."

Ian pushed his door open. She followed suit. The garage was heated, thankfully, because she didn't think her clothing was at all suitable for Colorado. Before she could grab her bag with its pitifully inadequate clothing, Ian shouldered it. She followed him deeper into the garage until they reached an elevator.

Two floors up and they entered a house that took her breath away. She had a feeling the views would take her breath away too, when she could see them, but for now she was caught by the beauty of the home. It was a lodge, with wood and marble accents, glass windows that soared two stories high, and a kitchen the size of a small gym.

There were wood beams that crossed high above, and a

rock fireplace that dominated one wall. The furniture was what she expected. Sleek and modern, and somehow perfect in the space.

But the house had no heart.

That's what she'd noticed in his last house too. There was nothing personal, nothing homey.

No Christmas tree. No decorations. Everything looked as if a designer had picked it out of a showroom and put it together. Impeccable but not personal.

Even the Venetian palazzo lacked the personal touch. It was just that it had so much history and was spectacular in its own right that you missed it. Where was Ian Black's heart and soul? Why did he hide them from view?

He appraised her with a cool gaze. An impersonal gaze that somehow hurt more than it should. She'd liked it when he'd looked at her with heat sparking in those eyes. With a look that said he could eat her up and make her scream with pleasure if only she asked him to.

Now he looked at her like she was one of the fixtures. Not important and not special.

You tried to kill him. What do you expect?

"You can go anywhere you like in the house," he said coolly. "The elevator won't operate for you, and the garage is part of a bomb shelter so the doors can't be forced. You could drop over the balcony, but the nearest neighbor is about twenty-five miles away. The only signal out here is satellite. There are no phones other than mine. If you try to leave, you won't make it. And if you try to kill me in my sleep, the settings in the house are linked to my watch. If my heart stops beating, you'll be locked in until my team shows up. I think you know what'll happen then."

Her heart hammered. She wasn't used to being help-less. Not in many years now.

"Then I guess I'd better hope you don't have a heart

attack or burst an aneurysm," she said acidly, forcing herself to be braver than she felt.

"Yeah, guess you should."

She folded her arms over her chest. She felt very small in this house, and it got to her. "Does heart disease run in your family? Should I prepare myself for imminent demise if you eat one fried chicken wing too many and keel over?"

If she'd thought he might laugh, she was mistaken. This Ian wasn't nearly as quick to humor as she was accustomed to. She missed his humor more than she expected.

"Relax. I'm healthy."

She blew out a breath in frustration. "Why are we here, Ian? What's the difference between here and the house in Maryland? Why did you bring me all this way when Daria is in Switzerland? You can't rescue her from here. My child is going to die if I don't succeed at my mission, and you aren't doing anything about it!"

"Why don't you go take a hot shower? I'll find something for us to eat. I assume you can eat now?"

She gulped down her emotions and stared at him, willing herself to find her control. She was on edge, and he acted like it was nothing. But her stomach didn't rebel at the thought of food and she needed to eat to keep up her strength. "I think I can eat. I don't need a shower. And you still haven't answered the question."

"I know." He dropped her bag on the floor and went into the ridiculously huge kitchen. It had a professional range that would make Gordon Ramsey proud, an island you could stage a play on, and two industrial-sized refrigerators. It occurred to her a few seconds later that one of them was a freezer.

"You aren't going to answer me, are you?"

"When I'm ready."

She wanted to strangle him. Instead, she clenched her

fists and willed herself to wait for this impossible man to tell her his plan. "Can you even cook?"

"Well enough not to starve. But not well enough to warrant this kitchen," he replied as he opened the refrigerator door. He came out with a block of cheese and some grapes. "If we've got crackers, then here's something quick and easy."

Natasha pulled out a chair and sat at the island while he disappeared into the pantry. When he came out again, he was holding a box of crackers. Her stomach rumbled loudly enough that he heard it. He sliced cheese, rinsed grapes, and prepared a tray that he put in front of her. He grabbed two bottles of Perrier from the fridge and took a seat at an angle to her.

Natasha put cheese on a cracker and bit into it. Her stomach didn't rebel when she swallowed, so she popped the whole thing into her mouth and grabbed another.

"How do you feel?" he asked.

He was looking at her with more softness than he had since she'd tried to assassinate him. Butterflies swirled in her belly, but they had nothing to do with nausea.

"Better than I did. The nausea meds are helping."

He put cheese on a cracker and ate it. "When did you suspect you were pregnant?"

Natasha fixed another and didn't look at him. "A few days ago. I've never had terribly regular cycles. And then…"

"And then?" he prompted when she didn't finish.

"There have been other close calls," she said matter-of-factly. "I thought I couldn't get pregnant."

There, she'd said it. Most of it anyway. If she shared things with him, maybe he'd share his plans with her.

He frowned. "You tried to get pregnant before?"

"No, I've never tried." The cracker tasted like paste

suddenly. She sipped the Perrier. More than anything, she wanted to retreat. But that's not how she reacted to life. She'd never had that luxury. She barreled ahead instead. "I was in a prison, Ian. Use your imagination."

She could see when understanding dawned. If she thought he'd been angry before, she'd been mistaken. She realized she'd never seen him truly angry until this second. It would have been frightening if she hadn't known it was *for* her and not *with* her.

She didn't expect it to last, but it was nice for the moment.

"Jesus Christ," he swore. "I should have—. Goddammit, Natasha. Why didn't you tell me before?"

She tossed her hair and thrust her chin up. "When would I have done this? When we first met? Any of the times we talked since? Or how about the night in Venice, when all I wanted was to keep feeling what you were doing to me? Yes, that would have been perfect. Right before you thrust your cock into me—Ian," she said breathily, pitching her voice higher. "I need to tell you about my previous sexual experiences."

He closed his eyes as if reining in his temper. His hands were fists on the counter. "I should have taken better care that night."

"We both should have."

"But we didn't, and now there's a baby on the way."

She should have said they could fix that, but she didn't want to. It didn't seem right. "There's also Daria. She's mine in all the ways that count. I can't fail her."

"I intend to get her back for you."

Her heart wanted to soar at the conviction in his voice, but she couldn't let herself believe. Not yet. The fall would be too far if he couldn't do it. And she didn't see how he could. The Syndicate didn't let people who'd failed them live. They didn't let families live either. One person's sin was paid in blood by everyone that person loved.

If she'd succeeded in killing Ian and been killed in return, Daria would be safe. But failing? That was a death sentence for everyone.

"How does bringing me here accomplish that?" she asked. "She's in Switzerland, and you aren't dead. From where I'm sitting, it's not looking good at all."

"I could be dead."

She reared back to stare at him. "That's not funny. Besides, you've told me more than once why that's a bad idea for me."

"I didn't say you'd actually kill me. I said I *could* be dead. For the Syndicate."

She shook her head. "No. They wanted proof of death for you. A photo." It was gruesome to say it aloud.

"So we arrange a photo."

"The poison would have blackened and swollen your skin."

"I see." He sipped the Perrier. "I suppose you'll need to meet Dax. Or be formally introduced since you've seen him a couple of times recently."

"Who?"

"My computer specialist. He can fake anything. Deep fake and so fucking good nobody can tell the difference. If we need me to look like a blackened puffer fish, he can do it."

She tried to ignore the little kernel of excitement growing inside. It couldn't be that easy. Nothing was that easy. She couldn't get her hopes up, no matter what he said. Hope was brutal, especially when crushed.

"And then what happens?" she asked him. "I can return home and collect Daria when I send the photo, but the instant they realize you aren't dead, they're coming for all of us."

He shook his head, the movements slow and deliberate. "I told you, Natasha. You're mine now. You aren't going anywhere. My team and I will get your daughter back."

She stared at him in shock and anger—and frustration. So much frustration. "You expect me to do nothing while my daughter's life is in danger? No. No fucking way," she sputtered.

"You stay." His voice was iron.

Her belly twisted as fury bubbled. She tried to think of how to convince him—and then she decided fuck it. Fuck this shit all the way to hell and back.

"I have skills you can use. You take me with you, or I will absolutely stab you the first chance I get. And this time I won't miss."

Chapter Twenty-Three

Natasha had been pretty subdued for most of the day, but now she'd come alive. Her eyes flashed fire and her chin jutted stubbornly. It hadn't been difficult to keep an emotional distance from her. She'd tried to kill him—and she'd intended to terminate her pregnancy before he'd found out she was carrying his child—and that tended to harden a man's heart like nothing else.

Yet the way she looked at him now, the way she threatened him for the sake of her daughter, he couldn't help but feel another small chink growing in his armor.

Natasha Oliver wasn't just an assassin. She was a mama bear protecting her cub.

Fucking hell. Nothing got to him like a mother who would do anything to save a child. Nothing.

"I'm not taking you," he growled. "You're pregnant."

"I'm barely pregnant—and now that this nausea is under control, I can help. I need to help, Ian. I can't stay here, locked away, and do *nothing* while you go up against the Syndicate."

"Not negotiable, Natasha."

She threw her head back and screamed. The sound shocked him. When she finished, she glared at him. If looks could kill, she wouldn't have needed poison.

"Why are you so pig-headed? You're just like every other man in this world. You think because I'm a woman that I'm weak and helpless, that I *need* you to save me. I *don't.* I just need your help to get Daria and Lissette back."

He frowned. "Who's Lissette?"

"Daria's nanny."

"For the record, I don't think you're weak and helpless. Far from it. Tell me what happened the day they took Daria."

She closed her eyes. He didn't think she was going to say a word, but then she started talking.

"It was the day I realized I might be pregnant. I usually walk Daria to school when I'm home, but Lissette could tell I didn't feel well so she said she'd do it. I went to the pharmacy to buy a test, then returned home and took it. Lissette didn't come home but I figured she had errands to run. She cooks and does the housekeeping. I went into Zurich—" Her words choked off.

"You already told me you live in Switzerland," he reminded her. "When you were pretending to be Anna."

"I guess I did. I didn't think you remembered."

Now probably wasn't the time to tell her he remembered everything about her. Every encounter, every freckle on her skin, every sigh and moan, every thrust of his body inside hers.

Jesus.

"I keep an apartment downtown," she continued. "For my work. Disguises, weapons, that kind of thing. I don't want it in our house where Daria could find it. Or Lissette, since the conversation would be awkward. Anyway, I was thinking about what I was going to do, if I could escape and take Daria with me. But I got a text from my handler. He said you were the target and to terminate. He sent a picture of the two of them and said they would be enjoying their stay at a luxury hotel until I returned."

"Is that standard procedure?"

"Taking Daria and her nanny? No. It's the first time."

"Why do you think they did it?"

She spread her hands on the counter, studying them. "I've wondered if they somehow knew about me and you. But if they did, I doubt they'd wait two months to act. I also thought it might be because they've finally figured out I was the one who killed the Butcher. It's a message to behave and do as I'm told."

"The Butcher—you mean Roberto Broussard."

She nodded.

"That wasn't authorized?"

"No."

She was complex, this woman. Young and beautiful and so fucking complex that he'd never learn all her secrets. Much like him, she had a lot of them. He remembered that night with clarity, the way she'd shot Broussard and then stolen his helicopter to make her getaway. In the dark, like a fucking warrior queen.

"Why did you do it then?"

She snorted. "You have to ask? He was an evil, disgusting, horrifying madman. He would have carved Tallie Grant's interesting eyes from her head. He would have made her beg for death before he was through."

Anger pulsed in his soul. "How do you know?"

She stared at him. Her jaw worked. Then she jerked her sleeve up, showing him those scars he'd only seen the night they'd spent together. But he hadn't seen them well because it'd been dark. The mermaid tattoo was a brilliant cover job, but you could see where the artist had worked the shiny skin into the design when you looked.

"Daria's mother was the only friend I had after I went to prison, and the Butcher killed her. But not before he promised he could fix the blinding headaches she'd been getting. He was the one giving her the headaches, using experimental drugs on her, playing with her mind. He performed drug-induced hypnosis on her—and on me. He went through a phase where he found that fun. I gave these scars to myself because he told me to. Lena sliced her wrists to the bone because that's what he told her to do. There were others, but Lena is the one I cared about."

Ian thought it was a very good thing Broussard was dead. Because he wouldn't have shot the man before he'd made him suffer brutally. And he would have made him suffer for a *very* long time.

"Was this in the prison or after?"

"Both. We were recruited for a special training program with promises to commute our sentences if we agreed. Of course we did. Broussard joined the program after it was in progress. Lena had just given birth to Daria about four months prior. Her parents had been allowed to take Daria, and Lena got to see her often. We thought we were being given this awesome second chance at working for our country, that we'd be free to live our lives. We were all lifers, you see. Traitors and murderers, mostly. But it wasn't a second chance at all. It was them. The Syndicate. When Lena and the others died, Broussard left. I stayed in the program because it was all I had."

Her cheeks were red with anger and she clenched her fists in her lap, breathing evenly to calm herself. "When I started work for the Syndicate, I was full of rage and I did whatever they asked. I also killed some of the guards who'd hurt me in prison. But then Lena's parents both got cancer and died within months of each other, and I took Daria. She was three then. Everything I've done since has been to keep her safe and happy."

Ian digested everything. Good God, this woman. The things she'd suffered. The things she'd done. She didn't think she was worthy. He knew that. Recognized it because deep down he felt the same way. There was something about being unable to prevent the tragic death of someone you loved that changed you.

Something about feeling unwanted and unloved that affected your whole life, even when you had good people in it who tried to fix that for you.

"And what about you, Tasha? Do you want to be safe and happy?"

Chapter Twenty-Four

HE'D NEVER SHORTENED HER NAME LIKE THAT BEFORE. He'd called her Calypso, he'd called her angel or kitten, and he'd called her by her name. But somehow calling her Tasha felt more intimate.

"Doesn't everyone?" she replied.

He nodded. "Then let me do that for you."

Her heart stuttered in her chest. What was he asking of her? To trust him? Or to close her eyes and leap without knowing where bottom was? Some people would say those were the same, but she knew they were two separate things. Trust had levels. Leaping had none.

"I wish you could," she told him honestly. "But I don't see how. The Syndicate has people everywhere. Even inside your organization. You can't hide me. You can't hide yourself. A faked photo will buy time, but not an infinite amount."

He arched an eyebrow. "Whether you like it or not, you're on my side now. I'm the only one who can save you. Best to tell me everything you know about them."

She closed her eyes. She'd spent so many years keeping

things inside. It was safer that way. She'd seen what happened when people betrayed the Syndicate. She'd carried out the orders herself sometimes. They would come for her and her child, and they would not be merciful.

Ian had dropped into the middle of her life and turned it upside down. She should have found a way to kill him months ago. It would have made everything easier. Except that her heart now ached at the thought. The tiny life inside her seemed to throb even though she knew that wasn't possible.

The truth showered over her like ice water: she no longer wanted him dead.

She was tired of revenge, tired of making choices that never brought her peace in the end. She'd killed the Butcher and she'd been satisfied—but she hadn't stopped dreaming of Lena's death. Killing him had fixed nothing other than ridding the world of his evil. A good thing, but not enough.

She didn't really believe Ian was going to make the Syndicate go away. But maybe he'd buy enough time for her to hide. She'd have to escape him, but if she could just take Daria—and the baby—and reinvent herself... It might be enough. With the Syndicate focused on him, she might have a chance.

"Even if I tell you, you aren't letting me help rescue Daria, are you?"

"No, I'm not."

"What makes you sure you can do this?"

Her voice was barely more than a whisper as her heart throbbed. Daria was her world. If anything happened to her sweet daughter—hers because Lena had made her promise to keep Daria safe always—she wouldn't be responsible for what she did.

And now there was a baby to consider as well. Hers and his. She put her hand over her abdomen beneath the countertop where he couldn't see it, spreading her fingers over her still flat belly. She wanted this baby. Fiercely. She wanted Daria to have a sister—or a brother—and she wanted to live like other people. She wanted her most pressing problem to be making it to the school pickup line on time, not jetting halfway around the world on a mission.

She was tired. So damned tired.

That desire to lay down her burdens and let someone else be the strong one flared inside. But she knew she couldn't give in to it. She couldn't rely on anyone but herself. Life had proven that to her again and again.

Ian reached across the island and tipped her chin up, forcing her to look at him. Long seconds passed where he said nothing. Where she didn't ask again.

His expression was hard, dark, and confident. Desire for him whipped into a froth before she tamped it down. It shocked her to feel desire when it hadn't been so long ago she couldn't hold down a meal.

His voice was dark and seductive. "You've been under their control for a very long time. I understand that. The Syndicate, and your handlers, are all you've known. But you don't know everything, and you don't know how deep my network goes—or who owes me favors. I'm calling in every last one of them if I have to. For you. For Daria. For our child. You're going to be safe. I promise you."

She wished it could be true—but she didn't believe it for a second. Life had taught her that no one was ever safe and nothing was certain. Promises, no matter how pretty, were nothing more than empty words.

Chapter Twenty-Five

IAN WOKE WITH THE DAWN, DESPITE GOING TO BED LATE. After Natasha had told him everything she knew about the Gemini Syndicate, he'd worked on his computer late into the night. She thought she didn't know anything useful, but she knew more than she realized.

Like the fact her training had started in Russia, and that Roberto Broussard had been there. There were plenty of oligarchs in Russia, but only a few who had the kind of ties Ian was looking for. Rich men with dark agendas who took satisfaction in world turmoil. But not too much turmoil lest they lose their fortunes.

When he drew the lines outward from there, he made other connections. It wasn't that he and his people didn't know some of the players who were a part of the Syndicate. They knew the identities of some of them, and they were literally sprinkled around the globe. No single country had a monopoly on rich douchebags. To all outward appearances, he was one of the rich douchebags.

But someone at the center of the organization knew better.

And they'd sent Calypso to take care of him.

A mistake to send her. She thought they'd taken her daughter and nanny because of Broussard, but Ian thought it was more likely that someone knew she'd been in contact with him. It could have happened in Venice, or it could have happened earlier.

He'd thought of the incident with Tommaso Leone that night, but it didn't seem likely Leone had recognized her. If he had, he wouldn't have approached her the way he had. No sane man put his hand on the ass of the notorious Calypso without permission.

It was possible Leone had realized her identity after the fact. But he hadn't seemed the sort of man with the patience to wait two months after he'd been humiliated to get his revenge.

Ian had made calls to Dax, to Jace, and to others. BDI had operations across the globe, some of them questionable, but all of them with a single purpose. To stop greedy men—usually men, though not always—from seizing power and ruining the world. Dictators, crime lords, arms dealers, drug runners, human traffickers. All disgusting, and all deserving of ruin.

He'd told Natasha he would burn the world down to protect her, and he hadn't been lying. Even if he wasn't sure what all this complicated shit rolling around in his head was, he focused on the one thing he *was* sure of. She was pregnant with his child.

Pregnant. With. His. Child.

He would protect her with his life because of that alone, though he hoped it didn't come down to it. He'd told her she was his, and he meant it. He would never abandon his child, which meant he would never abandon her. There was more to what he was feeling, but he wasn't ready to sort it out.

She was a compulsion. An addiction. He didn't know *why*. Didn't change what he had to do, though.

He didn't know what to think about fathering a child either, but he'd like to see the baby born. Like to see it grow up.

Yeah, he was fucking crazy. He'd never expected to be a dad. Never wanted to be.

Bad shit could happen to kids, even with the best parents in the world. His mother was never far from his mind when he thought about how vulnerable kids were. How they could be taken advantage of, their entire lives ruined over one mistake.

He wasn't going to let that happen to his kid.

Ian got out of bed and hit the shower, letting the hot water run over his body and ease the tension in his muscles. Once he dressed, he headed into the kitchen to fix coffee. He'd brought Natasha to this location because it was remote and hard to get to—or escape from—but he was going to have to leave her soon. He had an operative who could stay with her. Jamie Hayes was formidable in her own right, and she wouldn't let Natasha get the jump on her. He didn't think Natasha would try anything with so much at stake, but he couldn't be absolutely certain.

It would take two, maybe three days to extract Daria and her nanny from the Syndicate's clutches. He knew the Grand Hotel Schoenburg, and he was in the process of mapping their security and surveilling the surroundings. Things you could do with a global team at your disposal.

He wouldn't order it done without being there himself. He had to see it through for Natasha. He'd promised her over a year ago that he would help her if she switched sides, and he meant to keep that promise.

Especially since he'd forced her into it.

Not that forcing her bothered him. He'd given her time. Plenty of it. But time was up.

Ian poured coffee and went outside onto the deck. It was cold and snow blanketed the ground as far as the eye could see. There was a mountain range in the distance, but clouds obscured it. The snow draping the trees was beautiful. The house sat on a summit, and a field stretched out below. A group of deer moved into view, snuffling for grass.

He leaned against the railing, his breath frosting in the air, and watched them.

A few minutes later, the door slid open behind him. He glanced over his shoulder at the woman coming to join him. Natasha's blond hair was a cloud of messy gold that she'd tucked behind her ears. She wore an oversized pair of red silk pajamas with thick socks. He was glad to see she'd gone searching in the drawers and found them. He'd forgotten to tell her that he kept the house stocked with a variety of clothing since BDI used it as a safe house from time to time.

She had a blanket around her shoulders and she carried a cup of coffee. "Morning," she said.

"Morning. Did you sleep well?"

"I did." She yawned. "Do you have any news?"

He shook his head. "Not yet. I've got my people researching the hotel's security and the situation on the ground. As soon as they know something, I'll tell you."

She frowned and took a sip of coffee as steam wreathed her face.

"It's caffeinated," he said.

"I know. I won't have much. Lena said a cup a day was fine, and Daria is perfect so I believe it."

"You didn't mention Daria's father."

"I don't know who he is. She never told me." Her eyes were troubled.

"But you have an idea."

She nodded. "There was one particular guard in the prison who seemed to have feelings for her. He wasn't one of the ones I went looking for when I was tracking guards down, in case you were wondering. To my knowledge he's alive."

"You don't want to know if he's Daria's father?"

"No. He was married and had kids already. What would he do for Daria? Besides, though he had some feelings, he also used his position to coerce female prisoners into sex. They all did."

"I'm sorry, angel."

She shrugged. "What's done, is done. I wasn't a virgin, thank God, and I learned how to deal with the violation thanks to Lena. Honestly, she took the brunt of it. She'd been a sex worker before she was convicted of murder, and she had a different attitude about sex than I did."

It pissed him off to imagine Natasha being helpless in prison. To imagine other men touching her, forcing their way into her body. He had to push the images away before he lost himself in the inferno of his anger.

"I think you're remarkable."

"I'm not. But there are only so many things in the past I can dwell on, and that's not one of them. I don't deny what happened, but it doesn't define me. It took a long time afterward to go to bed with a man, but eventually I did. And I discovered that when I choose the man, it's a far more pleasant experience."

"I wish I'd known."

Her expression hardened. "Why? So you could treat me like glass? Like I would break at any moment? No, that's not at all what I wanted from you. I got what I wanted exactly the way I wanted it."

He couldn't stop himself from reaching out and

running his fingers over her cheek. He was still so fucking angry with her, but it wasn't enough to keep from touching her. "Apparently, you also got a bonus. I'm sorry I didn't take better care."

"I seem to remember begging you not to stop. I think we were both careless."

Everything inside him tightened at the memory. Anger didn't stop the want. The need. "Maybe we should try it again," he said, his breath frosting in the cold. "See if you beg me this time."

"Or maybe you'll beg me." She arched a slim brow as she gazed up at him.

"I might."

They stared at each other for a long moment. Her eyes closed and her face tilted up. He told himself not to do it. Not to succumb. For all he knew, she was still willing to kill him. Willing to sacrifice both their lives—and their unborn child's—for Daria's.

But it wasn't enough to stop him. His lips sealed to hers, her mouth opened, and he almost forgot to breathe.

Chapter Twenty-Six

WHAT ARE YOU DOING?

Natasha ignored the panicked voice in her head as Ian drew her against him. They both had cups of coffee, and she was also holding the blanket in place. She had no hands free to push him away.

Or pull him to her.

She wanted to do both. Her mind warred with her heart on the subject. Meanwhile, her body melted as his tongue slipped into her mouth and stroked hers. He tasted like coffee, rich and dark and delicious. His body heat wrapped around her. She shivered, but not from cold.

Ian's hand trailed down her spine, into the small of her back. The kiss deepened, and she melted even more. She hadn't thought she could, but she did.

She'd told this man about prison, about being at the mercy of the guards, and now they were kissing and her body was responding with so much need. Just like the last time.

Ian wasn't other men. He was himself, a law of his own.

She thought his hand would keep traveling downward, but instead it traveled up and cupped her cheek. She couldn't say why, but that nearly broke her. His care for her. His tenderness when he had every right to be murderously angry with her.

He stopped the kiss and gazed down at her. She realized with a start that his eyes were a pale shade of turquoise this morning. She hadn't actually spent any time looking at his face yet. She'd looked at the view, at her feet, at the coffee in the cup, but she hadn't locked gazes with him until right before he'd kissed her.

And she'd been so focused on what he was about to do that the color didn't register.

It did now. Turquoise. Not deep blue, not brown, not gray. She hadn't seen this color before. She thought she would have remembered. Though maybe she was wrong. Maybe she wouldn't have. How long had it taken her to notice this morning?

"I'm not going to take advantage of this situation," he said, his voice deep and growly, sending little lightning bolts of desire racing through her. "I don't want you to think you have to sleep with me for my help."

"I don't think that."

He tucked a lock of her hair that had come free behind her ear again. "Maybe not right now. But when you realize I'm not letting you go even if you do, you might change your mind."

Her heart flipped. She should be raging against that statement.

And yet she wasn't. Something inside her was comforted by it.

Crazy since she didn't really know what he meant by it. Did he mean she was his in every way for the rest of their lives? Or did he mean he wasn't letting her go until the baby was born?

Her natural rebellion flared in response to her confusion. "You can try to keep me, but even you make mistakes, Ian Black. And when you do, I'll be ready."

Because when it was all said and done, she needed to escape. Needed to make a life for her and Daria and this baby where no one could find them ever again. She'd find a way. Somehow.

He laughed softly. "Sometimes. Problem is, you have to guess if I've made one or if I'm testing you."

She shivered again and he frowned. "Let's get you inside."

She resisted his effort to move her, dropping the blanket to put her palm against his cheek. He hadn't shaved, and she liked the roughened stubble. He waited patiently.

"What?" he finally said as she studied him.

"I'm trying to decide if those are your eyes."

"And?"

"I think they are. I've never seen you with this color. And I can't find a contact rim."

He took her hand and pulled it away from his face. But he didn't let go as he wrapped his hand around hers. Instead, he picked up her blanket, then led her inside and shut the door behind them. He sat her down on the couch and tucked the blanket around her. She didn't protest. She didn't think any man had ever done such a thing for her before. She liked it.

When he had her tucked in, he went over to the fireplace and picked up a remote control from the mantel. A moment later, a fire blazed.

"What do you think you could eat this morning? Eggs? A bagel? Cereal? Waffles?"

Natasha sipped the coffee, which had gotten a little cool, and shrugged. Outwardly she was calm. Inwardly she was a mess. "I think they all sound good. You pick one."

"Hmm, I'm thinking buttery waffles with gooey maple syrup."

Her stomach rumbled. "Sounds amazing to me. Want help?"

"Nope. You stay here. I've got it."

"Ian," she called when he walked away.

"Yeah?" He turned, a question in his gaze.

"I hope you're as good as you say you are."

He nodded solemnly. She didn't have to explain. He knew she wasn't talking about sex or food.

"I am."

She closed her eyes as he turned away again. She only needed him to be as good as rescuing Daria and Lissette. After that, she'd figure out how to disappear and take them with her.

Chapter Twenty-Seven

IAN'S PHONE VIBRATED. HE CHECKED HIS MESSAGES TO SEE that Dax and Ty were arriving soon.

He hadn't told Natasha he'd sent for them earlier this morning. She wasn't relaxed around them and he hadn't wanted her to think about what would happen when they arrived. Instead, he'd made her waffles, which she'd eaten without incident, and then he'd heated canned soup for lunch.

She'd fallen asleep on the couch for a while, but eventually woke and disappeared into her room. When she returned, she wasn't wearing the army surplus gear. She'd found leggings and a flannel shirt that covered her tattoo, and she still wore the thick socks. Her hair was sleek and shiny, and her cheeks were pink. Her eyes were no longer hazel. They were green. He'd been right that she had more contacts in her jacket.

She looked the most relaxed he'd ever seen her, but he knew it was a façade. She was still keyed up and she would be for as long as it took to rescue Daria and the nanny. Then she'd worry about the Syndicate catching up to her.

He couldn't fix the worry, so he concentrated on what he had to do to fix the situation.

He sat in one of the big club chairs with his laptop and phone, working, while Natasha watched a sappy Christmas movie about a small town romance. She sniffled from time to time, but she didn't cry.

Hard to reconcile the woman engrossed in a Christmas movie with the assassin Calypso. Where Calypso was cold, calculated, and utterly confident, the Natasha he'd seen the past couple of days was vulnerable and wary. He wished Jace could see his sister now. Maybe he'd be a little more understanding of her if he did.

Ian didn't kid himself she'd stay this way. She was still getting used to the hormones in her system and the nausea pills. Once she equalized, she'd be hell on wheels again. Natasha was a trained operative, same as he was, and she wouldn't be content to take orders and stay out of the action. No matter how pregnant she was.

Ian had guessed there was a child the Syndicate used to keep her in line, but to know it for certain—to see Natasha's fear and concern for the girl and to hear her desperation—made him more determined than ever to help her escape the life she'd been leading since she was nineteen.

She was stronger than anyone he knew. His operatives had all been through some shit in their lives, but none had endured what she had. Imprisonment, rape, grueling training, the death of her parents and best friend. It went on and on. There weren't many who would have survived the emotional turmoil she'd been through.

Sometime later she asked, "Why don't you have a Christmas tree?"

He looked up to see the credits of her movie rolling. She watched him curiously.

"Uh, because I didn't expect to be here?"

She shook her head. "You didn't have one at the other house either."

"I'm busy."

"You're a rich man. You could pay people to take care of it for you."

That much was true. "Low priority. I didn't think about it."

"Not sure I buy that. I don't think there's much you don't think about."

"Some things. Christmas trees being one of them. Once you get them up, you just have to take them down again."

In truth, he tried not to think about Christmas. He much preferred January when everyone was back at work and ready to get shit done.

"I know, but I don't have much choice with a little girl at home." She closed her eyes. "I'm trying not to think about it, but it's impossible."

"Of course it is," he said gently.

His phone buzzed at that moment, letting him know that one of the garage doors was opening. Dax sent a text to confirm he'd used the code. Ian closed the laptop and stood.

"We're about to have company."

Natasha blinked up at him before she scrambled upright from her lazy position on the couch. "What? Who?"

"It's Dax and Ty. We need photos."

Her mouth dropped open. "I thought this Dax person was making the fake for you already."

"With what? I need to pose. It's not like I have photos of me lying on the ground with my eyes open and vacant."

"I could have snapped them with your phone since you took mine."

"You could have, but it's better this way. Dax will get exactly what he needs. Gonna need you to help with the composition. Make sure it looks like what you expected."

She hugged herself, her expression darkening. "I'm not sure I'm happy about this."

"Understand, but if you want it done right, then you need to help."

"Like I have a choice."

"Sorry, but no, you don't. Not if you want your daughter back."

She dropped her gaze and muttered beneath her breath as the elevator chime sounded on his phone. Maybe it was a cheap shot, but he wasn't above cheap shots if it meant his ends were achieved.

A few moments later, Dax and Ty strode in with suitcases containing photographic equipment and computers as well as their clothing and other things they'd need in order to stay for a day or two.

"You're alive," Ty said, infusing his voice with mock surprise.

"I'm alive, asshole. Which you knew before you walked in." They all knew the house alarms would have gone crazy if his vitals had stopped registering. Not that he'd been worried about it. Natasha needed his help, and she knew it. He'd backed her into a corner and there was only one way out. One sane way.

He didn't kid himself she wouldn't go the insane route if she felt she had no choice left. She'd kill him and let his people kill her. He intended to take that option off the table. The sooner the better.

"Yeah, I know," Ty said, sliding his gaze to Natasha. "Howdy, Calypso."

"Howdy yourself," she replied, annoyance oozing from her pores.

He knew that her prickliness was partly an act to protect herself. He wasn't sure how much of it was, but he suspected a lot. Natasha's soft spot was Daria, and maybe the child she carried. He'd seen an emotional side to her lately that would have surprised anyone else in his employ.

"Natasha, the other guy is Dax Freed. You've not been introduced yet, though you've seen him before."

"Hey," Dax said, nodding. Dax was as cool as they came. If he didn't like Natasha, and he probably didn't, he wouldn't let it show.

"Jared sent the poison report," Ty said. "I don't know if you've seen it yet."

"I saw it."

"Nasty stuff," Ty continued. "You'd have been dead inside five minutes if she'd connected."

"But she didn't." Ian's voice was cool. "And now that she knows we're her only hope of getting her daughter back, she won't be trying again."

"I wouldn't give her a vial of that shit though," Ty muttered.

"No intentions of it. Can we get on with this without all the chit chat? There's a little girl in Switzerland who would like to be reunited with her mother before Christmas."

"You got it, boss," Dax said. "Ready to die a gruesome death?"

Chapter Twenty-Eight

THE WORST PART OF THE AFTERNOON TURNED OUT TO BE giving her opinion on Dax's Photoshop job.

It'd only been yesterday that she'd almost injected him, but already she couldn't believe she'd tried to go through with it. The thought made her queasy. She knew that's what it was because otherwise she was fine and food no longer bothered her.

The sight of Ian's handsome face blackened and swollen, mouth open, eyes rolled back in his head, was almost more than she could stand.

"How about this?" Dax asked her for the millionth time, clearly enjoying the technical challenge. He was no longer connecting the photo to the man the same way she was.

"Yes, that's good," she said.

"Not quite like what I found on the internet," Ty said. "Needs a little more swelling. And some cracks in the skin."

"I can do that." Dax clicked the mouse, intent on the screen.

Natasha was beginning to shake. She didn't know why.

She turned and walked away, swallowing to keep her stomach from rebelling.

What is wrong with me?

She'd always done the job, no questions, no regrets. But now she couldn't stop thinking about what would have happened if she'd succeeded. What if Ian really were dead? If she'd done the job, her daughter would be safe.

But him dead was a thought she could no longer bear. How was it possible to want him alive when doing so doomed her, Daria, and the baby?

She heard Ian's footsteps. He put his hands on her shoulders. She wasn't expecting it. Despite her best intentions, she turned blindly into him, burying her face against his chest. He slid his arms around her while she breathed him in and worked to regain her composure. She shouldn't be doing this, shouldn't let anyone see her vulnerable, but stepping away from him would have taken more willpower than she currently had.

Eventually, when she could breathe without shaking, she broke away from him and wrapped her arms around herself.

Ty and Dax dropped their gazes the instant she glanced at them. She could see the confusion and speculation as they stared at the computer and didn't speak. Ty shot a glance at Ian, then focused on the computer again. Dax didn't take his eyes off the screen.

Nobody said anything and the work continued. She wasn't unaware of the curiosity burning in the room, and she knew they were sneaking speculative looks at her when they thought she didn't know. The third time she caught them, she lost her cool. She couldn't help it.

"Yes," she burst out. "It's *exactly* what you think."

"Uh, I don't know what you're talking about," Dax said.

"Me neither," Ty added, shrugging. *Asshole.*

"Then let me tell you the truth," she ground out. "I'm having Ian's love child and we've decided to get married. He's leaving BDI forever, selling everything to buy an RV for us to live in and travel across the country, and we're getting a dog. Then we're having sixteen children and naming all of them after you two. Even if they're girls. You're invited to the wedding, but only if you keep your mouths shut the whole time."

Ian snorted. Ty and Dax blinked. They got on her damn nerves, and she wasn't accustomed to putting up with it. Any other time, she'd twist some balls or shove a gun in someone's mouth. This time she had to settle for sarcasm.

"Better be a big RV," Ian murmured.

"You can afford it."

"Especially once I sell everything."

"Exactly."

"I think it's done," Dax said, ignoring them both. "Natasha, do you agree?"

She stomped over to look at the screen. She was ready for it this time. The photo was a gruesome sight, but it was fake. The man himself stood nearby, healthy as a horse. It confused her to be grateful for that, but she was.

"It's done," she said. "Now I need to send it. Or do you plan on doing that for me?" She directed this last at Ian.

"Dax has your phone," he said. "And he can break the code to get in. But it'd be easier if you unlock it for us."

"But you aren't letting me send it, are you?"

"I didn't say that. You can send it. Send whatever message you typically send. But not yet."

She wanted to growl. "Why not? Time is running out."

"We need a bit more information about the situation at the hotel."

"How much more do you need? I told you where they are. Go get them."

"It's not that easy and you know it."

Her heart throbbed. She did know it. What looked simple on the outside might be simple. But sometimes it wasn't, and if you pulled the trigger on the plan too soon, the whole thing was shot to hell. Sometimes with disastrous consequences. She couldn't afford that.

She'd told Ian how she worked. How jobs could sometimes take a couple of weeks or more to set up. Logically, she knew the ticking clock on her mission hadn't counted all the way down yet. Pluto wasn't expecting her to get it done in forty-eight hours, or even seventy-two hours.

But he was expecting information about her progress.

"I need to make contact. I've been out of touch for too long."

Ian walked over to Dax and held out his hand. Dax slid a look toward her before he reached into his computer bag and pulled out a metal box. Her phone was inside. Ian took it and sauntered over.

His eyes—deep blue again—sparked as he held it out. "Send your message, kitten."

She took the phone, her fingers brushing against his. Her heart thudded. "You aren't afraid I'll send a coded message?"

One eyebrow lifted in that sardonic expression she'd come to associate with him. "Nope. You want Daria out of their hands once and for all. You know I'm going to do that for you."

She swallowed. It would be worth it if he got Daria free. She could hide her daughter somewhere in the world, give them both a new identity. Once the Syndicate realized she hadn't killed Ian as ordered, they'd never stop hunting her.

But if she got a head start…

They would hunt him down too, no matter what he thought, but she couldn't think about him. She had to think of Daria and the baby. And Lissette if she could figure out how to take her along too. It was more difficult with the Frenchwoman in the mix, but maybe not impossible.

Natasha powered the phone up, holding her breath as she did so. A red number one stood out against the message app. She clicked on it. The sender was identified by the code name he used. Pluto, for the god of the underworld.

Status report.

The message was twelve hours old. She met Ian's gaze. "He wants a status report."

"Give it to him."

She didn't type anything at first. "Don't you want to watch me do it?"

"No."

That didn't mean he trusted her. It was just that there was no advantage to telling Pluto she'd been captured, which Ian knew as well as she did.

Target located. Observing.

She hit send. She wasn't expecting a reply, but one came swiftly.

Pluto: *Where have you been for the past 12 hours?*

Natasha pulled in a breath. Let it out. Told herself to be calm. *I picked up a stomach bug. Left my charger on the plane. Bought a new one and just got juice. In position now.*

Pluto: *How careless. Is the great Calypso losing her touch?*

His question rankled. *No. If I hadn't been ordered to use poison and send proof of death, I could finish it in a couple of hours. The man lives in a house with huge windows and plenty of cover on the property. Let me shoot him.*

Pluto: *The order from above is unchanged. Do as you've been instructed.*

Natasha tapped out a reply: *Understood.*

She wanted to ask about Daria and Lissette, but doing so would give him ammunition. She handed the phone to Ian before she could change her mind and beg for an update.

He read the exchange, then gave the phone back to Dax. She didn't blame him, and yet the evidence of his mistrust was like a thorn prick to her heart. She would have done the same thing in his position. It was the smart thing to do. So why did it bother her?

Because she was a hopeless idiot sometimes, that's why.

"You've bought us some time," he said softly. "That's a good thing."

"I can't help but think he's suspicious."

"Do you always answer immediately?"

"No. It's not possible in some situations. He knows that."

"Then trust that he knows it now. So long as you do the job, that's what matters. Don't borrow trouble."

"Boss," Dax said.

The tone of his voice made Natasha's heart squeeze.

"Have you got something?"

Dax shot her a look, then focused on Ian again. "Just heard from the team in Switzerland."

"And?"

"The girl and her nanny are gone."

Chapter Twenty-Nine

Ian wasn't sure what Natasha's reaction would be. He took a step toward her, but she moved away as if she didn't want to be touched this time.

She turned her back to them and wrapped her arms around her body. He could hear her breathing in and out, working on controlling her emotions.

He thought she might crumble, but she didn't. That well of strength she pulled on to see her through the dark times of her life hadn't failed her. She whirled around again a few seconds later, eyes hard and angry.

"What else do you have? Surely your people were watching the hotel? They must have seen something?"

Dax cleared his throat. "They have a couple of leads. They're following up."

"When did they discover Daria and Lissette were no longer there?" she demanded.

He let her do it because she had no control over the situation. If demanding answers helped her feel better, he could do that. Besides, they were the same questions he was going to ask.

Dax glanced at him. Ian nodded.

"An hour ago," Dax said. "We have an operative posing as a guest and one working as a valet. The guest saw them at dinner earlier. They were with a man. The other saw them get into a taxi a short while ago."

Factoring in the time difference, it was the middle of the night in Europe. An odd time to be leaving a hotel.

"A man," Natasha repeated. He could see her thinking, turning it over in her head. There was a lot to focus on in that report, but she'd focused on the biggest anomaly to her.

"Do we have photos?" Ian said.

Dax turned his laptop. Natasha went closer to inspect. The photos weren't close ups but they must have been good enough because her eyes widened in disbelief.

"That's Pluto."

Dax and Ty looked confused since they hadn't seen the texts on her phone.

"Her handler," Ian said. "I'm assuming you don't know his real identity."

"Of course not. I've only ever met him a handful of times over the years. He's my contact in the Syndicate, no matter where I go or what the job is. We don't engage in chitchat. But he's Eastern European. That much I'm sure of."

"And he's sitting at dinner with your daughter and her nanny. Have they ever met him?"

She looked bewildered. "No. I don't bring that side of my life home. I'm an international banker. It explains the travel and the money. But of course he knows who they are. It's the Syndicate's lever to use against me."

"The nanny doesn't look afraid," Dax noted.

"Which means either she's in on it or he's pretending

to be something he's not," Ian replied. "How much do you know about her?"

Natasha looked stunned. "In on it? No. Lissette loves Daria. She's been with us for more than two years now. She doesn't have any family other than us. Her mother is dead and she doesn't talk to her father at all. I researched her thoroughly before hiring her and she came with effusive references. Besides, if Pluto presented himself to her as one of my bank colleagues, she wouldn't have reason to be afraid of him. And it's likely that's exactly what he did. It's what I would have done in his place."

She had a point. Her handler would know details about her that he could use to ease his way with the nanny. "We need to find out what name he used at the hotel. I doubt it's his real one, but it's a start. I assume we're tracking the taxi down?"

"Finn followed them as far as he could. They went to the *Bahnhof* and boarded the train to Munich."

"Munich!" Natasha frowned. "Was there anyone with them? Anyone waiting for them?"

"He couldn't tell."

"Did he board the train?" Ian asked.

Dax shook his head and shot a glance at Natasha. "He was blocked. He doesn't know if it was intentional, but he didn't make it to the platform in time."

"We need to get someone on that train at the earliest possible location," Ian ordered.

"It's being done. We're researching all the stops and seeing where we can get an agent onboard."

"They could disembark before your people get on," Natasha said coldly. "I thought you had this under control? You promised me she would be well. *Promised.*"

She was so upset she was shaking. Ian went over and put his hands on her shoulders. "It *is* under control. If I didn't have people at the hotel, you wouldn't know they'd left at all. We'll find them."

There were two spots of red in her cheeks. Her nostrils flared with the effort to keep herself from coming unglued. "It doesn't make sense. If I send the photo like they want, then what? I should be able to return home and get my daughter back right away. But she's on her way to *Germany*. What are they doing with her?" She shook her head. "I should text Pluto again."

"And say what? That you want to know why he was having dinner with your daughter and her nanny? That you want to know why they're on the way to Germany?"

The color in her cheeks didn't recede. He knew she was struggling with what her heart wanted and what her head told her she had to do.

"Maybe I could ask for an update on them. Just a quick one while I wait for you to leave your house so I can kill you."

"And you feel like that's a normal thing for you to do?"

She closed her eyes and dropped her chin to her chest. "No."

"Exactly."

She didn't say anything more and he pulled her against him, holding her while she worked to accept what was happening. Not only that, but she also had to accept that it wasn't instantly fixable. He knew she would in the end because that's what Calypso would do. It was Natasha who was struggling.

"I'm not giving up," he said, putting his mouth against her hair. "This is a minor setback, that's all. You've encountered them many times, I'm sure. But you always improvised and came out on top. You aren't a quitter, Tasha. Neither am I. We fight for those we care about. We don't stop fighting, and we don't give up."

"I can't lose her, Ian."

"You aren't going to. Trust me."

She didn't answer but he didn't expect her to. She didn't trust him. Not yet.

He thought of her reaction to the photo Dax had been working on. He didn't think she was squeamish, considering her profession. He'd felt her trembling when he'd held her, and he'd wondered if it was because of him. Because of how she'd felt seeing *him* like that.

Now he was holding her again, and he liked it.

She slipped her arms around his waist, and emotion flared in his heart.

Was it desire? Happiness? Something else?

He didn't know what it was. He only knew it felt right.

Chapter Thirty

Two hours later, Natasha put a steaming meatloaf, homemade mac and cheese, green beans, and fresh-from-scratch biscuits on the island in the kitchen. Three pairs of eyes watched her in shock.

"It's not poisoned," she growled. "What would I use? There was some bleach under the sink, but I thought you'd taste that right away, unfortunately."

Ty and Dax blinked. Ian laughed and grabbed a plate.

"Uh, boss," Ty said.

"Relax, dude," Ian replied. "If it makes you feel better, wait for her to take a bite."

Natasha rolled her eyes. She hadn't intended to fix an entire meal from scratch, but she'd needed something to do to keep her anxiety at bay. Being stuck in Colorado with these three men, without a way to contact Lissette while the nanny and her daughter traveled across Europe—possibly in the company of her handler—was enough to make her lose her mind if she had to dwell on it.

She'd dwelled on cooking instead, putting together an

American meal like her mother used to fix sometimes. Lissette tended to do most of the cooking at home, but Natasha still enjoyed preparing meals when she got a chance. She'd found everything she needed to whip up a homemade meal in the pantry, fridge, and freezer.

"You two don't deserve to eat any of this," she said primly, picking up a plate and taking a slice of meatloaf for herself. Then she spooned up a big helping of mac and cheese, some green beans, and grabbed a hot, fluffy biscuit. "But I'm sharing with you because it's Ian's house and his food."

She set the plate down, shoved her fork in, and took a big bite. Then, just because she felt like being a jerk, she started choking and clasping at her throat. Ty and Dax were filling their plates but stopped to stare at her in horror.

Ian was trying not to laugh. Or so she thought since he'd dipped his chin and turned to the side.

She wheezed as she reached for her water bottle. "I forgot to take it from the middle," she gasped out. "That was the part I didn't poison. Goodbye, cruel world..."

Ian snorted finally. "Jesus, Tasha, way to scare the shit out of these two." He forked up a bite of meatloaf and downed it. "You could have gone into show business."

Natasha straightened and shrugged. "It wasn't an option."

"For fuck's sake," Ty grumbled.

Dax laughed. "Don't make me like you." He sounded like a parent scolding a child and trying not to crack up as he did so. "I don't want to like you."

"Don't worry, it won't last. My existence will piss you off again soon enough."

Dax filled his plate and took a seat. "I don't know. You're kind of fun."

She tried not to feel the glow of that simple statement. She didn't need him to like her. Didn't need anyone to like her. But it felt kind of good letting her goofy side out. She was only ever goofy at home, and probably not often enough because she always felt like she had so many worries pressing down on her that she couldn't let go and have fun.

It was hard to forget that someone could order you to leave everything and go halfway around the world at the drop of a hat. She tried not to think about all she'd had to do to survive, but sometimes it was like balancing on a teetering pile of bricks. Lose your focus and the pile would topple and crush you in the avalanche.

Despite everything she'd done for the Syndicate, they were still going to crush her if they got a chance. She just hoped she could escape before they did.

"Damn, this is good," Dax said after he took a bite of meatloaf.

"It is good," Ian said. "I'm kind of ashamed of what I've made for you now that I've tasted this."

Okay, so that glow inside was kind of addictive. She told herself not to dwell on it too much.

"I appreciate that you cooked for me."

"I put waffles in a toaster and heated a can of soup. Not too hard."

And yet the fact he'd done so added to the glow. "It's not the difficulty. It's the fact someone took the time to make a meal for you. That's what I appreciate." She glared at Ty. "So you be grateful, asshole."

He shoveled mac and cheese in his mouth and managed not to look pissed off or wary. She'd take that as progress.

"It's delicious," he said. "Not better than my grandma's, but really good."

"Thank you." She slathered butter and honey on her biscuit. Because that's the way she liked it and she didn't care if it seemed odd with this meal.

They spent the next hour sitting around the island, eating good food and talking about life and work. Natasha didn't say too much, but Ian tried to include her. She learned that these men were more than simply employees to Ian. And he was more than a boss to them.

They were a family. They had shared jokes, shared experiences, but even when they disagreed, they found a way to still care about each other. Listening to them made her heart hurt when she thought of what she'd lost.

Her parents and her brother. Yes, she missed her big brother. He used to fight for her on the playground, and he'd read her stories at night. She'd loved him so much. Idolized him.

That person was gone now, and the one in his place didn't like her at all. He'd told her yesterday that he would shoot her if he had to. Considering she'd actually shot him last year, she couldn't exactly get upset about it.

But it still hurt.

Then there was Lena. Her friend through thick and thin. Her only family after her parents were executed.

But now she was gone too and all Natasha had was Daria. And Lissette, though Lissette had only been around for a couple of years.

Daria and Lissette, who were on a train to Germany instead of spending Christmas with her at their home in Zurich.

Natasha chewed the inside of her lip. She couldn't figure it out. Pluto had dinner with them, and now they were on a train. She wasn't worried about their immediate safety, but she *was* worried. What was going on was outside the norm of her experience with the Syndicate.

"I should check my phone again," she said.

The room went silent. She hadn't realized she'd interrupted until the conversation ceased so abruptly.

Ian was looking at her. Assessing her.

"Not to communicate," she added. "I know better. You were right. But he could have sent a message. It's been a couple of hours."

Ian nodded at Dax who went to get her phone from the metal box. She knew why they used metal. It was to keep signals from going in or out.

Dax handed the phone to Ian. She thought he might turn it on and look at it but he held it out for her. She took it carefully, praying there was something that would help her make sense of what was happening as she pressed the power button.

The lock screen came up. She keyed in the code to open it. There was no red number to indicate she'd gotten a message, but she clicked the app anyway.

Nothing. Her stomach sank to her toes. The last text from Pluto was all there was.

"Nothing new?" Ian asked.

"No." She thrust the phone at him before she could do something rash.

"Sorry, angel."

"I should have made dessert," she said, looking at the empty plates. "I still could. Who wants a cake?"

The men exchanged glances. She didn't wait for them to speak. She jumped up and headed for the walk-in pantry. Hadn't she seen cake mix in there?

There wasn't cake mix, but there was a big box of brownie mix. She walked out of the pantry with the box held high in triumph.

"We're having brownies, gentlemen. Better come watch me carefully so I don't add any of those Tide pods I found in the laundry room."

Dax got to his feet. "Let's clean this up, Ty. Ian can help Natasha if he wants."

Ty seemed to hesitate, but then he got up too. "Sure, why not?"

They gathered plates and took them to the sink. Then the two of them did dishes even though Ian had a perfectly adequate dishwasher they could have used. She told herself not to be touched by it but, hell, she was overly emotional lately and it made her eyes sting.

Stupid hormones.

Ian fetched eggs, oil, and water for her. When she started to beat the mixture by hand, he said, "There's a stand mixer in the cabinet."

"I know," she said, working the thick batter until her hand and arm ached. "I prefer this."

Anything to stay busy.

"Okay."

"You could put the leftovers away. And turn on the oven to three-fifty."

"Got it. Anything else?"

She shook her head, but she didn't take her eyes off the batter. He went to do as she said, and she appreciated that he didn't argue or try to give her reasons she shouldn't be upset. After she beat the hell out of the batter, she poured it into an oiled pan, shook it to make everything even, and put it in the oven.

Then she stared at the pan behind the glass door and wondered what activity she could do next. She heard a phone ring, but she didn't turn around to see whose. It wasn't hers. That was all she knew.

It was Ian's voice, but his words were low enough she couldn't understand what he said.

And then he was beside her, his arm touching hers. She

turned her head. He wasn't smiling, but he didn't look as if anything terrible had happened either.

"We have an agent on the train. Daria and Lissette are still there, but they're not alone."

Chapter Thirty-One

"Is it him?" Natasha asked.

"It seems to be."

"What the *fuck* is he up to?"

"I don't know. I have agents in Munich. We'll be waiting for them."

Her eyes clouded. "There may be more hired guns with him. You wouldn't know who they were. But if your people try to take Daria and Lissette, they could get hurt in the fight that would inevitably follow."

"I know. We aren't doing an extraction until we know where they're going and how many of them are involved."

"I don't like it, Ian," she said, her voice tight. "I don't like not doing everything possible to get my daughter in Munich, but I also fear what would happen if you did."

He put his arm around her and rubbed her shoulder. He needed to touch her. Needed to comfort her, if it was possible. "I know. I feel the same. But I agree that we shouldn't do anything hasty. We don't know what we're up against. And it seems as if someone wants them alive and well. I know it's no consolation, but my agent on the train says your nanny doesn't seem stressed. That's not a lot to go on, but it's something."

"I don't understand what's happening, or how he got her to agree to it. Dinner is one thing, but this?"

Ian had been thinking about that. "What if he's romancing her? He could have targeted her at the hotel— or even in Zurich when you weren't around. Did you ever feel like she was seeing anyone?"

Natasha looked thoughtful. "No, never. She didn't have any reason to hide it from me. I wouldn't have cared if she'd had a boyfriend, but she never asked for time to see anyone. Even if he'd told her to keep it secret, I feel like she would have let it slip somehow. She's shy when she doesn't know you, but when she warms up to you she talks a lot about all kinds of things. The only man she's ever talked about is the one at the bakery who slips her extra pastries. She's still not sure if it means anything, or if he's just being nice. I've heard about it more than I care to, believe me."

"Then if it's a romance with your handler, it's a whirl-wind one."

She turned to face him, frowning. "It could be—but you don't believe it is, do you? You think he's been grooming her for longer than that."

"It doesn't matter what I believe. What matters is the truth—which we won't know for a while yet, I'm afraid."

"Right." He could see the gears grinding in her head. "If I'm wrong and he's been grooming her, then I can only think of one reason. They know about us. And the more I think about it, it's the only thing that explains any of this. Sending me to kill you, demanding proof, holding my daughter hostage to make sure I complete the mission."

He nodded. "You could be right."

"I thought it was because I killed the Butcher. But I've

gone over it again and again. The only people who saw me at the monastery were your people. The rescue of Tallie Grant pointed at you, not me. I abandoned the helicopter at an airfield where no one knows my identity. So either you have a mole, or it's not Broussard at all."

"I don't have a mole. Not on that team."

"But on other teams?"

He smiled thinly. "Yes. I know who they are, though. By design, BDI hires some of the scumbags. They don't get close to the important work."

He had to hire them to protect his cover in the underworld. Someone in the inner circle of the Syndicate may have cracked it, but his reputation was still intact in the wider community. He knew because his people monitored the dark web and the chat rooms where the nasty jobs were discussed. So did Phoenix, his staunchest ally and oldest friend at the CIA.

Natasha looked worried. "And you're positive the agents you have tracking my daughter are the good ones?"

"Yes."

"You've asked a lot of me, you know. From the very beginning. And you don't give me answers. You just want me to do as you ask."

"It's how I operate, angel. The less I tell anyone, the less that person can be used against me. Besides, is it any different from the Syndicate?"

"No. But you promised that BDI was different."

"It is different."

Her gaze drifted to where Ty and Dax were finishing the dishes. "They've put me in the scumbag category, you know."

"I know. But that's not where I put you."

"Even though I tried to kill you?"

"You did a shitty job of it. I'm pretty sure that wasn't your best effort."

"Not at all…" The indignant look faded from her expression. "I think someone's been watching me. I'm not sure how long, but certainly before Venice. How else would they know?"

"You know that was Tommaso Leone you humiliated in Venice, don't you?"

Her eyes widened. "I didn't. I've never met him before, though I know who he is. His father is Ennio. He's rumored to be part of the Syndicate."

"Tommaso or Ennio?"

"Both of them, though Ennio is the one with the power. And I have met him."

"You didn't mention that when you were supposed to be telling me everything you know."

"I didn't think about it. I've met Ennio precisely once. He gave a party at his Lake Como estate. Pluto told me to go, so I did. I kept expecting it was a job, but it wasn't. I enjoyed the food and the view, and then took a train home. It was nothing."

Nothing.

"When was this?"

"April. But I'm no one to the Leones. Why would they watch me? Or have me watched?"

"I don't know that they would. I'm just trying to figure out what the connections might be."

She gripped his hands in hers. "You have to take me with you when you go to Europe. Or wherever Daria and Lissette end up."

He squeezed gently. "Why would I do that, Tasha? You'd just be one more person I'd have to watch out for."

"As if I can't take care of myself! Who do you think I am anyway?"

171

He loved the way her eyes flashed fire at him. It made him want to kiss her and see if the touch of her lips sizzled the way her eyes did. He thought that he really should be a whole lot more pissed off at her than he was, but the more time he spent with her—the more he saw her vulnerable side—the harder it was to stay angry.

Natasha was a mama bear trying to protect her cub in the only way she knew how. He couldn't really fault her for that, even if he'd been the target.

"I know who you are, and I know what you're capable of. I also know you're pregnant and you aren't on your game. If I have to worry about you, then my focus is split. I don't want anything distracting me from getting Daria back to you."

Her nostrils flared with emotion. "Fine, don't let me go on the mission. But take me to Europe with you. I know you have safe houses there. You probably have one in Munich. Stash me there. Chain me up if you have to. But take me with you so I'm not stuck out here in the middle of nowhere with no communication, worrying about what's happening and if Daria is safe."

Ian had a picture in his head of chaining her to the bed. Naked. Not quite what she was asking, but he enjoyed it.

Taking her with his team wasn't impossible. It was just easier not to. Easier to leave her in this house with Jamie Hayes to watch over her. Less to think about.

But was there really? He'd still be thinking about her. And he'd be wondering if she'd try to pull something on Jamie. If she'd get hurt doing it, because Jamie was a badass in her own right. Maybe not as badass as Calypso when she was on her game, but right now she wasn't. How long would that last, though? Natasha wasn't permanently incapacitated. She was dealing with stress and pregnancy hormones, but she wasn't helpless and she damned sure wasn't harmless.

If he took her with him, he could keep her out of the action. It was entirely possible. Then he'd be able to keep an eye on her himself. There was every chance he wouldn't have to leave her at all once they reached Europe. He could send the team to extract Daria and Lissette, and he could stay with Natasha. She wouldn't have to wait for hours to see her daughter again. They could be reunited and on a flight back to the US before the Syndicate could react.

"I'll think about it."

"Ian—"

"No," he said firmly. "No more. That's the best I can do."

"You're being stubborn!"

"Don't push me," he growled. "You won't like the result."

She glared at him for a moment and he thought she might try again. But whatever she saw in his face must have stopped her.

"Go away," she said imperiously. "If I have to look at you for another second, I'm going to do something that will upset Ty and Dax."

He was almost amused. "And you care what they think now?"

"Hell no. But I'd rather not get tackled by your fan club when I knee you in the balls."

Chapter Thirty-Two

NATASHA THOUGHT SHE MIGHT HAVE TROUBLE SLEEPING, but she was out almost the instant her head hit the pillow.

When she woke sometime later, it was still dark. Since she didn't have a phone or a watch, and there was no alarm clock in her room, she didn't know what time it was.

She stretched, only to be confronted by her bladder. Wasn't it too soon to be peeing all the time?

She had no choice but to take care of it. When she was done, she twisted her hair onto her head and secured it with an elastic band before wrapping herself in a blanket and heading for the kitchen.

Now that she was awake, she wanted another brownie. Assuming those Neanderthals hadn't eaten them all after she'd gone to bed. She'd had to make a second pan because they'd devoured the first. If they'd eaten that one too, then she might just dig out those Tide pods for the next batch.

The house was dark and quiet. When she walked into the living room, a full moon hung high in the sky, shining through the tall windows and illuminating a narrow band of wooden flooring and furniture. Outside, the snow shone pristine and peaceful. It snowed a lot in Moscow too, but she'd rarely thought it was peaceful when she was growing up.

That snow didn't stay pristine. In a city, it got dirty quicker. Though Red Square was impossibly gorgeous when it snowed. St. Basil's Cathedral and the Kremlin, along with Lenin's tomb and the State Historical Museum, made for stunning landmarks against a white backdrop.

She turned toward the kitchen, dismissing thoughts of Moscow. It snowed in Zurich—but she didn't want to think of that either.

She found the pan sitting on one end of the island. When she uncovered it, half was left. Not bad for Neanderthals.

Natasha took a big piece and sighed as she bit into it.

"Sneaking brownies, kitten?"

She jumped and squeaked at the sound of his voice. "Ian! You scared me."

He moved into the shaft of light and she realized he must have been sitting in the living room the entire time. Her heart pounded.

"I didn't mean to. I thought you saw me."

"I didn't. You should announce yourself if you're going to lurk in dark corners."

His laughter was as rich as the brownie. "You should know better than anyone that's not how it works. Never draw attention to yourself when you have the tactical advantage."

"No, but this isn't combat."

"Isn't it?"

She turned away to retrieve a glass from the cabinet. Then she took milk from the fridge and poured it. She

LYNN RAYE HARRIS

didn't ask him if he wanted any. He could get his own damn milk.

"It shouldn't be," she said.

"And yet you threatened my balls earlier."

"You were being unreasonable."

The milk was cold and the brownie was gooey. Perfect. But still not enough to calm her jitters.

"Maybe. Maybe not. It's not unreasonable to want to protect the woman who's pregnant with my child."

She wasn't used to being someone who needed protection. She was the storm, not the house made of flimsy boards that would fly away when the storm hit. She was Calypso, legendary assassin and formidable opponent. She was not the swooning female who needed a man to keep her safe.

She hadn't failed to notice that he'd called her the woman pregnant with his child. It annoyed her. She wasn't the woman he cared about. Wasn't first in the equation at all. And why would she be? They'd had wild, partially unprotected sex and there were consequences.

She wasn't important to him for any other reason. It wasn't her he was worried about when he decreed she couldn't help rescue Daria. It was the baby.

Knowing his reasons shouldn't hurt, but it did. She should be used to playing second fiddle by now, but apparently she wasn't. If she and Jace had been a priority to their parents, they'd have never done anything that got the whole family deported to Russia. Or maybe they would have never left Russia in the first place, and she would have been born there. Her life would have been vastly different.

It made her feel suddenly, fiercely protective of the baby she carried. And angry too, because a moment of carelessness had led her to this place where everything was different for her.

176

"I wouldn't be pregnant if we'd used our brains that night," she snapped. "But I am, and now everything is changing for me. But not for you. You still get to be the mighty Ian Black, the man who men fear and women want. You give nothing of yourself, but you expect concessions from everyone else."

"Is that what you think?" he said, his voice low and dark.

"Yes. What do I know of you? You are a mysterious man, rich beyond imagination, and yet you throw yourself into work it would be so easy to ignore for a man in your position. You could take your money and lie on a beach somewhere, but instead you bash your head against the rocks as you fight a cabal of people who stand for all the things you hate—while pretending to be like them, I might add." She sucked in a breath hot with emotion. "You won't win, you know. They will chip away at you, like rainwater on a glacier, and you will grow smaller and smaller. *If* you manage to survive once they find out you're still alive."

Her emotions whipped higher, but she couldn't seem to stop them. Every word she spoke stabbed into her and made her feel desperate to stop the outcome she predicted. She knew what it was to feel aching loss, and she would not do it again. Not that she ached for Ian Black. Never that.

But they were bound together now, so long as this child inside her existed.

He came closer, until he stood so near she could smell him. That unique scent that was Ian. He smelled like hellfire and brimstone, damn him, and he smelled like pine and leather and fine Scotch. He was determination in the flesh. How had she resisted him for as long as she had?

"What do you want to know?" he asked, his voice darkly seductive and raw. "Ask me and I'll tell you."

Chapter Thirty-Three

NATASHA BLINKED. WAS HE SERIOUS? SHE CAST ABOUT, thinking for what she most wanted to ask him before he changed his mind. "Why are you so determined to fight them? And why do you think it matters?"

He didn't say anything at first. And then, "It matters."

"Why?"

He sucked in a breath and she could tell he was struggling with it. But she wasn't going to let him off the hook. She wanted to know why he risked so much when he didn't have to. There was no one holding his feet to the fire, no one pulling his strings. Even if he worked for the CIA, which the dossier had said he did, he was wealthy enough to walk away if he wanted to.

"Because innocent people get hurt when others do nothing," he began. "Every day, everywhere, there's a young woman who doesn't know any differently getting sucked into a situation she can't possibly fathom. And when she does know, it's too late. She's been dragged into something she can't escape on her own. The Syndicate has the slave auctions for rich men, but that's not all they do. They also have their fingers in the pies of smaller operations that happen across this country and others. The operations where sweet little Becky from next door is ignored at home, but finds acceptance when a man a bit older makes her feel special. He could be a coach, a youth pastor, or someone she met at the mall. These days he can be online, hiding behind a computer screen, which is even more insidious. Nevertheless, he's someone different from anybody else in her life. Someone exciting. Eventually she's running away from home to join him, but the reality she finds isn't what she was promised. She's not special. She's just a cog in the wheel, and now she's using drugs and selling her body to line the man's pockets with money.

"And *if* she gets away—a big if—life doesn't always return to normal. Sometimes she has mental health issues, and they don't get better, no matter how much therapy or anti-depressants her family throws at her. And then one day, when she feels at her lowest point, she'll take that gun that her father keeps in the bedside drawer and she'll blow her brains out. But not before she threatens to take her three-year-old son with her. Fortunately, he won't remember much about that day. He won't remember her putting the gun to his head, though he'll remember the crying and the talking—and the noise when she finally did it. Jesus, the noise a gun makes…"

He paused, and she didn't know what to do, but then he kept talking.

"He'll also remember the fear and the helplessness of all those around him after it was over. When he's old enough, he might make a vow to do everything he can to stop another Becky from getting sucked into the cycle. At the very least, he'll try and put a stop to the people who exploit the Beckys of the world.

"He knows it's an endless task, but he also knows it's worth it if he can save just one Becky and her child."

Natasha's heart squeezed painfully tight. She couldn't speak. The brownie was sawdust in her mouth as she digested everything he'd just said. She wanted to wrap her arms around him. And she was afraid because what if he pushed her away?

"I'm sorry, Ian," she finally said. "I shouldn't have asked."

He put his hands on the counter and pressed down, as if grounding himself. "It's okay. Like you said, I've asked a lot of you."

She found the courage to reach over and squeeze his hand. "I know that had to be difficult to share. But thank you."

He shook his head. "I didn't really share it though, did I? I was purposely vague. But yes, that's exactly what happened to my mother. She was fourteen when she disappeared, and seventeen when her parents found her again. She was also pregnant with me. She was in and out of rehab, in and out of counseling, but it was too much in the end. She put a gun in her mouth and pulled the trigger, and I was sitting on the floor at her feet when it happened. It was ten days before Christmas. I remember the lights."

His voice was hoarse when he said that last, and tears welled in her eyes. He'd been a child. A sweet, helpless child. Christmas was supposed to be beautiful for children, not ugly. And here she'd asked him why he didn't have a tree. She understood now.

She closed the space between them and wrapped her arms around him. His body was big and hard and warm, but she could feel the tremor rolling through him. She pressed her cheek to his chest and squeezed him tight. He looped his arms around her and held her gently, and she hated herself for ever thinking she wanted to kill him.

"I'm so sorry. I don't know what else to say."

He stroked her hair. "It's enough."

"It's really not." She tipped her head back to look up at him. "I'm sorry for what happened to you, and I'm sorry for trying to k-kill you."

She had to press her lips tightly together to stop herself from crying. Her heart pounded and her head whirled with so many thoughts and recriminations that it was impossible to try and follow them all.

"You were trying to save your child. I don't hate you for that."

"But I wasn't thinking of you, or *our* child. I was only thinking of Daria's safety—but I should have found another way. I should have asked you to help me." She paused to gather her chaotic thoughts. "This is not about me. I don't want to talk about me."

"You have more questions?" he asked, a trace of humor in his voice.

"Yes, definitely."

"Such as?"

He was still holding her, and she didn't mind being held. She liked it. "Beach or mountains?"

"Depends."

"Seriously?"

"Yes. It all depends on the time of year and how I'm feeling. If it's fall, then I want mountains. The colors are beautiful, plus there's hiking and crackling fires outside in the evening. If it's winter—dark, cold, and rainy—then give me the beach."

"Okay, you make a good point. I'll concede that the beach isn't the most perfect place all the time, but I still prefer it. I like walking on the edge of the water and picking up shells. I like watching the tide come in, and sunsets. Oh, and sunrises too. Those are perfect."

"True."

"What's your middle name?"

He laughed. "What's yours?"

"Not about me," she said, shaking him a little bit. "Middle name."

"Gabriel."

"Ah, so you're the angel then. Not me."

"It's my father's name. My grandfather," he added. "My grandparents adopted me when I was five. It was better legally, especially since I had a birth father out there somewhere. They wanted to be sure he couldn't take me away from them if he ever showed up. For the record, he never did."

"Does that bother you?"

"No. My parents were terrific people. They gave me every advantage."

"They're gone now." She knew it was true because it'd been in the dossier Pluto had sent.

He nodded. "Mom died two years ago after a brief illness. She was eighty-two. Dad was eighty-six, and he followed within a month. Didn't want to live without her. They were still in their home, believe it or not."

Her heart hurt for him. She remembered what it had felt like to be told that both her parents were gone. Under different circumstances, sure. But she wouldn't say her loss was worse. Just different.

"I'm sorry for your loss." She'd always thought those words sounded so empty, but what else was there to say? There was nothing that made it better. Nothing that could.

"They had a good life."

"Where did you grow up?"

"South Carolina. My parents owned a popular furniture chain there. Black's Fine Home Furnishings. It's still in the family, though it's a cousin running it now. Mom was an interior designer. She did work for some of Charleston's finest families. Including the Campbells, who were good friends, though a little bit younger."

"I'm afraid I don't know who the Campbells are," she said, enjoying standing in the circle of his arms and chatting like it was something they did all the time. "Should I?"

He laughed softly. "They live in the White House now."

She blinked. He really did know people in powerful places. "Oh."

"Preston Campbell is a good man. He and the First Lady came to Mom's funeral. He was out of the country on a diplomatic trip for Dad's, but Helena was there."

"That was good of them."

"Like I said, they were friends. My parents put money into Preston's first campaign for Senator, and they supported him over the years, donating, participating in fundraisers. The Campbells don't forget things like that."

She wasn't sure what to say. She didn't dare to think his connection to the American president could help her situation in any way. She was nobody to President Campbell. Less than nobody.

"The dossier I got on you said that you speak at least twelve languages fluently. Is that true?" she asked.

"I speak twelve fluently because I use them most often. I can get by in almost any language after a few days study."

"How is that even possible?"

He shrugged. "It's always been something that comes easily to me. I went to Harvard to study languages and political science."

"And then you joined the CIA."

"That was in your dossier, huh? What else did it say?"

She noticed that he didn't confirm it. "That you inherited a fortune from your parents, and that you have never been married. Possibly bisexual, but no confirmation."

He barked a laugh. "Why ask me where I grew up if you had a dossier? I'm sure Harvard was in there too. I inherited a fortune, but I've also made one of my own. And while I've never been married, I've also never had sex with another man. Got close once in college, but turns out it's not how I roll."

Her mind was reeling. "I asked because I wanted to hear you tell me. What if the dossier was wrong? And I think I'm relieved you aren't bisexual. But, um, *how* close?"

Because the thought of two big alpha males together was sort of hot.

He laughed. "It was college. I was drunk. There was a dare."

"But you've had another man's dick in your hand? Or was it your mouth?"

"Does the thought make you hot, kitten?"

She shrugged. "A little. Maybe. I don't know."

She was lying because there was a definite flood of heat and wetness between her legs.

He laughed again. "I touched a dick through jeans. It didn't do anything for me. Satisfied?"

"I think so. Was there kissing?"

He snorted. "I said I was drunk, right?"

She shivered a little. *Dear heaven.* "Well, it's nice to know Ty and Dax aren't competition. Unless you'd like to try again?"

He tugged her closer suddenly, until she could feel the press of his cock against her abdomen. Her breath shortened, her insides liquifying. The need was practically overwhelming. Maybe it was the hormones, or maybe it was simply that she knew how good sex with him could be.

"No, I don't want to try. They're definitely not competition. Not a chance. There's only one place I want to be, and it's definitely not with either of those hairy assholes."

Her pussy ached. All she had to do was say yes, and he was hers for the night. Him and his magical tongue. Not to mention his magical dick.

Maybe she should say no and keep this thing between them from growing more complicated, but she really didn't want to. She wanted mind-blowing orgasms, and she wanted a warm body beside hers in the cold night. She didn't want to be alone. Not when she could be cherished and held close for a few hours.

She knew it wasn't permanent. It couldn't be, but that didn't mean she couldn't enjoy it for now.

She stepped back, out of the circle of his arms, and took his hand. Then she led him to her room.

Chapter Thirty-Four

Ian closed the bedroom door behind him and leaned against it, watching her with hot eyes.

Natasha didn't turn on a light, but she didn't need to. The full moon shone through the transoms at the top of the windows and made the room seem almost like daylight to people whose senses were attuned to darkness. She'd lost the blanket she'd wrapped around herself to walk out to the kitchen, but she was warm for the moment.

Hot with the desire coursing through her. How could it feel like this?

New, exciting, maybe even a little dangerous.

"Are you coming over here?" she asked, the backs of her knees against the side of the bed.

"I want to. More than anything."

Her stomach fell a little. "You don't trust me? You think I stole a knife from the kitchen so I could lure you here and finish the job?"

He shook his head. "Not at all. But it's a little hard to forget that it was only two days ago when you felt miserable. It seems a little soon to do what I want to do to you."

Her pussy ached at the thought of what he might want to do. "I *was* miserable. Jared's miracle pill did the trick. Though it also makes me sleepy, but I'm not sleepy right now. And I'm not nauseous either." She started to unbutton the silk pajama top. "I want you, Ian. I want to feel good, and I want to stop worrying. Just for a little while. Reality will hit me again soon enough."

He moved a lot faster than she expected him to. It was as if he'd been held back by an invisible force that suddenly released when she said those words.

His mouth crashed down on hers, his tongue tasting, his hands seeking to divest her of clothes as she frantically worked to do the same with his. When they were naked, when there was nothing left between them but skin and heat, they fell to the bed together. Ian rolled her until she was pinned beneath him, and then he started work on her body, tasting the skin of her neck, nibbling her collarbones, then fastening his mouth over one distended nipple as she cried out and curled her fists into his shoulders.

"Ian... Don't tease me..."

"Not teasing you, angel. I'm tasting you. I fucking missed this. Missed every beautiful inch of you."

He dragged his mouth to her other nipple while he continued to softly pinch the one he'd just left. Natasha writhed beneath him, biting her lip to keep her moans at a reasonable level, but she feared it wasn't going to work for long.

She wanted to be loud. Wanted to let go and feel what he did to her without any self-consciousness creeping in. "I missed you too," she said. Or panted, really.

By the time he reached her abdomen, she was thrashing her head on the pillow, knowing what came next and wanting it so, so badly. When he settled between her legs, he didn't immediately start licking her.

"Look at me, Cinderella."

She did as he commanded, forcing her eyes open to gaze at the sight of dark-headed, utterly sexy Ian Black lying between her legs with his face only inches from her pussy. "Cinderella?"

"Yeah, you ran away and left me with no idea how to find you or where you'd gone the last time. That's not happening this time."

"No."

He traced a finger over her core, and she bowed up off the bed. "You realize you're mine in every way, right? You aren't getting naked with another man ever again. There's no leaving. No escaping. You belong to me."

His words made her shudder deep inside. No one had ever claimed her before. Not like he was doing.

"Is that a proposal?"

"A proposal implies there's a choice. I'm not giving you a choice. I'm stating a fact."

Her heart thumped. The first chance she got, she was taking her daughter and going into hiding. But that didn't mean she couldn't enjoy the idea of being his for a while.

"You don't know that you won't want me to go away. What if I'm a complete bitch and make you miserable?"

"I'm sure we'll make each other miserable, but then we'll go to bed and make each other happy. It'll all work out in the end."

He dipped his head and licked his way around her clit, holding her down with his shoulders as she tried to get his mouth where she wanted it most. He obliged her, but he took his time.

Natasha gasped. It turned into a moan. "So long as you make it up to me like this, I'm not going to complain."

He blew on her wet flesh. Goosebumps prickled her

skin as she sucked in a breath. How could she want him so much it hurt?

"Do you want me to make you come?" he murmured, his hot breath tickling her.

"Yes. Please, please, yes."

"Better hang on tight, then."

He went to work on her clit with the kind of expertise that came from lots of experience. Whatever idiot had put together the dossier on him had clearly missed the part where Ian Black was a sex god.

A flipping sex god. That was the thought foremost in her mind as he nibbled and sucked and devoured her pussy in all the right ways. Natasha spread her legs wider, moaning as the pressure built inside her. Right before she was ready to explode, he pressed two fingers inside her, fucking her slowly. Then he stopped sucking her clit and she wanted to scream.

"Don't stop," she begged him, uncaring that she sounded desperate.

"Not stopping, angel. Prolonging the pleasure."

"I don't want prolonged. I want it now."

"You're going to get it. All of it. Patience." He crawled up her body, sucking her nipples as he continued to fuck her with those two maddening fingers.

And then he was there, big and hard at her entrance. "I want to feel you coming around my cock. I've dreamed of it for the past two months."

"Ian," she whispered, spreading her legs wide, welcoming him.

He pushed inside. He went slowly at first, but she was so wet that he was soon deep inside her, their bodies joined completely.

"Heaven," he whispered. "Why would I ever want to leave?"

She couldn't disagree, but her brain wasn't capable of forming words at just that moment.

He pulled out slowly and returned just as slowly. Natasha gripped his bare ass and thrust her hips up into his. His groan made her happy.

"Too slow for you?" he asked as he stubbornly continued the glacial retreat and return.

"Ian," she begged.

He kissed her. Her body was a quivering mass of sensation as she waited for him to start moving the way she wanted him to move.

And then he did, and she lost herself to his hard thrusts. He reached for her hands, first one and then the other, trapping them above her head, his fingers wound into hers. His cock drove into her again and again as she moaned beneath him.

Her orgasm built even higher than when he'd been eating her. Then she'd thought she needed to come or die. Now she wanted to come, but she also wanted this feeling to keep building.

She writhed against him, trying to free her hands so she could touch him, but he held her fast, as if he knew that restraining her made the pleasure that much better. She knew he'd let go if she told him to. That was what made it work. What turned her on.

"Just feel what I do to you," he said. "Don't fight it, Tasha. *Feel.* Let me take care of you. Let me soothe the ache inside you."

She gazed up at him, their eyes locking as he somehow managed to take it up another level, fucking her so good she thought she might cry with the intensity of it. They'd had fabulous sex in Venice. But this was different. Better somehow.

"I love the way you feel," he said, his voice a sexy

growl. "The way you taste. You're perfect, Tasha. Beautiful. So fucking sexy it hurts."

She closed her eyes, but he commanded her to open them again. She did as he told her. She couldn't fathom disobeying him for even a second.

"Good," he said as their gazes tangled again. "I want to see your eyes when you come."

He pumped into her with abandon, driving them both to impossible heights. She teetered on the edge, and then her orgasm exploded through her in a wave of heat and sensation that stole her breath and left her gasping his name.

"Fuck," he groaned a moment later, his hips slamming into hers, his cock driving deep. And then she felt him coming inside her, hot semen coating the walls of her pussy as his hips jerked against her. His eyes were still locked on hers, and she found his expression in that moment to be the most achingly beautiful thing she'd ever seen. Pain and pleasure intermingled. She didn't know what it meant, and she didn't know how to ask.

Ian let go of her hands, but she couldn't find the strength to move them from above her head. They lay together for long moments, their bodies still joined, but she grew chill as the air cooled the beads of perspiration on her skin. Eventually, he levered himself up and off her.

A fresh chill made her flesh prickle with goosebumps. The chill on her skin was nothing compared to the chill inside her as Ian walked away. Despite everything he'd said about her belonging to him, she thought he was simply amusing himself with her. Saying what felt good in the moment rather than meaning it.

He didn't pick up his clothes, however. He went into the bathroom and returned with a warm washcloth, which he used to clean the semen that spilled from her. It seemed odd to let him do it, but his movements were tender and quick—and she had no inclination to move. When he finished, he climbed into bed with her and tugged the covers up until they were cocooned inside.

She turned into him, burrowing against his body as his arms came around her. They didn't speak, but they didn't need to. They both knew that everything had changed.

Chapter Thirty-Five

Natasha woke him shortly after dawn, her fingers and mouth bringing him to life achingly fast. Ian let her take the lead this time. When she climbed astride him and lowered herself onto his cock, it took all his control to keep from blowing too soon.

As her movements grew more frantic, her breasts bounced up and down, her pussy gripped him tighter and tighter, and he cursed as he felt the tingling in his balls. He wanted it to last, but as soon as she ground her hips down on him and cried his name, he lost his ability to hold on. He came deep inside her, loving the fact there was no barrier between them.

They fell asleep again and when he woke a second time, Natasha was still sleeping. He watched her, thinking he could stay in bed with her for days, his cock buried inside her sweet pussy, listening to her moans and sighs, making her beg him to let her come. Losing himself in the sensations and exploring the way she made him feel.

But the world wasn't going to wait while they ignored it.

It was going to keep on burning, same as always. And he had fires to put out.

He got up and grabbed his clothes. A glance at his watch told him it was seven-thirty. He made the trip back to his room, showered and dressed, and went into the kitchen to fix coffee. Ty was already there. He looked up when Ian walked in, a scowl fixed firmly on his face.

"What's going on, Ian?"

Ian got the coffee from the pantry. "Meaning?"

"I came out here last night."

"And?"

"I had to walk down the hallway. Past Calypso's bedroom door. She's gorgeous, I'll grant you that. But tapping that ass could be dangerous to your health, don't you think?"

Ian stopped in the act of spooning coffee into the filter. "I'm going to stop you right there before you say another word about her. My house, my life. Got it?"

"Does Jace know?"

Ian speared the other man with a look. "Did we die and wake up in the Middle Ages? Because so far as I know, I don't need her brother's permission for anything. Her permission is all that counts."

"She kidnapped Maddie and Angie and shot Jace and Colt. He's not going to be happy about you and her. And what about the fact she's pregnant? There has to be a father out there, and she's cheating on him with you."

Ian couldn't do anything but stare at the other man. Ty looked indignant. Almost affronted at the idea Natasha was cheating on the father of her child. It was oddly old-fashioned in a way. And probably a good thing that Ty hadn't connected the dots yet. Ian was going to have to tell his team, but he wanted to be back at HQ when he did it.

"She's not cheating on the father," Ian said.

"Cheating on what father?" Dax asked as he came into the kitchen.

"Nothing," Ty said. "Mere hypothetical conjecture."

Dax shrugged. "Any coffee?"

"Making it now," Ian said, popping the filter basket into the in-wall coffee maker and pressing the *on* switch.

"Man, that was some great food last night," Dax said, yawning. "Any brownies left?"

"There's a couple," Ty said.

Dax reached for the pan and uncovered it. "You think we could talk her into making breakfast?"

"There's easy stuff in the pantry," Ian said. "Waffles in the freezer. You can manage."

"Fine," Dax grumbled. "But I bet she could make something better."

"Maybe so, but it seems she's still in bed. You want to wait until she wakes up and then talk her into it?"

"Point taken."

Ian exchanged a look with Ty while Dax rummaged in the freezer. Ty shrugged. He might disagree about Ian sleeping with Natasha, but he wasn't going to share what he'd heard. One of the things Ian loved most about his team was that they pushed back when they thought it was necessary, but ultimately they had each other's backs.

He didn't want yes people. He wanted people who told him what they thought.

Ty had done that, and now he was leaving the subject alone. He'd speak up again if he thought it warranted.

When Natasha emerged a couple of hours later, Ian's belly tightened at the sight of her. She came into the kitchen and smiled shyly at him. He was sitting at the island with Dax and Ty and their computers, but he had a dark urge to sweep her up and return to bed. If they'd been alone, he'd have bent her over the kitchen island and made her beg for his touch.

"Is there any news?" she asked as he got up and poured coffee for her. He handed her the cup, heavily laced with cream.

Their fingers touched and a tingle of electricity slipped into his balls. She blinked at him and bit her lip, and he knew she'd felt it too. They stared at each other for a few moments, neither one speaking or moving. But then she smiled again and dropped her gaze shyly, and that dark urge pounded into him.

Make her yours. Make her yours.

He shook himself. She *was* his. He'd already claimed her.

Tell her she's yours. Tell her it's about more than the baby.

He shoved the thought away. "They're in Vienna. They've checked into a hotel."

Natasha's gaze sharpened. "Any sign of Pluto?"

"Not since the train reached Munich. He's not in Vienna with them. Or not yet, anyway."

"What else?"

"They're being watched by more than my people, but we knew that."

"I should check for any messages."

He gave Dax a look that had the other man retrieving Natasha's phone from the metal box. He started to hand it to Ian, but Ian motioned to Natasha. She took it with a smile of thanks and powered it up.

"There's a message," she said as she touched the screen. "It's from him. He says at the conclusion of this mission, I'm to report to Vienna. What the fuck?"

"That's all it says?"

She turned the phone around so he could read it. *Once*

target eliminated, report to Vienna. Will give further instructions when you text your arrival.

She didn't look happy about it.

"What usually happens after you complete the mission?"

"I go home. The money is wired into my account, and I get back to daily life with Daria until the next time."

"But you've been sent to other locations after a job in the past?"

"Sometimes. But this close to Christmas when I have a young child? Never before."

The furrows in her brow bothered him. He wanted to smooth them out, kiss her, and tell her it would all be well.

He made a decision. "We need to return to DC. Today."

"Should I phone HQ and tell them to send Jamie?" Dax asked.

"No, we don't need Jamie here."

Dax and Ty exchanged looks. "Okay, so which one of us is staying?" Ty asked.

"Neither of you. The plan's changed. Natasha's going with us."

Chapter Thirty-Six

When Ian had said she was going with them, Natasha hadn't quite known what that meant. She certainly hadn't thought he meant to BDI's headquarters.

They'd landed at the executive airport half an hour ago and now they were walking into BDI, where she'd once been a prisoner. But he'd given her her freedom that time, and all he'd asked was that she consider joining him and turning against her Syndicate masters.

She hadn't done it because she knew her life—and Daria's—were forfeit if she did. She would never have done it if he hadn't forced her into it.

She stared at Ian's back as they walked through the parking garage, thinking that he clouded her reason. He made her hope. Such dangerous hope.

And then there was what he did to her. Just a few hours ago she'd been spread out beneath him, begging him to let her come. He'd driven her mad with pleasure, and she couldn't wait for the next time.

Ian Black was an addiction. A dark, dangerous addiction that would get her killed if she didn't escape.

Except she didn't want to escape. She wanted to stay.

All the more reason to go. Go before he crushes your heart.

As if it was that easy. As if she could walk out of here on her own power whenever she wanted. She didn't have her phone, didn't have a computer, had no money and no access to transportation. She didn't even have a passport. They'd confiscated it all.

Think, Natasha. There must be a way.

They reached the elevator, but instead of taking it up to one of the office floors, Ian led her through the steel stairwell door and into a hallway. Ty and Dax were behind them. When they reached another door, Ian turned to her.

"I'm going to apologize in advance for the welcome you're about to receive."

"I understand."

"Maybe so, but I'm still apologizing."

Before Ian could reach for the door, it opened. Jace stood on the other side, looking more than a little pissed off. "What is she doing here?"

Ian waved impatiently and Jace stepped back, though he was still scowling. Ian turned and took her hand in his, holding it firmly as he led her into the room. Natasha gaped. It was… a bar. There was a pool table, game machines, tables and chairs, music playing over the speakers—and a pirate at one end of the bar. A sign proclaimed this place *The Pirate's Cove*.

He'd brought her to a bar, but not just any bar. A bar in the basement of the building that housed his organization. There were other people in the room, men and women, and they were all staring at her.

Staring at her and Ian, who hadn't let go of her hand. She resisted the urge to move closer to him for moral support and lifted her chin. She was the assassin Calypso, feared and respected the world over. She would not cower in front of these people.

A little voice inside her head told her she didn't want to be Calypso anymore, but she pushed it down and focused on being the woman people feared. She'd put in her contacts because it was habit, but she hadn't worn a wig. She was mostly herself, and that made her feel more vulnerable than she'd like.

Disguises were a part of who she was, and it was difficult to face these people without more of one.

She recognized Maddy Cole, soon to be Kaiser, and Angie Turner. Colt Duchaine was there as well. Neither he nor Angie were smiling. Jace definitely wasn't. Maddy, however, was. It surprised Natasha since she hadn't been kind to Maddy the first time they'd met. Maybe Maddy was smiling at Ty or Dax, but they'd moved into the room and were no longer standing behind her and Ian.

She wanted to turn and look behind her, but she didn't.

Tallie Grant got up and walked toward them. Natasha thought she had the friendliest face in the room. And why wouldn't she? Natasha had saved her from the Butcher's fortress in Spain. Her eyes—one green and one blue—were just the sort of thing that had fascinated him. He would not have been kind to Tallie had he gotten his chance to 'play' with her.

"Hi, Natasha," she said in her soft Southern accent. "I'm happy to see you."

"Thank you." She sounded stiff, but she didn't know how to relax in a situation like this one.

Tallie was still smiling. "I'm Southern and we hug. Is it okay if I give you a hug?"

She seemed so sincere that Natasha nodded. She wasn't accustomed to hugs from anyone but Daria. And Ian, though his hugs were so much more.

Tallie wrapped her arms around Natasha's shoulders and gave her a quick hug and pat. It felt nice, actually. Natasha felt awkward, but she patted Tallie with her free hand, unwilling to let go of Ian's hand long enough to use both.

"Can I get you anything, sugar?"

"Thank you, no. I had water on the plane."

What a dumb reply. But Tallie wasn't phased.

"Okay. Let me know if you change your mind."

She sashayed back to Brett Wheeler's side, who was frowning but didn't say anything. Jared Fraser and Libby King were there too. Libby smiled and waved. Natasha nodded, convinced Libby was only doing it to be nice. She wouldn't have forgotten that ugly scene in Ian's house.

There were other people in the room, men and women, but she didn't know them. Most of the gazes were unfriendly. Not a surprise, really.

"Thanks for coming," Ian said. "I'm sure you're wondering why I asked you here today. I need to say a couple of things, and I'd rather do it once instead of through several conversations."

He turned his head and gazed down at her for a second before looking at the assembled crowd of operatives and their significant others. "What I'm about to say is confidential. If you're in this room, then I trust you to know it."

She didn't know if the pause was dramatic, or if he was still working himself up to saying the words. But then he said them, and it wasn't what she'd thought he might say.

"Natasha and I are expecting a baby together."

The shock in the room was palpable. There were whispers and gasps. Jace half stood and then sat again when

Maddy put a hand on his arm and said something in his ear.

"A couple more things," Ian said, squeezing her hand quickly. "It's no one's business how or why it happened. Unless you'd like to share the details of your private life with everyone here, then you have no right to ask me to share mine. I won't be explaining to *anyone*. Natasha and I are adults. We don't need approval to have a relationship."

There was utter silence in the room.

"I realize there are some hard feelings toward her for some of you, and I don't expect you to get over it like it never happened. I'm simply asking you to give her a chance."

Natasha dropped her gaze. Her heart pounded and her stomach twisted. She had done terrible things to some of these people. She could wish it had been different, but it hadn't. She'd done what she'd had to do to protect those she loved. And she didn't need anyone to like her because she wasn't staying.

"Will she still be Calypso, or is she going to stay home and bake cookies now?"

Natasha's head snapped up. It was Jace, of course. She was getting better at thinking of him as that instead of Nikolai.

"I don't know," Ian said, that bizarre undercurrent of humor in his voice. Bizarre because she didn't always understand why things amused him. Perverse man. "Tasha?"

"I guess it depends. Are you staying home and baking cookies now that you're engaged to Maddy? Or do you expect her to bake the cookies? I'm trying to understand how having a relationship means someone has to bake cookies all the time. Or perhaps that's a euphemism for sex? My English isn't the best…"

Her English was perfect and he knew it. He glared. She glared back. Maddy elbowed him.

"Sorry," he muttered, glancing at Maddy.

"Then I accept your apology," she said, though her face was still hot with anger. She rushed on before she could change her mind. "I'm sorry for what happened last year, and I'm sorry I hurt you and the ones you love. I won't give you excuses, but I did what I thought I had to do. I miss you, Nik—Jace. I miss how we used to be, but I understand why we can't go back. We are not those same kids anymore."

Ian looped his arm around her shoulders and hugged her to his side. His lips brushed her temple. "Well done," he murmured. "I know it's not easy."

No, it wasn't. Her eyes pricked, but she wouldn't let any tears fall. She stared clear-eyed at the room until Ian spoke again.

"Okay, kids, that's the news. Natasha is one of us, like it or not. We take care of our own, and right now we're going to plan how to rescue her daughter and the nanny from the Syndicate. If you don't want to participate, I won't hold you to it. You can walk out of this room without recriminations. Your job isn't in danger. If you stay, then I'm going to assume you'll put everything you have into helping retrieve the child and her nanny."

He turned his back on the main part of the room and led her over to a barstool. When she was seated, he asked, "Need anything?"

"No. I'm good."

He gave her one of those half-grins of his that made her belly flip. "It's going to be okay, kitten. This is the part where you trust me to do what I said I was going to do."

She nodded. Fragile hope flared again and she tried to snuff it out. Better that way.

But it wouldn't die.

He winked at her as if he knew, then turned around. Not a single person had left the room.

Chapter Thirty-Seven

THEY HAD A PLAN.

After two hours of discussion, war gaming scenarios, and studying maps, Ian knew the plan was solid. Intel from Vienna indicated that Pluto still hadn't been seen, but there were at least three men watching the hotel. The Vienna team had an eye on them and knew their routine. Right now, they were waiting to see if more arrived or if three was it.

There might be someone on the inside too, but they hadn't identified that person. Daria and her nanny hadn't left their room, but they'd been seen by Ian's spy in room service and seemed fine.

The team was on the lookout for Pluto, aka Julian Nowak.

That was the name he'd used at the Grand Hotel Schoenburg and on the train. A Polish name, which meant nothing because it was also the most common surname in Poland. Dax was combing the web for Julian Nowak even now, but there was a lot to sort through with a name like that.

A jet was standing by. Ian and his men were arming for battle before heading for the airport. Natasha had gone to the armory with them. She was also arming for battle, but of a different kind. Ian could see it in her eyes as she glared at him.

"I have skills you can use," she said. "You need to take me with you."

"No. You're staying. For all the reasons I told you before."

And because he wasn't going to lose her. He couldn't bear the thought.

"Ian—"

He grasped her shoulders and held her firmly, putting his face in hers. "I can't have my attention divided out there. I can't concentrate on what needs doing, and on you at the same time."

Her expression didn't soften. "Stubborn man," she growled at him. "I'm as skilled as you are. I'm a trained combat operative. What makes you think you have to worry about me at all?"

He wanted to shake her. And kiss her. "You're pregnant, Tasha. And you're off your game because of it. You know it as well as I do. For once in your stubborn life, listen to your gut and do what it tells you to do. Stop fighting me when you know I'm right. If you make a mistake out there, it could be fatal for more than just you."

Her frown grew more pronounced. Then she yelled something unintelligible to no one in particular. The other men in the room glanced over at her before turning back to their tasks.

Ian watched her with admiration and no small measure of desire. Her cheeks were red, her blond hair wild as she spun toward him. But he could see the surrender in her eyes. Still green. Not hazel at all. He was sure hazel was her real color, but he hadn't seen it in a while.

She stuck a finger in his face, an inch from his nose. "If you fuck this up, I will kill you."

"Not intending to fuck it up, angel."

"And don't you get killed either. You haven't left me any money to raise this kid alone."

He shoved a weapon into the bag. "Is that the only reason you don't want me dead?"

She dropped her gaze. When she looked at him again, she didn't appear any softer than before—but he could see heat of a different kind in those eyes. "No. Who would scratch my itch if something happened to you?"

"Good enough," he said, thinking about all the ways he'd like to scratch her itch right this minute. He shook himself before the blood drained from his head to his dick. No time for that.

"You should still take me. I could wait on the plane. Or in your safe house. I know you have one there."

"I don't want you anywhere near Vienna." He finished packing what he needed in a gun case and locked it. The other guys were finishing up too. Not one of them had asked to stay behind. He hadn't expected they would, but he'd had to offer the option. In the end, he'd asked Jared and Brett to stay so they could keep an eye on Natasha and keep her safe.

"How will you find out what Pluto wants from me if I don't go?"

"I don't care what he wants. He's not getting it."

"You went to all the trouble to make that photo and now you aren't going to use it."

"I didn't say we weren't using it."

She blinked at him. He could tell when understanding dawned. Fury clouded her features all over again. "You're going to *pretend* to be me. You're going to text him the photo and text him when you get to Vienna—you *do* care what he wants! You just don't want me along."

"Bingo, Cinderella. The photo's already been sent, and he's demanded your presence in Vienna. Stupid not to use code words to verify the identity of the sender, you know. Amateur."

She folded her arms with a huff. "The first chance I get, I'm going to feed your balls to you."

He snorted. God he loved how prickly she was. How fiery. So long as she wasn't trying to kill him with that fire. She made life interesting, no doubt about it. "No you won't. You hurt my balls, you don't get your itch scratched."

She tilted her nose up. "There are plenty of men in this world. I'll find one with better itch scratching abilities."

He let his gaze slide down her body and back up again. Slowly. He could see her squirm, though she tried not to. No matter what she said, she wanted him every bit as much as he wanted her.

"Good luck with that."

"You are so certain of yourself," she said, her voice barely more than a whisper.

"I am. If there was time, I'd prove it to you."

"You could be replaced with a good dildo."

He laughed. "Doubt that."

Jamie Hayes entered the armory. She was dressed in army surplus gear, and she'd donned a short black wig and blue contacts. "Hi," she said as she walked over to where they stood separate from the others. "You must be Natasha."

Natasha studied Jamie. "I am. Are you supposed to be me?"

Jamie spread her arms. "One of your iterations. Will I pass the test?"

"I don't know," Natasha said in Russian. "What if Pluto speaks to you?"

"Then I'll answer him," Jamie replied flawlessly.

Natasha turned her gaze back to him. She still looked pissed off. "You're an asshole, Ian Black. All this trouble, and you could just take me to do the job."

He caught her around the waist and pressed a kiss to her forehead. She didn't try to stop him. Jamie moved discreetly away and busied herself talking to Jace, who was eying them hard and pretending not to.

"Any other time and you'd be right. But not now. We've discussed this. Do you really plan to keep fighting me?"

She sagged against him, but the movement was so slight no one else would have noticed. "I'm not used to being irrelevant."

"You are anything but irrelevant to me."

He was still sorting out how he felt, but she definitely wasn't irrelevant. Her safety and security were paramount, hence the trouble he was going to in order to keep her from the fight.

She gazed up at him, her fists curling in his shirt. "What happens when this is all over?"

"We've got time to figure it out, kitten. All you need to know is I'm going to fix everything for you. Then I'm keeping you and Daria safe for as long as it takes the Syndicate to lose interest."

She sniffed. He'd come to realize that Natasha didn't show her emotions if she could help it. He didn't either, but something about her made him more willing to do so.

"Pluto isn't an idiot," she said, picking at his shirt. "She will have to be very careful if she intends to impersonate me. We haven't met often, but he won't be oblivious to mistakes in tone or inflection."

"She knows. She's very good at what she does. Like you."

"It feels wrong not to go with you."

"I know. But you have to take care of the baby, Tasha. That's the most important job you have right now."

He felt her stiffen in his arms, but the movement was slight. She didn't like being sidelined, and he understood that, but it was the right thing to do. It was also the only option that made him breathe easier.

"Yes, of course."

She sounded stiff. He didn't know why and he didn't have time to sort it out.

"I'll send updates. Stay out of trouble, Tash."

"I am trouble," she grumbled without meeting his gaze. "And I don't like this one bit."

He tipped her chin up and forced her to look at him. "Better get used to it. You aren't alone anymore. Your fights are my fights. And my fights are BDI's fights, so you get a team of operatives on your side whether you like it or not."

"You're crazy if you think this will work," she whispered.

"Yeah. Better get used to that too."

Chapter Thirty-Eight

Natasha hated waiting. It was not her strong suit and never had been.

She'd returned to Ian's house with Brett and Jared, who watched her every move. They hadn't left her alone for a moment, and she hadn't expected them to. They didn't say much, and she didn't try to make conversation with them. When they gave her an update, it was brief and to the point—and spectacularly lacking in information.

What she wanted to hear was that Ian had Daria and Lissette in his custody, and that they were on the way back. But that update remained frustratingly absent, even after almost forty-eight hours, so Natasha paced and fretted.

When she discovered Ian's home gym in the basement that afternoon—she'd tried the door the day before but it'd been locked—she climbed onto one of the three treadmills and worked out her frustrations that way. She didn't have appropriate shoes so she did it barefoot. The Chucks would've killed her arches.

Jared swaggered in a few moments later, taking the treadmill beside her and ratcheting up the speed every time she did. She refused to let him win so she kept going. Faster, harder, running like Satan himself was chasing her down.

"Hey, slow it down, Natasha," he called out after they'd been running for ten minutes. "You're pregnant."

"I fucking know that," she yelled, sweat dripping down her torso and between her breasts. She needed the exertion, though. Needed to outrun her demons and *do something* while Ian sat on his high horse and refused to let her help.

A moment later, Jared reached across the treadmill and started to lower the speed. She slapped his hand but he didn't let up, slowing her to a crawl. She jumped off the machine and faced him with murder in her soul.

He was big, but she could take down big. She'd done it before. Many times.

His eyes narrowed a split second before she attacked. He was too slow, though, and she swept his legs from under him and dropped him onto the mat before dancing out of the way.

He propped himself on an elbow and glared at her. "That wasn't called for."

"Oh yes it fucking was," she growled. "You do *not* fuck with my treadmill. I'm pregnant, not incapacitated. And I know my body. I train hard all the time. That was nothing for me."

He got to his feet, frowning. "What you don't understand is that Ian will kill me if you hurt yourself. You're scary, but he's scarier."

"We'll see about that," she said. She went over to the punching bag and began to bareknuckle it, adding in some kicks for variety. She knew how to hit the bag without hurting herself, knew not to go at it full force, but the workout was still intense as she pummeled it with her hands and feet.

"Natasha," Jared said after a few minutes, moving closer. "Stop."

She whirled on him, panting. She needed to expend excess energy like she needed to breathe. It was helping, but this asshat wanted to stop her. She wasn't going to let him.

"I'm busy. Leave me alone."

Brett Wheeler stood in the door watching. He crossed his arms and grinned as Jared kept closing the distance. Natasha almost felt like he was on her side. Almost.

"I'll fucking kick your head off if you come any closer," she said when Jared was within an arm's length of her.

He stopped moving. He held his hands out to either side of his body as if trying to soothe her. "I'd really rather you didn't. Come back upstairs and watch one of those Christmas movies or something."

"I'd rather kick your ass."

"I can't let you do that."

"You won't have to let me, big man. You won't be able to stop me."

She saw the emotions warring across his face. He didn't want to rise to the bait, but a man like him—former military, competent, highly trained—had trouble backing down from a good challenge. He sneered as he gave her a disdainful once-over.

"I was special forces, little girl. I'll eat you for breakfast if you fuck with me."

Game on, asshole.

Natasha stopped bouncing on her heels and shrugged as if giving in. "Right. Because Ian would approve of you kicking my ass while he's gone."

Jared relaxed his fighting stance and she turned her back on him, watching for movement from her periphery. When he turned toward Brett and started to say something, she whirled and flew at him, getting off a good kick to his side and a punch to his gut before dancing out of reach again.

"Jesus H. Christ," he yelled.

"I barely connected," she said. "Stop being a pussy."

Brett laughed. "You can't stop her, Knight. You won't use your full strength on her because Ian would kill you if you accidentally hurt her, and you aren't going to be able to stop her from kicking your ass if you pull punches. And even if you don't pull punches, she might still win. Better give up."

Jared huffed a breath and threw his hands in the air. "Fine, I give up. Run until you drop, Calypso. But if you make yourself sick, you won't be ready to see your daughter when she gets here."

Natasha frowned. The fight leached out of her by degrees. He was right. If she ran herself into a stupor, or worked out so hard everything hurt, she wouldn't be in any shape to greet Daria.

And she had to believe that she *would* be greeting Daria, or she'd work out until she dropped.

"I'll dial it down," she said. "And I won't run for more than thirty minutes. How's that?"

He nodded. "That will work. But I'm staying here to watch."

She got on the treadmill again and started to walk before turning up the speed a few notches at a time. By the time she was done, she'd still managed to run six miles. She was sweaty and tired, but she felt better. Not happy, but not so keyed up either.

She sauntered from the gym, Jared on her heels, and went to her room, firmly closing the door behind her.

Then she took a hot bath, leaning back against the tub with her eyes closed. What Ian had said to her before he'd left played in her mind.

He'd told her that her most important job was the baby. And Jared had said he couldn't let her workout hard because she was pregnant. Because Ian would kill him if she hurt herself and, by extension, the child.

Which meant that her worth to Ian was the fact she carried his baby. It wasn't surprising, but it still managed to hurt. Because the more time she spent with him, the more she cared about him. He got to her in ways no one else ever had.

He'd also said he wasn't letting her go, but what did that mean precisely?

She didn't know, but it didn't matter in the end. She couldn't change her plans. If she was going to survive— and Daria and the baby with her—she had to figure out how to disappear for good.

Chapter Thirty-Nine

Natasha finished her bath, dressing in a sweatshirt she'd found in one of the drawers, and her jeans. The sweatshirt was gray and said *Property of U.S. Navy* on it. Didn't much matter what she wore since she wasn't going anywhere, so long as it covered her tattoo.

She put her Chucks on and blowdried her hair until it was damp, put in the brown contacts, and wished she had her makeup so she could contour her face and make it look different. Not that it mattered since these guys had seen her mostly looking like herself, but she felt naked without her disguises when she was used to wearing them around people.

After frowning at her reflection in the mirror—because she looked too much like herself—she headed for the family room where Ian had a television. Cheap bastard needed to put one in the guest room. She could have avoided these jerks if she'd had a TV to watch or a computer to surf.

She supposed she could read. Thought about it for two seconds before admitting she really wanted to be near

Jared and Brett. If they heard from Ian, she wanted to know about it. Hiding in her room would mean they could ignore her, and she wasn't taking a chance.

Jared was sitting in a chair, reading a book. Brett was surfing his laptop. They looked up as she walked in.

"Anything?" she asked.

"Nothing," Brett said.

She flopped onto the couch with a grumble and picked up the remote. She almost hit the button to turn it on, but hesitated. "Do you mind if I watch something?"

Jared looked surprised before he quickly masked it. "Go ahead. I can move if it bothers me."

Brett shrugged. "Fine with me."

Natasha turned on the TV and started flipping channels, still annoyed as hell at everyone, but also tired enough that she might just take a nap. Running and hitting the bag—not to mention hitting Jared—had helped take the edge off.

If Ian wasn't back soon, she'd be doing it again in the morning. This time she might actually wrap her fists and really go at the bag while she visualized his face. And Pluto's face, too. Couldn't forget him, the slimy bastard.

"I'm sorry if I hit you too hard," she said suddenly, needing to get her mind off her handler.

Jared lifted his gaze from the book. "I'm fine."

"Good. Don't try to stop me next time."

He shook his head. "Ian can't get back soon enough," he muttered.

"Amen, brother," she said. "Hey, maybe we can hit the range, have a contest. You'll have to loan me a gun, though. Most accurate shooting gets a prize."

Jared and Brett both looked at her like she'd grown another head. "No way in hell," Brett said before Jared could respond.

LYNN RAYE HARRIS

"Aw, after I rescued Tallie for you? Really?"

Brett's jaw flexed. "I would have gotten to her in time."

"Maybe." Natasha sighed, not really enjoying ribbing these guys anymore. "I didn't do it for you. I did it for her. Nobody deserves what that evil bastard would have done to her if he'd had the chance."

Brett swallowed, hard. "I appreciate what you did. But I can't let you have access to a weapon."

She lowered her gaze to study the remote in her fingers. "I know. I'm just... worried. That's all. I need something to do."

"Ian will get your daughter," Jared said. "And I'll spar with you if you really want me to."

She snorted. "You won't. You'll constantly be thinking that Ian will be angry with you, so you won't actually do anything except try to stay out of my way."

He grinned. "True enough."

"Hey," Brett said. "Can I ask you something?"

Her stomach flipped. This was the stuff she didn't do. Small talk with people she hardly knew. "I guess so."

"You asked me to pass a message to Ian that day in the Brenner Pass when you warned me and Tallie about the bounty on our heads. You said you wanted what he promised you. I thought you planned to change sides, especially after you went to get Tallie in Spain—but you never did. Why not?"

She didn't owe him an answer. But maybe responding would make these guys a little less hostile, which certainly couldn't hurt. She didn't have to give details. "I wanted to. But leaving the Syndicate has consequences for more than just me. I decided I couldn't risk it."

"Fair enough. You should know that we'll all do whatever it takes to make you and your daughter safe, no matter what you believe we think about you."

"I appreciate that." She didn't tell him that she thought it was a futile endeavor, though.

He didn't say anything else. Neither did Jared. She thought about heading to the kitchen to cook something and busy herself that way, but she'd actually tired herself out enough that a nap might happen. She found a mindless Christmas movie about a prince and let it play. But she kept glancing at Brett's laptop, wondering how she could talk him into letting her look at it. She couldn't come up with a single excuse he'd accept.

She didn't want to contact the Syndicate. She wanted to log into her bank account in the Caymans and make some arrangements. The Syndicate thought they knew everything about her, but there were some things she'd kept secret. Just in case. All she needed was enough money to buy a car and start driving.

She should have made arrangements before going straight to Ian. She could have bought a car and stashed it, bought more clothes, squirreled away her back up passport and some money until she could make a getaway.

She hadn't been thinking clearly, though. All she'd been thinking about was getting to Ian and somehow going through with the job so she could get her daughter back. Besides, it wasn't like she could have known she'd fuck the whole thing up so spectacularly that Ian would basically hold her hostage while he jetted off to rescue Daria. How could you be prepared for a thing you didn't even know was a possibility?

When Jared's phone rang, her heart leapt. But it wasn't Ian. It was Libby, judging by the way he lit up and said, "Hey, babe. What's up?"

Natasha focused hard on the movie and tried not to let her emotions get the best of her. At some point, she fell asleep. It wasn't until the doorbell rang that she woke with a start. Her training kicked in and she rolled from the couch, reaching for her weapon.

Except she didn't have a weapon.

"Relax, Calypso," Brett said with a laugh. "It's friends with food, nothing more."

Natasha blinked as she straightened. Brett started for the entrance. Jared was already gone.

Laughter and feminine voices echoed in the entryway. A moment later women spilled into the kitchen that adjoined the family room, carrying boxes and bags and chattering. Natasha recognized them, but stood awkwardly in place, unsure what to do. Tallie Grant came over, a big smile on her face.

"Hey, honey," she said. "Libby and Jared were having a party tonight, but she decided to cancel and bring the party here instead."

Natasha frowned as she glanced over at Libby King, who was handing a box to her fiancé in the kitchen and telling him where to put it. It was her fault that Libby had to cancel the party. They all knew it, too. Yet another thing for them to dislike her for.

"Do you need any help?" she asked. Dear God, could she sound any stiffer? Why didn't she know how to talk to this woman?

"Sure, honey. Come on over and help us put the food on the island. Then fix yourself a plate. We're going to have fun, just us—hey, is that the one where the party planner marries the prince?"

Natasha glanced at the TV. "Yes, I believe so."

"Oh, I like that one!" She laughed. "Actually, I like them all. I'm a sap for Christmas romances. How about you?"

"I've enjoyed the ones I've seen. I don't believe they're very realistic though."

Tallie laughed. "Well, when you consider how that woman just kind of bumped into the prince when he snuck away from his security detail, definitely so. And then there are all those big city women who end up in cute little villages where there's always a hunky, unattached mountain man type who she has to team up with to save the town. Of course they fall in love and she moves to the town to raise goats with him or something."

Natasha was more or less thinking that nobody fell in love that easily, or that you should believe it would last just because you'd planned a Christmas pageant together. Reality was bound to intrude sooner or later.

"Hey, you two coming or what?" Libby called. "There's food all over the place in here!"

"Coming," Tallie called back. "Natasha?"

She felt very self-conscious in the jeans and sweatshirt she wore, but she followed Tallie to the kitchen. She was still dressing as the college kid home for the holidays, and it felt very wrong when she got a look at the other four women. They wore festive clothes, heels, and full makeup. What she wouldn't give for her palettes right now. She could make herself look like anyone with those, but she'd traveled light this time. She'd expected the fake teeth, wigs, and grungy clothes would be good enough.

Or maybe she'd sabotaged herself before she'd begun. That thought didn't sit well.

Maddy smiled at her, and so did Libby. Angie's was more forced than real. Natasha understood why. She was surprised that Maddy wasn't more stand-offish, but Maddy seemed to be the kind of woman who got over things and moved on.

Natasha wished she had more of that, but she didn't. She held grudges.

The food on the island was plentiful, and the oven light

was on too, which meant they'd put stuff in there. Brett and Jared were piling up plates for themselves as Libby handed her one. "Eat as much as you want. I don't think there's anything you shouldn't have. Jared?"

He looked up. "Nothing I can see, but I'm not the expert on pregnancy."

"You're the only medical person we have at the moment."

"There's always Google," Angie said coolly.

"I'm fine," Natasha said. "There's no sushi or moldy cheeses. Any tuna?"

"No tuna."

"Then it's all good."

She fixed her plate quietly, though the other women chatted as they put food on theirs. When she would have gone back to the family room and her movie, Maddy pulled out the chair beside her and patted it.

"Please sit with us."

Natasha felt like she had in school when she'd been a child. She'd been shoved into a Russian school after living in America her whole life and she hadn't spoken a word of the language. She'd been scared and out of place, and she hadn't understood anything that was said to her unless it was in English. Then her teacher forbade anyone from speaking English in order to make her learn Russian faster, and she'd been miserable. An outsider.

She was still an outsider. That was the feeling foremost in her heart at the moment. But Maddy smiled patiently and Natasha didn't know how to refuse, so she took the seat and started to quietly eat.

The women talked around her, though they tried to include her. All of them except Angie. Natasha didn't know what to say, so she didn't say much of anything. When she was done, she pushed back and stood.

"Thank you for the food. It was delicious."

"Don't go, honey," Tallie said. "We want to get to know you."

Natasha blinked at the women. "Why would you want to do that?"

Tallie and Maddy shared a look. "Because you're one of us."

"I am not one of you. You don't have to pretend."

"We aren't pretending," Maddy said.

"I am," Angie replied. "But you know that. They aren't, though. I promise you that. These three women are ridiculously sweet and forgiving. I'm going to need more time."

Natasha swallowed the sudden lump in her throat. It was surprising how much she wanted to belong. But she didn't, and she couldn't let herself believe it was possible. She needed to harden her heart so she didn't get hurt when they rejected her. Which they would eventually.

Maddy reached out and took her hand before she could turn away. "I know you don't trust us. Why should you? Especially me. You did bad things to me and the ones I love. You might think I'm seeking revenge, but I'm not. I don't think like that."

"I do." She had to be truthful.

Maddy nodded. "I understand. I don't think you've had many people you could trust in your life. I'm sorry your brother is such a jerk to you, but he'll get better. And while I'm not asking you to trust me—us—I am asking you to talk to us. Doesn't have to be about anything too personal. Maybe tell us about your sweet little daughter while we wait for our guys to get her back for you."

The lump in her throat swelled. She wasn't accustomed to feeling so much damned emotion. And definitely not in front of other people.

"We all know what it's like to wait for news," Libby said softly.

"And what it's like to be scared for your life while you wait for rescue," Angie added tightly.

"Ang," Maddy said. "Not helpful."

Angie blew out a breath. "You're right. I'm sorry. I just get a little salty when I think about it."

"Tell her the other part," Maddy said. Insisted, really.

Angie rolled her eyes. "Fine." She speared Natasha with a look. "If you hadn't shot Colt, and I hadn't spent a lot of time with him after that, then maybe we wouldn't have fallen for each other."

"Not that you were bright enough to get together with him right away," Maddy added.

Angie pushed her friend lightly. Maddy snorted.

"Fine, right. I had some hang-ups and it took months. But I was drawn to him—we were drawn to each other—during his recovery."

"And now you're going to be a freaking French countess! It all worked out."

Angie laughed. "You will never let me live that down."

"Nope."

Natasha nibbled the inside of her lip. Then she carefully took her seat again, though she was ready to bolt at the first opportunity. "You would have gotten together anyway," she said. "It's not because of me."

Angie shrugged. "We'll never know, because it happened how it happened."

"I have an idea," Libby said. "Let's make some hot chocolate and go sit in the family room where we can spread out and be more comfortable. We can keep talking, and the guys can put away the food."

Jared and Brett looked up from their end of the island, where they'd very carefully avoided getting involved in the conversation at all—and, indeed, had pretended they couldn't hear it. Obviously, they could.

"No problem, baby," Jared said. "You go ahead."

Fifteen minutes later they'd settled in, steaming mugs of hot chocolate in hand, when Jared strode in, phone in hand. He held it out to Natasha.

"It's Ian. He wants to talk to you."

Chapter Forty

"Is she okay?" Natasha asked. They were the first words out of her mouth. Ian could hear the tension and the bravery in that one small question. She could have waited for him to speak first, to tell her what she wanted to know, but it wasn't her style.

Natasha took charge and demanded answers. He loved that about her.

"Yes," he said. "I have them both. We're on the plane, and we should be airborne in a few minutes."

"Oh thank God."

He waited for her to break down, but she didn't. Of course she didn't.

"Is everyone okay?"

"Everyone is fine. Not a scratch on them."

He thought she sniffled. "Thank you, Ian."

"You're welcome, Tasha. Do you want to speak to Daria?"

"Yes. Please, yes."

He gave the phone to the child with the dark, braided hair and bright eyes.

"Mommy!" she cried in English. "Mr. Ian says we're going to America I've never been to America are you there too do you have a Christmas tree?"

She ran all the words together so fast that Ian didn't know how Natasha was going to sort them out, but he didn't suppose she cared. The nanny sat beside the child, her expression far more sober. She had dark hair, and she wore no makeup. She was a plain, sturdy woman who could blend into the background. Ian had yet to question her in detail about Julian Nowak, or how they'd ended up in Vienna.

First, he'd had to let Natasha know her daughter was safe. And now he had to let her talk as long as she wanted. There would be time for questions later.

Eventually, Daria thrust the phone at him. "Mommy wants to talk to you."

"Yes?" he said. The word was not adequate for all he wanted to say to her right now. He'd had a lot of time to think, and he'd been thinking about her. Her and their baby. The future. He didn't know what it held, but he wanted her in it. He was going to marry her.

"What happened?" she asked briskly.

He knew she would be direct. He moved away from the little girl and her nanny and entered the onboard command center.

Dax was at the computer, searching for information. He'd found nothing on Julian Nowak. The name was too common. He'd been searching for Lissette Alarie as well. She checked out. Her mother was dead and she was estranged from her drunken, abusive father. She worked as a nanny for a firm in Paris, and had done for the past six years. Twenty-seven, from Strasbourg—which meant she spoke French and German both—with a list of impeccable references before she started work for Natasha. No red flags at all.

In addition to being rather plain, she was also an introvert and didn't talk much. Until she got to know you, according to Natasha. She was polite though, and maybe a little overwhelmed if the way she'd been looking wide-eyed at Ian and his team was any indication. He could see her being easily manipulated by a man who paid her the slightest bit of romantic attention.

Maybe he should have Dax or Ty question her. Flirt with her, make her feel desired.

Ian took a seat at one of the consoles. "We watched and waited, and when we determined it was safe, we went in and got them."

"Did you meet resistance?"

He knew what she was asking. Had anything happened that needed to be explained to Daria. "A little, but not much. We neutralized the opposition without shots, and without witnesses."

"Pluto?"

He didn't like the answer he was about to give. "Not there."

"Did your operative meet with him?"

"No."

"What was his response when she told him I was in Vienna?"

Ian sighed. There was no stonewalling this woman. She pelted him with questions and didn't let up. Not that he'd expected differently. It's what he got for making her stay in Maryland with Jared and Brett for guard dogs.

"He told her to meet him at the hotel where Daria and Lissette were, though he didn't mention it was the same hotel. He never showed. Jace and Ty shadowed Jamie for two hours beyond the meeting time while she waited."

Natasha made a noise.

"They know better than to be seen. It wasn't their presence that kept him away," Ian said.

"You don't know that."

"Pretty sure I do. They're professionals, Tasha. We all are. Just like you."

"Okay, fine. What else?"

"After two hours, I decided we needed to grab our targets and get out."

He'd gotten a bad feeling when Nowak didn't show, and he hadn't wanted to wait for the Syndicate to send reinforcements. He and his team took out the three men stationed in the hall, then breached the door with a master key to find Daria and Lissette putting on coats. Heading to the *Weihnachtsmarkt* for some shopping, according to Daria, who was a chatty source of information on a great deal of things.

"What did you tell Lissette?"

"That you'd sent us to bring them to America."

"And she accepted that?"

"Not at first. I couldn't exactly wait for her to work it through, could I?"

"Tell me you didn't force her to leave with you."

"Kinda. She calmed down when I apologized for the inconvenience and promised she could speak to you."

"She didn't speak to me though."

Ian grinned. "Told you Jamie was good. I dialed her phone from the car and she mimicked your voice. Told Lissette how sorry she was for the inconvenience but she'd see her soon. I'm afraid the call dropped after that. Bad signal. But here we are again and now you've spoken to your daughter."

"That was risky," Natasha said. "You could have just called me."

"It needed to happen fast, and you'd have asked too many questions."

She huffed a breath. She knew he was right. "I don't like that Pluto didn't show. That's not like him. He must have known Jamie wasn't me."

"I don't see how. Not without talking to her first, which he didn't." He sighed. "Shit happens, kitten. He might have been making you wait on purpose, and I pulled the plug too quickly. But let's focus on the most important thing, which is that your people are safe. I'm bringing them to you, and you're going to spend Christmas together."

"You're right. We aren't going to solve it over the phone." She made a noise. "Oh, crap. I promised Daria a tree and you don't have one. And then there are the presents to consider. Hang on…"

He could hear voices suddenly in the background. Women's voices. Jared had told him the ladies were there. He'd been pleased about that. They were making an effort, though he didn't kid himself that it was easy for them. Not for Angie anyway. She was more likely to hold a grudge. Kind of like Natasha.

"Okay," she said brightly, but he didn't think she was talking to him. And then she was. "Never mind, Ian. Tallie and Maddy say we're going to fix all that."

"Don't leave the house." There was steel in his voice.

"For fuck's sake, do you really think your two guard dogs would let that happen?"

No, he didn't. But she'd started talking about fixing the fact he didn't have a tree, and he'd had visions of the women all driving to Target or Home Depot together. Her incensed tone amused him though.

"You're right, they wouldn't."

"Then calm down." Her voice lowered and he knew she was trying to talk to him without the others hearing.

"Also, I'm sorry about the tree and all. I know you don't really want one."

"It's fine. Daria is a child, and Christmas is for children."

"I know, but…"

"It's okay, angel. Really." And it was. Putting up a tree hadn't been a priority in years, but a child in the house changed things. Time to get used to that, he supposed.

"Thank you."

"It's an easy thing to give to you both. I'll be okay. It's not like we didn't have trees when I was growing up."

"I would just hate for you to be uncomfortable in your own home."

"I won't be. Trust me."

"I think I do," she said softly. "And that scares me."

Chapter Forty-One

IAN'S HOUSE WAS A WINTER WONDERLAND. MADDY, LIBBY, Angie, and Tallie had gotten to work immediately.

Natasha wasn't used to relying on others, but she'd had no choice. Libby and Tallie had gone to get a tree and the trimmings. Maddy and Angie went shopping for a few things to put under the tree. Natasha told them the things Daria had asked for, items she had at home in Switzerland waiting to be wrapped, and the two women said not to worry, they'd take care of it.

They had. She'd been teary-eyed, and pissed off about being teary-eyed, when they'd returned bearing decorations and presents. Teary because oh my God they were doing something sweet for her daughter. Pissed off because it softened her attitude and made her vulnerable.

She didn't want to like these women. Didn't want to put herself out there and get hurt when it inevitably went to shit.

When they'd left a few hours later, the house was beautiful—and she was grateful. She'd even helped decorate. It'd been fun, and it'd taken her back to when she was a child with her parents and Jace. They'd had such lovely Christmases filled with traditions like baking special desserts, singing carols, and going for sleigh rides. There had been many happy holiday memories made before everything changed.

It was almost three in the morning when Ian returned with Daria and Lissette. Natasha had napped on the couch, because she refused to be anywhere else, and she heard them come in. She didn't roll off the couch and reach for a non-existent weapon this time, though.

Jared was in a chair reading his book. His turn to watch her, apparently. He closed it and got to his feet at the same time she did. A moment later, she heard Daria's voice and she took off at a run.

"Mommy!" the little girl cried when she saw Natasha.

Natasha dropped to her knees and opened her arms. Daria hurtled into them and Natasha hugged her tight, kissing her dark head, her heart beating fast. My God, she'd thought she would lose her sweet girl when she'd failed her mission. She lifted her gaze to Ian's and they stared at each other. She'd said she trusted him, and she did. In more ways than she should, probably.

He did something to her insides. Something that made her feel gooey and restless. But it was more this time. He'd sworn he would get her child back for her, and he had. She was grateful, and she was happy. She wanted to hug him tight, press her cheek to his, and not let go for a long time. She wanted the little boy who'd ultimately lost his mother because of traffickers to know that what he did mattered. That *he* mattered.

It would have to wait, though. Right now she had to take care of Daria.

It took a couple of hours for the little girl to grow tired. Until then, she chattered excitedly about everything—

though not about any travel companions on the train, Natasha noticed. When she started to droop, Natasha settled her into the room next to hers. As much as she wanted to keep Daria close and not let go, she didn't want to upset the girl's sense of normalcy by letting her panic show. Daria was looking at the entire thing as a fun adventure she'd gone on with Lissette, and Natasha didn't want to inject any stress by clinging to her. Having Daria in the next room was going to have to be enough.

Not to mention there were things Natasha needed to know that only Ian could tell her. She needed to talk to him, and she couldn't do that if she was with Daria. Not even in Russian because Daria had learned it from her grandparents. Natasha didn't speak it to her at all these days, but that didn't mean the child couldn't understand.

Lissette had been given a room across the hall from Daria, and she'd already turned in. The hours of travel and stress had done their work on her. She'd seemed bewildered by everything that'd happened over the last few days. One minute she'd been walking Daria to school. The next she'd been whisked away to an Alpine hotel, then cajoled onto a train to Munich, then sent to Vienna, and then an entirely different man burst into her room and told her she was going to America.

She'd chattered about all of it in rapid French whenever she could get a moment with Natasha alone, but that hadn't been often. Natasha had questions, but she decided they could be asked later when Lissette was rested and calm.

After Natasha tucked Daria in and said goodnight, she closed the door and went to her room. Ian sat on the bed waiting for her, elbows on his knees, head in his hands. He looked up when she walked in. Exhaustion was written on his face. She wrapped her arms around him, pulling him against her, and pressing his face to her chest. She stroked his hair, and he looped his arms loosely around her.

Tears of relief pricked her eyes. She hadn't realized until that moment just how much of her worry had been for him. She'd hated that he'd been so far away, and that she hadn't been there to help. To watch his back.

Damned stubborn man. He should have taken her with him.

She tugged his head backward with a fist in his hair and pressed her mouth to his. He squeezed her ass—and her pussy ached. She was tired, so damned tired, but she needed this. It wasn't what she'd intended, but now that he was there she could imagine nothing else. She tugged his shirt up, splaying her hands on his chest, and pushed him back on the bed.

He didn't argue with her. He let her undress him, let her kiss her way down his body, until she reached his cock. When she took him in her mouth, he let out a sexy little groan that made her even wetter. She wrapped a hand around him and stroked while she sucked—but when she thought he might be close, he growled and flipped her over as if she weighed nothing.

"I'm going to be in you when I come," he said, tugging her clothes off until she was naked beneath him.

"I wanted to make you feel good," she whispered. "Just this once, let me take care of you."

"You are taking care of me," he said. And then he impaled her and she moaned softly as he kept moving.

"Ian," she gasped. "I missed you."

"I missed you too, my angel. So fucking much."

He kissed her, and she lost herself to the rhythm of his body inside hers. It was slow, and then it was fast. Gentle and hard. It was everything as he rocked into her over and over, knowing just how to make her feel as if there was nothing in this world but him and her and this thing between them.

She came hard, her eyes squeezing shut. Her heart hammered and her pulse raced—and it hit her suddenly that everything she'd felt for this man, all the anger and hate and blame, had become something else entirely.

Love.

Chapter Forty-Two

Ian startled awake. For a moment he didn't know where he was, but his senses quickly attuned to the body beside him. Natasha was curled into a ball, facing away from him.

A naked, delectable ball. He ran a hand over her hip and down her ass, thinking about how good it had felt to be inside her. Of all the things he'd hoped for when he got home, that was the best. And the most surprising since he'd expected she would be too focused on her daughter to have anything left for him.

A check of his watch told him it was almost eight. He didn't know how long Daria would sleep, but he didn't want to be there when the little girl came looking for her mother. Reluctantly, he sat up and scrubbed two hands through his hair. Natasha stirred, rolling over and opening her eyes.

She smiled, and something inside him ached in response.

"Morning," she said, her voice raspy with sleep.

"Morning, kitten." He bent to kiss her forehead. "You

need to sleep. It's still early considering what time we got to sleep."

"Where're you going?"

"Do you want Daria to find me here?"

She frowned. "Maybe not yet. Better to explain first."

"That's what I thought." He kissed her again. Her eyelids drooped. "Go to sleep."

"Mkay…"

Ian got up and tugged on his clothes, then went to his own room to shower and change. When he was done, he went to the kitchen to make coffee. But he stopped in the family room, taking in the changes that five women had wrought over the course of a few hours. There was a tree —a live one—decorated with ornaments and garland. Christmas pillows and throws on the furniture. There were presents under the tree, and the mantel was draped in garland. It was like Christmas had thrown up in his house. Strangely, he discovered that he didn't mind it.

The woman he'd called Mom for most of his life had loved Christmas, and she'd gone over the top every year with her decorating. She started planning it months before the season, and the house had been featured in magazines over the years. Even with her perfectionism about her decor, she'd never told him he couldn't touch something as a child.

He'd asked her once when he was older how she'd managed to throw herself into the holiday when her daughter had committed suicide so close to Christmas. She'd told him that it didn't change the meaning of the season, and she hoped that her child—his mother—was in heaven looking down and loving the lights and displays. She also thought that maybe it was God who'd stopped his birth mother from killing him the day she'd decided to take her own life. He was her Christmas present, she'd always said.

Ian had tried to be like her, but as he'd gotten older, he'd associated the lights and decorations with things he didn't want to remember. What was in his house now wasn't fancy even though Tallie Grant was an interior designer. He didn't doubt she'd directed the whole thing, but instead of magazine-like perfection, it was pretty and festive, and it looked kid-friendly. He liked it.

He'd always thought that ignoring the holiday was best for him, but now he couldn't. And part of him was glad.

Ty was in the kitchen when Ian got there. The other man looked up and muttered a greeting.

"Did you even sleep?" Ian asked.

"A little." Ty yawned and scrubbed a hand over his head. "My cousin has been texting me."

"Anything wrong?"

Ty poured coffee into a mug. "She's fine. She has a friend who's been getting threatening emails or something. She wants me to take care of it."

"Do you plan to?"

Ty scowled. "No. I told her that's what the police are for. She won't stop, though."

Ian got a mug out for himself. "Do you know the friend?"

"My cousin says she went to our high school but damned if I remember her." He shook his head. "Trust me, that was the wrong thing to say. Pissed her off even more."

Ian laughed. "Maybe you should give it some attention just to satisfy her and get her off your back."

Ty shrugged. "Maybe. If she keeps bugging me, I'll escalate."

Dax wandered in, a laptop tucked under his arm. "What are you two doing up so early?"

"My cousin's texting me," Ty said. "I don't know what Ian's problem is. What's yours?"

Dax was bleary-eyed. Hell, they all were after the past seventy-two hours plus. "Chasing down leads online. I keep thinking I'm nearly there, but then it turns into a dead end."

"All the more reason to sleep," Ian said.

"I isolated the video feed of Julian Nowak, sharpened it up, and loaded it to the database for possible matches. So far nothing. He must have been in disguise when he met the nanny for dinner."

"He's out there somewhere. We'll find him," Ian replied. He'd had Dax try to talk to Lissette on the plane, but the nanny hadn't said anything useful. She'd just been doing what she was told by her employer's 'bank coworker'. Since she'd lost her phone shortly after they arrived at the the Grand Hotel Schoenburg, she hadn't tried to call Natasha—Miss Weiss—for confirmation. Besides, the man knew everything about her schedule and he showed her texts from Miss Weiss that indicated she should trust him.

She hadn't heard from him since he'd left the train in Munich. Dax said she'd dropped her chin at that point and wouldn't look at him. Her cheeks had turned red, which very likely indicated embarrassment. Nowak had very likely romanced her and abandoned her.

But why?

"I don't know how he figured out Jamie wasn't Natasha considering she makes herself look different all the time. But he must have been watching the café and bailed when he decided Jamie wasn't the right person for some reason," Ty grumbled. "Jace and I didn't blow our positions. We didn't see anyone coming or going, other than the staff, and no one made us."

"I know." He'd said as much to Natasha too.

"Hi!"

Ian, Ty, and Dax pivoted toward the hallway where a little girl stood. Her hair was messy and she still wore her pajamas. Christmas pajamas with snowmen.

"Hi," Ian said. "Are you looking for your mommy?"

He was pretty sure Natasha had told the little girl her room was next door when she'd put her to bed a few hours ago.

Daria skipped into the kitchen and made a beeline for his side. She put her hand in his. It was surprising, but also nice. She gazed up at him, her eyes bright and wide awake.

"No. Mommy's still asleep. So's Lissette. But I have to ask before I can watch TV. Plus I don't know how to turn it on. You don't have a remote on the table."

"I don't, huh? Guess we'd better find it."

"That would be wonderful."

Her English was accented, but it wasn't thick. He figured Natasha would have taught her English, and of course she would study it in school. All Europeans studied English these days. She probably also spoke German, specifically the Swiss German dialect, and French. Maybe Russian too.

As they started toward the family room where the television was, she stopped and turned back to Ty and Dax. "You can come too. We can watch together."

Ian lifted his gaze to the two men who were blinking at the little girl and each other as if caught off guard.

"Uh, sure," Ty said. "Sounds good."

"I'll be there in a few minutes," Dax replied. "Have to grab some coffee."

Daria grew excited. "Oh, can I have some too?"

Ian suppressed a laugh. "You drink coffee?"

"Mommy lets me have a little bit when she's home. But I need lots of cream and sugar, please."

"You heard the lady," Ian said to Dax. "Small cup. Lots of cream and sugar. Though maybe not too much sugar."

"You got it," Dax said.

Ian and Daria started toward the family room again with Ty following along. "I'm not going to get in trouble with your mother for letting you have that, am I?"

She shook her head. "Only if you let me have more than one. Mommy says it makes me climb walls."

Ian didn't laugh, but he wanted to. When they reached the family room, Daria got onto the couch and snuggled beneath one of the Christmas blankets. Ty flopped into a chair with his coffee, looking a little bewildered at how he'd gotten roped into joining them.

Ian took the remote off the mantel and clicked it on. "What do you want to watch?"

"Something about Christmas."

"Okay."

"You have a very pretty tree," she said as he flipped through the channels.

He didn't know where to find Christmas shows for kids so he kept on flipping. "Thank you."

"I saw my name on the presents. But I didn't shake them."

Ian looked at her. "That's very good of you."

"I wanted to, but it's not my house and Mommy wouldn't like it."

"A good reason not to do it then."

"I have a mommy in heaven. Did you know that?"

Ian found a Christmas movie and stopped. The Muppets were in it. Surely that was appropriate. "I did not," he said, though he did.

"Uh huh. She watches over me and keeps me safe. My mommy was her best friend and when she died she gave me to my mommy I have now."

"That was smart of her."

"It was. I wish she was still here though. It would be nice to have two mommies so I'd always have one at home with me when one is traveling for work."

"That sounds very reasonable," Ian said. "But you also have Lissette."

"Oh yes, but then she wouldn't be alone when one of my mommies is gone. She gets scared sometimes."

Ian frowned. "Does she? Why?"

Daria shrugged. "I don't know. I hear her on the phone and she cries about being alone. I'm not supposed to mention it, so I don't. It makes her feel bad."

Ian filed the information away. "That's very thoughtful."

"Mommy says you have to be nice to other people if you can. So long as they are nice to you. If someone tries to hurt you, then you're supposed to not be nice. I'm always nice." She smiled at him. "You can sit beside me. I don't mind."

He didn't know what else to do, so he sat. Ty met his gaze and shrugged, and they settled in to watch Michael Caine and Kermit the Frog in *The Muppet Christmas Carol*. Dax arrived a little while later with his laptop under his arm and two cups. He put his cup and computer down, then grabbed a coaster and placed it on the table beside Daria. He set the coffee there and Daria thanked him primly before asking him to sit and watch the show.

Which was how three grown men ended up watching an entire movie with a little girl who laughed, drank her half cup of coffee, and charmed them all with her questions and observations. Daria was a bright, sweet little girl who managed to be both a typical six-year-old and somehow mature beyond her years.

By the time Natasha found them, they'd finished the Muppet movie and moved on to *Emmet Otter's Jug-Band Christmas*. She stood in the entry and stared at them—three men and a little girl in Christmas pajamas—as if she couldn't quite believe what she was seeing.

"Mommy! Come watch with us," Daria said. "It's Emmet Otter!"

Natasha strolled into the room wearing the jeans and T-shirt of her college kid persona, and Ian told himself he was buying her new clothes today. He wanted to see her in a soft sweater. Cashmere. Leggings and booties. She'd look smashing in red. Or pink. Even sky blue. He needed to call his assistant and get a start on that.

Natasha twirled a finger in her daughter's hair. "What did you eat for breakfast?"

"Nothing. We had coffee and we watched Muppets."

Natasha arched a brow. "Did you? How fun. How much coffee?"

Daria leaned her head back on the cushion. "Only half a cup. I told Ian that was all I could have."

Natasha met his gaze. He nodded. "Yep, she did. Dax fixed it with cream and sugar."

"Did you thank Dax?" Natasha asked.

"Yes, Mommy."

"Very good. Now what about breakfast?"

"Can we have cookies?"

Natasha blinked. "No, sweetie. We need something more nutritious to start the day."

"Cake?"

Ian had to give the kid points for trying.

"No cake. I'll go see what Ian has in the kitchen."

"I'll help," Ian said.

Natasha's smile made his pulse skip. It also made his balls tighten. Was this what it was going to be like to wake up every morning with Natasha and Daria in his life? He hoped so, because he hadn't been kidding when he'd told her she was his. He was all in now. Wedding bells and baby carriages and all that crap.

Jesus.

"Thank you," she said.

Ty started to shift in his seat, and Daria speared him with a look. "You aren't leaving are you, Ty?"

He settled down again. "Uh, no. Of course not. We need to find out what happens when Emmet enters that contest."

"He doesn't win," she said as Ian followed Natasha from the room. "But he learns something even better."

Ian grabbed her hand when they were out of sight of the others. Then he spun her into in his arms and kissed her. He was going to have to tell her they were getting married, but he'd do that later. After he got a ring.

She wrapped her arms around his neck and arched into him, and he groaned softly at the feel of her curves pressing against him. He had a brief thought about picking her up and taking her to his room so he could strip her and make love to her, but a little girl needed breakfast first. Ian broke the kiss and set her away from him.

"Keep kissing me like that and Daria won't eat until lunch," he growled.

Natasha laughed. "Oh, she'd eat. But she'd talk one of those Neanderthals into giving her cookies."

Ian took her hand again and tugged her toward the kitchen. "Then we'd better make sure that doesn't happen."

"A good plan, Mr. Black."

"Most of my plans are."

She grinned at him. His breath felt tight in his chest. He didn't know why.

"I don't know about *all* of them," she teased, her mood lighter than he thought he'd ever seen it. She was happy, and that made him happy. "But some of them are good."

"How do you feel about the ones involving you and me naked?"

Her grin turned sly. "Those are my favorite ones of all."

His too. In fact, most plans with her—whether they involved being naked or not—were his favorites.

Chapter Forty-Three

THE DAY PASSED IN A WHIRLWIND OF HOLIDAY ACTIVITY until everyone was gathered at the dinner table that evening. Natasha glanced at Ian as he said something to Ty and Dax, and her stomach flipped like she was a teenager experiencing her first crush.

All day, she'd asked herself how she could be in love with Ian Black. She didn't know the answer, but she was. She just was. Somehow, she'd fallen for him. Somewhere between the flirting and the fighting and the fucking, she'd dropped headlong into feelings so intense and hot that they couldn't be anything else.

He'd risked his life for her child. He'd shared personal things with her that she knew he didn't find easy to talk about. He was a dangerous man, and a lost little boy at the same time.

He was just like her in so many ways.

She'd thought the romantic Christmas movies were wrong, but the joke was on her. She was living in one. So long as you added in a murderous criminal syndicate and a very unhealthy dollop of danger, that is.

It made her shudder to think how close she'd come to killing this man. How intent she'd been on completing the mission when she'd arrived only a few days ago. To save Daria and herself. She still wanted to save them—and she wanted to save him too. That was the most shocking part of all.

But she didn't know how. As happy as she was—and she *was* happy—she couldn't forget that the Syndicate was out there. That Pluto knew by now she'd betrayed them. He would be looking for her. All the best assassins in the Syndicate would.

That made her shiver.

Natasha looked at the people gathered around the table. So long as she was here among them, they were in danger too. A few days ago, she wouldn't have cared. Now she did. She felt—if not precisely like she belonged—that at least she wasn't unwelcome.

What a difference a few days made.

Ty no longer glared at her. He was too busy listening to Daria tell him about her doll that she'd left at home. Once, he lifted his head and caught her eye. Instead of the usual dislike, she saw curiosity. As if he was considering that she might actually be human after all.

She nodded. He nodded back. Then he dropped his attention to Daria again.

Dax was speaking to Lissette, who had seemed out of sorts earlier today but was beginning to rally.

Natasha wanted to know everything that had happened since the moment Lissette had walked Daria to school more than a week ago, but she had to be careful. Lissette still thought she was a banker, and now she thought that Natasha was involved with a rich client.

Lissette had walked into the kitchen that morning and seen Natasha in Ian's arms as they were waiting on bacon to cook. It had been a little awkward. Lissette turned beet red and stammered apologies, but Natasha had stopped her from fleeing and steered the conversation to questions about how she was feeling that morning.

Ian had told her what Lissette said to Dax on the plane, but Natasha still had questions. She'd considered stripping away the veneer of her polite banker persona and letting Calypso emerge to demand answers, but she couldn't do that to Lissette. Not after two and a half years when the Frenchwoman had been the only person she could count on to care for Daria while she was gone. To keep Daria happy and loved and safe.

Besides, it was almost Christmas, and Daria was hyperfocused on that event. Natasha was relieved that Daria didn't seem to be traumatized by her adventures and planned to do everything she could to make the holiday wonderful for her daughter. Making Lissette cry wasn't part of the plan.

Christmas in America was different from Christmas in Switzerland, and Daria was endlessly fascinated by those differences. She asked Ty questions. Then she asked Dax. Once she'd questioned them, she focused on Ian. Then back to Ty.

And so on.

No matter how Ty the Terrible had glared or growled at Natasha since the first day she'd arrived, the way he treated her daughter softened her feelings toward him considerably.

A new thought hit her as she sat there. What if it could stay like this? What if they could spend evenings around the table with Daria and this new baby, laughing and talking and enjoying being together? Not just her and Ian, but his team as well.

Her brother would be there too, and maybe he wouldn't hate her anymore.

Except that it was a pipe dream. So long as the Syndicate existed, she couldn't relax her vigilance. She couldn't stay and put all these people in danger. She had to get access to her bank account so she could make things happen. She had to get out of there. Soon.

"Hey," Ian said, leaning toward her, his fingers squeezing her knee beneath the table. "Is everything okay?"

Natasha pasted on a smile to reassure him. She'd been perilously close to tears as she thought about leaving. She'd been taught to hide her emotions, to bury them deep. For them to be so close to the surface now was disconcerting.

"I'm fine," she said, keeping her voice low so no one else could overhear them talk. "Just happy to have Daria with me. She's enjoying herself, and everyone is patient with her."

"She's a great kid. Funny and sweet. She's got Ty and Dax wrapped around her finger."

"And you?"

He laughed. "And me."

Natasha chewed the inside of her lip. "I'm worried, Ian. The Syndicate isn't finished with us. They won't let me leave them so easily. And they aren't going to give up trying to kill you when they figure out you aren't really dead—if they haven't already. This is the calm before the storm."

She didn't expect them to attack Ian's compound, or make any moves in the next few days, but silence didn't equal inaction. He needed to be prepared. And she needed that escape plan no matter how much she wanted to stay.

The look in his eyes was hard. Determined. "No, they aren't finished with us. But I'm not finished with them either. I swear to you I'm not as easy a target as they'd hoped. Neither are you. When I told you I could protect you, I meant it. Have faith."

She took a deep breath. "I'm trying, but I need something from you, too. I need freedom. I need my access back. I need to know what they're up to, and for that I need my phone, my laptop—"

He squeezed her knee again. "I know, but we're going to have to talk about it first. It's not that simple."

"I know it's not simple, but you can't keep me a prisoner forever."

"You aren't a prisoner, Tasha. And we need to talk about this later when we aren't at the table with everyone, okay? It's complicated, and it's going to take time."

Her heart thumped. She couldn't expect that he would just hand everything back, no questions asked. That he was even willing to discuss it was a good thing.

"Soon," she said firmly.

"Soon."

Chapter Forty-Four

IAN DIDN'T LIKE THE IDEA OF NATASHA GETTING BACK online, but he couldn't prevent it forever. She needed a phone, and she needed the kind of everyday access that most people had.

He'd told himself that her being online where the Syndicate could track her wasn't a good idea, but he knew that wasn't the only thing holding him back from giving her access. He didn't want her online because he wasn't sure how much he could trust her. He didn't really think she'd try to return to the Syndicate, but he wasn't sure she wouldn't attempt to make alternative plans. The kind where she tried to use her skills to disappear.

Not that she would succeed because his people would track everything she did online. She wasn't going to like that, but they were going to have to discuss it. It was the only way to see if anyone was trying to hack into her accounts or trace her location. If he didn't tell her, then yeah, deep down he feared she'd use her new freedom to deceive him.

And that wasn't the kind of betrayal he was ready to experience.

Like he'd told her, complicated.

After dinner, Daria put her hand in his and led him to the family room so he could turn on the television. He'd shown her how to do it that morning but she insisted she'd forgotten. It wasn't until he found a program and then found himself sitting beside her that he realized he'd been conned. Daria was a very social child and wanted people around her. She hadn't forgotten a thing about how to turn on the TV.

It made him want to laugh. Bested by an adorable six year-old.

Lissette and Natasha entered the room, but Lissette soon excused herself to go for a walk down to the water's edge. She and Natasha had taken Daria to the water to see ducks earlier, and Natasha had said that Lissette chattered nonstop about how beautiful it was. She asked Natasha and Daria if they wanted to go again, but neither did. Daria was too caught up in a Christmas cartoon to want to get bundled up and go outside. Besides, it was dark, and though the moon glinted on the snow, they weren't going to see ducks this time.

"Lissette likes walks," Daria said matter-of-factly once the alarm sensor chirped to signal Lissette's departure.

"She does," Natasha agreed, sitting on Daria's other side. She met Ian's gaze. They both knew Lissette would be fine. Ian's house sat on five acres, and the property was fenced and patrolled. Not only that, but Dax and Ty refused to go home, so one of them was watching to make sure she was safe. As if on cue, Ty slipped out the back door.

"Daria," Natasha said softly, and the little girl turned her head.

"Yes?"

"We need to talk about something we've never talked about before."

He knew what it was because Natasha had mentioned it to him when they'd been clearing up dinner dishes. She wanted Daria to be comfortable with the idea of them being affectionate with each other. She didn't want to go so far as to talk about anything permanent, but she wanted her daughter to understand what it meant for adults to like each other. He'd give her that space for now, but the talk about permanency was going to have to happen soon.

They'd have to tell Daria about the baby before long, and the fact they were getting married. Not that he'd told Natasha yet, but she had to have guessed. He'd told her she was his, and that meant the ring and the ceremony. Though maybe he should actually *ask*.

Except, what was the point? He wasn't an idiot, he knew women liked to be asked, but this situation was different. He could ask where she'd like to be married, and when —but not if. There was no if.

"We talk about everything, Mommy," Daria said.

"Well, yes, we do. But this is new." Natasha drew in a breath. "Sometimes, adults get lonely."

"I know. Lissette is lonely."

"Is she?" Natasha seemed to consider it. "She's never said so, but yes, I can see it. Sometimes, single ladies like Lissette and I want boyfriends."

He was enjoying this more than he should. And not helping at all because it wasn't his place to help.

"Lissette has a boyfriend, Mommy."

Natasha frowned. "Do you mean the man who had dinner with you at the hotel?"

Daria nodded. "Yes. He was on the train too. They held hands."

Alarm crossed Natasha's features. Ian's senses tingled. Nowak was clearly a smooth operator.

"Have you ever seen him before?" Natasha asked.

Daria cocked her head to the side. "Ummmmm… nope. Just that time. He was very nice, and he made Lissette smile."

Romancing her, Ian mouthed. They'd dug deep on Lissette, and she was what she seemed. But she was also not the sort of woman who attracted a lot of male attention, which meant male attention mattered to her when it happened. Nowak had exploited that for his own purposes and then disappeared.

Natasha nodded. "Okay, honey."

"Please don't tell Lissette I told you. She said I shouldn't."

Ian could see fire flash in Natasha's eyes. She didn't like that Lissette was using her daughter to keep secrets from her. "Why did she say that?"

"Because she said she would tell you when the time was right." Daria frowned. "I messed up, didn't I?"

Natasha squeezed her daughter's hand. "You didn't mess up. And I won't say anything, don't worry."

"Good. I wouldn't want to ruin a surprise." She cocked her head. "Do you want a boyfriend too?"

Ian smirked. Perceptive kid.

"Actually, I think I do."

"Okay, well I think it should be Ty. He's funny and I like him."

Ian put a hand over his mouth to cover a laugh. He shrugged at Natasha as if the kid's pronouncement meant he was out of the running.

She gave him a mock glare. "Well, I kind of like Ian better than Ty, baby. Ty is nice, but Ian is better in my opinion."

Daria swiveled her head to look at him. Then she smiled. "I like you, too. Do you want to be Mommy's boyfriend?"

Ian had never experienced such complicated feelings to such a simple question. But there was really only one answer to give.

"I do want to be her boyfriend."

"Okay," Daria replied before turning her attention back to the television. That seemed to be the end of the matter to her.

Natasha still gazed at him over Daria's head. He grinned at her. She grinned too. He reached for her hand on the back of the couch and threaded his fingers through hers.

Right. That was the word that popped into his head when they touched.

It was *right.*

Natasha, Daria, and their unborn child all hanging together and watching a Christmas cartoon. It was positively domestic. General John Mendez would laugh if he knew. Phoenix would smirk. The secretive CIA officer had gone her whole career without domestic entanglements. Prided herself on it, in fact.

But Ian liked it more than he thought he would. It was… comforting. The idea of time stretching before him with a wife and children—damn, it felt good.

What the hell?

Eventually, Natasha got up to make hot chocolate and popcorn. She made enough for Ty and Dax as well. Both men accepted without hesitation. Though Ty sniffed his drink first. Natasha took his cup and sipped it, then handed it back with an eye roll.

He grinned at her and took a big swig.

"Asshole," she said.

"Assassin," he replied, still grinning.

"Bang bang," Natasha said, sauntering into the family room with a laugh.

Daria was oblivious, her attention firmly fixed on the television.

"I should probably check on Lissette," Natasha said before she sat down again. "Make sure she knows she can join us."

Lissette had gone to her room after her walk and hadn't come back. Natasha left him on the couch with Daria, then returned a few minutes later with a shrug.

"She says she's still fighting jet lag. She was sick when they first arrived in Vienna, and she thinks she's still feeling the effects of it." Natasha frowned. "I think it's stress."

She dropped her gaze to Daria's head. Daria was engrossed in a movie about Santa Claus and didn't notice a thing.

"Got it," Ian said. Lissette could be anxious because of the drama of the last week—or it could be because Nowak had ghosted her.

As soon as they finished the movie, Daria wanted to watch another. Natasha told her it was time for bed.

Daria frowned. "Just one more? Please?"

"No, baby. You've been watching television all day, and we don't usually do that, do we? It's time for bed. Christmas Eve is tomorrow."

Daria perked up. "Are we making Christmas cookies like always?"

Natasha smiled. "I'm sure we can. Ian might not have everything we need, but he'll get it for us if we ask him nicely."

Daria's head swiveled. "Please, Ian, can we make Christmas cookies? Mommy makes a mess, but I don't. I'm very neat."

Ian laughed. "Sure, you can make cookies. Your mommy can give me a list of what she needs and I'll make sure you have it."

"What about dinner, Mommy? We always have fondue. Can we have fondue in America?"

Natasha smoothed Daria's hair. "I'm not sure that's what everyone wants for Christmas Eve dinner, but I'm sure we can make something delicious. And maybe have a small pot of fondue for an appetizer."

"Okay."

"Come on," Natasha said, standing and holding out her hand. "Let's get you ready for bed."

Daria turned and flung her arms around his neck. He was shocked, but he hugged her back. "Goodnight, Ian. Thank you for being Mommy's boyfriend."

"Goodnight, kiddo. And you're welcome."

Natasha's eyes glittered suspiciously as she led Daria toward the bedrooms. Ian shook his head and laughed. Kids, man. They really did surprise you with the stuff that came out of their mouths.

"Guess you'd better get used to that kind of thing." Ty was standing between the kitchen and the family room, snacking on popcorn.

"Guess so."

"I think I could learn to like her," he said. Ian knew he didn't mean Daria. "Seeing that kid, the love between them—I think I understand why she felt she had no choice but to carry out her orders. She's not evil. She's like the rest of us—looking for peace and safety, and doing all she can to protect the innocent child in her care. Still don't entirely trust her with a vial of poison or a weapon, but she's growing on me."

"And yet you're still not going home so you can wake up on Christmas morning in your own bed," Ian replied.

Ty shook his head. "Are you kidding me? They're making cookies tomorrow. And dinner. I'm staying."

"Like you don't have GrubHub on speed dial."

"Not the point, boss. Not the point at all. Cookies. Homemade. Big difference between that and store bought."

"Cookies?" Dax asked as he walked in with his laptop open in one hand. "Who has cookies?"

"Natasha and Daria are baking tomorrow," Ty said. "I told Ian I'm not leaving."

"Hell no I'm not leaving," Dax practically yelled. "Motherfucking cookies, man."

Ty elbowed him.

"Oh shit, better watch the language, huh? Yummy cookies. Yum-my."

Ian could only roll his eyes. "Got something there?"

"Oh, yeah," Dax said, lifting the laptop. "Not a hundred percent sure, but it looks like the Syndicate might have an exclusive event scheduled for New Year's Eve. There's a lot of talk in the chatrooms."

By event, he meant a sex slave auction.

"Where?" Ian asked.

"Vienna."

Chapter Forty-Five

It was Christmas Eve and Natasha had impulsively said to Ian that he should invite Jace and Maddy to dinner. They were arriving in half an hour, and she was beginning to wish she hadn't suggested the gathering.

What had she been thinking? Jace was hostile, and though Maddy had been sweet the night they'd decorated Ian's house, she might have changed her mind since then. It was idiocy to want them here, but Natasha blamed her softened mood on Daria's enthusiasm for Christmas.

They'd baked cookies and listened to Christmas carols, and Natasha had such a strong memory of spending the holiday with family when she'd been Daria's age that she'd suddenly wanted her brother to come. Even if she couldn't tell Daria that Jace was her uncle just yet.

And now she was feeling like an idiot for that moment of weakness.

She looked in the mirror at her appearance. At least she would look like an adult tonight. Her college drab was gone. Ian had insisted she needed new clothes, and though she hadn't wanted to let him buy her clothing, he'd convinced her that letting his executive assistant handle everything was easiest in the end.

She'd used his phone to text her measurements to someone named Melanie, skeptical that the woman would come up with anything Natasha would approve of. But then the clothing arrived in designer shopping bags, and Natasha had held up buttery-soft cashmere sweaters with awe. She'd tried on fine-spun merino wool leggings, silk blouses, a jersey wrap dress, and a variety of shoes that went with each outfit. There were jeans—stylish ones, not poor college kid chic—and delicate knit shirts that were so much finer than her T-shirts.

They were the kind of clothes she would have chosen for herself if she'd been free to wander into shops. Though she had a variety of things in her disguise wardrobe, her personal tastes ran to simple and chic. Melanie had delivered that in a big way.

Natasha donned a red sweater with a v-neck, black leggings, and a pair of suede booties. She didn't wear disguises with Daria, so she'd put the contacts and wigs away. Yet another reason to regret inviting company. Her blond hair hung free, her skin glowed with pregnancy hormones, and Daria pronounced her beautiful the moment Natasha walked into the family room.

What more could she ask for?

Other than a perfect dinner, of course. Lissette had pitched in to help with the cooking. Between them, they were making a beef tenderloin roast, scalloped potatoes, roasted broccoli, and dinner rolls. There was a fondue appetizer, and a blackberry crumble for dessert. Plus all the cookies that she'd made with Daria earlier.

That had been fun. Ian had joined them as they'd mixed and rolled and cut.

Ty and Dax wandered in at some point and Daria

recruited them to work. They'd laughed and indulged her, clumsily rolling out dough and squeezing piping onto finished cookies.

It made them more likable in Natasha's eyes.

When Maddy and Jace arrived, Maddy hugged her. Jace ignored her for the most part, shaking hands with Ty, Dax, and Ian. The men broke out the Scotch, and Maddy helped get the food to the table. They sat down in a candlelit dining room and shared a meal that everyone praised. Lissette was predictably quiet, but Natasha worked to include her.

For two and a half years, it'd been just the three of them. Lissette had come to her from another family, highly recommended, but she'd needed the change because she didn't thrive in high pressure environments. Her last family had five kids, two of which were twins, and all had been boys. Rambunctious didn't begin to describe it.

She'd wanted to work in a quieter family, and Natasha and Daria fit the bill. Especially because there were no social engagements, no parties, and no polite chitchat required. They'd settled into a groove.

A groove that was now turning inside out as Lissette had to sit at a table with five people she didn't really know and engage with them. She started to open up as Dax chatted with her. She seemed taken with him, darting her gaze away shyly and then back again whenever he turned to speak to someone else.

Natasha sighed to herself. Lissette was the sort of woman who was easily led by a man, especially if he was flirtatious. She wouldn't have stood a chance with Pluto.

After dinner, everyone adjourned to the family room where the tree glowed with lights and the Christmas music played. There was no television, and Daria didn't ask. That wasn't how they spent Christmas Eve in Switzerland.

Instead, they drank *glühwein* and coffee—and chocolate for Daria—and shared Christmas memories. Natasha knew that Ian and the others were doing this for Daria, and her heart warmed. Daria believed in Santa Claus, because that's who Natasha had been raised to believe in, but in Switzerland it was Father Christmas or the Baby Jesus who brought presents. Natasha let Daria open one gift, but the rest were for tomorrow.

Daria sat by the tree and played with the American Girl doll she'd been given while the adults talked. Lissette was quiet, contemplating the fire that Ian had turned on with the touch of a button. Maddy chatted about wedding plans, because Ian had asked, and Jace sat with his arm around his fiancée, sipping his spiced wine slowly.

His gaze met Natasha's at one point, and her heartbeat quickened. He didn't look away, and neither did she. They studied each other. She wondered what he saw, what he was thinking, but she couldn't ask. His gaze strayed to Daria and back again. He nodded once, and the tension she'd been feeling began to ease. Maybe he understood now. Or maybe he didn't, but at least he knew *why*.

Jace and Maddy left around eleven. Ian carried a sleepy Daria to bed and Lissette said goodnight at the door to her room before closing it quietly behind her. Ty and Dax had disappeared to the guest rooms they were staying in. Natasha helped Daria into her Christmas jammies and tucked her in while Ian sat on the opposite side of the bed and told her a story because she insisted she was awake enough.

She was out before he finished, and they tiptoed out of her room as quietly as possible. Natasha pulled the door closed with a long sigh. Ian took her hand and led her to the master bedroom. She thought maybe she should protest that she needed to be closer to Daria, but if the little girl needed anything in the middle of the night and Natasha wasn't there, she'd go to Lissette.

Ian undressed her slowly, kissing his way over her skin. Instead of pushing her onto the bed and making love to her, he lay her down in her panties and bra and began to massage her shoulders and back. Natasha groaned.

"You worked hard today," he said, his voice like warm honey.

"I wanted Daria to have a normal day. We have traditions."

"Yes, but it was more than that. You wanted to take care of everyone with food. You wanted them to have a good time and enjoy what you prepared."

She sighed. "It was Lissette and me both."

"She was a big help, but you were driving the bus. It was your menu, your direction. You were worried about it not working out."

"I always am. But I like to cook. It's something I enjoy, even if Lissette usually does most of it at home."

He ran his fingers down her spine, digging in to release the tension that had gathered. Natasha moaned. It felt so good to be touched by him. Cared for. No one else paid this much attention to her needs. No one else noticed that she was nervous, or that she worked hard to do something for people.

She was the cold-hearted assassin Calypso. She didn't have feelings or needs, and she didn't care about others. That's what the world thought.

It's not what Ian thought.

"I could tell." He dipped down to press a kiss to her shoulder blade, his warm breath tickling her skin. "People think you don't care. I think you care too much. It's why you let Lissette cook at home even if you'd like to more often. It's also why you care if people like what you make, and if they've had enough to eat. Though cooking isn't the only way in which you care."

It was as if he'd read her thoughts. She rolled over to gaze up at him as he sat on the edge of the bed. He was still fully dressed in a black button-down shirt and black trousers. The silver at his temples was slight, a mere sprinkling, but it distinguished him.

And it turned her on. Crazy on. He was so hot. So beautiful. She loved him utterly.

But she couldn't tell him that. Not when he didn't feel the same.

"We still haven't discussed a phone and computer," she said, forcing her thoughts away from getting him naked. "Don't think I haven't noticed."

He laughed. "I don't think there's anything you don't notice, Tasha. Is that really what you want to talk about right now?"

She let her gaze slide from his hot, dark eyes to the obvious bulge in his trousers. "Maybe not."

"Then what *do* you want?"

"I want you," she whispered, her throat tight with emotion. It was so much more than sexual for her. She wished it was for him too, but she couldn't ask. No way.

His grin was wicked. "I'd hoped you would say that because I'm hard as a rock after touching you. But I didn't touch you for that reason. I'm prepared to sleep beside you tonight and not do a thing. You're tired—and that little girl's going to be up at the crack of dawn."

She laughed as she pushed up to loop her arms around his neck and arched into him. "She will be. But I want *my* present now."

"And what present is that?"

Tease.

"You. Inside me. Making me come."

"Well, if you insist…"

He reached behind her to unsnap her bra, then divested her of bra and panties both. His shirt disappeared, and then his trousers slid down narrow hips, revealing his beautiful cock in all its glory. She reached for him, cupping his balls as he groaned and closed his eyes.

How could she ever leave him?

"Is it true you're ordained?" she asked as she stroked him.

His eyes popped open. "Where did that come from?"

"I heard you officiated at a wedding not too long ago."

"And that's what you're thinking about as you hold my dick in your hand?"

She grinned. "Oh, I'm thinking a lot of things. Dirty things. But first I was thinking that your middle name fits you. The angel Gabriel. That got me to priests and weddings."

His breath hissed in as she squeezed. "I'm ordained. I was undercover for a year in a tiny principality in the Urals. It no longer exists. But part of my cover was entering a monastery for warrior monks. I studied. I took ordination. Any other questions, beautiful, or can I make you scream now?"

"Oh please," she said with a shiver. "Please make me scream."

That's exactly what he did.

Chapter Forty-Six

FOR THE FIRST TIME IN HIS ADULT LIFE, IAN WAS DRAGGED out of bed at the ass crack of dawn on Christmas morning so he could watch a little girl tear through wrapping paper. Daria was delighted with everything she received, and Ian was thankful that he'd been able to deliver her safely to her mother in time for the holiday.

Watching Natasha was almost as fun as watching her daughter. She *oohed* and *aahhed* as Daria opened presents, she made waffles—homemade, not toaster—and topped them with a blueberry sauce that she also made, and she even managed to make Ty laugh at one point.

There was laughter, food, and friends, and Ian decided that he liked it. He'd been avoiding throwing himself into Christmas for years. It wasn't that his mother hadn't made the holiday special, but he'd always known that his parents were sad for their lost daughter. He'd felt their grief, no matter how they tried to hide it, and he'd been sad for the birth mother he barely remembered. Her life had been cut short far too soon, which was why he'd vowed to do his damndest not to let that shit happen to other young women.

His entire adult life, unless he accepted a dinner invitation from someone or went home to be with his parents for the holiday, he didn't put up trees or decor. He didn't play the music or watch movies. He didn't buy presents either. His executive assistant did that for him when it was necessary.

He'd certainly never done the excited kid thing before.

It was an interesting experience, and not without its benefits. He pictured future Christmases with a child that belonged to him and Natasha both, and he was nearly overcome with emotion.

Not like him at all—but he fucking loved it.

That's what he'd been missing for so long. The excitement and wonder of Christmas, the companionship of a woman he cared about. Because he did care about Natasha. It was more than the coming child that bound them. It was that itch beneath his skin, that magnetic pull when their eyes met, that singular desire that lit him on fire and made him need to possess her.

He wanted to be with her. He wanted to wake up with her in the morning, and go to sleep with her at night. He wanted to make love to her as often as he could, and he wanted to watch her belly grow big with their child. He couldn't think of anything better than just being with her every day.

But first he had to stop the Syndicate from coming after her. And him, though he didn't worry nearly as much about himself. There'd been no mention of his 'death' on the dark web, which meant someone in the organization was either holding the information close, or they didn't believe it.

Julian Nowak hadn't shown up to the meeting with

Jamie Hayes after the mission, which seemed to indicate he'd realized something was wrong. But nothing was certain at this point.

Nothing except the fact Ian needed to end the threat to his family. *His family.*

Damn, that felt good to admit.

For the next four days, he worked his connections like crazy—from home and discreetly since the Syndicate was supposed to think he was dead—and his team worked to locate the auction venue. The information Dax had found said Vienna. But where in Vienna? And was it really Vienna or one of the outlying villages? That's what they didn't know.

Ian was working on it when Natasha walked into his office without knocking. He minimized the screen and smiled. "What's up?"

She came over and sat on his lap. He didn't mind. Or, he did kind of mind since he couldn't take advantage of her in the middle of the day with a house full of people— Daria, Lissette, Ty, Dax, and now Rascal, who'd returned from his latest assignment in a subdued mood. He'd led a team into Mexico to rescue a wealthy man's daughter and her friends from a drug cartel, and he hadn't shaken off the mood of that trip yet. Ian didn't ask. He understood dark moods and needing time to clear his head.

"I'm stuck in limbo," she said. "I can't return to my home or get my things. Daria needs to start school again, and Lissette is withdrawn and out of sorts. I think she misses home. And I'm *still* not able to access my online accounts."

Ian skimmed his hand over her thigh and up her arm to cup her cheek. Then he pulled her down to kiss her. "It's not safe to return to Zurich. You know that."

"I know. I'm not used to being idle, though. And you

still haven't given me access." Her eyes flashed. "Not to mention that you keep ignoring my requests about it. I'm getting impatient, Ian."

He sighed. "It's not safe yet, Tasha. You know that. They've very likely tagged all your accounts and they'll be looking for a login."

Her color was high. "Do you think I'm so stupid I wouldn't have a secret account somewhere?"

"Do you?"

"Do *you?*"

"Secret accounts are failsafes. You know it was well as I do. Are you planning to run away?"

She tried to push herself off his lap but he held on tight and wouldn't let her go. That was pretty much all the answer he needed and they both knew it.

It hurt, but he also understood. She'd been conditioned that no one was going to take care of her but herself. Trusting anyone else with her safety—her child's safety—wasn't an easy thing to do.

She stopped struggling and glared. "You asked me over a year ago to join BDI and you promised to protect me if I did. I'm here, but you haven't let me *do* anything. It's frustrating."

"When I asked you to flip on the Syndicate, I didn't think about you being pregnant with my child. That kind of changes things."

"Meaning you won't let me do any work for you."

"Meaning the kind of work I'm going to let you do is more limited than it would have been before."

Her nostrils flared. "That's very caveman of you."

He traced the part of her collarbone that was exposed in the loose neck of her pink sweater. She didn't stop him, but she didn't soften either. "Not trying to be a caveman, angel. But having you enter active missions where you could be in physical danger isn't going to work for me right now."

He wasn't sure it would ever work for him. But saying that was a sure way to piss her off.

"You told me in Colorado that you also hire scumbags to work at BDI, but you keep them separate from the important stuff. I feel like I'm one of the scumbags. Less than one since you haven't told me anything."

"That's not what's going on here. I don't let those people anywhere near the inner sanctum. You've been to our headquarters building, and you've been in on mission planning. Believe me when I tell you I don't let just anyone be a part of that."

"Then what are you working on?" she challenged.

He studied her for a moment. He didn't want to worry her, but not telling her was only going to frustrate her more. Natasha wasn't stupid, and she had a right to know what was going on. Especially since she was still in danger. The Syndicate hadn't forgotten about her and they both knew it.

"There's supposed to be an exclusive sex-slave auction on New Year's Eve. In Vienna."

She reared back on his lap. "Vienna?"

"Yes."

"Lissette and Daria were sent to Vienna. I was told to go to Vienna. What the fuck?"

He could feel the shudder moving through her body. He wasn't sure if it was fear or fury. "We haven't confirmed anything yet."

"And if you do?"

"Then I'll send people in to disrupt it."

He could see her processing what he'd said. "It's no wonder they hate you," she replied. "You've cost them a lot of money over the past few months."

"I intend to cost them a lot more."

"You can't stop everything, Ian. The Syndicate is more than trafficking. They're drugs and guns and taking over vulnerable countries. They're disinformation and stoking the flames of populism to get what they want. They have people everywhere. Even in Congress."

His gut churned. "I know they do. And I still intend to stop what I can. That's what the good guys do. They keep fighting the bad guys."

"I want to fight too."

He tucked her hair behind her ear. God he loved touching her. Loved that he had the right to do so. "I know you do, but there's nothing you can do right now. Trust me, if I need your help, I'll take it."

"Will you really?"

He heard the challenge in her voice. The doubt. He made an X over his heart. "Yes, Natasha, I will. Promise."

"I'm not entirely certain I believe you, but you need to know that if you fuck this up, I'll never trust you again."

He felt the conviction in her words and he knew he was going to have to be careful. He didn't want to involve her, would do all kinds of gymnastics to avoid it—but if he hit a wall that only she could help scale, then he'd turn to her. "Understood."

"I want to know why they wanted the three of us in Vienna. Pluto told Lissette that we were going to spend Christmas there. But why?"

"I'm not sure." He had an idea, but he didn't want to say it.

She studied him. He could tell when she'd worked it out by the way her eyes widened. "Holy shit. They were going to kill me anyway. But they were planning to punish me first. Maybe by forcing me to watch Lissette and Daria go through the auction."

He hated every last motherfucker involved in that organization right now. All the ones he knew about, and all the ones he didn't. He'd set fire to them and listen to them scream for help if he could. Without an ounce of regret.

"I'm sorry, Natasha."

"You agree with me?"

"Unfortunately, I do. It's how cartels operate. Punish the guilty by punishing their family too. Send a message to anyone else who might get out of line."

She squeezed her eyes shut. "I should have realized how it was meant to go when they took Daria and Lissette. I didn't."

"What could you have done differently?" he asked gently.

Her eyes were hard and angry, yet somehow soft when she looked at him. "I could have trusted you sooner."

Chapter Forty-Seven

"I CAN MAKE MY CHOCOLATE GANACHE CAKE," LISSETTE said. "If you like."

Natasha looked up from where she was busy rolling out dough to make her own pasta. After her conversation with Ian earlier, she'd needed something challenging. She was still shaken inside. She was pissed too. More than anything, she wanted to return to her Zurich apartment and arm herself for battle.

She was ready to stride into the middle of that auction and start shooting every motherfucker who dared to think he could buy a human being. She'd never worked for the traffickers. Her jobs for the Syndicate were always about revenge. People who did bad things and tried to screw over the Syndicate in the process.

Idiots like Daniel Weir, who'd tortured Libby King, killed her friend, and nearly got away with it when the law got involved. Natasha had been sent to silence him, and she'd done so. Good riddance.

But innocent women? Little girls and boys? On auction blocks?

No. Hell no.

"Are you okay, madame?"

Natasha focused on Lissette. "Yes, sorry. Just thinking about this dough and wondering if I have enough. I think everyone would love your cake. Thank you."

Lissette smiled. "I checked the pantry earlier and realized everything I needed was there."

"Daria will be very excited."

"She does love my cake."

Lissette went into the pantry and returned with flour, sugar, vanilla, and chocolate chips. She got butter from the fridge, and eggs, and set them on the counter. She went back for the heavy cream and set that on the counter too.

"How are you feeling?" Natasha asked.

Lissette had returned to her room this morning after breakfast, complaining of a headache. She sometimes got migraines, and Natasha knew there was nothing she could do except take her medicine and rest for a while. She didn't get them often anymore. When she'd worked for the family with all the boys, she'd had them frequently.

"Better. It was just a headache." She smiled and held up the bag of chocolate chips. "Good enough to make cake."

"I'm glad."

Natasha rolled the dough out until it was as thin as she wanted it, then began cutting strips. She might need to make more. Fine with her since it kept her busy. And since Ian wasn't giving her a phone or a computer today. She should have known he would see through her request to what was really driving her.

When he'd asked if she'd planned to run away, she couldn't form the words to answer. The hurt in his expression had been too much to bear. The last thing she ever wanted to do was hurt him.

But she didn't want Daria to get hurt either. Or Lissette. That Pluto had been manipulating Lissette while planning to harm her was infuriating. Not that she knew the Syndicate planned to sell Daria and Lissette, but it seemed like a pretty strong possibility.

"I'm sorry for all the stress of the past couple of weeks," Natasha said as Lissette began to beat the cake batter.

The other woman looked up, a soft smile on her face. "It's okay. You have always had to travel at a moment's notice. We're used to it."

"Yes, but you don't typically have to travel anywhere when I do."

She had to be careful, because she didn't know exactly what Pluto had said and she didn't want to blow her bank cover story. Not that Lissette was going to be able to leave Ian's house and return to Europe anytime soon, but telling her the entire truth might send her into hysterics. Finding out your employer was an assassin with a price on her head wouldn't be easy for anyone.

Not to mention, the last thing Natasha wanted was the kind of tension Daria could sense. If Lissette knew the truth, how would that affect Daria? Her daughter loved the nanny, and vice versa, and Natasha wasn't going to ruin that for either of them.

"I didn't believe the man in the limousine when he said you'd sent him to get us since you did not text me, but he said you'd wanted it to be a surprise and would be in touch soon. And then we went to the Grand Hotel Schoenburg, and it was magnificent and I could see how you wouldn't want to ruin that surprise for Daria. There were clothes waiting, and everything else we would need too. But then your coworker came to us and said that your plans had changed and we were to meet you in Vienna. So we took a train north."

"I'm so sorry for all the confusion," Natasha said. "The man in the limousine was a different person than my coworker?"

"Yes. He did not give a name, but he was driving a limousine. It was very luxurious. Exactly the kind of thing you would send if you wanted to treat us."

"I did want to treat you. I'm glad they sent the best limo for you." She rolled the dough a little too hard and had to stop before she made it too thin. "Which coworker of mine came to see you? I talked to more than one, I'm afraid, and I was never quite clear on who took care of you for me."

Lissette frowned at her. "It was Julian. He said you've worked together for years. He said you asked him specifically."

Natasha forced a smile. "Well yes, I did. But I didn't know if he sent someone. He's very busy and travels a great deal as well. I did try to text you," she added.

"I lost my phone. I don't know where. I just didn't have it when we checked into the Grand Hotel. There was nowhere to get a new one right away and I figured it didn't matter anyway. You could call the hotel if necessary. I meant to get a new one, but then we left Switzerland and I was unwell. Julian read your texts to me and I sent answers back. I told you about the phone then."

"Yes, I know," she lied. "I didn't realize you'd lost it so soon."

If she could find Pluto, he'd be the first one to die. Theirs had been a professional relationship, nothing more, but to deceive Lissette like that. To pretend to romance her while knowing that he—or someone—intended her harm. It was unforgivable. Lissette hadn't mentioned that he'd romanced her, but Natasha didn't expect her to. He'd held her hand and flattered her at dinner and on a train simply to get her to do his bidding. He hadn't intended to carry on with it beyond that.

It infuriated her. Lissette was a sweet girl, not much younger than she was, but far more simple in her experience and tastes. Natasha wasn't entirely certain that Lissette hadn't been taken advantage of by the husband in her last post, but she'd never found out for certain.

And it wasn't her business anyway. Lissette wanted a quiet life with a little girl and her mother in Switzerland, and that's what Natasha had given her.

Lissette busied herself with preparing the cake and Natasha made more pasta dough. She had a sauce simmering on the stove and the smells eventually lured the men into the kitchen. Ty was first. He sniffed and asked what she was making.

"Homemade fettuccine with bolognese sauce," she said. "Extra Tide pods for you."

Lissette had put the cake in the oven and gone into the family room to play with Daria, so Natasha wasn't worried about what she said.

Ty snorted. "If it tastes the way your cooking usually tastes, then keep doing whatever it is you do with those Tide pods. Mmm, flavor."

A tiny flare of happiness burst inside her. That dangerous feeling of belonging was more prevalent these days. Every day, she felt as if she were becoming a part of Ian's little work family.

She told herself to be careful. Ty might have gone from hating her to tolerating her and even making jokes, but that didn't mean he liked her. He probably still expected her to do something diabolical, and he'd still make good on his threat to put a bullet in her if he thought she had. She couldn't lose sight of that for a moment.

Dax was next. He'd never openly disliked her the way Ty had, but she knew he hadn't trusted her. Probably still didn't. He strolled in, sniffing the air.

"What on earth is that? It smells freaking divine."

She told him what she'd told Ty. Minus the Tide pods.

"Damn, girl, when did you have time to get so good at that, er, job you do—did—and learn to cook like a chef too?"

She glanced at Lissette checking her cake. The other woman didn't seem to notice what he'd said.

"I make my own schedule unless I'm traveling. Lots of work from home, which means domesticity."

"Who would have thought it?" he said with an air of disbelief.

Last to arrive was Ian. Her heart squeezed with love and longing when he strode in. He was dressed in a pair of faded jeans that hugged him in all the right places and a dark navy henley with enough of an open throat that she fixated on that spot for a few moments as she imagined pressing her mouth there.

Mmmmm….

"Smells delicious," he said as he came over to stand behind her, wrapping his arms around her and pulling her against him.

A shiver of delight slipped through her. Her hands were sticky with dough or she'd reach around and squeeze his ass. She knew if she did that he'd be pressing a hard cock against her backside. Not that they could drop everything and disappear with so many people around, but a little taste of what was waiting for her when bedtime came was always appropriate. Even when she was annoyed with him, she wanted him.

"It will be," she murmured as he pressed his lips to her throat.

"You smell delicious too."

Lissette was stirring her chocolate ganache and very deliberately not looking at them. Natasha thought the other woman's cheeks were red. Poor Lissette. She wasn't exactly pretty, but a little makeup would do wonders if she learned to apply it. Maybe Natasha should offer to teach her. Subtly, of course.

"Thank you," she said.

"When's dinner?"

"About an hour. Are you hungry?"

He flexed his hips against her backside and she felt the hard press of his cock. It was everything she could do not to moan softly. "So hungry," he said. "Starved, in fact."

A moment later he stepped away. She didn't want him to go, but she was glad too. Another minute of that and she'd embarrass herself by moaning in front of Lissette.

"He is a very handsome man," Lissette said when Ian left with a wink and a smile.

"Yes."

"And good with Daria."

"He seems to be."

"You never mentioned you were seeing anyone." Lissette sounded almost hurt.

"It's complicated. Ian and I aren't… We weren't…" She sighed. "It just kind of happened, I guess. I wasn't expecting it."

Lissette turned off the burner and lifted her spoon. Chocolate drizzled from the wood into the pan.

"There are a lot of things we don't expect," Lissette said. "Sometimes they are good things. Sometimes bad. And you never know which one you'll get, do you?"

Chapter Forty-Eight

IAN SPENT THE NEXT HOUR WITH HIS TEAM, RESEARCHING rumors and possible locations for a human auction scheduled to take place in just four days while delicious cooking smells wafted through the house. Definitely not the norm, and definitely something he could get used to.

The smells, not the part where he had to find human traffickers. He would never get used to knowing there were people in this world who could sell women and children into sex slavery. Ty, Dax, and Rascal were still with him, still unwilling to go home and leave him alone with two women and a child.

Except now Ty expressed concern about the Syndicate's plans for Natasha instead of worrying that she planned to kill him the first chance she got. *Progress.*

They sat in his home office and linked up with Jared, Brett, Jace, and Colt, who were at BDI HQ and monitoring the situation from there. They also had the command center staff busy chasing leads and doing research.

"Mobilize Finn and his team," Ian said. "They're

already in Europe. Get them to Vienna. And start putting out disinformation on the dark web. Suggest it's a setup, an Interpol sting designed to sweep up everyone who attends."

"They could move the location if we do that," Rascal said.

"Exactly," Ian replied. "To move it fast, information is bound to leak. And even if they don't move it, there's going to be talk. We'll find something."

They talked a bit longer, then wrapped it up when someone knocked on the door to his office. Dax was closest so he answered it.

Daria stood there with shiny pigtails and a sweet smile. "Mommy said to tell you that dinner is ready."

Chairs scraped as men hastily stood. Ian chuckled to himself. For guys who'd been reluctant to eat anything Natasha cooked a week ago, they sure couldn't wait to get to the table these days.

Dinner was turning into something he really looked forward to. His mother had insisted on dinners at the table every night, but since leaving home and heading to college, Ian hadn't concerned himself with meals at a table in years. Unless he was eating in a restaurant with people, or at someone's house, he ate at the kitchen island or at his desk.

Yet here he was, sitting at the head of the table in his own home, surrounded by friends and enjoying the kind of camaraderie that a good meal and good wine could provide. Natasha glowed as she accepted the compliments the men gave her. They shoveled in homemade pasta and sauce with shaved parmesan and garlic bread made for them by one of the world's most dangerous assassins and didn't blink twice. A week ago, they'd have watched her prepare it and then made her taste it first just to be sure.

Natasha looked content for the moment, but he knew she seethed beneath the surface.

Like a brewing storm, she was going to explode when the pressure got too much. He knew he was going to have to make his peace with using her skills at BDI. He'd always intended to use her skills, but then she'd gotten pregnant and he'd lost his objectivity.

He still hadn't found it, but he was trying. For her. Because he wanted her happy, and because she wasn't the sort of woman who was going to be satisfied on the sidelines. He wasn't taking her to Austria, but he could use her knowledge in the command center. That might not be enough for her, but they'd work on it.

Lissette seemed happy tonight, too. She didn't glow, but she smiled more. Shyly, but at least it was a smile. He knew why she was happy when she served her cake. It was rich, chocolatey, and decadent, and everyone praised her skills. She blushed and thanked them all, offering more cake to those who wanted it and pouring coffee into cups.

Ian didn't finish the whole slice she'd given him because it was a little too rich, but it was delicious. He could almost forget they had a ticking clock in the background, driving them to find the Vienna location so they could free the women and return them to their lives and families.

It wasn't until he noticed Ty slurring his words that the tingling started in his gut.

Ian tried to stand, but nothing happened. He couldn't get his legs to work. They wouldn't function. His hands didn't work either. He lifted them to the table but couldn't move them further.

Ian worked hard—so damned hard—to turn his head to Natasha. She was beside him, and turning his head was almost impossible.

He did it though. He didn't know what to expect. If she would be affected too, or if she'd done this to him and his men for some reason. Maybe it was because he'd told her that he knew why she wanted to access her secret account. Maybe she was desperate to get back on the Syndicate's good side and save her child.

But her eyes were open, glassy. She wasn't moving. Beside her, Daria slumped as if sleeping.

"Nooo," he slurred. "Tash…"

Lissette dabbed her lips with her napkin and stood. "She's alive," she said in a cold voice. "For the moment."

He stared. Lissette was still plain, but she no longer looked shy. She looked hard and cold. Mean.

Ian wanted to demand answers, tried to demand them, but the words didn't sound right.

His eyelids were so heavy. He forced them open again and again, but each time was harder than before. His heart thumped, his ears roared, and he wondered if this was it. If this was how his life ended.

He wasn't ready to go. He had a baby on the way. A woman he planned to marry.

A woman he loved.

He'd finally found it. Finally knew what it was that men like Jace, Colt, Brett, and Jared felt. Men like Johnny Mendez, who'd sacrificed so much for Kat.

And then there was Kat, who'd been willing to die for the man she loved. Who'd thrown herself in front of a bullet for him.

Ian would die for the woman he loved. He knew it in his bones. He'd choose death in a split second if that's what it took to save her.

But not like this. Not when he couldn't be sure she was going to be okay.

He blinked. A lone tear slid hotly down his cheek. So

much left undone and unsaid. So many damned regrets. And then there was the anger…

"Tashhhh…"

Lissette fisted his hair and dragged his head backward, exposing his throat. She wrapped her hand around his neck. Her fingers were cold. "The mighty Ian Black, brought low by a drugged cake. Who would have ever thought?"

"Lissss…"

"You should be unconscious, but of course you aren't. You didn't eat the whole slice. Always different, aren't you?" She lowered her head until her cheek was beside his. Her skin was cool. Repulsive. "I'm afraid this is goodbye. You won't wake up again. But know this before you go— Natasha will pay for what she's done. There will be no peaceful end for her. She will suffer for betraying us."

Lissette squeezed his throat until black spots swam in his eyes. He wanted to stop her, but he couldn't. His hands dropped to his lap as she pushed him back. And then he felt the edge of a leather band on his wrist. His fingers fumbled numbly as he tried to press the crown of his watch. He needed to send the signal…

He kept trying, kept pressing, but it was too late.

The blackness blotted his vision. The world went silent.

Chapter Forty-Nine

IT WAS UTTERLY DARK WHEN IAN SNAPPED AWAKE. HIS HEAD throbbed. An odor of rotten eggs crawled over him, growing stronger every second.

"Ty," he croaked.

There was no reply.

"Dax!"

Nothing.

"Rassscll…"

Still nothing.

He despaired. Lissette had drugged them. She intended to kill them. He realized that the rotten eggs meant she'd turned on the gas before she'd left. He had to assume she was gone, though maybe only a few moments had passed. He coughed as he flipped over onto his hands and knees and forced himself toward the kitchen. If he could reach the emergency shut off valve and get a window open…

But the smell was strong and his coughing intensified. He had to go the other way, had to get outside and revive enough to try the shut off valve again.

There was something else he needed to do, something he couldn't remember.

And then it hit him. He stopped in mid-crawl and groped for his wrist, intending to send an emergency alert through his watch. But the scream of sirens suddenly split the night, which meant he must have succeeded when he'd tried before.

He needed to call Jace and tell him to go after Natasha and Daria, but first he had to find his phone. It wasn't in his pocket. Maybe it was on the table, or the floor where he'd fallen.

Before he could drag himself back to search for it, the doors burst open and black-clad bodies hurtled inside. He wondered for a moment if maybe he hadn't succeeded in sending an emergency alert after all. Maybe it was the Syndicate, come to finish him off.

Flashlights swept over the floor until they found him, and then he was being carried outside into the fresh night air. Someone put an oxygen mask over his nose and mouth and he breathed deeply. Dax, Ty, and Rascal were carried out and laid on the grass.

There was shouting and movement but Ian sucked in oxygen and tried to think while his team took care of things.

Someone knelt beside him and pushed off the balaclava covering his head so Ian could see a face.

It was Jace. "What happened?"

Ian pulled the oxygen mask off. "Natasha," he croaked.

Jace's eyes hardened. "Goddammit, I knew she couldn't be trusted."

"No," Ian forced out. His throat was raw from coughing, and his head hurt like hell, but he wasn't going to let Jace blame her. He sucked in oxygen again. "It wasn't her. It was Lissette."

"Lissette! Jesus, I thought she was scared of her own shadow."

Ian shook his head. "Drugged the cake. Don't know with what. Took Natasha and Daria."

"Fucking hell."

"Need to access the security cameras. Find out how she got them out."

Jared walked over and thrust an object at Ian. "Your phone. Found it on the kitchen island with everyone else's."

"How are they?" he asked, nodding toward the grass where Ty, Dax, and Rascal lay with oxygen masks over their faces.

"Their vitals are stable. They should be fine. We got here just in time."

Ian nodded as he pulled up his security system, accessing the cameras with a couple of taps. A car had driven up to the front of the house and a man got out. His face wasn't visible because he wore a hoodie and a mask that covered the lower half of his face. The door opened and Lissette stood in the entry. The man went inside and the two of them came back out a short while later carrying Natasha and Daria. They put them in the car, got in, and drove away.

Next, Ian pulled up the cameras from inside. He could watch later to see how Lissette drugged the cake if he wanted, but right now he wanted to see what she did when the man entered. The man shoved his mask down. They threw themselves at each other and kissed passionately before breaking apart and going into the dining room.

Once there, they were all business, grabbing Natasha and Daria and carrying them back to the front door. They left the two limp bodies while they quickly and efficiently went about collecting phones and moving them to the island, then turning on the gas while they speculated how long it would take for the place to blow when the gas built up enough that the pilot light in the fireplace triggered an explosion.

"Motherfuckers," Jace said. "If you hadn't sent the alarm, they would have succeeded."

Ian looked at the time stamp on the video. "It's only been twelve minutes since they left. They couldn't get that far. Where's the gate guard?"

Jared and Jace exchanged a look. "He didn't make it, boss. He was still in the shack, shot through the head with a small caliber pistol. Probably shot him on the way in."

Ian growled. "They made a mistake not shooting me when they had the chance."

"They must've figured blowing you up was good enough."

"We have to find them. They intend to make Natasha suffer for betraying the Syndicate. I don't know what that means, but I'd lay odds it involves Vienna."

Jace's expression was grim. "They could be taking her anywhere, boss."

"I know. We need to track that vehicle down, see if we can catch them before they board a plane." He coughed, his throat feeling like razor blades lined it. "Run the security footage against Dax's video of Nowak. I expect it'll match. Lissette's fingerprints are all over the house since she's been here a few days. Run them and see what comes up."

"On it, boss," Jace said, throwing a nod at Colt who turned and went back inside the house.

Ian swallowed the despair threatening to overwhelm him and focused on what he'd learned over a lifetime of fighting the bad guys—and pretending to be one of them. He didn't have time to feel the chaotic emotions brewing inside. The sense of loss and despair that wanted to overwhelm him. He only had the mission. It was how he survived and how he got the job done.

It was going to be how he got his family back, too.

"I want every resource we have focused on finding Natasha and Daria. I'm not letting the Syndicate have them, Jace." He sucked in a breath and forced down the panic inside. "I failed your sister once before, and I won't do it again."

He couldn't lose her. Not when he finally knew what she meant to him. Her and Daria and the baby were his family, and if anyone harmed them, he wouldn't be responsible for the level of damage he'd do. Nuclear level damage that would take out high placed officials if he had to. He'd burn every bridge he had, and then burn the damned boat on top of it. Whatever it took to punish those responsible.

Jace put a hand on his shoulder and squeezed. "I failed her too, and I'm one hundred-percent with you on this. I don't care whose dick we have to suck or whose asshole we have to lick—I want my sister and her kid back."

Ian scrolled through his phone. "Time to call in some favors," he muttered as he clicked on a name he hadn't spoken with in months.

She answered on the first ring. "Hello, Odysseus," Phoenix said in that smoky, no-nonsense voice of hers. "I've been waiting for you to call."

Chapter Fifty

NATASHA WOKE SLOWLY, HER HEAD ACHING. SHE BLINKED into the overhead light, wondering if Ian had carried her to bed and forgot to turn it off.

But no, he wouldn't forget. He was very attentive to her comfort, always asking her if she felt all right, if she had any nausea or tiredness. He brought her drinks if she was sitting down, he checked on her if she was cooking to make sure she hadn't exerted herself or to see if she needed help. He carried things from the pantry, fetched from the refrigerator, and made sure she had everything she needed before he went back to his office with his team.

She'd resented being left out of the action, but she'd also realized it was going to take time for him to come to terms with letting her participate. It wasn't easy for her, but she'd decided to give him that time.

Some of it, anyway, because at the end of the day she was damn sure going to ask what he'd learned about Vienna. And she was going to keep asking him every day, whether he liked it or not. He might want to sideline her because she was pregnant, but she wasn't going to let it happen.

She'd worked hard to cook today's meal because she'd wanted to be busy, but Ian had been there often to ask what she needed. She'd had to shoo him away with threats to his balls if he didn't stop treating her like she was helpless. He'd laughed but he'd gone away. Despite her annoyance with him, she'd glowed inside at the attention.

Even Ty had come to ask if she need help. She hadn't been annoyed with him. She'd been touched considering how they'd started off. Even if Ian had sent him, the fact he asked and would have helped was more than she could have expected from him a week ago.

They'd all gathered at the table and eaten the pasta, and it had been as wonderful as she'd hoped. She remembered the compliments and the warmth as everyone seemed content. Lissette had served her chocolate ganache cake. Natasha remembered digging into her slice, though she was fairly full already, and exchanging a wink with Daria who loved chocolate most of all.

Everyone had eaten cake and been happy.

What'd happened next? That's what she wasn't quite sure of. It was… fuzzy.

She shifted on the mattress. It was so hard. Why was it hard? And what was that damp, musty smell?

Her belly tingled with apprehension. Something wasn't right. She knew it wasn't right, but she was still groggy. She blinked and fought the feeling until she could turn her head to look at something besides the light.

A chill swept through her, freezing the marrow in her bones.

"Daria," she forced out.

Her daughter was across the room, lying on a thin

mattress on the floor. There was a chain running from Daria's wrist to a ring in the concrete wall. *What the hell?*

Natasha rolled. She had to get to her child.

But a sharp pain bit into the skin of her wrist. Her stomach turned upside down as reality intruded on her.

She was chained, too. Too far from her daughter to hold her. Too far to check on her and make sure she was okay.

Daria was still. So still. Natasha stared hard, blinking back tears, trying to see—and there it was, the soft movement of Daria's chest. She was alive. Drugged most likely, but alive.

Natasha turned her head again and tears rolled down the sides of her face, into her hair. Where were they? What had happened to them? The Syndicate had taken them, she had no doubt—but how?

Another dark chill flooded her then. *Ian.*

Where was he? What had they done to him? Was he chained up, too? Or had they killed him?

The scrape of a key in a lock had her struggling to sit up. She managed to get her back against the wall and inch up it until she was halfway sitting. The door swung open on creaky hinges.

"Lissette?" The name came out as a croak. But if Lissette was here, then maybe it would be okay. Maybe she was dreaming and she wasn't chained to a wall.

Lissette came over and hunkered down beside her. She didn't look as meek as she usually did. Or as plain. This version of Lissette was harder, grimmer. She wore makeup, and her features were transformed by it. Natasha cursed herself. She of all people knew how a person could change who they were, how they could hide inside a different identity.

"If only you had resisted that man, Calypso. If you

had killed him as you were supposed to, then perhaps you wouldn't be here right now. Perhaps you would be at home, cozied up in your lovely home, with your sweet little girl."

Natasha's heart hammered. *How had she been so blind?* "Who are you?"

Lissette reached out and traced the line of Natasha's jaw before tucking her hair behind her ear. "I was sent to watch you. They never trusted you, you know. Coming from a family like yours? Traitors, all of you. But you were useful, that's certain. Until you failed to bring in your brother—I recognized him, by the way. It's very obvious you and Jace are related." She rolled back on her ass and crossed her arms over her knees. "It was only a matter of time before someone persuaded you to betray those who saved you, wasn't it? You and Ian Black. And now you're pregnant with his baby. I knew it when you started puking every morning and sleeping in, though you didn't have any idea, did you? You had to go get a test before you had a clue. Very careless, Calypso. Very careless indeed."

If this was a nightmare, then Natasha desperately wanted to wake up. But no amount of trying to force herself awake worked. In the end, she had to accept that she wasn't dreaming.

She really was chained to a wall in a room somewhere dank and cold. The woman she'd trusted with her child was taunting her. A woman who wasn't at all who she'd said she was.

And Natasha had never noticed. She squeezed her eyes shut as fear and regret—and self-loathing—sliced through her. She'd let herself get too soft. Worse, she'd failed to protect Daria the way she'd promised she would. She'd trusted this woman, and she was going to pay for it. But Daria shouldn't. She was innocent.

"You spent over two years with us," she croaked. "How

can you do this to Daria? She's just a child! Do what you want to me, but please don't hurt her."

Lissette sighed. "I'm sorry, Natasha, but it's not up to me. It hurts me to see her like this. It really does. But I know what the price of crossing the Syndicate is. You should have known it too."

She did know. That was the awful part. She knew that if you betrayed them, they didn't kill only you. They killed your entire family. It was one of the ways they kept people in line. For many people, the threat to loved ones was harder to ignore than threats to themselves. You could rebel if you thought you were the only one paying the price, and that your rebellion was worth the sacrifice in the end.

That was why it was easier not to love anyone when you did what she did for a living. But she hadn't had a choice with Daria. Maybe she should have found a family to take Lena's toddler instead of keeping her. If she'd done that, Daria wouldn't be here now.

"You can save her. Please."

Lissette shook her head sadly. "I can't. But take heart, she's not going to die. Someone will pay a steep price for such a lovely little girl. If she's lucky, they'll simply want a sweet little daughter of their own. If they want something more, well, she'll still be alive, won't she?"

Bile rose in Natasha's throat at the thought of what a pedophile might do to her child. She turned her head to retch, but nothing came up. It must have been hours since they'd been taken. Hours in which they'd been drugged and chained up. Hours in which they'd been moved from Ian's house.

If she had any strength at all, if she could get free, she would kill this woman. Without hesitation.

But she had no strength, and hope was a withered thing in her soul.

"What did you do to Ian and the others?"

Lissette shrugged. "They're dead."

Despair threatened to swallow her whole. *Not Ian. Please not Ian.*

And not just him, though his death hurt the worst. She loved him and she'd never told him. She'd let fear and pride hold her back when she should have taken the risk. She'd give anything to have another chance to say what she felt, but that's not how it worked. She knew that better than anyone.

And then there were the others. She'd started to care about them. Ty the Terrible with his curly hair and his faded scar. Dax the computer nerd who was way more handsome than a nerd should be. Rascal, who she hadn't known long but who'd made Daria giggle with his impressions of cartoon characters.

Tears threatened, but Natasha dug down deep and found the coldness that lived inside her. The emotional detachment she'd relied upon for so long. She would fall apart later, but now she needed information. She thought back to the last time they'd all been together. Sitting at the table, enjoying dessert.

"You drugged the cake. You pushed it around your plate and didn't actually eat any."

She hadn't realized that Lissette hadn't eaten any at the time, but looking back, it was obvious.

"True. I couldn't risk killing you and Daria so I had to be careful with the tranquilizers. I needed everyone to sleep at once so I could get you both out of there. Ian didn't eat his entire slice though. He fought it when he realized what was happening, but it wasn't enough."

Oh, Ian. I told you not to cross the Syndicate. I told you it wasn't that easy.

"What's the plan for me?"

"I'm not quite certain. Someone higher up wants you for himself. He'll decide what to do with you."

Natasha dragged in a breath. The room smelled moldy and dank, but she felt stronger every moment as the drugs faded from her system. If taking deep lungfuls of stale air helped, then so be it.

"You had better hope he kills me," she said softly. "Because I'll be coming for you if he doesn't. And I won't be nice if I do."

Lissette pushed to her feet, laughing. "Empty threats, Calypso. You aren't leaving this castle alive. If you do, it won't be for long."

The door clanged shut. Hot tears clogged Natasha's throat and stung her eyes. She hugged her knees to her chest and rocked back and forth. She'd never thought she'd find herself back in this place—imprisoned, threatened, and brutalized.

But here she was, and now she had two innocent babies with her and no way to help them. Ian was dead, and her brother would never risk his life for her after what she'd done to him.

No one was coming. Unless she thought of something, this was how it ended.

She squeezed her eyes shut and tried to come up with a plan.

Chapter Fifty-One

"CASTLE HIMMEL, LOCATED JUST OUTSIDE VIENNA," DAX said. "It's owned by Ennio Leone, but his son Tommaso is the one who frequents it."

Ian's gut churned. It'd been six hours since Natasha and Daria had been taken, and they were just now getting into the air. But they'd had to wait until they had confirmation of the location. The Syndicate could have been throwing out misdirection for his benefit and they'd needed to be sure.

Now they were.

As the plane reached cruising altitude, Mandy Parker, his airborne communications director, turned from her screen to face him. "It's Phoenix. Would you like me to patch her to your private line?"

"No," Ian said. "I want everyone to listen."

Mandy nodded. A moment later, Phoenix's smoky voice filled the cabin.

"I ran your video of Julian Nowak, and the prints for Lissette Alarie. They're both in the CIA database."

He'd figured as much. That was one of the reasons

he'd called her. "I'm listening. So's my team."

She laughed. "I suspected. Hello, team. Who's with you? Jace and Ty, I bet. Rascal? Dax, of course."

The men blinked. They didn't know Phoenix's identity, but they knew she was powerful within the shadow world of the CIA. That she knew them by name had to be a bit of a shock. They'd met Samantha Spencer before and probably hadn't thought too much about it. Sam came across as a harmless—though feisty—desk jockey type, but she was so much more than any of them realized.

She was capable of giving her voice different inflections. He remembered that she'd spoken with an almost exaggerated Southern drawl the day she'd met with his team. There was no trace of it now.

Ian couldn't help but shake his head at the way she teased them. "They're here. Colt, Jared, and Brett, too. We're all invested in getting Natasha back."

"You mean Calypso, don't you?"

Ian gritted his teeth. Of course she would know. There wasn't much she didn't know. "Yes, I mean Calypso. Is that a problem?"

He could hear her blow smoke from her e-cigarette. "Not at all. In fact, I find it amusing that the woman who has your attention is called Calypso. The nymph Calypso and the warrior Odysseus have quite a history in Greek mythology. I don't think it worked out, though."

"I'm aware." Calypso had tried to convince Odysseus to stay with her forever. He'd stayed seven years. "But they're just names. Like Phoenix."

She laughed. "True. I'd like to talk to Calypso sometime. Think you could arrange it?"

"I'm sure I could." He loved that she was so positive of his success. He was trying to believe they weren't too late, but it was difficult when his heart was on the line. He'd found the woman he loved, and she'd been ripped away before he'd told her how he felt. Before he'd told her what he really wanted from her.

Natasha was his, and not just because she was pregnant. She was *his*. When he thought of how it felt to lie in bed beside her, her hand twined in his, her leg thrown over his, he was almost overcome. How had he not realized what it all meant sooner? Love didn't always announce itself with explosions and sirens blaring. Sometimes it snuck in on tiptoe, its power evident in the quiet moments that made life feel full.

Johnny Mendez was going to laugh his ass off the next time they met. Ian had spent so much time teasing the Hostile Operations Team commander about being a new dad in his fifties, and getting domesticated, while swearing it would never happen to him.

Joke was on him because it had. And damned if he was going to let anyone take that away from him.

"Great," Sam said. "I'll send the files. I think you'll find them interesting."

"Thank you. I owe you."

"You always owe me."

"I know. It's why you keep me around."

That and the fact he was still technically a CIA asset. He would never stop working for them, even if they no longer signed his paychecks. Even if the spy world thought he'd done something so terrible he'd been disavowed by them. Didn't matter what anyone thought. The people on this plane knew the truth. A few others. That's what mattered.

She snorted. "Too true. Let me know if you need anything else."

"I will."

The call ended and Dax refreshed his screen, waiting

for the files. When they popped into the inbox a moment later, he opened them on the central screen so they could all see.

There was a photo of a woman. It was the woman they knew as Lissette, if Lissette wore makeup and looked like she had no soul. The name beside the photo said Lucienne Vernier.

"French, thirty-two, from a town called Sarreguemines, right across the border from Germany." Dax whistled. "There was a Lissette Alarie who was a nanny, but she went missing a couple of years ago."

He typed something and another photo appeared beside Lucienne's. "The real Lissette Alarie."

Ian's gut churned. He could imagine what they'd done with her. She was a pretty girl, and she was either dead or she'd been sold into servitude. The Syndicate had gone to a lot of trouble to make sure her photo had disappeared from her employment records, too, because the photo Dax had originally found when he'd researched Lissette was Lucienne's.

"Lucienne served in the Gendarmerie before marrying a Polish national she met at Interpol in Lyon. Szymon Gorecki, aka Julian Nowak," Dax continued.

"Szymon and Lucienne have always been working together," Ian said, stating the obvious. "Pluto, her handler, and Lissette, her nanny. Jesus."

Jace blew out a breath. "The Syndicate didn't trust her, even from the beginning. Our parents," he added for those who weren't following along. "We have a history of double and triple agenting in the Oliver-slash-Orlov clan."

"That's a lot of trouble to go to, isn't it?" Ty asked. "Recruit and train your sister from prison, then watch her closely for any hint of disloyalty?"

"It is, but I disappeared without a trace and they might

have thought we were still in touch. I was an intel officer in the *Spetsnaz*. If they believed I went to the CIA, they might have thought she was a means to get to me. She would bear considerable watching under those circumstances. Though it could also be simpler than that. Someone might have wanted to kill us both. Wipe out our branch of the family as a means of revenge. Let her lead them to me, then take us both out."

"Which she nearly did," Ian said. "The reason doesn't matter. Cartels don't trust anyone in their employ, not really, so sending a nanny to watch her movements and send back reports, while also having access to the person Natasha loved most, isn't outside the norm."

"And now she's very likely being held in a castle owned by the Leones."

"With a human auction scheduled to happen tomorrow night," Ian growled. He didn't know if the Syndicate planned to put Natasha onstage, but he wasn't going to let it happen. Not her. Not Daria. Not anyone.

"We're lucky they think we're all dead," Ty said. "If they thought you were alive, they'd go underground and we'd never find her or the kid."

He had Phoenix to thank for that. She'd put the information out that he and his men had been killed in an explosion at his house. In reality they'd shut off the gas and cleared the area, but Phoenix had sent in a special team from the CIA who'd staged an explosion. His house hadn't burned down, but she'd made it appear that it had. Not literally, but in the news and online. The truth would leak out soon enough, but hopefully not before they'd accomplished their mission and rescued his woman and children.

Yes, children, because he'd already fallen for Daria. She was a delightful kid and he wanted her to grow up calling him Dad. He wanted to tuck her in at night, and he wanted to intimidate the first guy she brought home who thought he could date her. Most of all, he wanted to keep her safe from the kind of scumbags who preyed on innocents and did them harm.

"We know who they are now," Ian said, focusing on the photos of Lucienne and Szymon. "And we're pretty sure we know where we're going to find them. Pull up a schematic of the castle and let's get to work on a plan. There won't be any time to lose once we land."

Chapter Fifty-Two

THE SOUNDS OF FIREWORKS REACHED INTO THE ROOM where Natasha and Daria were being held. There was no window, and Natasha's body clock was all wrong, but she figured it must be dark if the fireworks were being set off.

Daria had awakened a few hours ago. She hadn't cried at first. She'd been curious about where they were and why they were chained up, and when they might be let go, but once the curiosity wore off and the cold and hunger set in, she started to cry.

It broke Natasha's heart. She cried too, because she couldn't help her child, but deep inside the dark, hard ball of hate swelled bigger. She wasn't only deadly with weapons. She was also deadly with her hands. Perhaps Lissette didn't know that. Or perhaps she thought it unlikely Natasha would find an opportunity.

But if she got the ghost of a chance, she would make Lissette—and whoever else was responsible—pay for harming Daria.

"Mommy, I'm hungry."

"I know, honey."

"I want to go home."

"I do too, baby."

"Where is Lissette? Is she okay? Did the bad people get her too?"

Natasha gritted her teeth. "I don't know where she is, but I'm sure she's fine."

"I don't like it here."

"I don't either, honey."

"Will Ian come get us?"

Natasha's heart ached. A sob caught in her throat. "I hope so." Because what else could she say? She wasn't telling the little girl that Ian was dead. There was always a chance, no matter how remote, that Jace would come. Except he probably thought she was the one who'd killed Ian and his friends. And how could she blame him if he did? Not that long ago, it's exactly what she would have done.

A key scraped in the lock. Daria huddled in a ball and Natasha steeled herself for whatever was on the other side of the door. She hoped it wasn't Lissette. She didn't think she could bear it if Daria realized that Lissette was the reason they were here.

But she wasn't that lucky. Lissette and another woman came through the door. Daria scrambled up excitedly. "Lissette! The bad men didn't get you!"

"Hi, honey," Lissette said, smiling like nothing was wrong. "No, they didn't get me."

"You look sort of different. Are you here to save us?"

Lissette went over to the little girl and gave her a quick hug before she inserted a key in the cuff around Daria's wrist. "I had a makeover—and of course I'm here to save you! It's all been a big misunderstanding, but you are perfectly fine now. I want you to go with my friend so you can have a makeover too. She's going to take you for a hot bath and some food, then we'll get you into a lovely dress so you can go to the New Year's Eve party."

Daria's eyes shone with excitement. "A party? Can I stay up late and everything?"

"I think you can, yes. But go with Ursula and she will get you fixed up."

Daria wrapped her arms around Lissette's torso, and Natasha wanted to growl. She bit the inside of her lip and didn't say anything, though her eyes stung and hatred grew in her heart. "Thank you, Lissette. Can Mommy come too?"

"Your mommy will see you later, okay? She's going to go to her own room and have a bath and dinner, all right? Then she has to get ready for the party too. It will be such a surprise when you see her later!"

Daria seemed uncertain, but she was nothing if not an extrovert at heart and she soon warmed to the idea. She had no notion that anyone would hurt her, especially since Lissette was clearly okay and wanted her to believe it was all a mistake. Lissette, who'd been in her life for as long as she could remember.

"I'll see you later, baby," Natasha said. "Remember to be good."

Natasha hated to tell her that, but she feared for the child's safety otherwise. She wanted to tell Daria to fight like hell if anyone tried to touch her inappropriately or tried to make her do something she didn't want to do, but she'd only scare the girl if she did that. And it might get her killed.

"Okay, Mommy."

Ursula took Daria by the hand and led her from the room. Natasha deflated. Lissette turned back to her, eyes hard. "I'm taking you to a room where you'll bathe and dress. If you try anything, Daria will die. Try to overpower me, she dies. Try to escape, she dies. Do anything but walk meekly to your room, and she dies. Do you understand?"

"Clearly."

Lissette came over to open the cuff. Natasha dreamed of wrapping the chain around her neck and pulling it tight, but fear for Daria stopped her. She wouldn't risk it. Not yet. She needed more information about where she was and what the security was like. Getting her and Daria out of there alive was her sole focus, and she wasn't going to let herself be defeated before it was over.

Every moment she was breathing, she had a chance. That was her plan for right now.

Keep breathing. Keep thinking. Find the weak spot and strike hard.

It was the only way to survive.

Chapter Fifty-Three

THE ROOM SHE WAS TAKEN TO WAS A STUDY IN MODERN medieval luxury, with silk wall hangings and a big fireplace where logs blazed in the hearth. There was a huge bed piled high with pillows and furs and draped with heavy curtains. The walls were stone, and the windows were broad and let in a lot of light.

A copper tub, filled with steaming water, sat beneath one window. Natasha thought about drowning Lissette in that tub, but there were two other women in the room who would either try to stop her or run for help.

"Take your clothes off and get in," Lissette said.

"So you can shove me under?"

"Not today, Calypso."

Natasha ground her teeth together, but the two women didn't blink. Either they knew who she was, or they didn't care. Lissette took a seat on a chair not too far from the tub and sighed.

"Clothes. Now."

"Or what?" Natasha said, folding her arms over her chest.

"Do you want to see Daria again or not?"

Natasha wanted to fly at this woman. Instead, she ripped her sweater over her head and dropped it. Then she took off her booties and leggings, her underwear, and stood stiffly.

"That's some tattoo," Lissette said, getting up to come over and look closely. "You never really let me see it before."

The mermaid perched on her arm from her inner elbow to her wrist, the tail curling halfway around her forearm. The thin scars of her cuts were worked into the design so that it looked like they were part of it. She'd always loved the tattoo, even though she'd known it was a liability for someone who needed to be unobtrusive. But how much more noticeable was it than her naked scars had been?

"You should step back, Lissette," she seethed. "The temptation to kill you is a bit much."

Lissette laughed, and hatred for the woman boiled in her belly.

"You could try. It wouldn't work out."

Natasha bared her teeth as the other woman returned to her seat. "Guess we'll never know, will we?"

Lissette shrugged as if bored. Natasha could hardly credit she was the same person who'd spent over two years in her employ.

"In the tub."

Natasha thought about refusing, but after long hours on the floor in the damp cellar, she was ready for the warmth of the water. She stepped into the tub and the two women came over to begin washing her skin and hair.

She hated every moment that they touched her, but she closed her eyes and didn't fight. What she needed was answers, not a fight. Not yet anyway.

"Where is Daria?"

"Don't worry, she's having a very good time with Ursula. She won't know anything's wrong. She thinks it's all a grand adventure."

Natasha's heart throbbed. "How can you be so uncaring about what happens to her? You've raised her as much as I have. She loves you."

She opened her eyes to look at the other woman. Lissette didn't even look uncomfortable. She merely sighed and shrugged. "I don't like kids much, to tell the truth. I'll grant you that Daria is smart and much more interesting than I expected, especially as she's gotten older, but a job is a job. She's not even your kid, so why do *you* care so much?"

"Maybe I don't," Natasha said, taking a different path. What if she pretended like it didn't matter to her what they did with Daria? Maybe she'd learn something that could help her get them out, or maybe they'd lose interest in putting Daria in the auction.

Who are you kidding? They won't lose interest. She'll bring too much money.

Lissette laughed. Natasha was beginning to hate that laugh. "Oh, you definitely do. I saw you when Ian Black took us to his house, remember? You were overcome with emotion."

"I might have been faking it. Like you've clearly been faking everything about yourself. Were you even a nanny at all? Or was that just a very good fake?"

"Lissette Alarie was a nanny. I was not."

Natasha gritted her teeth. Of course. The Syndicate had been using Daria against her from the beginning. They wouldn't think twice about killing some poor girl and having one of their operatives assume her identity.

"And as for fakes, what about the proof of Ian's death,

hmm? You almost had us with that one. Until he showed up to collect me and the kid."

Way to go, Dax. His photo had been good enough to fool them, but it'd all been ruined when Ian appeared in the flesh. Lissette—or whatever her name was—would have seen him when she arrived in Maryland anyway, but maybe she'd have had a harder time getting a message out to whomever had helped her.

"How did you communicate with them from Ian's house?"

"One of the gate guards. Not everyone who works for Mr. Black wants to kiss his ass, you know."

"You sure know a lot for someone who was relegated to a fake nanny job for two and a half years," Natasha said with a sneer.

Lissette's eyes flashed. "Maybe it wouldn't have gone on quite that long if you'd handed your brother over like you were supposed to. Guess you failed that loyalty test though, didn't you?"

Anger and hurt swirled inside her. She'd only failed because Ian's people had caught her before she could deliver Nikolai into the Syndicate's hands. And thank God they had, really. Her brother was alive and happy, and she'd met the man she loved. Even if it had taken far too long to realize he was the one she was meant to be with.

Not that she'd ever see him again in this life, but if she could get out of here, she had a piece of him that would live on. And so long as she was breathing, there was a chance. For her, for Daria, and for the baby she carried.

"Maybe I did fail. But at least no one forced me to sit in the background and do something I despised for over two years, did they? Seems as if your worth to them isn't all that important."

Lissette shot to her feet, glaring. Her face was red and

her eyes narrowed. She'd always been so good at the blushing. It'd helped her seem shy or embarrassed, but maybe she simply couldn't control when she blushed. Maybe it was any strong emotion that made it happen.

Maybe it was anger. That would explain a lot of those shy moments. Pretending to be something she wasn't, wanting to break out of the role, and feeling trapped.

Natasha laughed. "Maybe they didn't trust me, but they certainly didn't think much of you, did they? Your job was to watch my kid, and to report on my personal life. Not very exciting."

Lissette prowled over to the tub. Natasha's pulse flared. Not from fear but from exhilaration. She'd gotten to this bitch and she loved it. She'd also figured out that no matter what Lissette said, she wasn't authorized to actually do anything. Someone wanted Natasha for himself. That's what Lissette had said.

Didn't mean the mystery man wasn't going to harm her, but it did mean that Lissette couldn't. Not yet anyway. Likely not at all if the way she clenched her fists in impotent fury was any indication.

"Go ahead and laugh, Calypso. You won't be laughing when you find out what's going to happen to you. I promise you that."

Chapter Fifty-Four

Security at Castle Himmel was tight, no doubt in response to the information Dax had planted that the event was meant to be a sting operation. Now Ian and his men had to intricately plan how and when to breach the fortress rather than storming in immediately and taking Natasha and Daria by force.

Which had him prowling like a tiger in a cage, scrubbing his hand through his hair and growling at anyone who got in his way.

He could see the damn castle from the window, and that didn't sit well with him at all. It squatted on a rocky outcrop at a bend in the river and commanded sweeping views of the snowy landscape in all directions. A full-on assault in broad daylight was not possible under those circumstances.

It had never been possible in all of Castle Himmel's history, which was why the castle had never been taken by enemy forces.

The castle was not technically in Vienna, but it was close enough that the kind of men who would attend could fly into Vienna's main or executive airports. A steady stream of limos had begun to move through the village where Ian and his men were holed up in a safe house that Finn MacDermott had scouted for his own team of three a few days ago.

They were currently waiting for information from someone Finn was paying on the inside. The longer they waited, the more impatient Ian became. It wasn't dark yet, but the sun was sinking in the sky and revelers were already shooting off fireworks from time to time.

Dax, Ty, Rascal, Jace, Brett, and Jared looked as grim as Ian felt. Fucking fireworks. They could mask gunfire or mimic it, and that wasn't what his team needed tonight of all nights.

The door opened and Finn strode in. His cheeks were flushed with exertion and his red hair stood up in places when he tore his knit cap off.

"She met me as planned," he said, and Ian breathed a sigh of relief. There'd been some question whether or not the woman, who worked in the kitchen when the Leones were in residence, would come through.

"And?" Ian demanded.

"There's only one child in the castle. A little girl of about six with dark hair."

"That's Daria," Ty said. "How is she? Did she say?"

Ian looked at the man, eyebrow raised. Ty was earnestly watching Finn. Waiting.

Ian squeezed Ty's shoulder as if to say *I feel you*.

Ty glanced over. "Sorry, boss."

Ian's throat was tight. "No, it's fine. Thank you for caring so much about her."

"Who couldn't care about that kid? She's fucking adorable," Ty said, his voice rough.

"She is. We're here to get her back."

Finn flopped into a seat and yawned. He'd been burning the midnight oil for days on this job, and he wasn't done yet. "She's okay. Katrina only saw her for the first time today. She was being treated like a little princess. There was a bath, and talk about the party tonight. Katrina served sandwiches and tea and observed the girl. She kept asking if her mother could join them, but the woman with her—Katrina thinks her name is Ursula—told her she'd see her mother later that evening at the party."

"The party," Ian growled. "Fucking hell."

"There aren't many guests at this one," Finn continued. "Katrina said it's a scaled down event from the norm. Not that I think she knows what they really do there, but she says there are fewer guests this time."

"Does she know how many women?"

Finn shook his head. "No. She thinks the parties are immoral bacchanalias, and that the women are sex workers brought in for the event. She doesn't want to know how many of those there are. She's also scandalized that a child is included, but she thinks she'll only be allowed at the start of the party and then sent to bed. She thinks the mother is probably a socialite, though she doesn't know who."

Finn took a piece of paper from his pocket and dropped it on the table. "The room where she served sandwiches. She believes it to be the room the little girl is staying in."

Dax took the paper and opened it. Then he compared it to the schematic of the castle. "There's a stairwell nearby. But this is only good if they don't move her."

"We'll use infrared cameras," Ian said. "We won't be able to pick out Natasha, but we can find the heat signature of a child."

Dax nodded. "We can do that."

Ian glanced at his watch. It was still about three hours until dark. The positives were they knew that Daria was there, which meant Natasha was most likely there as well. And they knew where Daria was for the moment.

Security was heavy, but his people were the best-trained and best-equipped in the business. And it was personal to them. They would storm the castle after dark like they were being sent in to depose a foreign head of state and take over a government.

Then they would locate Natasha and Daria, and get them the hell out.

Once Ian knew his girls were safe, he was hunting Szymon Gorecki and Lucienne Vernier down. If they weren't at the castle, he'd find them eventually. And when he did, he was going to make them pay for every moment of fear and pain they'd ever put his family through.

Chapter Fifty-Five

AFTER THE WOMEN FINISHED BATHING NATASHA, THEY dried and styled her hair, applied makeup, and helped her into a gorgeous, figure-hugging red dress that sparkled with tiny crystals. There was a slit cut up to her thigh, and narrow straps that held up the cinched bodice. They buckled four-inch heels onto her feet and gave her a white fur stole to put around her shoulders.

She wrapped herself in it, trying to drape it to cover her tattoo. She only partially succeeded.

Inside, she seethed. She'd accepted the attention without a word. She hadn't been silent at first, though. She'd pelted the women with questions after Lissette was gone, but they pretended she wasn't there and only spoke to each other. And only when necessary.

It was dusk when they left and locked the door behind them. Natasha explored the room, checking for secret doors set into the walls. It wasn't an impossibility in a castle, but there weren't any. She went over to the windows and looked out again. She was on a high floor, and there was nothing but sheer wall beneath her. Even if she wasn't wearing an evening dress and heels, she couldn't scale that wall without equipment.

And she didn't have any.

She could see two towers at what she assumed was a gate. A car came through and disappeared again, hidden by the structure. A round of fireworks burst into the sky and she jumped at the sudden bang. It was too much like gunfire. Every time she heard the sound, her hopes were raised that maybe Jace was coming to her rescue.

Behind her, the door opened and she whirled. A man walked in and shut the door behind him. He was dressed in a tuxedo, his dark hair slicked back, his expression filled with arrogance—and she knew exactly who he was.

She also knew the last time she'd seen him.

"Ah yes, red is so much nicer on you than white. And that mermaid—marvelous."

"What do you want?" she growled.

He sauntered into the room, hitching a thumb over his shoulder as he got closer. "There are armed security guards outside. If I make the slightest unusual sound— such as if you were to twist my arm like you did in Venice —they'll come through that door. And they won't be nice to you when they do."

"I'm sorry I didn't break your arm when I had the chance," she snapped.

"It's a good thing you didn't," Tommaso Leone said. "I would not have been as merciful with you as I am now being."

"You have my daughter. How is that merciful?"

His dark eyes sparked. They were cruel eyes. "She is not dead. I'd say that's very merciful."

Natasha seethed. Anger was a living thing inside her, but she knew she had to be careful. One wrong word. One wrong move. He would hurt Daria. She couldn't let that happen. She'd play along with him as long as she had to.

Do what he wanted. Whatever he wanted. Anything to buy time.

"Let her go. She has nothing to do with what I did to you."

"You know I can't do that. It's not how we work, is it? You've been a bad girl, Calypso. And not just to me." He stopped only inches away and took her chin in his fingers. He was not tender about it, either. "You've betrayed us all with that man. You told him things you should not. You gave yourself to him." His gaze dropped to her belly for a moment. "And you carry his child. *Tsk, tsk.*"

"That's not Daria's fault." There was a note of desperation in her voice. She hated it, and yet she would do anything to get this man to release her child.

He put a hand on her breast through the bodice and squeezed. "It could have been mine, you know. I would have treated you so well. Like a queen. Instead, you whored yourself to Ian Black."

There was nothing she could say. He would not appreciate if she disagreed with him, so she didn't. Part of her wanted to show him that he had a false sense of security with his men on the other side of the door, but she couldn't take the chance. If she killed him—and she could do it without letting him call for help or cry out—she still had to get past the men watching the room. That would be harder, and there'd be more of a chance she'd get caught.

"Nothing to say?" he asked, his cruel eyes studying her.

"What do you want me to say? That I made a mistake. That I should have chosen you instead of him? Because I should have. It's obvious. It's also obvious that I can't change what happened, so I don't know what you want me to do."

He seemed to consider it. "Beg."

She blinked. Then she dropped to her knees, which wasn't easy in the red dress, but she managed it. Tommaso let his gaze linger on the gap between the stiff bodice and her breasts. He repulsed her, and yet she wouldn't let it show.

"I'm begging you, Mr. Leone. Let my daughter go. I'll do whatever you want. However you want. As *often* as you want. Just let her go."

He didn't say anything as he watched her with narrowed eyes. Then he threw his head back and laughed.

The sound startled her. Eventually, he stopped laughing and speared her with a glare.

"Sorry, not good enough. You're damaged goods, Calypso. You were so strong and beautiful, you know. The legendary assassin. I was there when you shot General Popov on that rooftop terrace in Moscow. And then, when his security detail had you cornered—you stepped onto the edge of the building and fell backward, arms spread like an angel. It was amazing."

That mission had been just a few months ago. She'd been wearing a small parachute because she'd gamed the scenarios and knew that jumping off the building was a very likely possibility.

"Then you know I'm very useful," she said, her mind flying through possible outcomes to this conversation. "I still can be."

"I'm not so sure. We can no longer trust you, and that's a problem."

"You can trust me. Protect my daughter, and you'll have my unwavering loyalty."

"Will I? Because I know what you can do, Calypso. I've seen it with my own eyes. If you think you can turn on me, you will. Besides, it wouldn't send a very strong message to let you live. Others might begin to think they can disobey orders and get away with it."

"Why am I here then? Why not just kill me and be done with it?"

He stared down at her, his gaze dropping to her breasts again. "Because I can think of more interesting things to do with you. By the time I'm through with you, no one will ever disobey my orders. Now get up, Calypso. It's time to go and watch your daughter be sold to the highest bidder."

Chapter Fifty-Six

IT WAS FUCKING COLD AS IAN AND HIS MEN SCALED THE side of a cliff to reach the outer wall of Castle Himmel. His hands were frozen, his face was numb, and he'd already scraped a knee in the process.

They'd discussed and discarded scenarios until all that'd been left was climbing the rock face. Entry to the castle was tightly controlled tonight, and trying to pass as tradesmen, lost tourists, or last minute revelers wasn't going to work. Likewise, sneaking inside in the belly of a delivery van wasn't going to happen either. All deliveries were cut off as soon as it got dark.

The only way in was straight up.

When they reached the top of the wall, Jace lifted himself to look over it. Then he motioned to his teammates. Ian, Brett, Ty, Dax, Colt, and Jared finished the climb and vaulted over the wall. Finn and Rascal were in vans at the scenic overlook halfway up the mountain, waiting for the signal to head up so the team could make their escape once they'd rescued Natasha and Daria.

Once they were all on the ground and had stowed the ropes and gear, they moved toward the place in the wall where they'd been told there would be a door. When they flanked the door, Ian and Jace exchanged a look—and then Ian tapped in a serious of soft raps and scratches.

A second later, it opened. Jamie Hayes grinned at them. "Thought you'd never get here, boss."

"Have they started?" Ian asked as the men passed inside the inner wall of the fortress.

Jamie was dressed in a long black skirt with a black apron and a white button-down shirt with a bowtie. The uniform of a server. She looked cool, but he knew she was outraged by what was happening in the castle tonight.

"Soon. Daria might be first or she might be last. I couldn't get a clear answer on that. There are twelve girls, by the way. They're all young, though none as young as Daria. Sixteen to twenty, maybe."

"Jesus," Brett growled.

"Do you know where Natasha and Daria are?"

"Daria is where you were told. I haven't seen Natasha, but I know she's here. I overheard a couple of women talking about her. How they had to wash and dress her like she was some kind of queen."

Ian's gut squeezed. "Has she been hurt?"

"They didn't say so. Just that they gave her a bath while she traded insults with another woman that ended with that woman storming from the room. They were whispering back and forth pretty quickly. When they realized I was there, they shut up."

Ian felt light-headed for a moment. Relief that Natasha was alive. That he had a chance to find her and tell her what she meant to him.

"This whole event feels more wrong than usual," Jamie

continued. "Like it's not quite what they usually do, you know? It's normally about the money and getting the buyers gone as soon as they collect their prizes, but tonight they're supposed to stay. And they're being encouraged to, uh, share with each other. Whenever and however. They're also being told there's something special going to happen at midnight."

Ian's head wanted to explode. "That's not the norm at all. What the fuck is Tommaso doing? Is his father around?"

"No sign of him. It's just Tommaso."

"Lissette and Nowak?" He used those names since Jamie hadn't yet been briefed about their real identities. She'd already been in the village with Finn's team when they'd learned the truth, and then she'd been getting herself hired for the castle serving staff for tonight. This was the first time any of them had spoken to her in days.

"They're with Tommaso most of the time. It's almost like they're a part of his decisions instead of the hired help. But I might be reading too much into it."

Jamie stopped at a door and unlocked it. They passed into a darkened hall one by one. Dax took something from his backpack and handed it to Jamie. "Your comm link."

"Thanks," she said, inserting it in her ear. "I've felt naked without it. I've gotta get back to the kitchen and start serving some special drinks to security, if you know what I mean. Let me know what's going on."

"Let us know if you see Natasha or Daria anywhere."

"Copy that," Jamie said. "Good luck and happy hunting."

"All right, gentlemen," Ian said after Jamie disappeared down the corridor. "Let's go and fuck this place up."

"Copy that," everyone replied.

It took a few minutes to reach the tower where Daria's

room was. They were still about two floors away when the sound of cheering reached their ears. Jamie's voice came through the comm link a minute later. She sounded out of breath, as if she'd been running.

"They've started. It's Daria on stage—and the bidding just opened at half a million."

Chapter Fifty-Seven

IT WAS A NIGHTMARE. HER WORST NIGHTMARE COME TRUE.

Natasha stood in the wings, held tightly in a man's grip, a needle poised at her jugular as she watched her sweet little girl standing on a stage as men cheered and bid money to own her. Not just own her, but abuse her.

And there was nothing she could do except watch in horror.

Daria had been so excited to see her when she'd arrived with Tommaso before he'd gone to sit at his table. Lissette had been standing with Daria like everything was normal, hand on her shoulder, grinning like an evil fiend while Natasha had to pretend everything was okay for Daria's sake. She'd asked herself why she didn't take her chances and do something, but she couldn't bear for her daughter to see what would happen when she did. Even if she succeeded, they would kill her—and they'd do it in front of Daria.

It didn't matter that Daria's life was about to change—and not in a good way—Natasha had to preserve her daughter's innocence about the situation as long as she could. Because she still believed she would get a chance to act. Believed it with her entire being.

Daria stood on the stage with Lissette, her pigtails swinging as she looked at the men below her. Lissette whispered something to her and Daria broke out in song. Natasha's eyes flooded. Daria thought she was at a party and everything was supposed to be fun. Lissette turned to shoot Natasha a smirk, and hatred scoured her soul.

"That kid is your weakness, you know that? You had what it took to be great if not for her," Pluto said in her ear as he held the poison to her throat. Julian Nowak was the name she knew because Ian had told her, but that was only an alias. Still, it was more than she'd known before.

"Fuck you," she spat.

"Careful, Calypso. Do you want to die so soon? Be a good girl, and maybe Tommaso will let you live as his sex slave for a while." He licked the side of her face. "Or maybe he'll let you be mine. He's angry enough with you that he might."

The idea of having sex with any man but Ian made her want to heave. She'd do it though. She'd do what it took to survive another day. And then she'd kill them all if she could.

"Why did you send me to kill Ian Black? What was the point if it was all leading to this anyway?"

"Wasn't my idea, but maybe you shouldn't have humiliated Tommaso at Black's party in Venice. You damn near broke his wrist—and then you spent the night fucking Black and got yourself pregnant."

"First, I didn't know he was the one who thought he could put his hand on my ass and tell me he wanted to do dirty things to me. And second, how did he even know it was me? I was in disguise."

"But you were being followed by then. Everywhere.

You weren't disguised to me because I'd been watching you, and I told Tommaso." Pluto snickered in her ear. "You didn't even know I was at the party, did you?"

Her heart throbbed. She sniffed back tears, trying to keep her vision clear so she could see Daria. And so she could act when she got the chance. "No."

"Of course not. You were too busy trying to get laid."

"If that's what you think."

"Then why go?"

Because he kissed me and I had to know why. She didn't say that, though.

"Maybe because Ian wanted to trust me, and I was trying to get information. Did you ever think of that?"

"I might have if you'd ever told me about your meetings. But you didn't, did you?"

"I didn't think it was relevant until I had something."

Pluto laughed softly in her ear. "Such bullshit, Calypso. Even now you try to play me. But it's too late. You were sent to kill him and you didn't. You tried to fake it, though. Went over to his side and tried to play me."

Her eyes stung. Daria was still singing, and the men were lifting paddles to place their bids. Not all of them. Just the ones who sexualized children. It was too much to hope one of them was horrified and only trying to help.

"It was never about me doing the job," she growled. "It was about punishing me for stepping out of line."

"Very true. This—tonight—was always going to happen. From the moment you humiliated a Syndicate boss, you were marked for death. And your family along with you."

"Stupid reason to kill one of your best assassins," she said, her throat tight.

"Maybe so, but—"

The lights went out, plunging the room into darkness. An angry murmur rippled through the crowd.

Natasha stilled, listening hard. Pluto had stiffened. He too was listening. Hope made her heart beat too loud and she couldn't hear anything beyond the blood rushing through her ears.

Cell phones had been forbidden in the room so there were no screens coming to life. No phone flashlights.

The doors at the back of the room burst open and light beams swept across the crowd as the sound of booted footsteps echoed.

"Nobody fucking move," a man shouted.

Jace?

Natasha didn't dare move. She didn't feel the needle at her neck anymore, but that didn't mean he didn't have it.

"Time to say goodbye." It was Pluto's voice in her ear.

His grip on her tightened—but instead of shoving a needle into her, he dragged her in the opposite direction of the disturbance.

"Szymon," a voice hissed.

"Over here," Pluto hissed back. "Hurry the fuck up."

Szymon?

Natasha smelled Lissette before she saw a shape. Her scent today had been flowery and spicy. Natasha didn't know the exact perfume, but she recognized the scent.

"Mommy?"

"Shut up," Lissette hissed as they reached Szymon and Natasha.

Relief flooded her nonetheless. "I'm here, baby," she whispered. And then she decided to take a chance as Szymon and Lissette whispered back and forth about getting away and taking her and Daria as insurance.

She bent as low as she could and whispered in rapid Russian, praying that Daria understood the words. "As soon as you can, run to those flashlights. Lissette isn't our friend anymore, baby. Just run."

There was a chance Szymon would understand, but she didn't think Lissette would. And if she did, well, the plan would go nowhere because Lissette would hold on tight.

Natasha held her breath for a split second as Szymon jerked her back, away from Daria. And then Lissette cried out as Daria took off at a run.

Natasha's knees turned to jelly, but Daria kept running and Lissette didn't go after her. She still had to face Szymon's anger as he shoved her toward the door that Lissette threw open.

"Fucking bitch," Lissette hissed as Natasha tumbled through the door, barely keeping her feet.

These damned shoes...

"Kill her," Lissette said. "Just kill her and let's get out of here. Or give me the syringe and I'll do it. That brat smashed her foot down on my instep—because this bitch told her to!"

"Shut up, Lucienne," Szymon grated. "If that squad of commandos is here for her, then she's our insurance. Stop being dramatic and get moving."

Szymon dragged her down the corridor, away from the room where the auction had been taking place. Lissette/Lucienne hooked an arm through Natasha's and helped drag her by forcing her to move faster than she could have with four-inch heels impeding her progress.

"I don't know who that is out there," Lissette/Lucienne said, "but they aren't here for *you*. You're still going to die."

They rounded a corner—and came face to face with three bright lights that shone in their faces and made them throw their hands in front of their eyes.

"Want to bet?" a familiar voice grated.

Chapter Fifty-Eight

Szymon Gorecki and Lucienne Vernier stood on either side of Natasha. Szymon started to move, but Ian fired and Szymon went down. He would not be getting up again.

Lucienne cried out as she dropped to her knees beside her husband. Natasha stumbled toward him and he dropped the light just enough so that she could see him better.

Maybe not the best plan because she halted, her eyes widening. "Is it really you? I thought I was hearing things."

"It's me, Tasha," he said, his voice tight with emotion.

"Oh my God." She put her hand to her mouth, choking back a sob. "They told me you were dead."

She wobbled then and Ian took a step toward her.

"No!" Lucienne yelled, launching herself at Natasha from behind. Ian caught a glimpse of something silver glinting in the light. He didn't know what she had, but he had an idea. And he had to stop her at all costs.

"Tasha, move!"

His shot was blocked by her body. Ty and Colt didn't have a clear shot either because neither of them fired.

Ian sprinted toward Natasha, intent on pushing her out of the way. If he got a clear shot then, he'd fire. And if he didn't, then he'd take the brunt of Lucienne's attack. Even if it meant his life.

Time slowed. Natasha turned her head toward Lucienne, as if just realizing the woman was coming after her. Before Ian could close the distance, he saw her entire body stiffen—

And then something happened. The shaky, frightened woman in the tight red dress became another person entirely. She became Calypso. She was liquid grace as she shifted to the side just in time to throw off Lucienne's center of gravity. Lucienne hit the ground, then scrambled to turn and lunge again.

But Calypso was already in motion. She pivoted like a bullfighter swirling a cape at an angry bull, her colorful tattoo catching the light as she moved. She caught Lucienne from behind and shifted left. Ian, Ty, and Colt saw everything in the lights they held, but they would never be able to fully describe how Natasha moved.

Lucienne cried out in agony as her arm snapped. The syringe hit the ground and rolled away. Calypso whirled like a ballerina—and another arm snapped. Lucienne started to beg for her life then.

Natasha stopped in mid-motion, Lucienne's head wrapped in her arms. Tears rolled down the woman's face as she blubbered her pleas.

There was a knot in Ian's throat as the woman he loved met his gaze. Her eyes were hazel. Her hair was blond, long where it'd fallen from the french twist they'd put it in. Her tattoo stood out against her pale skin. This was the real Natasha Oliver, aka Orlova, aka Calypso. She was mighty and fierce and he loved her utterly.

"You wish me to spare you?" she hissed, dropping her attention to Lucienne again.

"Yes, please. I didn't want to—they made me—I would never hurt Daria, I swear it. Please, please. I'll tell you anything you want to know. I'll cooperate."

"Do you know what I can't forget?" Natasha said, ignoring Lucienne's words. "The way you told me that even if some sick, twisted man abused her innocence, she would still be alive. After everything else you did, I might have forgiven you if you'd showed even a shred of compassion for my daughter."

"I had to do it," Lucienne cried. "I had to. They would have killed me."

"Yes, I know," Natasha replied, her voice almost tender. "They would have killed you. For years, I did everything I could to protect my child. Not because they might kill me, but because they might kill her if I did not. As we both know, I didn't do a perfect job of it. But I never put myself first. Do you understand what I'm telling you?"

"Holy shit," Ty whispered behind him. "I never thought of it like that."

"I had to," Lucienne wailed. "They made me, they made me."

"You made your choice, Lissette," Natasha said. "And I've made mine. For Daria."

In a move that would have been beautiful if not for the result, the assassin Calypso snapped the neck of her former nanny. She didn't drop her to the ground though. She let her down gently, then dropped to her knees beside her and wept for the woman she'd thought Lucienne Vernier had been. A woman who'd shared her life for over two years, and who her child had loved. A woman who wasn't real.

Ian sank beside Natasha and wrapped an arm around her shoulders. "We have to go, angel. We can't stay. The *Polizei* are on the way. There will be questions we don't want to answer."

She looked up at him, her face tear-streaked. "Daria is okay?"

He skimmed his fingers over her cheek. "She's with Jace. She's perfectly fine."

"He came too?"

"We all did," Ty said gruffly, stepping from the shadows.

Natasha smiled at him. "Ty the Terrible. I've got a syringe over here somewhere if you'd like to confiscate it."

"Already on it, Boss Lady."

"Boss Lady?" she asked, turning back to Ian.

He shrugged. "I think it's inevitable, don't you?"

And then, because he couldn't wait another second, he kissed her.

Chapter Fifty-Nine

IAN'S PLANE WAS A WELCOME RETREAT AFTER THE HELL OF the last couple of days. Natasha lay in the bed in the back of the plane, Daria in her arms, and stared at the ceiling after her daughter fell asleep. Jared had checked them both out and they were physically unharmed.

Natasha didn't know about how Daria was going to be mentally, though. They'd had to have a difficult conversation about adults and how sometimes people you thought were your friends were really your enemies.

Daria had cried, but she was also remarkably resilient. She said that Lissette had been mean sometimes, and that she didn't always like her. It made Natasha wish she'd kept Lissette—Lucienne—alive a while longer so she could've made her suffer some more.

She worried that Daria would have trouble trusting anyone in the future, but the only thing she could do about that was shower her daughter with love and always be the person she *could* trust.

Ian stepped into the cabin and their eyes met. Her heart flooded with so many emotions. Love, happiness, relief, desire, gratitude—the list went on and on. Carefully, she disentangled herself from Daria and stood. She was no longer wearing the red dress. Ian had produced a sweatshirt, leggings, and a thick pair of socks for her to change into courtesy of Mandy Parker, who she'd just met tonight. No shoes, but it was better than the four-inch torture devices she'd worn at Tommaso Leone's fortress.

She went into Ian's arms and hugged him tight. He pressed a kiss to the top of her head, and she squeezed him tighter. Her eyes flooded with hot tears. She'd thought she'd lost him. She'd thought she was doomed, and Daria with her, and all the time he'd been alive and he'd been coming for her.

"You found us," she said against his chest, her eyes blurry.

"I will always find you, Tasha. Because I'll always look for you. Wherever you go, whatever trail you take, I'll be searching for you."

She snorted because he said that last bit in song. And it sounded like a particularly stalkery song by a band called The Police. "You're too much, Ian Black."

"Too much what? Too much awesomeness? Too much manly man? Too much of an arrogant jerk?"

"All the above." She curled her fists in his shirt and tipped her head back to look up at him. His eyes were turquoise. "You're showing me your real eyes. I love them, by the way."

He smiled down at her. "You sure they're the real ones?"

"I'm sure." She ran her fingers along his jaw and he closed his eyes, shuddering at her touch.

Then his eyes snapped open and he turned her palm so he could kiss it. "You know me better than anyone. I thought I'd never find someone like you, but I did. And when you said you had that secret account and you wanted online access, I knew you were going to try to leave me. I wanted to howl, Natasha. Just fucking howl. Then Lucienne drugged us and took you, and I thought my world was at an end."

Her throat ached. There was so much in that statement that she needed to process. "I didn't want to leave you. I wanted to protect Daria from the Syndicate. That's all it was ever about."

"I know." He kissed her palm again, then tipped her chin up and kissed her on the mouth. Not a hot kiss, but a sweet one. Didn't matter because it made her wet anyway. He could make her want him with the slightest touch. Probably always would.

"We still aren't safe, Ian. Tommaso Leone is still out there. Still angry that I chose you over him in Venice." She told him everything that Pluto had said to her about that night. "He wants revenge. I can't fathom it, but that's what he was angry about when he came to see me."

Ian's expression grew hard. Dangerous. "Tommaso Leone isn't getting revenge on anyone."

She searched his gaze, her heart racing. "How can you say that? What do you know that you aren't telling me?"

"Come with me." He took her hand and led her toward the door. She hesitated, throwing her gaze at where Daria lay curled on the bed.

"She'll be fine, Tasha. We're close if she needs us."

She took a deep breath and followed him. Ty was sitting in a chair near the door to the cabin. "Can you keep an eye on Daria while I take Natasha to the command center?" Ian asked.

"You got it, boss." He steered his gaze to Natasha. "Just in case you had any doubts, I'm Team Natasha now."

Her grin shook at the corners. Was this what it felt like

to belong with people who genuinely had your back? Maybe. It would take her time to get used to it, to stop looking for the catch, but she would. Eventually.

"And I'm Team Ty. Because you'll always have Ian's back, no matter what, and that means a lot to me."

He nodded. "I'll have your back, too. Just so you know."

She reached out and patted his shoulder as they walked by because she couldn't trust herself to speak. Ian squeezed her hand. "You okay?"

She sniffled. "Yes. Just… overwhelmed."

He smiled down at her. "It's only going to get better from here."

Then he swung the door to the command center open and they walked inside. Jace stood immediately and came to where she stood. He loomed over her, just like he'd always loomed over her when they'd been children. "Jesus, Tash—I'm sorry."

She blinked. "Why are you sorry? I'm the one who shot you. I shot Colt too. And I kidnapped Angie and Maddy. You don't have anything to apologize for."

He threw his arms around her and hugged her hard, and she started to cry. "Dammit," she whispered. "After all the work those two silent bitches did to fix my makeup, too."

Jace laughed as he let her go. He still held her by the shoulders. "I'm sorry I didn't try harder to understand what you were going through. I should have known there was something driving you. Something besides hate and anger."

"That was a factor, Nicky. I'm sorry, I mean Jace. I was angry, and I thought I hated you for leaving me in that place. I didn't know you thought I was dead."

"I heard about the firing squad through channels.

They said it was you, Mom, and Dad along with the rest of the 'traitors' who were shot that day. I believed it, but maybe I shouldn't have. I also believed you were irredeemable when we met again, and I'm ashamed of that."

"How could you know? I was pretty pissed at you, and I nearly took you in. Would have done it if your boys hadn't swooped in to save you."

"Do you know who put a price on my head?"

Ian had asked her at the time and she'd refused to share a name. But the truth was that she hadn't known the answer. "I don't. All I know is that it came from somewhere in the FSB. They wanted you back. I realize now that they sent me because they thought we were still connected somehow." She frowned. "Lissette said she recognized that you were my brother. I don't know who she might have told."

He nodded. "It's okay. We'll deal with it."

"We're monitoring channels," Ian said. "If the news is out there, we'll find it and we'll do something about it."

Natasha stood on tiptoe and kissed Jace's cheek. It felt good to be able to do that again. "I want you to be an uncle to Daria. I want her to know you that way. And Maddy, too. Whenever you're ready. It'll take time to get her accustomed to these changes, but I want a family for her."

He grinned. His eyes were suspiciously shiny. "Yeah, I'd like that. But just so you know, she has a lot of uncles in here. Ty would walk across hot coals for that little girl. Any of us would."

"You don't have to walk across hot coals. You risked your lives for her tonight. I can never repay you."

"We didn't just risk our lives for her," Colt said, standing up so she could see him. He looked fierce. "We did it for you, too. Because Ian asked us to. You're one of us now."

"Thank you. I won't let you down. I swear it."

Ian tugged her to where Dax was and made her sit. "We know you won't, kitten." He kissed the top of her head. "Show her, Dax."

Dax pulled up a breaking news site. Natasha leaned forward and started to read.

ITALIAN BILLIONAIRE'S SON AT CENTER OF CHILD TRAFFICKING SCHEME

Tonight the Austrian police and Interpol raided Castle Himmel, near Vienna, and made several arrests. They'd received an anonymous tip earlier in the day that underage girls were being sold as sex slaves. Twelve girls were rescued from the castle and will be returned to their families. Tommaso Leone, the son of Italian plastics billionaire Ennio Leone, was arrested for conspiracy to traffic children. The elder Leone, when reached for comment, replied that his son could rot in hell for all he cared. Mr. Leone has pledged twenty million euro toward the prevention of human trafficking and states that he will contribute more in future.

Two bodies were also found at Castle Himmel. It's rumored that the pair were co-conspirators with Tommaso Leone, and that he killed them out of fear they would expose his involvement...

NATASHA REARED back in her seat. "How in hell did you make that happen?" she asked Ian.

He laughed. "I told you I have connections. But I didn't have anything to do with Ennio. That's all him. He knows a public relations nightmare when he sees one."

She considered it. "Ennio Leone struck me as a shrewd businessman the one time I met him. Tommaso, on the other hand, was always reputed to be a loose cannon."

"A loose cannon who was somehow obsessed with you. I don't know how or when that began, or how he got your handler to do his bidding, but I suspect Tommaso used his father's authority to get things done. Ennio won't make the mistake of letting that happen again."

It made sense. And yet… "That doesn't mean we're clear, Ian. They could still come for us."

"They aren't coming for any of us, babe. I told you I'd burn the whole fucking thing to the ground to protect you and Daria. There are people who'd rather I didn't." He laughed. "Too many secrets that could be exposed, too many lives ruined, and for what? To eradicate one woman and her child simply because someone's manhood was insulted? Not happening."

Natasha didn't dare to hope—but it grew like a tiny flame in her soul anyway. "What about you? You were on the list, too."

"That was Tommaso's idea. It wasn't an authorized or sanctioned operation within the Syndicate ranks, according to them. That could be a lie, but it'd be too dangerous to come after me now. The people who need to know it, know it."

"But the photo Dax made… don't they think you're dead already?"

Dax laughed. "I attached a script designed to delete the photo after forty-eight hours. From everywhere. It's gone."

Natasha could only stare. "That's not possible."

Dax winked. "Not for ordinary mortals, maybe."

Jace laughed and slapped Dax on the arm. "You hang around long enough, Tasha, and you'll realize how genius this dude is."

Hang around? She didn't ever want to leave. "I can

never thank you enough for what you've done for me and Daria. All of you." Her voice got caught in her throat.

Ian put an arm around her and she leaned into his strength. "I don't know how many times I'm going to have to say this, but I'll keep saying it until you believe me. You're one of us and we take care of our own. Get used to it, kitten, because this is one crazy family you've joined. But you're safe with us. Nobody will ever ask you to do something you don't want to do, and nobody will ever threaten you if you don't do it."

She turned in his embrace and put her arms around him. Happiness filled her. So much happiness. It was a warm, glowing thing in her soul. Whenever she'd felt it before now, she'd always squashed it, afraid that someone would take it away like they had so many times in the past. She'd thought she didn't deserve to be happy. But she was beginning to believe.

"I love you, Ian Black. For so many reasons, but most of all because you make me believe."

He smiled down at her. "Believe what?"

She shrugged. "That's it. Just believe."

He cupped her face in his hands, his thumbs caressing her skin. She'd put her heart on the line, but she wasn't worried. His next words proved why she didn't need to be.

"For the record, I'm crazy about you. You make me believe too. Believe that I don't have to go through this life alone, that I'm not *only* what I do, and that I can still make a difference without feeling guilty because I can't save everyone. I love you, Natasha. I can't wait to welcome our child into the world, and I can't wait to be a dad to Daria. I told you that you were mine, and I meant it—but I realize it's only proper to give you the choice."

He dropped to one knee and she started to laugh and sob at the same time. There was a chorus of *awwww* from the command center, and at least one "Welcome to the dark side, my friend." She didn't know who said it because all she could see was Ian. His dark hair with the sprinkling of silver, his turquoise eyes, and the love that shone from them. For her.

"I don't have a ring because I honestly wasn't planning to do this here with all these nosy people watching—but will you marry me, Natasha?"

Everyone was holding his or her breath. That was the only reason there was no sound other than the plane's engines droning. But Natasha couldn't look at any of them. All she could do was look at the man she loved with every last breath in her body.

"Yes. A million times, yes."

Ian surged to his feet and swept her in his arms, kissing her while everyone cheered. When he finally put her down, Ty was standing in the entrance to the command center, looking confused. "What did I miss?"

"Ian proposed to my sister," Jace said, grinning happily. He kissed her on the cheek even though Ian was still holding her.

"Aw, man, I missed *that?*"

"You won't miss the wedding though," Ian said. "We're doing it soon, though I guess I have to let the future Mrs. Black decide where and when and what she wants for her big day."

Natasha cupped his cheek and kissed him. "All I want is you." Then she gazed at the people in the command center. Her new BDI family. "And all of you, too. I don't care what else we do, so long as our friends and family are with us."

"My thoughts exactly," Ian murmured against her cheek. "God, I love you."

"I love you. So much."

"That makes me happier than you know…. Guess we'd better go tell our daughter the good news, huh?"

"Yes, I think we should."

Ian didn't put her down as they headed for the back of the plane. Natasha looped her arms around his neck and laid her head against his shoulder, sighing.

It had been a long journey, but she was finally home.

Epilogue

WHAT A DIFFERENCE A COUPLE OF MONTHS MADE. IT WAS the last week in February, it was still somewhat cold out—okay, there was snow on the ground—and Ian was getting married.

Outside.

The minister was none other than General John Mendez, dressed in his finest Army dress uniform. He'd ribbed Ian for precisely one minute before clapping him on the back and congratulating him on his impending fatherhood. That had been a month ago, once Natasha decided when and where she wanted to get married, and Ian had decided that the best person to marry them was the HOT commander.

He admired Mendez, respected him, and it appealed to his perverse sense of humor that the man who'd once been his enemy was now an important enough friend to perform his wedding. Mendez had said yes, of course.

The *when* was today, the last Saturday in February, and the *where* was his, Natasha, and Daria's house with the view of the Chesapeake Bay. Or, rather, their back yard with the view.

When Ian had mentioned the potential cold temperature, Natasha had said they could get tents and heaters. She'd been right, and they had.

When it'd started to snow two days ago, he'd told her they might have to move things inside. She'd said no way. And what Natasha wanted, Natasha got.

It was overcast, which meant the snow wasn't blinding, and the clouds looked as if they might drop even more snow on the event. The white tents were heated inside, and there was flooring set up so that people could walk comfortably without crunching in snow. There were enough round tables, set with white linens and white plates with silver accents, to seat everyone at BDI Headquarters, as well as some of the Hostile Operations Team people.

Natasha had decided, after much deliberation, that she was only getting married once in her life and she wanted a wedding to remember. He could deny her nothing.

"You ready for this?" Mendez asked as the appointed hour came and the string quartet that'd set up on a heated stage nearby began playing the wedding march.

"Past ready," Ian said, resisting the urge to straighten his bow tie. He was wearing a tuxedo and a long black coat, because Natasha had insisted that she wanted a winter wedding, and she didn't want anyone to be cold. Everyone was wearing coats and gloves, and there were heaters nearby to prevent anyone from getting too chilly, though they weren't near enough to melt the snow.

A path had been cleared down the aisle to the arbor draped in fairy lights where Ian and Mendez stood, and Daria appeared with a basket of deep purple flower petals. Where had Natasha found purple? It reminded him of her mask in Venice the night he'd fallen head over heels for her.

Because, yes, *that* was the moment he'd tumbled into something so much deeper than the desire he'd always felt for her. Hindsight was always 20/20.

Ian smiled at Daria and she smiled back. Then she began her walk up the aisle, sprinkling her petals as she glided toward him. The little girl was wearing a cream-colored coat with faux fur trim, a matching hat, gloves with faux fur around the wrists, and a dress with cream tights.

She'd had nightmares after they'd returned home, but she was such a sweet kid and so forgiving that she'd managed to move on from those more quickly than he would have thought possible. She'd had some trouble with Lissette's betrayal, and she'd wanted to know where Lissette had gone. Natasha had told her that Lissette was not coming back ever again. She'd said that Lissette had gone to heaven. Ian had asked Natasha about it later and she'd shrugged and told him that telling the child her nanny had gone to a bad place wasn't going to help her heal.

She'd been right, of course. They'd gotten a psychologist to spend some time with Daria, to listen to her talk about things she might not want to tell her mother or him. The woman had every confidence that Daria was going to be fine.

The music swelled and Natasha appeared with Jace at her side. Ian's heart thumped. She was beautiful. She wore a long, white velvet dress with a matching white cloak. The hood was trimmed in faux fur and draped artfully around her face. She wore white gloves and beneath her dress he got a peek at white Uggs as she moved up the aisle on Jace's arm.

Her brother beamed. Ian was relieved that the two of

them had started to repair their relationship, but he'd had to give Jace a stern speech when the man had attempted to work out just how and when Natasha had gotten pregnant.

It was Ty who'd figured it out in the end. "Venice," he'd said, his eyes wide. "The woman who made Tommaso Leone scream like a little girl—that was Natasha!"

Ian had rolled his eyes. "Honestly, I'm not sure you guys are worth what I pay you sometimes." He'd pointed his finger at them. "Not another word. That's the woman I love and I'm not talking about our private life with you."

That had been the last word said about any of it. Tommaso Leone wasn't going to be contracting hits on anyone ever again. He'd hanged himself in an Austrian prison while awaiting extradition to Italy. Ian figured that Ennio had had enough and sent someone to get the job done. Usurping Ennio's authority and colluding with Szymon and Lucienne was more than a top Syndicate boss could allow. Besides, the man had two other sons, though they were young, and he probably thought they'd be less trouble when the time came to pass on his empire.

Ennio hadn't communicated with Ian, but he'd sent a message through channels that basically said he considered any orders given by his son to be illegitimate. There'd been more words exchanged, indirectly of course, but ultimately Natasha and Daria were safe from further harm. The assassin Calypso was dead and gone.

In her place, the warrior goddess Athena would rise from the ashes to work by his side whenever she was needed. She liked her new code name very much, and that pleased him.

The closer Natasha got, the more Ian's heart thumped. God, he loved her. So damn much. And he'd almost lost her. He sometimes woke up at night thinking about how close it'd been.

But then he recalled the utter beauty of her when she'd transformed into Calypso to deal with Lucienne Vernier. She'd never been helpless. She still wasn't.

He wasn't about to let her go into battle pregnant, but he knew she could if she had to. She was barely starting to show now, but even if she had a basketball belly, she'd be able to take care of herself. His Athena was more than capable.

Jace stopped and Mendez asked who gave this woman in marriage. Jace replied that he did. It was more traditional than Ian would have thought she'd want, but he also knew his bride. She didn't need anyone to take care of her, but she liked it when she got to make the choice—and she'd chosen to have her brother give her away because it would please them both.

Jace put her hand into Ian's and he felt the lightning down to his toes. She smiled at him.

"Hello, kitten," he said softly. "You look beautiful."

"And you look devilishly handsome, Mr. Black."

"Dearly beloved," Mendez began, and Ian couldn't stop the grin that spread across his face. Damn, life was crazy good right now. And he was happy. More than happy.

Content. Things he'd never thought he would be.

The ceremony was short and sweet. Natasha said her vows and placed a ring on his finger. Mendez turned to him and asked him to repeat a bunch of stuff that Ian only half heard.

Then the big moment came.

"Do you take this woman to be your lawfully wedded wife?" Mendez asked.

"I do," Ian said. "With all my heart and with everything I am."

Ian slipped the ring on Natasha's finger as she sniffled and tried not to cry.

"You may kiss the bride."

Ian pulled her into his arms and tipped her chin up with a finger. Then he pressed his mouth softly to hers, intent on doing this right. He'd eat her up later, but right now he intended to be well-behaved.

He heard cheering in the background and his bride shivered in his arms. He tightened his hold on her for a brief moment, but reminded himself it was long hours until the day was over, and that she deserved this day. He gently broke the kiss.

"You wanted to pick me up and take me to bed, didn't you?" she whispered.

He arched an eyebrow. "That obvious?"

"It is to me."

He grinned. "Let's hope it's only obvious to you."

She put an arm in his and they turned to greet the world as Mr. & Mrs. Black. Two hearts beating as one. Two broken souls healed because they'd found each other. Two futures that were no longer empty and bleak.

Against all odds he'd found her. His sweet, tender, dangerous wife.

The only woman in the world for him.

Bonus Epilogue

NATASHA HAD MUCH TO LEARN ABOUT BEING PREGNANT, BUT many of the things she'd read simply didn't happen to her. After the initial nausea was taken care of, she sailed through the months, her baby's checkups perfectly normal and routine. She still exercised, which the doctor told her was very good—though no more running like her hair was on fire for a while—and she ate a healthy diet. She also did not grow very big. Though the baby was due next month, her belly wasn't huge. She had a belly finally, and people knew she was pregnant, but they typically thought she wasn't due for months.

Today was her baby shower, a thing she'd read up on when Maddy and Tallie had approached her about it because she wasn't very familiar with it. She'd said yes because of course she wanted to experience everything. She'd thrown herself into her American life, and she loved it. She would always be Russian too, but she could be both. Unlike her parents, she wasn't conflicted about it. But then she wasn't a spy either.

She worked at BDI, advising teams, supervising some

of the training, and teaching disguise techniques. She and Ian often had fun disguising themselves and blending in with the crowd in public venues where members of their team were supposed to find them. So far, it was Mr. & Mrs. Black in the winning column.

After the baby was born, she would do more. She was never going to be the type of woman who stayed home with the children all the time. She needed work, and she and Ian had discussed how best to provide that for her. She would take the baby to work with her because Ian was putting in a daycare facility. His employees were thrilled since many of his support staff were married and had children. Having onsite daycare would help everyone.

Ian had shaken his head and wondered aloud why the hell he hadn't thought of it before.

"Because it wasn't about to happen to you," she teased. "But now you have a baby on the way and you need daycare since you and your wife are going to split childcare duties."

He'd hugged her close, laughing. "I can't wait," he'd said, kissing her.

When it was time for the shower, Ian helped her into the big SUV he'd bought—because you needed a big vehicle with two children, apparently—and they drove over to Maddy and Jace's house. Daria was already there, helping her Aunt Maddy with decorations.

When they turned onto the street, Natasha gaped. "This can't be for us."

Ian looked as surprised as she felt. She knew that he'd agreed to go along because the women had asked him to come, but he hadn't expected anything more than a few ladies and some games. "Nah, surely a neighbor's having a party too."

But it wasn't a neighbor. It was all for them. Ian and

Natasha walked into Jace and Maddy's house and confronted a space teeming with men and women. Daria came running over and yelled "Surprise!" before wrapping them both in a hug.

"I'm... wow," Natasha said, unable to get anything out.

Maddy sashayed over with two fruity drinks in decorative glasses. "Non-alcoholic punch," she said. "There's no alcohol allowed at this party. We're all in the same boat together today."

"What have you done, Maddy?" Natasha whispered as she accepted the drink.

Maddy looped her arm through Natasha's. "My dear sister-in-law, this is a proper baby shower for the littlest Black. But don't you worry, the ladies are going to go into the family room and the men will head outside to cook dinner on the grill." She slanted a glance at Ian. "They might also have a bit of fun with your husband, I suspect."

"Damned straight," John Mendez said, wrapping an arm around a stunned Ian. "How you doing, Black? Ready for your baby shower?"

Ian's gaze roamed the room, taking in the grinning men from BDI and the ones from HOT that she recognized—and then he snorted. "Dang, you guys are going to roast my behind, aren't you?"

Natasha appreciated that he was careful with the language since Daria was there. There were other kids in the room, too, which meant lots of little ears to pick up bad words. Nobody wanted that.

"You have no idea, sweet cheeks," Mendez said gleefully. "After all the, uh, crap you've given us over the years? Yeah, buckle up, buttercup. We're about to have some fun."

Ian gave her a quick kiss on the cheek. "I think this is

about to be painful for me," he told her. "But you, Mrs. Black, are going to have a marvelous time."

And she did. The women retreated to the family room and Natasha was seated in a cushy chair where she opened gifts and ate lovely appetizers and played silly games such as trying to pick tiny safety pins out of rice, baby shower bingo, or trying to guess what baby item was inside each of ten plain paper bags. The women showered her with gifts for the baby, and the ones who were mothers gave advice about how to use the things she'd gotten. There was also a lot of serious talk about taking care of children, and about the men who shared the duties.

And there were children who interrupted, because moms have answers that dads don't, but Natasha didn't mind. She loved all of it.

Angie sat down beside her after the gifts and games were done and the women were talking in little groups of two or three. When Angie took her hand and squeezed, Natasha felt tears rising in her throat. Angie had warmed up to her over the months and the hostility had ceased, but she'd never touched Natasha. She hugged her friends and she touched their arms or hands, but she never did that with Natasha.

This was new, and it made Natasha emotional.

"I understand and I forgive you," Angie said. "I told you it would take me some time, and it has. But I wouldn't say the words if I didn't mean them."

"Thank you," Natasha replied. "It means a lot. For what it's worth, I don't like who I was back then. I'm ashamed of her."

Angie's eyes widened. "Ashamed? Honestly, I think you were amazing when I look back on it. A strong, badass woman doing what it took to survive and protect her vulnerable child." She dropped her gaze a moment. "I was, um, assaulted by a man. Once and briefly, but it took me months to stop being scared of my own shadow. Yet you were a badass bitch who kicked ass and took names."

Natasha could only stare. "I did what I had to do."

"I know," Angie said. "You didn't quit and you didn't shut down. I did for a while. It took Colt's love to bring me to my senses again."

Natasha squeezed back. "Listen, to come back from anything like that takes strength. You are strong and badass too, Angie Duchaine. I've seen that lead pipe in the case down in the Cove. That took a badass, you know. You survived and you *are* a warrior."

Angie laughed through the tears that had sprung to her eyes. "Flatterer."

Natasha laughed too. "Maybe, but it's true."

Angie hugged her then and the two of them cried a little. Maddy was there suddenly. "Hey, what's this? What are you two crying about? Did I mess up the charcuterie board? I told Jace that Americans put cheese and crackers and stuff on there too, but he insisted that charcuterie means meat in French and that's the only thing allowed. Darn him!"

Natasha and Angie broke apart, laughing. "Don't you mean a Shark Coochie board?" Angie asked.

Maddy giggled. "Obviously, I do."

Natasha got the joke because when she'd seen the Shark Coochie board advertised online, she'd had to ask Ian what the hell that meant. It was stupid funny now that she knew, and she laughed along with the other two.

Maddy perched beside them, her gaze sweeping the crowd of women. "I hope you enjoyed your shower, Natasha."

"I really did. Thank you so much."

"You still don't know if it's a boy or a girl, huh?"

Natasha shrugged. "No. Ian knows, but I told him not to tell me. I want to be surprised."

"Not me," Maddy said. "When I get pregnant, I want to know. I'm going to go crazy decorating the nursery."

"Of course you are," Angie said. "Look at this house and all you've done."

"It's beautiful," Natasha said. Maddy and Jace's house had belonged to her grandmother, who was in an assisted living facility now. It wasn't a huge house, but they'd added an addition and renovated to make it their own. It was cozy and felt like home.

Just like her home with Ian and Daria. It wasn't small, but there was heart in the home now. Daria's drawings were on the refrigerator, the furniture had been changed to things more comfortable and kid-friendly, and there was laughter. So much laughter.

When it was time to go home, Ian opened car doors for his two ladies and then got in the driver's seat.

"What did they do to you?" Natasha asked. She'd wanted to know but couldn't ask until they were alone.

Daria was in the back seat with her headphones on, singing to a kid's show that she watched on the television screen hanging from the center of the roof.

"They gave me a baby doll and a pack of diapers and timed me," he said with a shudder. "And that was the nicest thing they did."

Natasha laughed. "How did you do?"

"Uh, I have some things to learn."

"I think you're going to get plenty of practice. Don't worry, the next time it happens you'll ace the challenge."

He glanced at her. "The next time, Mrs. Black? Are you saying you want more babies with me?"

"I want everything with you, Ian."

He reached over and took her hand, kissing it reverently. "I love you, Natasha. You're the best thing that's ever happened to me."

"I love you, too. You saved me from myself."

"I think we saved each other, angel. Without you, I'd be a shell of what I am now."

She sniffled. "Stop saying such beautiful things to me. You know I cry at everything these days."

Stupid hormones.

"I'm never going to stop, Tasha. Loving you, saying beautiful things to you, worshipping the ground you walk on. Never."

They held hands on the center console for the rest of the ride home, then spent the evening with Daria, playing board games at the kitchen island and chatting about everything and anything as a family. After tucking Daria in, they retreated to their bed where Ian showed her with touches and kisses exactly how he felt about her.

Natasha fell asleep in his arms, thinking that though they'd only been married for a few short months, it was still just the beginning of their story together...

Books by Lynn Raye Harris

HOT Heroes for Hire: Mercenaries
Black's Bandits

Book 1: BLACK LIST - Jace & Maddy

Book 2: BLACK TIE - Brett & Tallie

Book 3: BLACK OUT - Colt & Angie

Book 4: BLACK KNIGHT - Jared & Libby

Book 5: BLACK HEART - Ian Black!

Book 6: BLACK MAIL - Tyler Scott

The Hostile Operations Team ® Books
Strike Team 2

Book 1: HOT ANGEL - Cade & Brooke

Book 2: HOT SECRETS - Sky & Bliss

Book 3: HOT JUSTICE - Wolf & Haylee

Book 4: HOT STORM - Mal & Scarlett

Book 5: HOT COURAGE - Noah & Jenna

The Hostile Operations Team ® Books
Strike Team 1

The HOT SEAL Team Books

Book 1: HOT SEAL - Dane & Ivy

Book 2: HOT SEAL Lover - Remy & Christina

Book 3: HOT SEAL Rescue - Cody & Miranda

Book 4: HOT SEAL BRIDE - Cash & Ella

Book 5: HOT SEAL REDEMPTION - Alex & Bailey

Book 6: HOT SEAL TARGET - Blade & Quinn

Book 7: HOT SEAL HERO - Ryan & Chloe

Book 8: HOT SEAL DEVOTION - Zach & Kayla

The HOT Novella in Liliana Hart's MacKenzie Family Series

HOT WITNESS - Jake & Eva

7 Brides for 7 Brothers

MAX (Book 5) - Max & Ellie

7 Brides for 7 Soldiers

WYATT (Book 4) - Max & Ellie

7 Brides for 7 Blackthornes

ROSS (Book 3) - Ross & Holly

Filthy Rich Billionaires

Book 1: FILTHY RICH REVENGE

Book 2: FILTHY RICH PRINCE

Who's HOT?

Strike Team 1

Matt "Richie Rich" Girard (Book 0 & 1)
Sam "Knight Rider" McKnight (Book 2)
Kev "Big Mac" MacDonald (Book 3)
Billy "the Kid" Blake (Book 4)
Jack "Hawk" Hunter (Book 5)
Nick "Brandy" Brandon (Book 6)
Garrett "Iceman" Spencer (Book 7)
Ryan "Flash" Gordon (Book 8)
Chase "Fiddler" Daniels (Book 9)
Dex "Double Dee" Davidson (Book 10)

Commander
John "Viper" Mendez (Book 11 & 12)

Deputy Commander
Alex "Ghost" Bishop

Strike Team 2

Cade "Saint" Rodgers (Book 1)
Sky "Hacker" Kelley (Book 2)
Dean "Wolf" Garner (Book 3)
Malcom "Mal" McCoy (Book 4)
Noah "Easy" Cross (Book 5)
Ryder "Muffin" Hanson
Jax "Gem" Stone
Zane "Zany" Scott
Jake "Harley" Ryan (HOT WITNESS)

SEAL Team 1

Dane "Viking" Erikson (Book 1)
Remy "Cage" Marchand (Book 2)
Cody "Cowboy" McCormick (Book 3)
Cash "Money" McQuaid (Book 4)
Alexei "Camel" Kamarov (Book 5)
Adam "Blade" Garrison (Book 6)
Ryan "Dirty Harry" Callahan (Book 7)
Zach "Neo" Anderson (Book 8)
Corey "Shade" Vance

Black's Bandits

Jace Kaiser (Book 1)
Brett Wheeler (Book 2)
Colton Duchaine (Book 3)
Jared Fraser (Book 4)
Ian Black (Book 5)
Tyler Scott
Thomas "Rascal" Bradley
Dax Freed
Jamie Hayes
Mandy Parker (Airborne Ops)

Melanie (Reception)
? Unnamed Team Members

Freelance Contractors

Lucinda "Lucky" San Ramos, now MacDonald (Book 3)
Victoria "Vee" Royal, now Brandon (Book 6)
Emily Royal, now Gordon (Book 8)
Miranda Lockwood, now McCormick (SEAL Team Book 3)
Bliss Bennett, (Strike Team 2, Book 2)
Angelica "Angie" Turner (Black's Bandits, Book 3)

About the Author

Lynn Raye Harris is a Southern girl, military wife, wannabe cat lady, and horse lover. She's also the New York Times and USA Today bestselling author of the HOSTILE OPERATIONS TEAM ® SERIES of military romances, and 20 books about sexy billionaires for Harlequin.

A former finalist for the Romance Writers of America's Golden Heart Award and the National Readers Choice Award, Lynn lives in Alabama with her handsome former-military husband, one fluffy princess of a cat, and a very spoiled American Saddlebred horse who enjoys bucking at random in order to keep Lynn on her toes.

Lynn's books have been called "exceptional and emotional," "intense," and "sizzling" -- and have sold in excess of 4.5 million copies worldwide.

To connect with Lynn online:
www.LynnRayeHarris.com
Lynn@LynnRayeHarris.com